21/1

THE DEATH OF SLEEP

Also by Anne McCaffrey in Orbit

DINOSAUR PLANET

SURVIVORS (Dinosaur Planet II)

TO RIDE PEGASUS

SASSINAK (with Elizabeth Moon)

ANNE McCAFFREY
and JODY LYNN NYE

THE DEATH OF SLEEP

Volume Two of
THE PLANET PIRATES

ORBIT

An Orbit Book

First published in the United States in 1990 by Baen Books

First published in Great Britain in 1991 by
Orbit Books, A Division of
Macdonald & Co (Publishers) Ltd
London & Sydney

Copyright © 1990 by Bill Fawcett and Associates

The right of Anne McCaffrey and Jody Lynn Nye to
be identified as authors of this work has been asserted.

A CIP catalogue record for this book is available
from the British Library

ISBN 0 356 20308 5

Printed and bound in Great Britain by
BPCC Hazell Books
Aylesbury, Bucks, England
Member of BPCC Ltd.

Orbit Books
A Division of
Macdonald & Co (Publishers) Ltd
165 Great Dover Street
London SE1 4YA

A member of Maxwell Macmillan Publishing Corporation

BOOK ONE

Chapter One

The single engaged engine of the empty spherical ore carrier thrummed hollowly through the hull. It set the decks and bulkheads of the personnel quarters vibrating at a frequency which at first, depending on one's mood, could be soothing or irritating. After four weeks aboard the Tau Ceti registered mining vessel *Nellie Mine,* Lunzie Mespil had to think about it to remember that the hum was there at all. When she first boarded, as the newly hired doctor for the Descartes Mining Platform Number 6, the sound drove her halfway to distraction. There wasn't much to do except read and sleep and listen, or rather, feel the engine noise. Later, she discovered that the sound was conducive to easy sleep and relaxation, like being aboard a gently swaying monorail passenger carrier. Whether her fellow employees knew it or not, one of the chief reasons that the Descartes Mining Corporation had so few duels and mutinies on delivery runs was due to the peace-inducing hum of the engines.

The first few days she spent in the tiny, plain-walled cubicle which doubled as her sleeping quarters and office were a trifle lonely. Lunzie had too many hours to think of her daughter Fiona. Fiona, fourteen, lovely and precocious in Lunzie's unbiased

3

opinion, had been left behind in the care of a friend who was the chief medical officer on the newly colonized planet of Tau Ceti. The settlement was surprisingly comfortable for one so recently established. It had a good climate, a biosphere reasonably friendly toward humankind, marked seasons, and plenty of arable land that allowed both Earth-type and hybrid seeds to prosper. Lunzie hoped to settle down there herself when she finished her tour of duty on the Platform, but she wasn't independently wealthy. Even a commodity as precious as medical expertise wasn't sufficient to buy into the Tau Ceti association. She needed to earn a stake, and there was little call on an atmosphere-and-gravity world for her to practice her specialty of psychological space-incurred trauma. There was no help for it: she was compelled to go off-planet to earn money. To her great dismay, all of the posts which were best suited to her profession and experience —and paid the most—were on isolated facilities. She would not be able to take Fiona with her. After much negotiation, Lunzie signed on with Descartes for a stint on a remote mining platform.

Fiona had been angry that she couldn't accompany her mother to the Descartes Platform, and had refused to accept the fact. In the last days before Lunzie's departure, Fiona had avoided speaking to her, and stubbornly unpacked Lunzie's two five-kilo duffels as often as her mother filled them up. It was an adolescent prank, but one that showed Lunzie how hurt Fiona felt to be abandoned. Since she was born, they had never been apart more than a day or so. Lunzie herself was aching at the impending separation, but she understood, as Fiona would not, the economic necessity that caused her to take a medical berth so far away and leave Fiona behind.

Their spacefare to Tau Ceti had been paid on speculation by the science council, who were testing the viability of a clone breeding center on the newly colonized planet. Lunzie had been approached by the ethics council to join them, their interest stemming from her involvement as the student advisor on a similar panel during her days in medical school which had resulted in an experimental colony. Surprisingly, the data on that earlier effort was unavailable even to the participants on the panel. Her former term-husband Sion had also given her his recommendation. He was becoming very well known and respected in genetic studies, mainly involved in working on controlling the heavyworld human mutations.

There were four or five meetings of the ethics council, which quickly determined that even so altruistic a project as fostering a survival-oriented genome was self-defeating in just a few generations, and no further action was taken. Lunzie was out of work in a colony that didn't need her. Because of the classified nature of the study, she was unable even to explain to her daughter why she wasn't employed in the job which they had traveled to Tau Ceti to take.

After the fifth or sixth time she had to repack her case, Lunzie knew by heart the few possessions she was taking with her, and locked her luggage up in the poisons cabinet in the Tau Ceti medical center to keep Fiona away from it.

By then, the protests had degenerated into a mere sulk. With love, Lunzie watched Fiona patiently, waiting for her to accept their parting, placing herself where she would be available to the troubled youngster when she decided she was ready to talk. Lunzie knew from experience that it was no good chasing Fiona down. She had to let Fiona come to her in her own time. They were too much alike. To force an early confrontation would be like forcing a nuclear pile to overload. She went about her business in the medical center, assisting other medical personnel with ongoing research which the colony had approved.

At last, Fiona met her coming out of the medical center one sunny day after work, and presented her with a small wrapped package. It was a hard triangular cylinder. Lunzie smiled, recognizing the shape. Under the paper was a brand new studio hologram of Fiona, dressed in her feastday best, an outfit in the latest style for which she had begged and plagued her mother to supplement the amount she'd saved to buy it from her allowance on their last planetary home. Lunzie could see how much of her own looks were reflected in Fiona: the prominent cheekbones, the high forehead, the warm mouth. The waves of smooth hair were much darker than hers, nearer black than Lunzie's golden brown. Fiona had long, sleepy eyes and a strong chin she inherited from her father that made her look determined, if not downright stubborn, even as a baby. The ruby-colored frock enhanced the girl's light skin, making her exotic and lovely as a flower. The translucent flowing cape which fell from between the shoulders was in the very height of fashion, a field of stars in pinpoint lights which swirled like a comet's tail around Fiona's calves. Lunzie looked up from the gift into her daughter's eyes, which were watching her warily, wondering what she would say. "I love it, darling," Lunzie told her, gathering her close and tucking the hologram safely into her zip pouch. "I'll miss you so much."

"Don't forget me." A broken whimper was muffled against Lunzie's tunic front.

Lunzie drew back and took her daughter's tear-stained face between her hands, studying it, learning it by heart. "I never could," Lunzie promised her. "I never will. And I'll be back before you know it."

During her remaining days planetside, she had turned over her laboratory work to a co-worker so she could spend all her time with Fiona. They visited favorite spots, and together moved Fiona's belongings and the rest of her own from their temporary quarters to the home of the friend who would be fostering the girl. They asked each other, 'Do you remember this? Do you remember that?', sharing precious memories as they had shared the events themselves. It was a glowing, warm time for both of them, too soon over for Lunzie's taste.

A silent Fiona walked her to the landing bay where the shuttle waited to transport her to the *Nellie Mine*. Tau Ceti's pale lavender-blue sky was overcast. When the sky was clear, Lunzie could often see the sun glint off the sides of visiting ships high above Tau Ceti in parking orbit, but she was just as happy that she could not now. She was holding back on her emotions. If there was any way to spare Fiona her own misery, she would do it. Lunzie promised herself a really good cry once she was shipside. For one moment, she felt like ripping up her contract and running away, telling Descartes to chuck it, and pleading with the Tau Ceti authorities that she would work at any job, however menial, to stay here with Fiona. But then, good sense took over. Lunzie remembered crude financial matters like making a living, and assured herself that it wouldn't be that long before she could return, and they would have a comfortable life thereafter with what she'd earned.

"I'll negotiate for an asteroid miner as soon as I can afford it," Lunzie offered, breaking the silence. "Maybe I'll stake a few." Her words echoed among the corrugated metal walls of the spaceport. There seemed to be no one there but themselves. "We'll strike it rich, you'll see. You'll be able to go to any university you like, or go for officer training in Fleet, like my brother. Whatever you want."

"Mm," was Fiona's only comment. Her face was drawn into a mask so tragic that Lunzie wanted to laugh and cry. Fiona hadn't used any makeup that morning, so she looked more childlike than her usual careful teenaged self.

It's manipulation, I know it, Lunzie told herself severely. I've got to make a living, or where's our future? I know she's grieving, but I'll only be gone two years, five at the most! The girl's nose was turning red, and her lips were white and pressed tightly closed. Lunzie started to offer another pleasantry, and then realized that *she* was trying to manipulate her daughter into foregoing her legitimate feelings. I don't want to make a scene, so I'm trying to keep her from acting unhappy. She pressed her own lips shut. We're too much alike, that's the trouble, Lunzie decided, shaking her head. She squeezed Fiona's hand tighter. They walked in silence to the landing bay.

Landing Bay Six contained a big cargo shuttle of the type used by shippers who hauled more freight than passengers. This craft, once nattily painted white with a broad red band from its nose to tail, was dinged and dented. The ceramic coating along the nose showed scorching from making descents through planetary atmospheres, but the vehicle seemed otherwise in good shape and well cared for. A broad-shouldered man with black curly hair stood in the middle of the bay, waving a clipboard and dispensing orders to a handful of coveralled workers. Sealed containers were being forklifted into the open top hatch of the shuttle.

The black-haired man noticed them and came over, hand out in greeting.

"You're the new doctor?" he asked, seizing Lunzie's free hand and wringing it companionably. "Captain Cosimo, Descartes Mining. Glad to have you with us. Hello, little lady," Cosimo ducked his head to Fiona, a cross between a nod and a bow. "Are those your bags, Doctor? Marcus! Take the doctor's bags on board!"

Lunzie offered Cosimo the small cube containing her contract and orders, which he slotted into the clipboard. "All's well," he said, scanning the readout on his screen. "We've got about twenty minutes before we lift off. Hatch shuts at T-minus two. Until then, your time's your own." With another smile for Fiona, he went back to shouting at one of his employees. "See here, Nelhen, that's a forklift, not a wee little toy!"

Lunzie turned to Fiona. Her throat began to tighten. All the things she wanted to say seemed so trivial when compared to what she felt. She cleared her throat, trying not to cry. Fiona's eyes were aswim with tears. "There's not much time."

"Oh, Mama," Fiona burst out in a huge sob. "I'll miss you so!" The almost-grown Fiona, who eschewed all juvenile things and had called her mother Lunzie since early childhood, reverted all at once to the baby name she hadn't used in years. "I'll miss you, too, Fee," Lunzie admitted, more touched than she realized. They clutched each other close and shed honest tears. Lunzie let it all out, and felt better for it. In the end, neither Lunzie nor any member of her family could be dishonest.

When the klaxon sounded, Fiona let her go with one more moist kiss, and stood back to watch the launch. Lunzie felt closer to her than she ever had. She kept Fiona in her mind, picturing her waving as the shuttle lifted and swept away through the violet-blue sky of Tau Ceti.

Now, with the exception of today's uniform, one music disk, and the hologram, her baggage was secured in the small storage chamber behind the shower unit with everyone else's. Lunzie had cropped her hair practically short as most crew members did. She missed the warm, fresh wind, cooking her own food from the indigenous plant life, and Fiona.

Without other set duties to occupy her, Lunzie

spent the days studying the medical files of her future co-workers and medical texts on the typical injuries and ailments that befall asteroid miners. She was looking forward to her new post. Space-incurred traumas interested her. Agoraphobia and claustrophobia were the most common in space-station life, followed by paranoid disorders. Strangely enough, frequently more than one occurred in the same patient at the same time. She was curious about the causes, and wanted to amass field research to prove or disprove her professors' statements about the possibility of cures.

She'd used her observations from the medical files to facilitate getting to know her fifteen shipmates. Miners were a hearty lot, sharing genuine good fellowship among themselves, but they took slowly to most strangers. Tragedy, suffered on the job and in personal lives, kept them clannish. But Lunzie wasn't a stranger long. They soon discovered that she cared deeply about the well-being of each of them, and that she was a good listener. After that, each of the others claimed time with her in the common dining recreation room, and filtered through her office, to pass the time between shifts, making her feel very welcome. With time, they began to open up to her. Lunzie heard about this crewman's broken romance, and that crewwoman's plan to open a satellite-based saloon with her savings, and the impending eggs of a mated pair of avians called Ryxi, who were specialists temporarily employed by the Platform. And they learned about her early life, her medical training, and her daughter.

The triangular hologram of Fiona was in her hand as she sat behind the desk in her office and listened to a human miner named Jilet. According to his file, Jilet had spent twelve years in cryogenic deepsleep after asteroids destroyed the drive on an ore carrier on which he and four other crewmen had been travelling. They'd been forced to evacuate from their posts, Jilet in one escape capsule near the cargo hold, the others in a second by the engine section. The other four men were recovered quickly, but Jilet was not found for over a decade more because of a malfunction in the signal beacon on his capsule. Not surprisingly, he was angry, afraid, and resentful. Three of the other crew presently on the *Nellie Mine* had been in cold sleep at least once, but Jilet's stint had been the longest. Lunzie sympathized with him.

"The truth is that I know those years passed while I was in cold sleep, Doctor, but it is killing me that I can't remember them. I've lost so much—my friends, my family. The world's gone round without me, and I don't know how to take up where I've left off." The burly, black-haired miner shifted in the deep impact lounger which Lunzie used as a psychoanalyst's couch. "I feel I've lost parts of myself as well."

"Well, you know that's not true, Jilet," Lunzie corrected him, leaning forward on her elbows attentively. "The brain is very protective of its memory centers. What you know is still locked up in there." She tapped his forehead with a slender, square-tipped finger. "Research has proved that there is no degeneration of memory over the time spent in cold sleep. You have to rely upon what you are, who you are, not what your surroundings tell you you are. I know it's disorienting—no, I've never been through it myself, but I've taken care of many patients who have. What you must do is accept that you've suffered a trauma, and learn to live your life again."

Jilet grimaced. "When I was younger, my mates and I wanted to live in space, away from all the crowds and noise. Hah! Catch me saying that now. All I want to do is settle down on one of the permanent colonies and maybe fix jets or industrial robots for a living. Can't do that yet without my Oh-Two money, not even including the extra if I want to have a family—a *new* family—so I've got to keep mining. It's all I know."

Lunzie nodded. Oh-Two was the cant term for the set-up costs it took to add each person to the bio-sphere of an ongoing oxygen-breathing colony on a non-atmosphered site. It was expensive: the contain-ment domes had to be expanded, and studies needed to be done to determine whether the other support systems could handle the presence of another life. Besides air, a human being needed water, sanitary facilities, a certain amount of space for living quar-ters and food synthesis or farming acreage to support him. She had considered one herself, but the safety margins were not yet acceptable, to her way of think-ing, for the raising of a child.

"What about a planetside community?" Lunzie asked. "My daughter's happy on Tau Ceti. It has a healthy atmosphere, and community centers or farm-land available, whichever you prefer to inhabit. I want to buy in on an asteroid strike, so that Fiona and I can have a comfortable home." It was a com-mon practice for the mining companies to allow freelancing by non-competitive consortia from their own platforms, so long as it didn't interfere with their primary business. Lunzie calculated that two or three years worth of her disposable income would be enough for a tidy share of a miner's time.

"Well, with apologies, Doctor Mespil, it's too set-tled and set on a domeless world. They're too—complacent; there, that's the word. Things is too easy for 'em. I'd rather be poor in a place where they understand the real pioneering spirit than rich on Earth itself. If I should have a daughter, I'd want her to grow up with some ambition . . . and some guts, not like her old man . . . With respect, Doctor," Jilet said, giving her an anxious look.

Lunzie waved away the thought that he had in-sulted her courage. She suspected that he was un-

willing to expose himself to the undomed surface of a
planet. Agoraphobia was an insidious complaint. The
free atmosphere would remind him too much of free
space. He needed to be reassured that, like his memories, his courage was still there, and intact. "Never
mind. But please, call me Lunzie. When you say
'Doctor Mespil,' I start to look around for my husband. And that contract ended years ago. Friendly
parting, of course."

The miner laughed, at his ease. Lunzie examined
the flush-set desk computer screen, which displayed
Jilet's medical file. His anger would have to be talked
out. The escape capsule in which he'd cold-slept had
had another minor malfunction that left him staring
drugged and half conscious through the port glass at
open space for two days before the cryogenic process
had kicked in. Not surprisingly, that would contrib-
ute to the agoraphobia. There was a pathetic air of
desperation about this big strong human, whose pal-
pable dread was crippling him, impairing his useful-
ness. She wondered if teaching him rudimentary
Discipline would help him, then decided against it.
He didn't need to know how to control an adrenaline
rush; he needed to learn how to keep them from
happening. "Tell me how the fears start."

"It's not so bad in the morning," Jilet began. "I'm
too busy with my job. Ever been on the mining
platform?" Lunzie shook her head. The corners of
Jilet's dark eyes crinkled merrily. "You've a lot to
look forward to, then, haven't you? I hope you can
take a joke or two. The boys are full of them. Don't
get to liking this big office too much. Space is tight in
the living quarters, so everyone gets to be tolerant of
everyone else real fast. Oh, it's not like we're all
mates right away," he added sadly. "A lot of the
young ones first coming along die quickly. It only
takes one mistake . . . and there you are, frozen or

suffocated, or worse. A lot of them leave young families, too."

Lunzie gulped, thinking of Fiona, and felt her heart twist in her body. She knew the seals and panels of her atmosphere suit were whole and taut, but she vowed to scrutinize them carefully as soon as Jilet left. "What are your specific duties?"

"We all take turns at whatever needs doing, ma'am. I've got a knack for finding lucky strikes when I'm on scout duty, so I try to draw that one a lot. There's a bonus for a good find."

"Maybe you're the one I'll pay to make my daughter's fortune for her," Lunzie smiled.

"I'd be proud to have your trust, D—Lunzie, only why don't you see if I can cut it, eh? Well, every asteroid's got ore, large and small, but you don't waste your time on everything you see. The sensors in a scout are unidirectional. Once you've eyeballed something you like the look of, either on visual or in the navigational scanning net, you can get a detailed readout of the asteroid's makeup. Scouts aren't big. They're fit for one man only, so he'd better like being by himself for days or weeks, even months, at a time. It's not easy. You've got to be able to wake up cold-eyed if the scanner net alarm goes off to avoid collisions. When you find a potential strike, you lay claim to it on behalf of the company, pending computer search for other claims of ownership. If it's small, like a crystal mass, you can haul it back behind you to the platform—and you'll want to: there's always a bonus on crystals. You don't want anyone jumping claim behind you. The mediums can be brought in by a tug. The big ones a crew comes out to mine on the spot. I don't mind being in a scout, because I'm looking straight down the 'corridor' between fields in the net, and the inside of the ship is small enough to be comfortable. It starts to bug me when I'm fixing one of the rotating tumbling shafts,

or something like that out in free-fall." Jilet finished
with his brows drawn down and his arms folded
tightly across his chest.

"Focus on the equipment, Jilet. Don't catch yourself staring off into space. It was always there before.
You just didn't pay attention to it then. Don't let it
haunt you now. What matters is what you are working on at the moment." Lunzie hastened to calm
him. She wanted him to verbalize the good facets of
his job. It was impossible to heal the mind without
giving it something positive to hang on to, a reason
for healing. Half the battle was won, whether Jilet
knew it or not. He had the guts to go back to his post
on the Mining Platform. Getting back on the horse
that threw him. "What do you look for when you're
scouting?"

Jilet's body gradually relaxed, and he studied the
ceiling through his wiry black eyebrows. "What I can
find. Depending on what's claiming a good price
dirtside, you'll see 'em breaking down space rock
into everything from diamonds to cobalt to iron. If
the handling don't matter, they slag it apart with
lasers and shove it into the tumbling chutes for
processing. If how it's handled makes a difference, a
prize crew'll strip it down. As much as possible is
done in vacuum, for safety, conservation of oxygen,
and to keep the material from expanding and con-
tracting from exposure to too many temperatures.
Makes the ore tough to ship if it has been thawed
once. It'll split up, explode into a million shards if it
warms too quickly. I've seen mates of mine killed
that way. It's ugly, ma'am. I don't want to die in
bed, but I'd rather not go that way, either."

With a rueful smile for her precise clinical imagination, Lunzie dismissed thoughts of trying to recon-
struct a splintered miner's body. This was the life
she was moving toward, at just under the speed of
light. You won't be able to save every patient, you

idealist. Help the ones you can. "What's a crystal strike look like? How do you find one?"

"Think I'd give all my secrets away, even to a friendly mindbrowser like you?" Jilet tilted one eyebrow toward her. Lunzie gave him an affable grin. "Well, I'll give you one clue. They're lighter than the others on the inside. Sounding gives you a cross-section that seems to be nearly hollow, bounces your scan around its interior. Sometimes it is. Why, I had one that split my beam up in a hundred different directions. The crew found it was rutilated with filaments of metal when they cut it apart. Worthless for communications, but some rich senator had it used for the walls of his house." Jilet spat in the direction of the nameless statesman.

They were getting off the track. Regretfully, for Jilet was really relaxing with her, Lunzie set them back on it. "You've also complained of sleeplessness. Tell me about it."

Jilet fidgeted, bent forward and squeezed his forehead with both hands. "It's not that I can't sleep. I—just don't want to fall asleep. I'm afraid that if I do, I won't wake up."

" 'Sleep, the brother of Death,' " Lunzie quoted. "Homer, or more recently, Daniel."

"Yes, that's it. I wish—I wish that if I wasn't going to die they'd've left me asleep for a hundred years or more, so that I'd come back a complete stranger, instead of everything seeming the same," Jilet exploded in a sudden passionate outburst that surprised even him. "After only a dozen years I'm out of step. I remember things my friends have forgotten long since, that they laugh at me for, but it's all I've got to hang on to. They've had a decade to go on without me. They're older now. I'm a freak to them, being younger. I almost wish I had died."

"Now, now. Death is never as good as its press would have you believe. You've begun making new

friends in your profession, you're heading toward a
job right now that makes the best use of your talents,
and you can learn some new techniques that didn't
exist when you started out mining. Give the positive
aspects a chance. Don't think of space while you're
trying to sleep. Let your mind turn inward, possibly
to a memory of your childhood that you enjoyed." A
chime sounded, indicating Jilet's personal time was
at an end, and he needed to get back to his duties.
Lunzie stood up, waited for Jilet to rise. He towered
easily a third of a meter over her. "Come back and
talk to me again next rest period," Lunzie insisted.
"I want to hear more about crystal mining."

"You and half the youngsters that come out to the
Platforms," Jilet complained good-naturedly. "But,
Doctor, I mean Lunzie, how can I get to sleep
without having this eating away at me? We're still so
far out, but the feelings are keeping me awake all
over again."

"I'd rather not give you drugs, though I will if you
insist after you try it my way first. For now, concentrate on what is here, close by and around you. When
you're in the rec area, never look out the window,
always at the wall beside it," Lunzie smiled, reaching out to press Jilet's hand warmly. "In no time,
you'll be so bored with the wall that mere yearning
for something new will set you to gazing at the stars
again."

After Jilet left, Lunzie got a carafe of fresh hot
coffee for herself from a synthesizer hatch in the
corridor, and returned to her office. While her observations on Jilet's case were still fresh in her mind,
she sat down at her desk to key in data to her
confidential files. She believed that in time he would
recover completely. He'd obviously been counselled
by experts when he first came out of cold sleep.
Whoever the psychology team was that had worked

with him, they were right on the ball when it came to rehabilitation counseling.

Jilet's agoraphobia had been triggered by an occupational hazard. Lunzie wondered uneasily how many latent agoraphobics there were in space who simply hadn't been exposed to the correct stimuli yet that would cause it to manifest. Others in the crew could be on the edge of a breakout. Had anyone else shown symptoms?

Immediately, Lunzie put the thought away. Wryly, she decided she was frightening herself. "I'll have to treat myself for paranoia soon, if I'm not careful." But the feeling of uneasiness persisted. Not for the first time, Lunzie wished that Fiona was here to talk to. She had always discussed things with Fiona, even when she was an infant. Lunzie turned the hologram in her hands. The girl was growing and changing. She was already as tall as her mother. "She'll be a woman when I get back." Lunzie decided that her dissatisfaction was because she was spoiling for a good chat with someone. Her remote cubicle was too lonely. Since "office hours" were over, she would run down the corridor to the rec area and see if anyone else was on break.

Abruptly, Lunzie realized that the everpresent hum of the engine had changed, sped up. Instead of the usual purr, the sound had an edge of panic to it. Two more growling notes coughed to life, increasing the vibration so much Lunzie's teeth were chattering. They were trying to fire up the dorsal and ventral engines!

"Attention, all personnel," Captain Cosimo's voice blared. "This is an emergency alert. We are in danger of collision with unknown objects. Be prepared to evacuate. Do not panic. Proceed in an orderly fashion to your stations. We are attempting to evade, but we might not make it. This is not a drill."

Lunzie's eyes widened, and she turned to her desk screen. On the computer pickup, the automatic cut-off devolved to forward control video, and showed what the pilot on the bridge saw: half a dozen irregularly shaped asteroids. Two that appeared to be the size of the ship were closing in from either side like pincers, or hammer and anvil, with more fragments heading directly for them. There wasn't room for the giant ship, running on only one of its three engines, to maneuver and avoid them all. Normally, asteroid routes could be charted. The ship's flight plan took into account all the space-borne debris to be avoided. At the last check, the route had been clear. These must have just crashed into one another, changing their course abruptly into the path of the *Nellie Mine*. The huge freighter was incapable of making swift turns, and there was no way to get out of the path of all the fragments. Collision with the tumbling rocks was imminent.

One of the asteroids slipped out of view of the remote cameras, and Lunzie was thrown out of her chair as the huge ship fired all its starboard boosters, attempting to avoid collision. Crashing sounds reverberated through the corridor, and the floor shook. Some of the smaller fragments must have struck the ship.

The red alert beacons in the corridor went off. "Evacuate!" the captain's voice shouted. "We can't get the engines firing. All personnel, evacuate!"

As the klaxon sounded, Lunzie's mind reached for Discipline. She willed herself to be calm, recalling all her training on what to do in a red alert. The list scrolled up in her mind as clearly as it would do on a computer screen. Make sure all who are disabled or too young to look after themselves are safe, then secure yourself—but most importantly, waste no time! Lunzie paused only long enough to grab Fiona's hologram off the desk and stow it in a pocket before she dashed out into the corridor, heading for her section's escape capsule.

The crew section was a curved strip one level high across the equator of the spherical freighter. When the ship was making a delivery run, she could carry as many as eighty crew in the twenty small sleeping cubicles, ten on either side of the common rooms. At intervals along the corridor, round hatchways opened onto permanently moored escape capsules. Lunzie's office was at the far left end of the crew section.

The ship rocked. They'd been struck again, this time by a big fragment. There was a gasp of life support fans and compressors speeding up to move the air in spite of a hull breach. All the lights in the corridor went out, and in the center of one wall, a circle of bright red LEDs chased around the hatch of the escape capsule, which irised open as Lunzie ran toward it.

She waited at the hatch, staring down the long corridor toward the center of the crew section to see if anyone was coming to board this escape shuttle with her. Her heart hammered with fear and impatience. The capsule iris would close and launch automatically thirty seconds after a body entered the hatchway, so she forced herself to wait. Lunzie wanted to be certain that there was no one else in this section that she would be abandoning if she took off alone in the capsule.

There was a deafening bang, and then a roar like thunder echoed in the corridor. A section of rock the size of her head burst through the bulkhead less than a hundred feet down the passage, cutting her off from the rest of the crew. Lunzie ducked the splinters, and grabbed with both hands at the edge of the hatchway, as the vacuum of space dragged the ship's atmosphere out through the tear in the hull. Gritting her teeth tightly, she clung to the metal lip, and watched furniture, clothing, coffee cups, atmosphere suits fly through the air toward the gap. The air dropped to near freezing, and frost formed swiftly on her rings and sleeve fasteners, and on her eyelashes, cheeks and lips. Her hands were growing numb with cold. Lunzie wasn't sure how long she could hang on before she, too, was sucked out into space through that hole. This was death, she knew. Then: a miracle.

She heard a rending sound, and her desk and chair flew out of her office door, ricocheted off the opposite corridor wall with individual bangs, and collided in the tear in the hull. The tornadic winds died momentarily, blocked by her office furniture. Lunzie grabbed the opportunity to save herself. She dove through the hatchway headfirst, tucking and rolling to land unhurt between the rows of impact seats. She arched up from the floor to punch the manual door control with her fist, then crawled to the steering controls, not bothering to right herself before sending the pod hurtling into space.

The capsule spun away from the side of the *Nellie Mine*. Lunzie was flung about in the tiny cabin. She caught hold of the handloops, yanked herself into the pilot's seat and strapped in.

The lumpy shape of the mining ship looked like another asteroid against the curtain of stars. The brief strip of living space raised across a 60 degree arc of the ship's midsection bloomed with other pinpoints of light as the rest of the crew evacuated in vessels like hers. She regretted that there hadn't been opportunity for anyone else to join her in the escape pod, company until rescue could reach them, but Space! when the alarm sounds, you go, or you die.

She could see where the gigantic asteroid had struck the *Nellie*. It had torn away a large section of the crew quarters at the opposite end of the strip from hers, creased the hull deeply, and sailed away on a tangential course. The second asteroid, the size of a moon, would do far more damage. The ship, still on automatic pilot, was slowly turning toward her, firing on all the steering thrusters down one side, so the jagged rock would take it broadside instead of a direct strike. She watched, fascinated and horrified, as the two immense bodies met, and melded.

Her little pod hurtled outward at ever-increasing speed, but much faster still came the explosion, the overtaxed inner engine kicking through the plating behind the living quarters, imploding the shells and then kicking the debris forward of the directionless hulk. Pieces of red-hot hull plating shot past her, some missing her small boat by mere yards. The planetoid deflected away, its course changed only slightly.

Lunzie let go of the breath she had been holding. The disaster had happened so quickly. Only minutes had gone by since the alert was broadcast. Her Discipline had served her well—she had acted swiftly and decisively. She was considered by her masters a natural Candidate, who had already achieved much on her own. Basic training in Discipline was recommended for medics and Fleet officers of command rank and above, especially those who would be going into hazardous situations—much like this. Over the years, Lunzie had achieved Adept status. It was a pity she hadn't been able to go on with her lessons since reaching Tau Ceti. Lunzie was grateful for the instruction, which had probably saved her life, but she realized that her capsule was still at least two weeks travel away from the Mining Platform. She switched on the communication set and leaned over the audio pickup.

"Mayday, Mayday. This is *Nellie Mine* Shuttle, registration number NM-EC-02. I repeat, Mayday."

A wave of static poured out of the speaker. Underneath it, she could hear a voice. The static gradually

died, and a man's voice spoke clearly. "I hear you,
EC-02. This is Captain Cosimo, in EC-04. Is that
you, Lunzie?"

"Yes, sir. Is everyone else all right?"

"Yes, dammit. All present and accounted for but
you. We thought we'd lost you when Damage Control reported a punchthrough in your wing. That was
one hell of a bang. I knew it would happen one day.
Poor old *Nellie*. Are you all right?"

"I'm fine."

"Good. We've been signalling, but there's no one
in immediate range. Before the blast, we sent off a
message to Descartes 6 advising them to send someone out for us. Lock in your beacon to 34.8 and
activate."

Lunzie found the controls and punched in the
command. "How long will it take for them to reach
us, Cosimo?"

There was more static, and the captain's voice
broke through it, fainter than before. ". . . flaming
asteroid interference. It'll be at least two weeks before the message reaches them, and I'd estimate it'll
take them four more weeks to find us. I am ordering
cold sleep, Doctor. Any comments or objections?"

"No, sir. I concur. It would be an emotional strain
for so many people to spend six weeks awake in such
close quarters, even providing the synthesizers and
recyclers hold out."

"That's for certain. There are two crew on this
shuttle, including the Ryxi, who're squawking about
their damned eggs and claustrophobia. I wish you
were here to oversee the deepsleep process, Doctor.
Hypodermic compressors make me nervous." Cosimo
didn't sound in the least distressed, but Lunzie was
grateful to him for keeping the mood light.

"Nothing to it," she said. "Just remember, pointed
end down."

With a hearty laugh, the captain signed off.

Inside the shuttle's medical supply locker were several vials containing medicines: depressants, restoratives, and the cold sleep preservative formula alongside its antidote. Lunzie removed the spraygun from its niche and loaded in a vial of the cryogenic. She would have only moments before the formula took effect, so she prepared a cradling pad from stored thermal blankets, and wadded up a few more under her head as a pillow. She fed instructions to the ship's computer, giving details of her identity, allergies, next of kin, and planet of origin for use by her rescuers. When all was prepared, Lunzie lowered herself to the padded deck. She could feel the adrenaline of the Discipline state wearing off. In moments, she was drained and exhausted, her strength swept away. In one hand she held the spraygun. In the other, Lunzie clutched the hologram of her daughter.

"Computer," she commanded. "Monitor vital signs and initiate cold sleep process when my heart rate reaches zero."

"Working," the metallic voice responded. "Acknowledged."

Her order was unnecessary, since the module was programmed to complete the cold sleep process on its own, but Lunzie needed to hear another Standard-speaking voice. She wished someone had been close enough in the corridors of the damaged carrier to have boarded the pod with her. For all her theoretical training, this was the first time she would experience the cryogenic process. Lunzie gazed into the lucite block, smiled into the image of Fiona's eyes. "What an adventure I'll have to tell you about when I see you, my darling." She pressed the nozzle of the spray against her thigh. It hissed as the drug dispersed swiftly through her body. Where it passed, her tissues became leaden, and her skin felt hot. Though the sensation was uncomfortable, Lunzie knew the process was safe. "Initiating," she told the computer indistinctly. Her jaw and tongue were already out of her control. Lunzie could sense her pulse slowing down, and her nervous responses became lethargic. Even her lungs were growing too heavy to drag air in or push it out.

Her last conscious thoughts were of Fiona, and she hoped that the rescue shuttle wouldn't take too long to answer the Mayday.

All lights on the shuttle except the exterior running lights and beacon went down. Inside, cold cryogenic vapor filled the tiny cabin, swirling around Lunzie's still form.

BOOK TWO

Chapter Two

When his scout ship was just two days flight out of Descartes Mining Platform 6, Illin Romsey began to pick up hopeful signs of radioactivity. He was prospecting for potential strikes along what his researches told him was a nearly untapped vector leading away from Platform 6. He was aware that in the seventy years since the Platform became operational, the thick asteroid stream around the complex had had time to shift, bringing new rock closer and sweeping played-out space rock away. Still, the explorer's blood in his veins urged him to follow a path no one else had ever tried.

His father and grandfather had worked for Descartes. He didn't mind following in the family tradition. The company treated its employees well, even generously. Its insurance plan and pension plan alone made Descartes a desirable employer, but the bonus system for successful prospectors kept him pushing the limits of his skills. He was proud to work for Descartes.

His flight plan nearly paralleled a well-used approach run to the Platform, which maintained its position in the cosmos by focusing on six fixed remote beacons and adjusting accordingly. Otherwise, even a complex that huge would become lost in the swirling pattern of rock and ice. It was believed that the asteroid belt had originated as a uranian-sized planet, destroyed in a natural cataclysm of some kind. Some held that a planet had never been formed in this system. The sun around which the belt revolved had no other planets. Even after seven decades of exploration, the jury was still out on it, and everyone had his own idea.

Illin held a fix on the vector between Alpha Beacon and the Platform. It was his lifeline. Ships had been known to get lost within kilometers of their destination because of the confusion thrown into their sensors by the asteroid belt. Illin felt that he was different: he had an instinct for finding his way back home. In more than eight years prospecting, he'd never spent more than a day lost. He never talked about his instinct, because he felt it would break his luck. The senior miners never twitted him about it; they had their own superstitions. The new ones called it blind luck, or suggested the Others were looking after him. Still, he wasn't cocky, whatever they might think, and he was never less than careful.

The clatter of the radiation counter grew louder and more frenzied. Illin crossed his fingers eagerly. A strike of transuranic ore heretofore undiscovered by the busy Mining Platform—and so close by—would be worth a bonus and maybe a promotion. Need for other minerals might come and go, but radioactive elements were always sought after, and they fetched Descartes a good price, too. What terrifically good luck! He adjusted his direction slightly to follow the signal, weaving deftly between participants in the great stately waltz like a waiter at a grand ball.

He was close enough now to pick up the asteroids he wanted on his scanner net. Suddenly, the mass on his scope split into two, an irregular mass that drifted gently away portside, and a four-meter-long pyramidal lump that sped straight toward him. Asteroids

didn't behave that way! Spooked, Illin quickly changed
course, but the pyramid angled to meet him. His rad
counter went wild. He tried to evade it, firing thrusters to turn the nippy little scout out of its path. It
was chasing him! In a moment, he had the smaller
mass on visual. It was a Thek capsule.

Theks were a silicate life-form that was the closest
thing in the galaxy to immortals. They ranged from
about a meter to dozens of meters high, and were
pyramidal in shape, just like their spacecraft. Illin's
jaw dropped open. Theks were slow talking and of
few words, but their terse statements usually held
more information than hundreds of pages of human
rhetoric. Not much else was known about them,
except their inexplicable penchant for aiding the more
ephemeral races to explore and colonize new planetary systems. A Thek rode every mothership that the
Exploratory and Evaluatory Corps sent out. What
was a Thek doing way out here? He cut thrust and
waited for it to catch up with him.

He was suddenly resentful. Oh, Krims! Illin
thought. Did I come all this way just for a Thek? The
other miners were going to have a laugh at his expense. He tapped his rad counter and aimed the
sensor this way and that. It continued to chatter out
a high-pitched whir, obviously responding to a strong
signal nearby. Were Theks radioactive? He'd never
heard that from anyone before. Had he discovered a
new bit of interesting gossip about the mysterious
Theks to share with the other miners? Yes, it would
seem so. But to his delight, the signal from the
asteroid he'd spotted continued. A strike! And a concentrated one, too. Should be worth a goodly handful of bonus credits.

In a few minutes, the Thek was alongside him.
The pyramidal shape behind the plas-shield was featureless, resembling nothing so much as a lump of
plain gray granite. It eased one of its ship's sides

against the scout with a gentle bump, and adhered to the hull like a flexible magnet. The cabin was filled then with a low rumbling sound which rose and fell very, very slowly. The Thek was talking to him.

"Rrrrreeeeeee . . . ttrrrrrrrrriieeeeevvvve . . . sssssshhhhuuuuuutttt . . . ttttlllleee."

"Shuttle? What shuttle?" Illin asked, not bothering to wonder how the Thek was talking to him through the hull of his scout.

For answer, the Thek moved forward, dragging his ship with it.

"Hey!" Illin yelled. "I'm tracking an ore strike! I've got a job to do. Would you release my ship?"

"Iiiiimmmm . . . perrrrrrr . . . aaaa . . . ttttiiiiivv vvvveee."

He shrugged. "Imperative, huh?" He waited a long time to see if there was any more information forthcoming. Well, you didn't argue with a Thek. Resigned but unhappy, he allowed himself to be towed along at a surprising speed through a patch of tiny asteroids that bounced off the Thek craft and embedded themselves into the nose of his ship. The outermost metal layer of a scout's nose was soft, backed by a double layer of superhard titanium sandwiching more soft metal, to absorb and stop small meteorites or slow and deflect bigger ones. Illin had only just stripped the soft layer and ground out the gouge marks in the hard core a week ago. It would have to be done all over again when he got back from rescuing this shuttle for the Thek—would anyone believe him when he told them about it? He scarcely believed it himself.

Behind him the starfield disappeared. They were moving into the thickest part of the asteroid belt. The Thek obviously knew where it was going; it didn't slow down at all, though the hammering of tiny pebbles on the hull became more insistent. Illin switched on the video pickup and rolled the protective lid up to protect the forward port.

A tremendous rock shot through with the red of iron oxide rolled up behind them and somersaulted gracefully to the left as the Thek veered around it, a tiny arrowhead against its mass. Illin's analyzer showed that most of the debris in this immediate vicinity was ferric, and a lot of it was magnetic. He had to recalibrate continually to keep his readings accurate. They looped around a ring of boulders approximately all the same size revolving around a planetoid that was almost regular in shape except for three huge impact craters near its "equator."

Nestled in one of the craters was a kernel-shaped object that Illin recognized immediately. It was an escape pod. As they drew closer, he could read the markings along its dusty white hull: NM-EC-02.

"Well, boy, you're a hero," he said to himself. Those pods were never jettisoned empty; there must be sleepers aboard. The beacon apparatus, both beam and transmitter, was missing, probably knocked off by the meteor that had shoved the pod into the cradle it now occupied. He didn't recognize the registry code, but then, he wasn't personally familiar with any vessels large enough to be carrying pods.

The Thek disengaged and floated a few meters away from his scout. It hadn't extruded eyes, or anything like that, but Illin felt it was watching him. He angled his ship away from the escape pod. The magnetic line shot out of the scout's stern and looped around the pod. The tiny dark ship twisted in his wake, showing that the net had engaged correctly.

Moving slowly and carefully, Illin applied ventral thrusters and steered his ship upward, over the ring of dancing giants. The Thek floated next to him.

He followed the small pyramid out of the thick of the field and back to his vector point. As soon as they were clear, he bounced messages to the beacons:

Scout coming in, towing escape pod NM-EC-02, intact, beacon damaged. Thek involved. He grinned jauntily to himself. That short message would have them fluttering on the Platform all right. He couldn't wait to see what a fuss he was stirring up.

Descartes Mining Platform 6 had changed a great deal in the many years since the first modular cylinders had been towed into the midst of the asteroid field and assembled. While the early employees had had to make do with barrackslike communal quarters, families could now claim small suites of their own. Amenities, which were once sold practically out of the backpacks of itinerant traders, could be found in a knot of shops in the heart of the corridors joining the cylinder complex near the entertainment center. With the completion date for the residential containment dome only five years away, Descartes 6 could almost claim colony status. And would.

Ore trains consisting of five to eight sealed containers strung behind a drone crossed back and forth between the ships ranged out along the docking piers. Some carried raw rock from the mining vessels to the slaggers and tumblers whose chutes bristled from the side of the Platform. Some carried processed minerals to the gigantic three-engine ore carriers that were shaped like vast hollow spheres belted top to bottom by thruster points. Those big slow-moving spheres did most of the hauling between the Platform and civilization. In spite of their dowdy appearance and obvious unwieldiness, the Company had never come up with anything better with which to replace them.

Ships belonging to merchants from the Federated Sentient Planet worlds were easily distinguished from the Mining Company's own vessels by their gaudy paint jobs. They were here to trade household goods, food, and textiles for small and large parcels of minerals that weren't available on their own planets, hoping to get a better price than they would get from a distributor. As Illin watched, one moved away from its bay with four containers in tow, turning toward the beacon that would help guide it toward Alpha Centauri, many months travel from here even at FTL. A personal shuttle with the colors of a Company executive shot out of an airlock and flew purposefully toward a large Paraden Company carrier that lay in a remote docking orbit somewhere over Illin's left shoulder.

Illin transmitted his scout's recognition code as he approached the Platform. The acknowledgment tone tweetled shrilly in his headphones.

"Good day, Romsey. That your Thek behind you there at .05?" Flight Deck Coordinator Mavorna said cheerfully from Illin's video pickup, now tuned to the communications network. She was a heavyset woman with midnight skin and clear green eyes.

"It's not my Thek," Illin said peevishly. "It just followed me home."

"That's what they all say, pumpkin. You've hooked yourself a geode, I hear."

"That's so," Illin admitted. A "geode" was a crystal strike that was seemed promising but couldn't be cracked in the field. Some of them panned out well, others proved to be deeply disappointing to the hopeful miner who found one. "I don't know who's in it. The Thek didn't say. It's still sealed."

"The Thek didn't say—ha, ha! When do they ever? I've got a crew and medics on the way down to the enclosed deck to meet you. Set down gently, now. The floor has just been polished. Remember, wait until the airlock siren shuts off before you unseal."

"Have I got a tri-vid team waiting to talk to me, too?" Illin asked hopefully.

"Sonny, there's more news than you happening today. Wait and see. You'll get the whole picture when you're down and in. I haven't got time to gossip."

With a throaty chuckle, Mavorna signed off. Her image was replaced on the screen with the day's designated frequency for the landing beacon. Illin tuned in and steered up toward the opening doors through which bright simulated daylight spilled. The Thek sailed silently behind him.

Tiny gnats were buzzing near her ears. "Lnz. Lnz. Dtr Mspw."

She ignored them, refusing to open her eyes. Her skin hurt, especially her ears and lips. Gingerly, she put out her tongue and licked her lips. They were very dry. Suddenly, something cold and wet touched her mouth. She startled, and cold stuff ran across her cheek and into her ear. The gnats began whining again, but their voices grew slower and more distinct. "Lunz. Lunzie. Dr. Mespil. That is your name, isn't it?"

Lunzie opened her eyes. She was lying on an infirmary bed, in a white room without windows. Three humans stood beside her, two in white medic tunics, and one in a miner's jumpsuit. And there was a Thek. She was so curious about why a Thek should be in her infirmary ward that she just stared at it, ignoring the others. The tall male human in medical whites leaned over her.

"Can you speak? I'm Dr. Stev Banus. You're on Descartes Platform 6, and I am the hospital administrator. Are you all right?"

Lunzie drew a deep breath, and let out a sigh of relief. "Yes, I'm fine. I'm very stiff, and my head is full of sawdust, but I'm all right."

"Iiiiinnnnnn-taaaaaaaaaccct?" the Thek rumbled. The others listened carefully and respectfully, and then turned to Lunzie. It must have been a query directed at her. She wished that she had more per-

sonal experience with the Theks, but none had ever
spoken to her before. The others seemed to know
what it was asking.

"Yes, I'm intact," she announced. She wished it
had a face, or any attribute that she could relate to,
but there was nothing. It looked like a hunk of
building stone. She waited for a response.

The Thek said nothing more. As the humans watched
it, the featureless pyramid rolled swiftly toward the
door and out of the room.

"What was that Thek doing here?" Lunzie asked.

"I don't know," Stev explained, puzzled. "I'm not
sure what it was looking for out there in the asteroid
field. They're not easy to communicate with. This
one is clearly friendly, but that's all we know. It was
instrumental in finding you. It pointed you out to
young Miner Romsey."

"I'm sorry I didn't thank it," Lunzie said flip-
pantly. She pulled herself up into a sitting position.
The human in white tunics rushed forward to sup-
port her as she settled against the head of the bed.
She waved them away. "Where am I? This is the
Mining Platform?"

"It is." The female medic smiled at her. She had
perfectly smooth skin the color of coffee with cream,
and deep brown eyes. Her thick black hair was in a
long braid down her back. "My name is Satia
Somileaux. I was born here."

Lunzie looked at her curiously. "Really? I thought
the living quarters on the Platform were less than
fifteen years old. You must be at least twenty."

"Twenty-four," Satia confessed, with a friendly and
amused expression.

"How long was I asleep?"

The two doctors looked at each other, trying to
decide what to say. Lunzie stared at them sharply.
The dark-haired young man in the coverall shifted
uncomfortably from one foot to the other and cleared

his throat. Banus shot him a sly, knowing look out of
the corner of his eye and turned to face him. "I
haven't forgotten you, Illin Romsey. There's a substantial finder's fee for bringing a pod in, you know
that."

"Well," the young man grinned, squinting thoughtfully. "It'll make up for losing that strike. Just. But
I'd'a brought her in anyway. If I was shiplost, I sure
hope someone would feel the same about bringing
me home."

"Everyone is not so altruistic as you, young man.
Self interest is more prevalent than your enlightened
attitude. Computer, record Miner Romsey's fee for
retrieving escape pod . . . ?" The tall doctor looked
to Lunzie for assistance.

"NM-EC-02," she said.

". . . and verify by my voice code. If a check is
necessary, refer requests to me."

"Acknowledged," said the flat voice of the computer.

"There you go, Miner," Stev said. "There's no
security classification, so if you want to beat the
rumor mill with your news . . ."

Illin Romsey grinned. "Thanks. I hope all's well
for you, Dr. Mespil." The young man dropped a
courteous bow and left the room.

Stev returned to Lunzie's side. "Of course, the fee
is nothing compared to the back salary that is owing to
you, Doctor Mespil. You were in the Company's
employ at the time you underwent deepsleep.
Descartes is honest about paying its debts. Come
and talk to me later about your credit balance."

"How long have I been asleep?" Lunzie demanded.

"You must understand where the miner found you.
Your capsule was not recovered when the other two
pods from the, er, 'Nellie Mine' were brought in.
Even they were difficult to locate. The search took
more than three months."

"Is everyone else all right?" she asked quickly,

immediately concerned for the other fourteen members of the *Nellie's* crew. Jilet had been so frightened of going into deepsleep again. She regretted not having ordered a sedative for him before he took the cryogenic.

Dr. Banus swiveled the computer screen on the table toward him and drew his finger down the glass face. "Oh, yes, everyone else was just fine. There are normally no ill effects from properly induced cryogenic sleep. You should be feeling 'all go and on green' yourself."

"Yes, I do. May I make use of the communications center? I assume you notified my daughter, Fiona, when we escaped from the *Nellie Mine*. I'd like to communicate with her that I've been found. She's probably been worried sick about me. Unless, of course, there is an FTL shuttle going towards Tau Ceti soon? I must send her a message."

"Do you think she's still there?" Satia asked, frowning at Stev.

Lunzie watched the exchange between the two. "It's where I left her, in the care of a friend, another medical practitioner. She was only fourteen . . ." Lunzie paused. The way the doctors were talking, it must have been a couple of years before they found the shuttle. Well, that was one of the risks of space travel. Lunzie tried to see Fiona as she might be now, if she continued to grow into her long legs. The adolescent curves must be more mature now. Lunzie hoped her daughter's mentor would have had the clothes-sense to guide the girl into becoming fashions instead of the radical leanings of teenagers. Then she noticed the overwhelming silence from the others, who were clearly growing more uncomfortable by the minute. Her intuition insisted something was wrong. Lunzie looked suspiciously at the pair. When an FTL trip between star systems alone could take two or three years, a cold sleep stint at that length would hardly provoke worry in modern psychologists. More? Five years? Ten?

"You've very neatly sidestepped the question several times, but I won't allow you to do that any more. How long was I asleep? Tell me."

The others glanced nervously at each other. The tall doctor cleared his throat and sighed. "A long time," Stev said, casually, though Lunzie could tell it was forced. "Lunzie, it will do you no good to have me deceive you. I should have told you as you were waking up, to allow your mind to assimilate the information. I erred, and I apologize. It is just such an unusual case that I'm afraid my normal training failed me." Stev took a deep breath. "You've been in cryogenic sleep for sixty-two years."

Sixty-two— Lunzie's brain spun. She was prepared to be told that she had slept for a year, or two or three, even twelve, as Jilet had done, but sixty-two. She stared at the wall, trying to summon up even the image of a dream, anything that would prove to her that amount of time had passed. Nothing. She hadn't dreamed in cold sleep. No one did. She felt numb inside, trying to contain the shock. "That's impossible. I feel as though the collision occurred only a few minutes ago. I closed my eyes there. I opened them here. There is no gap in my perception between then and now."

"You see why I found it so difficult to tell you, Lunzie," Stev said gently. "It isn't so hard when the gap is under two years, as you know. That's generally the interval we have here on the Platform, when a miner has an accident in the field and has to send for help. The sleeper falls a little behind in the news of the day, but there's rarely a problem in assimilation. Working cryogenic technology is slightly over a hundred and forty years old. Your . . . er, interval is the longest I've ever been involved in. In fact, the longest I've ever heard of. We will help you in any way we can. You have but to ask."

Lunzie's mind would still not translate sixty-two years into a perception of reality. "But that means my daughter . . ." Her throat closed up, refusing to voice her astonished thoughts. Fumbling, her hand reached for the hologram sitting on the pull-out shelf next to the bed. She could have accepted a seventeen- or eighteen-year-old Fiona instead of the youth she left, but a woman of seventy-six, an old woman, more than twice her own age? "I'm only thirty-four, you know," she said.

Satia seated herself on the edge of the bed next to Lunzie and put a hand sympathetically on her arm. "I know."

"That means my daughter . . . grew up without me," Lunzie finished brokenly. "Had a career, boy-friends, children. . . ." The smile in the Tri-D image beamed out at her, touching off memories of Fiona's laughter in her ears, the unconscious grace of a leggy girl who would become a tall, elegant woman.

"Almost certainly," the female doctor agreed.

Lunzie put her face in her hands and cried. Satia gathered her in her arms and patted her hair with a gentle hand.

"Perhaps we should give you a sedative and let you relax," Stev suggested, after Lunzie's sobs had softened and died away.

"No!" Lunzie glared at him, red-eyed. "I don't want to go to sleep again."

What am I saying? she thought, pulling herself together. It's just like Jilet described to me. Resentment. Fear of sleep. Fear of never waking again. "Perhaps someone could show me around the Platform until I get my bearings?" She smiled hopefully at the others. "I've just had too much relaxation."

"I will," Satia volunteered. "I am free this shift.

We can send a query to Tau Ceti about your daughter."

The Communications Center was near the administrative offices in Cylinder One. Satia and Lunzie walked through the miles of domed corridors from the Medical Center in Cylinder Two. Lunzie was taking in the sights with her eyes wide open. According to Satia, the population of the Platform numbered over eight hundred adult beings. Humans made up about eighty-five percent, with heavyworlders, Wefts and the birdlike Ryxi, along with a few other races Lunzie didn't recognize, making up the rest.

Heavyworlders were human beings, too, but they were a genetically altered strain, bred to inhabit high-gravity planets that were otherwise suitable for colonization, but had inhospitable conditions for "lightweight" normal humans. The males started at about seven feet in height, and went upward from there. Their facial features were thick and heavy, almost Neanderthal in character, and their hands, even those with proportionately slender fingers, were huge. The females were brawny. Lightweight women looked like dolls next to them. They made Lunzie nervous, as if they were an oversize carnival attraction. She had an uncomfortable feeling that they might fall over on her. Their pronounced brow ridges made many of the heavyworlders look perpetually angry, even when they smiled. She warily kept her distance from them.

Satia kept up a cheerful chatter as they walked along, pointing out people she knew, and talking about life on the Platform. "We're a small community," she commented cheerfully, "but it's harder to get away when you're feuding with someone. Privacy centers are absolutely inviolable on a deepspace platform. They help at most times, but Descartes really does detailed personality analyses to weed out the people who won't be able to get along on the Platform. There are community games and events every rest period, and we have a substantial library of both video and text. Boredom is one of the worst things that can happen in a closed community. I get to know everyone because I organize most of their children's events." Numbly, Lunzie kept pace with her, murmuring and smiling to Satia's friends without retaining a single name once the face was out of sight.

"Lep! Domman Lepke! Wait up!" Satia ran to intercept a tall, tan-skinned man in a high-collared tunic who was just disappearing between the automatic sliding doors. He peered around for the hailing voice, and smiled broadly when Satia waved.

"Lep, I want you to meet a new friend. This is Lunzie Mespil. She was just rescued from deepsleep. She's been lost for over sixty years."

"Oh, another deadtimer," Lepke said disapprovingly, shaking hands. "How do you do? Are you a 'nothing's changed' or an 'everything's changed'? Everyone is one or the other. That's nothing. Listen, Satia, have you heard the latest from the Delta beacon? Heavyworlders have claimed Phoenix. It must have been pirated!"

Satia, her mouth open to rebuke Lep for his insensitivity, stopped, her eyes widening with horror. "But that was initiated as an inhabited human colony, over six years ago."

"They claim not that the planet was empty of intelligent life when they got there, but there should be lightweights on that planet right now. No sign of them, or their settlement, or any clue as to what happened to them. Wiped clean off the surface, if they ever made it there in the first place. The FSP are releasing a list of settlers—the usual: 'anyone knowing the last whereabouts,' and so on." Lepke seemed pleased to have been first to pass along the news. "Possession and viability make a colony, so no one can deny their claim if there's no evidence the planet was inhabited before they got there. The Others only know who's telling the truth."

"Oh, sweet Muhlah! It must have been pirated! Come on, Lunzie. We'll hear the latest." Pulling Lunzie behind her, the slim pediatrician raced toward the communications center.

When they arrived, there was already a large group of people gathered around the Tri-D field, talking and waving arms, tentacles, or paws.

"They had no right to take over that world. It was designated for lightweight humans. They're adapted to the high-gee planets. Let them take those, and leave the light worlds to us!" a man with red hair expostulated angrily.

"It is not the first planet to be stripped and abandoned," said a young female with the near-perfect humanoid features a Weft shapechanger usually assumed when living among humans. Lunzie looked around quickly to find the Weft's co-mates. They always travelled in threes. "There was the rumor of Epsilon Indi not long ago. All its satellites were attacked at once. Phoenix is just the most recent dead planet brought to light."

"What happened to the colonists assigned to Phoenix?" a blond woman asked.

"No one knows," the communications tech said, manipulating the controls at the base of the holofield. "Maybe they never made it there. Maybe the Others got 'em. Here, I'll run the 'cast again for those of you who missed it. I'm patching down files as quickly as I can strip them off the beacon." The crowd shifted, as viewers who had already seen the report went away, and others pressed closer.

Squeezing between a broad-shouldered man in coveralls and a lizardlike Seti in an Administrator's tunic, Lunzie watched the report, which featured computer imaging of the new colony's living quarters

and their industrial complex. What had happened to
the other colonists? They must have relatives who
would want to know. Humans weren't raised in vacuum. Each of these was somebody's son. Or somebody's daughter.

"The FSP's official report was cool, but you could
listen between the lines. They are horribly upset.
Something's breaking down in their system. The FSP
is supposed to protect nascent colonies," the blond
woman complained to the man standing beside her.

"Only if they prove to be viable," the Weft corrected her. "There is always a period when the settlement must learn to stand on its own."

"It was their gamble," the Seti said, complacently,
tucking its claws into the pouch pockets on the front
of its tunic. "They lost."

"See here, citizens, if the heavyworlders can make
a go of it, let them have the planet." This suggestion
was promptly shouted down, to the astonishment of
the speaker, a florid-faced human male in coveralls.

"It's a good thing the FSP don't have an attitude
like yours," another growled. "Or your children won't
have anywhere to live."

"There are plenty of new worlds for all out there,"
the coveralled man insisted. "It's a big galaxy."

"Look at us, we're all acting like this is news," the
red-haired man grumbled. "Everything we get is
months or years old. There's got to be a faster way to
get information from the rest of civilization."

"Speed of light's all I've got," the tech smiled
wryly, "unless you want to pay for a regular FTL
mail run. Or talk the Fleet into letting us install an
FTL link booster on the transmitter. Even that's not
much faster."

Lunzie peered into the tank at the triumphant face
of the Phoenix colony's leader, a broad-faced male
with thickly branching eyebrows that shadowed his
eyes. He was talking about agreements made for

trade between Phoenix and the Paraden Company. All that was needed for a colony to be approved by the FSP was a viable population pool and proof that the colony could support itself in the galactic community. ". . . although this planet appears to be poor in the most valuable minerals, transuranics, there are still sufficient ores to be of interest. We have begun manufacture of . . ."

"The heavyworlders shouldn't claim that planet, even if the first colonists didn't survive," Satia declared. "There are many more planets with a high gravity than there are ones which fall within the narrow parameters that normal humans can bear."

"In my day," Lunzie began, then stopped, realizing how ridiculous she must sound, using an elder's phrase at her apparent physical age. "I mean, when I left Tau Ceti, the heavyworlders had just begun colonizing. They were mostly still on Diplo, except for the ones in the FSP corps."

"You know, there must be a connection there somewhere," the red-haired man mused. "There was never planet-pirating before the heavyworlders started colonizing."

A huge hand seized the man's shoulder and spun him around. "That is a lie," boomed the voice of a heavyworld-born man in a technician's tunic. "Planets have been found stripped and empty long hundreds of years before we existed. You want to blame someone, blame the Others. They're responsible for the dead worlds. Don't blame us." The heavyworlder glared down from his full seven feet of height at the man, and included Lunzie and Satia in his scorn. Lunzie shrank away from him. With a heavyworlder in its midst, the lightweight crowd began to disperse. None of the grumblers wanted to discuss Phoenix personally with one of the heavyweight humans.

The Others. A mysterious force in the galaxy. No one knew who they were, if indeed a race of Others, and not natural cataclysm, had caused destruction of those planets. Lunzie suddenly had a cold feeling between her shoulder blades, as if someone was watching her. She turned around. To her surprise, she saw the Thek that had rescued her waiting on the other side of the corridor. It had no features, no expression, but it drew her to it. She felt that it wanted to talk to her.

"Cccccooooooouuuurrrrr . . . aaaaaaaggggggeee . . . . Ssssuurrrrrr . . . . . vvvviiiiiiivvvveee . . . ." it said, when she approached.

"Courage? Survive? What does that mean?" she demanded, but the pyramid of stone said nothing more. It glided slowly away. She wanted to run after it and ask it to clarify the cryptic speech. Theks were known for never wasting a word, especially not on explanation to simple ephemerals such as human beings.

"I suppose it meant that to be comforting," Lunzie decided. "After all, it saved my life, leading that young miner to where my capsule was lodged. But why in the Galaxy didn't it rescue me sooner, if it knew where I was?"

In her assigned room, Lunzie made herself comfortable in the deep, cushiony chair before the cubicle's computer screen. She glanced occasionally at the bunk, freshly made up with sweet-smelling bedding, but avoided touching it as if it was her dreaded enemy. Lunzie wasn't in the least sleepy, and there was still that nagging fear at the back of her mind that she would never wake up again if she succumbed.

Better to clear her brain with some useful input. Once she had run through the user's tutorial, she began systematically to go through the medical journals in Descartes's library. She made a database of all the articles on new topics she wanted to read about. As she pored over her choices, she felt more and

more lost. Everything in her field had advanced
beyond her training.

As promised, Stev Banus had sat down with her
and discussed the credits owed to her by Descartes.
It amounted to a substantial balance, well over a
million. He recommended that she take it and go
back to school. Stev told Lunzie that a position with
Descartes was still open, if she wanted to take it.
Even without up-to-date training, he felt that Lunzie
would be an asset to his staff. With refresher courses
under her belt, she could be promoted to department head under Stev's administration.

"We can't restore the years to you, but we can try
to make you happy now you're here," he offered.

Lunzie was flattered, but she wasn't certain what
to do. She resented having her life interrupted so
brutally. She needed to come to terms with her
feelings before she could make a decision. Stev's
suggestion to seek further education made sense, but
Lunzie couldn't make a move until she knew what
had happened to Fiona. She went back to the file of
medical abstracts and tried to drive away her doubts.

Chapter Three

"Did you sleep well?" Satia asked Lunzie the next morning. The intern leaned in through the door to Lunzie's cubicle and waved to get her attention.

Lunzie turned away from the computer screen and smiled. "No. I didn't sleep at all. I spent half the night worrying about Fiona, and the other half trying to get the synthesizer unit to pour me a cup of coffee. It didn't understand the command. How can I get the unit fixed?"

Satia laughed. "Oh, coffee! My grandmother told me about coffee when I was off-platform, visiting her on Inigo. It's very rare, isn't it?"

Lunzie frowned. "No. Where, or rather when, I come from it's as common as mud. And sometimes has a similar taste. . . . Do you mean to say you've never heard of coffee?" She felt her heart sink. So much had changed over the lost decades, but it was the little things that bothered her most, especially when they affected a lifelong habit. "I usually need something to help me wake up in the morning."

"Oh, I've *heard* of coffee. No one drinks it any more. There were studies decrying the effects of the heavy oils and caffeine on the nervous and digestive systems. We have peppers now."

49

"Peppers?" Lunzie wrinkled her nose in distaste. "As in capsicum?"

"Oh, no. Restorative. It's a mild stimulant, completely harmless. I drink some nearly every morning. You'll like it." Satia stepped to the synth unit in the wall of Lunzie's quarters, and came back with a full mug. "Try this."

Lunzie sipped the liquid and felt a pervasive tingle race through her tissues. Her body abruptly forgot that it had just spent an entire shift cramped in one position. She gasped. "That's very effective."

"Mm—. Sometimes nothing else will get me out of bed. And it leaves behind none of the sour aftertaste my grandmother claimed from coffee."

"Well, here's to my becoming acclimated to the future." Lunzie raised her cup to Satia. "Oh, that reminds me. The gizmos in the lavatory have me stumped. I figured out which one was the waste-disposer unit, but I haven't the faintest idea what the others are."

Satia laughed again. "Very well. I ought to have thought of it before. I will give you the quarter-credit tour."

Once Lunzie had been shown how to work the various conveniences, Satia punched up a cup of herbal tea for them both.

"I don't understand these newfangled things perfectly yet, but at least I know what they do," Lunzie said, wryly self-deprecating.

Satia sipped tea. "Well, it's all part of the future, designed to make life easier. So the advertisements tell us. My friend, what are you going to do with your future?"

"The way I see it, I have two choices. I can search for Fiona, or I can take refresher courses to fit me to practice medicine in this century, and then try to find her. I had the computer research information for me on discoveries that were just breaking when I

went into cold sleep. Progress has certainly been
made. Those breakthroughs are now old hat! I feel
like a primitive thrust into a city without even the
vocabulary to ask for help."

"Perhaps you can stay and study with me. I am
completing my internship here with Dr. Banus. I
may do my residency off-platform, so as to give me a
different perspective in the field of medicine. Specifically, I am studying pediatrics, a field that is becoming ever so important recently—we're having quite a
population explosion on the Platform. Of course, that
would mean leaving my children behind, and that I
do not wish to do. Nonya's three, and Omi is only
five months old. They're such a joy, I don't want to
miss any of their childhood."

Lunzie nodded sadly. "I did the very same thing,
you know. I'm not sure what I want to do, yet. I
must work out where to begin."

"Well, come with me first." Satia rose and placed
her cup in the disposer hatch for the food processor.
"Aiden, the Tri-D technician, told me he wanted to
talk to you." Lunzie put her cup aside and hastened
after Satia.

"I sent your query to Tau Ceti last shift, Doctor,"
the technician said, when they located him at the
Communications Center. "It'll take several weeks to
get a reply out here in the rockies. But I wanted to
tell you—" The young man tapped a finger on the
console top, impatiently trying to stir his memory. "I
think I've seen your surname before. I noticed it,
I forget where . . . in one of the news articles
we've received recently. Maybe it's one of your
descendants?"

"Really?" Lunzie asked with interest. "Please, show
me. I'm sure I have great-nieces and -nephews all
over the galaxy by now."

Aiden keyed in an All-Search for the day's input
from all six beacons. "Here it comes. Watch the

field." The word **"Mespil"** in a very clear, official-looking typestyle, coalesced in the Tri-D forum, followed by **", Fiona, MD, DV."** Other words in the same font formed around it, above and below.

"My daughter! That's her name. Satia, look! Where is she, Aiden? What's this list?" Lunzie demanded, searching the names. "Is there video to go with it?"

The technician looked up from his console, and his expression turned to one of horror. "Oh, Krims, I'm sorry. Doctor, that's the FSP list. The people who were reported missing from the pirated Phoenix colony."

"No!" Satia breathed. She moved to support Lunzie, whose knees had gone momentarily weak. Lunzie gave her a grateful look, but waved her away, steady once again.

"What happens to people who were on planets that have been pirated?" she asked, badly shaken, trying not to let her mind form images of disaster. Fiona!

The young man swallowed. Bearing bad news was not something he enjoyed, and he desperately wanted to give this nice woman encouragement. She had been through so much already. He regretted that he hadn't checked out his information before sending for her. "Sometimes they turn up with no memory of what happened to them. Sometimes they are found working in other places, no problems, but their messages home just went astray. It happens a lot in galactic distant communications; nothing's perfect. Mostly, though, the people are never heard from again."

"Fiona can't be dead. How do I find out what became of her? I must find her."

The technician looked thoughtful. "I'll call Security Chief Wilkins for you. He'll know what you can do."

Chief Wilkins was a short man with a thin gray

mustache that obscured his upper lip, and black eyes that wore a guarded expression. He invited her to sit down in his small office, a clean and tidy cubicle that said much about the mind of the man who occupied it. Lunzie explained her situation to him, but judged from his knowing nods that he knew all about her already.

"So what are you going to do?" he asked.

"I'm going to go look for her, of course," she said firmly.

"Fine, fine." He smiled. "Where? You've got your back pay. You have enough money to charge off anywhere in the galaxy you wish and back again. Where will you begin?"

"Where?" Lunzie blinked. "I . . . I don't know. I suppose I could start at Phoenix, where she was last seen. . . ."

Wilkins shook his head, and made a deprecatory clicking sound with his tongue. "We don't know that for certain, Lunzie. She was expected there, along with the rest of the colonists."

"Well, the EEC should know if they arrived on Phoenix or not."

"Good, good. There's a start. But it's many light years away from here. What if you don't find her there? Where next?"

"Oh." Lunzie sank back into the chair, which molded comfortably around her spine. "You're quite right. I wasn't thinking about *how* I would find her. All her life, I was able to walk to any place she might be. Nothing was too far away." In her mind, she saw a star map of the civilized galaxy. Each point represented at least one inhabited world. It took weeks, months, or even years to pass between some of those star systems, and searching each planet, questioning each person in every city. . . . She hugged her elbows, feeling very small and helpless.

Wilkins nodded approvingly. "You have ascertained

the first difficulty in a search of this kind: distance. The second is time. Time has passed since that report was news. It will take more time to send out inquiries and receive replies. You must begin at the other end of history, and find out where she's been. Her childhood home, records of marriage or other alliances. And she must have had an employer at one time or another in her life. That will give you clues to where she is now.

"For example, why was she on that planetary expedition? As a settler? As a specialist? An observer? The EEC has records. You may have noticed"—here Wilkins activited the viewscreen on his desk and swiveled the monitor toward Lunzie—"that her name is followed by the initials MD and DV."

Lunzie confronted the FSP list once more, trying to ignore the connotation of disaster. "MD. She's a doctor. DV—" Lunzie searched her memory. "That denotes a specialty in virology."

"So she must have gone to University somewhere, too. Good. You would have wanted her to opt for Higher Education, I am sure. What did she do with her schooling? You have a great many clues to work with, but it will take many months, even years, for answers to come back to you. The best thing for you to do is to establish a permanent base of operations, and send out your queries."

"Stev Banus suggested I go back to school and update myself."

"A valid suggestion. While you're doing that, you'll also be accomplishing your search. If one line of questioning becomes fruitless, start others. Ask for help from any agency you think might be of use to you. Never mind if they duplicate your efforts. It is easier to have something you might have missed noticed by a fresh, non-involved mind. And it will be less expensive than running out to investigate prospects by yourself. It will be a costly search in any case, but you won't be in the thick of it, trying to make sense out of your incoming information without the perspective to consider it."

"I do need perspective. I've never had to deal on such a vast basis before. Her father and I corresponded regularly while she was growing up. It simply never occurred to me to think about the transit time between letters, and it was a long time! It's faster to fly FTL, but for me to think of traveling all that distance to a place, when I might not find her at the end of the journey . . . Fiona is too precious to me to allow me to think clearly. Thank you for your clear sight." Lunzie stood up. "And, Wilkins? Thank you for not assuming that she's dead."

"You don't believe she is. One of your other clues is your own insight. Trust it." The edges of the thin mustache lifted in an encouraging smile. "Good luck, Lunzie."

The child-care center was full of joyful chaos. Small humans chased other youngsters around the padded floor, shouting, careening off foam-core furniture, and narrowly missing the two adults who crouched in one of the conversation rings, trying to stay out of the way.

"Vigul!" Satia cried. "Let go of Tlink's tentacle and he will let go of your hair. Now!" She clapped her hands sharply, ignoring the disappointed "Awwwwww" from both children. She relaxed, but kept a sharp eye on the combatants. "They are normally good, but occasionally things get out of hand."

"They're probably acting up in the presence of a stranger—me!" Lunzie said, smiling.

Satia sighed. "I'm glad the Weft parents weren't around to see that. He's so young, he doesn't know yet that it's considered bad manners by his people to shape-shift in public. I'd rather that he learn to be himself with other children. It shows that he trusts them. That's good."

Beside Lunzie in his cot, Satia's infant son Omi twisted and stretched restlessly in his sleep. She picked up the infant and cradled him gently against her chest, his head resting on her shoulder. He subsided, sucking one tiny fist stuffed halfway into his mouth. Lunzie smiled down at him. She remembered Fiona at that age. She'd been in medical school, and every day carried the baby with her to class. Lunzie joyed in the closeness of the infant cradled in the snuggle pack, heartbeat to heartbeat with her. That perfect little life, like an exotic flower, that she'd created. The teachers made smiling reference to the youngest class member, who was often the first example of young humankind that an alien student ever encountered. Fiona was so good. She never cried during lectures, though she fretted occasionally in exams, seeming to sense Lunzie's own apprehension. Harshly, Lunzie put those thoughts from her mind. Those days were gone. Fiona was an adult. Lunzie must learn to think of her that way.

Omi snuggled in, removing the fist from his mouth for a tiny yawn and popping it back again. Lunzie hugged him, and shook her head aggressively. "I refuse to believe that Fiona is dead. I cannot, will not give up hope." She sighed. "But Wilkins is right. I've got to be patient, but it'll be the hardest thing I've ever done." Lunzie grinned ruefully. "None of my family is good at being patient. It's why we all become doctors. I have a lot to learn, and unlearn, too. Schoolwork will help me keep my mind in order."

"I'll miss you," Satia said. "We have become friends, I think. You'll always have a home here, if you want one."

"I don't think I'll ever have a home again," Lunzie said sadly, thinking of the vastness of the star map. "But thank you for the offer. It means a great deal to me." Gently, she laid the baby back in his cot. "You know, I went to see Jilet, the miner I was treating for agoraphobia before the *Nellie Mine* crashed. He's still hale and healthy, at ninety-two, good for another thirty years at least. His hair is white, and his chest has slipped into his belly, but I still recognized him on sight. Illin Romsey is his *grandson.* He prospected for some fifty years after his shuttle was rescued, and now he's working as a deck supervisor. I was glad to see him looking so well." Her lips twitched in a mirthless smile. "He didn't remember me. Not at all."

Astris Alexandria University was delighted to accept an application for continuing education from one of their alumna, but they were obviously taken aback when Lunzie, dressed very casually and carrying her own luggage, arrived in the administration office to enroll for classes. Lunzie caught the admissions secretary surreptitiously running her identification to verify her identity.

"I'm sorry for the abrupt reception, Doctor Mespil, but frankly, considering your age, we were expecting someone rather more mature in appearance. We only wanted to make sure. May I ask, have you been taking radical rejuvenative therapy?"

"My age? I'm thirty-four," Lunzie stated briskly. "I've been in cold sleep."

"Oh, I see. But for our records, ninety-six years have passed since your birth. I'm afraid your I.D. code bracelet and transcripts will reflect that," the registrar offered with concern. "I will make a note for the files regarding your circumstances and physical age, if you request."

Lunzie held up a hand. "No, thank you. I'm not that vain. If it doesn't confuse anyone, I can live without a footnote. There's another matter with which you can help me. What sort of student housing, bed and board, can the University provide? I'm looking for quarters as inexpensive as I can get, so long as it still has communication capability and library access and storage. I'll even share sanitary facilities, if needed. I have few personal possessions, and I'm easy enough to get along with."

The registrar seemed puzzled. "I would have thought . . . your own apartment, or a private domicile . . ."

"Unfortunately, no. I need to leave as much of my capital resources as possible free to cope with a personal matter. I'm cutting back on all non-essentials."

Clearly, the woman's sense of outrage regarding the dignity and priorities of Astris Alexandria alumni was kindled against Lunzie. She was too casual, too careless of her person. Her only luggage was the pair of small and dowdy synth-fabric duffles slung across the back of the opulent office chair in which she sat. Not at all what one would expect of a senior graduate of this elite seat of learning.

To Lunzie's relief, her cases had been kept in vacuum temperatures in remote storage on the Mining Platform, so that none of her good fiber-fabric clothes were perished or parasite-eaten. She didn't care what sort of state the University wanted her to keep. Now that she had acknowledged her goals, she could once more take command of her own life as she had been accustomed to doing. Austerity didn't bother her. She preferred a spare environment. She had felt helpless on the Descartes platform, in spite of everyone's kindness. This was a familiar venue. Here she knew just exactly how much power the authorities had, and how much was empty protest. She kept her expression neutral and waited patiently.

"Well," the woman allowed, at last. "There is a quad dormitory with only a Weft trio sharing it at present. There is a double room with one space opening up. The tenant is being graduated, and the room will be clear within two weeks, when the new term begins. One room of a six-room suite in a mixed-species residence hall. . . ."

"Which is the cheapest?" Lunzie asked, abruptly

cutting short the registrar's recitation. She smiled sweetly at the woman's scowl.

With a look of utter disapproval, the registrar put her screen on Search. The screen blurred, then stopped scrolling as one entry centered itself and flashed. "A third share of a University-owned apartment. The other two current tenants are human. But it is rather far away from campus."

"I don't mind. As long as it has a roof and a cot, I'll be happy."

Juggling an armful of document cubes and plassheet evaluation forms as well as her bags, Lunzie let herself into the small foyer of her new home. The building was old, predating Lunzie's previous University term. It made her feel at home to see something that hadn't changed appreciably. The old-fashioned textboard in the building's entryhall flashed with personal messages for the students who lived there, and a new line had already appeared at the bottom, adding her name and a message of welcome, followed by a typical bureaucratic admonishment to turn in her equivalency tests as soon as possible. The building was fairly quiet. Most of the inhabitants would have day classes or jobs to attend to.

Her unit was on the ninth level of the fifty-story hall. The turbovator whooshed satisfyingly to its destination, finishing up on her doorstep with a slight jerk and a noisy rattle, not silently as the unnerving lifts aboard the Platform had. Neither of her roommates was home. The apartment was of reasonably good size, clean, though typically untidy. The shelves were cluttered with the typical impedimentia of teenagers. It made her feel almost as if she were living with Fiona again. One of the tenants enjoyed building scale models. Several were hung from the ceiling, low enough that Lunzie was glad she wasn't five inches taller.

A little searching revealed that the vacant sleeping

chamber was the smallest one closest to the food synthesizer. She unpacked and took off her travel-soiled clothes. The weather, one of the things that Lunzie had always loved about Astris Alexandria, was mild and warm most of the year in the University province, so she happily shed the heavier trousers she had worn on the transport, and laid out a light skirt.

The trousers were badly creased, and could use cleaning. Lunzie felt she would be the better for a good wash, too. She assumed that all the standard cleaning machinery would be available in the lavatory. She gathered up toiletries, laundry, and her dusty boots.

In the lavatory, Lunzie stared with dismay at the amenities. Instead of being comfortably familiar, they were spankingly brand new. The building's facilities had been very recently updated, even newer and stranger than the ones Descartes furnished to its living quarters. If it hadn't been for Satia's patient help on the Platform, she would not now have the faintest idea what she was looking at. There were enough similarities between them for her to figure out how to use these without causing a minor disaster.

While her clothes were being processed, she slipped on fresh garments and sat down at the console in her bedroom. She logged on to the library system, and requested an I.D. number which would give her access to the library from any console on the planet. Automatically, she applied for an increase in the standard student's allotment of long-term memory storage from 320K to 2048K, and opened an account in the Looking-GLASS program. If there was any stored data about Fiona anywhere, the Galactic Library All-Search System, GLASS, as it was fondly known, would find it. As an icon to luck, she set Fiona's hologram on top of the console.

LOOKING-GLASS LOG-ON (2851.0917 Standard) scrolled up on her screen.

She typed in *Query Missing Person* NAME *Fiona Mespil* DOB/RACE/SEX/S,PO *2775.0903/ human/female/Astris Alexandria* She had been born right here at the University, so that was her planet of origin. *Current location requested.* LOCATION SUBJECT LAST SEEN? Lunzie paused for a moment, then entered: *Last verifiable location, Tau Ceti colony, 2789.1215. Last presumed location, Phoenix colony, 2851.0421.* The screen went blank for a moment as GLASS digested her request. Lunzie entered a command for the program to dump its findings into her assigned memory storage and prepared to log off.

Suddenly, the screen chimed and scrolled up a display of dates and entries, with the heading:

MESPIL, FIONA
TRANSCRIPT OF EDUCATION (REVERSE CHRONOLOGICAL)
2802 GRANTED DEGREE CERTIFICATE IN BIOTECHNOLOGY, ASTRIS ALEXANDRIA UNIVERSITY
2797 GRANTED DEGREE CERTIFICATE IN VIROLOGY, ASTRIS ALEXANDRIA UNIVERSITY
2795 ASTRIS ALEXANDRIA UNIVERSITY, GRADUATED WITH HONORS, M.D. [GENERAL]
2792 GRADUATED MARSBASE SECONDARY SCHOOL EDUCATION SYSTEM, GRADUATED GENERAL CERTIFICATE
2791 TAU CETI EDUCATION SYSTEM, TRANSFERRED
2787 CAPELLA PRIMARY SCHOOL EDUCATION SYSTEM, GRADUATED

Following was a list of courses and grades. Lunzie
let out a shout of joy. Records existed right here on
Astris Alexandria! She hadn't expected to see anything come up yet. She was only laying the ground-
work for her information search. The search was
beginning to bear fruit already. *Save*, she commanded the computer,

"I should have known," she said, shaking her head.
"I might have known she'd come here to Astris, after
all the hype I'd given the place." The first successful
step in her search! For the first time, Lunzie truly
felt confident. A celebration was in order. She surveyed the apartment, and advanced smiling on the
food synthesizer. One success deserved another.

"Now," she said, rubbing her hands together. "I
am going to teach *you* how to make coffee."

An hour or so later, she had a potful of murky
brew that somewhat resembled coffee, though it was
so bitter she had to program a healthy dose of a
mellowing sweetener with which to dilute it. There
was caffeine in the stuff, at any rate. She was satisfied, though still disappointed that the formula for
coffee had disappeared from use over the last sixty
years. Still, there was a School of Nutrition in the
University. Someone must still have coffee on record.
She considered ordering a meal, but decided against
it. If the food was anything like she remembered it,
she wasn't that hungry. Synthesized food always tasted
flat to her, and the school synth machines were
notoriously bad. She had no reason to believe that
their reputation—or performance—had improved in
her absence.

When time permitted, Lunzie planned to treat
herself to some real planet-grown food. Astris Alexandria had always produced tasty legumes and greens,
and perhaps, she thought hopefully, the farm community had even branched out into coffee bushes.
Like all civilized citizens of the FSP, Lunzie ate only

foods of vegetable origin, disdaining meats as a vestige of barbaric history. She hoped neither of her roommates was a throwback, though the Housing Committee would undoubtedly have seen to it that such students would be isolated, out of consideration to others.

Following the instructions of the plas-sheets, she logged into the University's computer system and signed up for a battery of tests designed to evaluate her skills and potential. The keyboard had a well-used feel, and Lunzie quickly found herself rattling along at a clip. One of the regulations which had not existed in her time was registration qualification: enrollment for certain classes was restricted to those who qualified through the examinations. Lunzie noted with irritation that several of the courses which she wanted to take fell into that category. The rationale, translated from the bureaucratese, was that space was so limited in these courses that the University wanted to guarantee that the students who signed up for them would be the ones who would get the most out of them. Even if she passed the exams, there was no guarantee that she could get in immediately. Lunzie gave a resigned shrug. Until she had a good lead on finding Fiona, she was filed here. There was no hurry. She started to punch in a request for the first exam.

"Hello?" a tentative voice called from the door.

"Come?" Lunzie answered, peering over the edge of the console.

"Peace, citizen. We're your roommates." The speaker was a slender boy with straight, silky black hair and round blue eyes. He didn't look more than fifteen Standard years old. Behind him was a smiling girl with soft brown hair gathered up in a puffy coil on top of her head. "I'm Shof Scotny, from Demarkis. This is Pomayla Esglar."

"Welcome," Pomayla said, warmly, offering her

hand. "You didn't have the privacy seal on the door, so we thought it would be all right to come in and greet you."

"Thank you," Lunzie replied, rising and extending hers. Pomayla covered it with her free hand. "It's nice to meet you. I'm Lunzie Mespil. Call me Lunzie. Ah . . . is something wrong?" she asked, catching a curious look that passed between Shof and Pomayla.

"Nothing," Shof answered lightly. "You know, you don't look ninety-six. I expected you to look like my grandmother."

"Well, thank you so much. You don't look old enough to be in college, my lad," Lunzie retorted, amused. She reconsidered asking the registrar to put an explanation on her records.

Shof sighed long-sufferingly. He'd obviously heard that before. "I can't help it that I'm brilliant at such a tender age." Lunzie grinned at him. He was hopelessly cute and likely accustomed to getting away with murder.

Pomayla elbowed Shof in the midriff, and he let out an outraged *oof*! "Forgive Mr. Modesty. They don't bother teaching tact to the Computer Science majors, since the machines don't take offense at bad manners. I'm in the Interplanetary Law program. What's your field of study?"

"Medicine. I'm back for some refresher courses. I've been . . . rather out of touch the last few years."

"I'll bet. Well, come on, granny," the boy offered, slinging a long forelock of hair out of his eyes. "We'll start getting you up to date this millisecond."

"Shof!" Pomayla shoved her outrageous roommate through the door. "Tact?"

"Did I say something wrong already?" Shof asked with all the ingenuousness he could muster as he was propelled out into the turbovator.

Lunzie followed, chuckling.

*　　　*　　　*

Looking-GLASS turned up nothing of note over the next several weeks. Lunzie submerged herself in her new classes. Her roommates were gregarious and friendly, and insisted that she participate in everything that interested them. She found herself hauled along to student events and concerts with them and their "Gang," as they called themselves, a loose conglomeration of thirty or so of all ages and races from across the University. There seemed to be nothing the group had in common but good spirits and curiosity. She found their outings to be a refreshing change from the long hours of study.

No topic was sacred to the Gang, not physical appearance, nor habits, age, or custom. Lunzie soon got tired of being called granny by beings whose ages surely equaled her own thirty-four Standard years. The subject of her cold sleep and subsequent search for her daughter was still too painful to discuss, so she lightly urged the conversation away from personal matters. She wondered if Shof knew about her search, seeing as he had already unlocked her admissions records. If he did, he was being unusually reticent in not bringing it up. Perhaps she had managed to lock her GLASS file tightly enough away from his prying gaze. Or perhaps he just didn't feel it was interesting enough. In most cases when someone started a query, she would carefully reverse the flow and launch a personal probe into the life of her inquisitor, to the amusement of the Gang, who loved watching Lunzie go into action.

"You ought to have taken up Criminal Justice," Pomayla insisted. "I'd hate to be on the witness stand, hiding anything from you."

"No, thank you. I'd rather be Doctor McCoy than Rumpole of the Bailey."

"Who?" demanded Cosir, one of their classmates, a simian Brachian with handsome purple fur and reflective white pupils. "What is this Rompul?"

"Something on Tri-D," Shof speculated.

"Ancient history," complained Frega, another of the Gang, polishing her ebony-painted nails on her tunic sleeve.

"Nothing I've ever heard of," Cosir insisted. "That's got to have been off the Forum for a hundred Standard years."

"At least that," Lunzie agreed gravely. "You could say I'm a bit of an antiquarian."

"And at your age, too!" chortled Shof. He clutched his hands over his narrow belly. He tapped a fist on it and pretended to listen for the echo. "Hmm. I've gone hollow. Let's go eat."

Lectures were, on the whole, as dull as Lunzie remembered them. Only two courses kept her interest piqued. Her practicum in Diagnostic Science was interesting, as was the required course in Discipline.

Diagnostic science had changed enormously since she had practiced medicine. The computerized tests to which incoming patients were subjected were less intrusive and more comprehensive than she would have believed possible. Her mother, from whom Lunzie had inherited the "healing hands," had always felt that to be a good doctor, one needed only a thoroughgoing grasp of diagnostic science and an excellent bedside manner. Her mother would have been as pleased as she was to know that Fiona had followed in the family tradition and pursued a medical career.

Diagnostic instruments were no longer so cumbersome as they had been in her day. Most units could be carried two or three in a pouch, saving time and space in case of an emergency. Lunzie's favorite was the "bod bird," a small medical scanner that required no hands-on use. Using new anti-gravity technology, it would hover at any point around a patient and display its readings. It was especially good for use in zero-gee. The unit was very popular among physicians who specialized in patients much larger than themselves, and non-humanoid doctors who considered extending manipulative digits too close to another being as an impolite intrusion. Lunzie liked it because it left her hands free for patient care. She made a note of the "bod bird" as one of the instruments she would buy for herself when she went back into practice. It was expensive, but not completely out of her range.

Once data had been gathered on a subject's condition, the modern doctor had at her command such tools as computer analysis to suggest treatment. The program was sophisticated enough that it gave a physician a range of choices. In extreme but not immediately life-threatening cases, recombinant gene-splicing, chemical treatment, or intrusive or non-intrusive surgery might be suggested. It was up to the physician to decide which would be best in the case. Types of progressive therapy now in use made unnecessary many treatments that would formerly have been considered mandatory to save a patient's life.

Lunzie admired her new tools, but she was not happy with the way attitudes toward medical treatment had altered in the last six decades. Too much of the real work of the physician had been taken out of the hands of the practitioner and placed in the "hands" of cold, impersonal machines. She openly disagreed with her professors that the new way was better for patients because there was less chance of physician error or infection.

"Many more will give up the will to live for lack of a little personal care," Lunzie pointed out to the professor of Cardiovascular Mechanics, speaking privately with him in his office. "The method for repairing the tissues of a damaged heart is technically perfect, yes, but what about a patient's feelings? The mood and mental condition of your patient are as important as the scientific treatment available for his ailment."

"You're behind the times, Doctor Mespil. This is the best possible treatment for cardiac patients suffering from weak artery walls that are in danger of aneurysm. The robot technician can send microscopic machines through the patient's very bloodstream to stimulate regrowth of damaged tissue. He need never be worried by knowing what is going on inside him."

Lunzie crossed her arms and fixed a disapproving eye on him. "So they're not troubled by asking what's happening to them? Of course, there are some patients who have never known anything but unresponsive doctors. I suppose in your case it wouldn't make any difference."

"That's unjust, Doctor. I want what is best for my patients."

"And I want to do more than tending the machines tending the patient," Lunzie shot back. "I'm a doctor, not a mechanic."

"And I am a surgeon, not a psychologist."

"Well! It doesn't surprise me in the least that the psychology professor disagrees with your principles one hundred percent! You're not improving your patient's chances for survival by working on him as if he was an unaware piece of technological scrap that needs repair."

"Doctor Mespil," the cardiologist said, tightly. "As you so rightly point out, the patient's mental condition is responsible for a significant part of his recovery. It is his choice whether to live or die after receiving quality medical care. I refuse to interfere with free will."

"That is a ridiculous cop-out."

"I assume from your antiquated slang that you think I am shirking my duties. I am aware that you have published in respected scientific journals and have a background in medical ethics. Commendable.

I have even read your abstracts in back issues of
Bioethics Quarterly. But may I remind you of your
status? You are my student, and I am your teacher.
While you are in my class, you will learn from me.
And I would appreciate it if you would cease to
harangue me in front of your fellows. However many
hands you wish to hold sympathetically when you
leave my course is entirely up to you. Good afternoon."

After ending that unsatisfying interview, Lunzie
stormed into the gymnasium for a good workout with
her Discipline exercises.

Discipline was a required study for high-level physicians, medical technicians, and those who wanted
to pursue deepspace explorations. The tests she'd
taken showed her natural aptitude for it but she
dreaded having to set aside the hours necessary to
complete the course. She had moved from the basic
studies to Adept training years ago. Discipline was
time-consuming but more than that, it was exhausting. She was dismayed to discover that her new
teacher insisted that at least six hours every day be
devoted to exercises, meditation, and practice of concentration. It left little time for any other activity.
The short months since she had practiced Discipline
showed in softened muscles and a shortened attention span.

After a few weeks, she was pleased to notice that
the exercises had put more of a spring back in her
walk and lessened her dependency on her ersatz
coffee. She could wake up effortlessly most morn-
ings, even after little sleep. She had forgotten how
good it felt to be in shape. Meditation techniques
made that sleep more refreshing, since it was possible to subsume her worries about Fiona by an act of
will, banishing her concerns temporarily to the back
of her mind.

Her memory retention improved markedly. She
found it easier to assimilate new data, such as the cur-

rent political leanings and policies as well as
the new styles and colloquialisms, besides the data
from her schoolwork. It was clear, too, that she
was in better physical shape than she had been in
years. Her bottom had shrunk one trouser size and
her belly muscles had tightened up. She mentioned
her observations to Pomayla, who promptly pounced
on her and dragged her out to the stores to buy
new clothes.

"It's a terrific excuse. I didn't want to mention it
before, Lunzie, but your garb is *dated*. We weren't
sure if that was the way fashions are on your
homeworld, or if you couldn't afford new clothes."

"What makes you think I can now?" Lunzie asked
calmly.

Pomayla, embarrassed, struggled to get her con-
fession out. "It's Shof. He says you have plenty of
credits. He really is brilliant with computers, you
know. Um." She turned away to the synth unit for a
pepper. With her face hidden from Lunzie, she admitted, "He opened your personal records. He wanted
to know why you look so young at your age. Were
you truly in cold sleep for sixty years?"

Lunzie refused to be shocked. She'd suspected
something of the kind would happen eventually. "I
don't remember anything about it, to be honest, but
I find it difficult to argue with the facts. Drat Shof.
Those records were sealed!"

"You can't keep him out of anything. I bet he
knows how many fastenings you've got in your un-
derthings, too. We get along as roommates because I
treat him the same way I treat my little brother:
respect for his abilities, and none for his ego. It's a
good thing he has a healthy moral infrastructure, or
he'd be rolling in credits with a straight A average.
Oh, come on, let go of a little money. All you ever
use it for is your mysterious research. Fashions have
changed since you bought that outfit. No one wears

trousers tight about the calves any more. You'll feel better about yourself. I promise."

"Well . . ." Shof must not have found her GLASS file yet. Thank goodness. There were other things in her records which she didn't want to have found, such as her involvement as a student on a clone colony ethics panel. Surely by now the laundered details of the aborted project had been made public, but she couldn't be sure how they would feel about her involvement in it. Clone technology was anathema to most people. Lunzie weighed the price of a few new garments against the cost of data search. Perhaps she had been keeping too tight a hand on the credit balance. Even though she hated the flatness of synth food she had even been eating it exclusively to save the cost of real-meals. Every fraction of a credit must be available for the search for Fiona. Perhaps she was allowing her obsession to run her life. It wouldn't make all that much difference, with the interest her credits were earning, to spend a little on herself.

"All right. We can shop for a while, and you can drop me off at the Tri-D Forum afterward. I want to see today's news."

Lunzie had taken to heart Security Chief Wilkins's advice to make use of every source of information she could. At the EEC office, she filled out hundreds of forms requesting access to any documents they had on Fiona, and asking how she was involved in the doomed Phoenix colony.

For doomed it was. In the interval since she had seen the first report about Phoenix, an independent merchant ship had made planetfall there to trade with the colonists and had sold its story to the Tri-D. The merchant brought back vid-cubes of the terrain, which showed the "smoking hole" where the lightweight camp had been. The merchant had also affirmed that the heavyweight humans now living there were possessed of no weapons of that magnitude and could not possibly have caused the colony's destruction. Lunzie, who had conceived a dislike for heavyworlders that surprised her, mistrusted such a blanket assurance, but the colonists had gone under oath and sworn the planet was vacant when they landed. In any case, they had proved the viability of their own settlement, and were now entitled to FSP privileges and protection. Looking-GLASS told her much the same thing.

The heavyworlders had their own disappointments, too. The original EEC prospect report, made twelve years before the original colony was launched, had stated that Phoenix had copious radioactive ores that could be easily mined because upthrust folds in the planet's surface had brought much of it in reach. Their rad counters didn't so much as murmur. The planet's crust had been swept clean of transuranics. If the Phoenix settlers were hoping to become a trading power in the FSP with a new source of the ever-scarce ores, they were frustrated. Rather than chalk the omission off to the unknown Others, as the Tri-D chat-show presenters were doing, the FSP was suggesting that the original report had been in error. Lunzie doubted it. Her resentment for the unknown planet pirates redoubled. Her hopes of finding Fiona alive were slipping away.

The University's Tri-D Forum was a public facility for use free of charge by any individual. Cheap entertainment on Astris was fairly limited beyond outdoor concerts and Tri-D, and Tri-D was the only one which was held in all weathers. The display field hovered several feet above the ground in a lofty hexagonal chamber lined with tiered benches. The Forum was seldom filled to capacity, except during reception of important sports events, but it was never completely empty. News broadcasts and reports of interest were received throughout the day and night, the facts recited in FSP Basic, with Basic subtitling over the videos of local language events. Astris University authorities tried to keep it from becoming a haven for the homeless, preferring to divert those luckless beings to shelters, but even at night there were usually a few citizens watching the broadcast: insomniacs, natural nocturnals, a few passing the time between night classes, or just those who were unwilling to let the day end. Lunzie noted that most of those who used the facility were older and more mature than the average. Entertainment Fora were available to the younger set who weren't interested in the current news.

Lunzie went there whenever sleep eluded her, but her usual time to view Tri-D was late morning, just before the midday meal. A dozen or so regulars smiled at her or otherwise acknowledged her presence when she came in after shopping with Pomayla. She kept her head down as she found her accustomed seat. Though she hated to admit it to herself, she was becoming addicted to Tri-D. Lunzie watched all the news, human interest stories as well as hard fact documentation. Nothing much had changed but the names in the sixty-two years since she was in the stream. Piracy, politics, disaster, joy, tears, life. New discoveries, new science, new prejudices to replace the old ones. New names for old things. The hardest thing to get used to was how old the world leaders and public figures of her day were now. So many of them were dead of old age, and she was still thirty-four. It made her feel as though there was something immoral in her, watching them, secure in her extended youth. She promised herself that when she was sufficiently familiarized with the news events of her lost years, she would quit stopping in to the Forum every morning, but she didn't count on keeping that promise.

The round-the-clock headline retrospective aired

at midday. Lunzie always waited through that to see if there was any story that might relate to Fiona, and then went on with her day. She had arrived at the Forum later than usual. The headline portion was just ending as she entered the dim arena. "There is nothing new since yesterday," one of the regulars, a human man, whispered as he stood up to leave.

"Thanks," Lunzie murmured back. The Tri-D field filled the room with light as another text file appeared, and she met his eyes. He smiled down at her, and eased his way out along the bench toward the exit. Lunzie settled in among her parcels. Watching repeats of earlier broadcasts didn't bore her. She considered Tri-D in the light of an extracurricular course in the interaction of living beings. She was instantly absorbed in the unfolding story in the hovering field.

Chapter Four

Lunzie had no classes that afternoon, so following her visit to the Forum, she decided to stop in at the EEC office. It had been nearly a Standard year since she filled out the forms requesting Fiona's records. So far, she hadn't been told anything, but every time she came in there were more forms to fill out. She was becoming frustrated with the bureaucratic jumble, smelling a delaying technique, and an irritating one at that. Her temper had reached the fraying point.

"You're just giving me more paperwork so you don't have to tell me you don't know anything," Lunzie accused a thin-faced clerk over the ceramic-topped counter between them. "I don't believe you've even advanced my query to the FSP databanks."

"Really, Citizen, such an accusation. These things take time. . . ." the man began, patiently, glancing nervously at the other clerks.

Lunzie held on to her temper with all of her will. "I have given you time, Citizen. I am Dr. Mespil's next of kin, and I want to know what she was doing on that expedition and where she is now."

"This information will be sent to you by comlink. There is no need to come into this facility every time you have questions."

75

"Nothing ever gets answered anyway. I've never had information passed on to me even when I do come here in person. *Have* you sent my queries on to the FSP databank?"

"Your caseworker should be keeping you posted on details."

"I don't have a caseworker," Lunzie's voice rose up the scale from a growl to a shriek. "I've never been assigned one. I've never been told I *needed* one."

"Ah. Well, if you'll just fill out these forms requesting official assistance, I will see who has room in their caseload for you." The clerk blithely fanned a sheaf of plas-sheets before her, and disappeared through the swinging partitions before she could fire off an angry retort.

Muttering furiously to herself, Lunzie picked up the stylus and pulled the forms over. More of the same nonsense. Heartless bureaucratic muckshovelers. . . .

Some days later, she was back filling out yet another form.

"Excuse me, Dr. Mespil." Lunzie looked up to find a tall man standing over her. "My name is Teodor Janos. I'll be your caseworker. I . . . haven't we met?" He sat down across from her and peered at her closely. His straight black brows wrinkled together.

"No, I don't think so—Wait a milli." She blinked at him, trying to place him, then smiled. "Never formally, I'm afraid. I've seen you at the Tri-D."

Teodor threw his head back and laughed. "Of course. A fellow viewer. Yes. You leave before I do most days, I think. I saw you, only a short time ago, on my way out. Good, then we have something in common. I am supposed to relate to you as closely as I can. But not too much. Officially." His smile was warm, and slightly mischievous.

"You're new at this," Lunzie guessed.

"Very. I've only been in this position since the beginning of the year. Would you prefer a case-worker with more experience? I can find one for you."

"No. You'll do just fine. You're the first person with any life in you I've seen in this office."

That set him laughing again. "Some would say that is a disadvantage," Teodor admitted humorously, showing even, white teeth. "Let us see. You wish information on your daughter, also a doctor, whose name is Fiona, and who was involved in the Phoenix expedition, which ended in failure."

"That's right."

He consulted an electronic clipboard. "And the last time you had contact with her was when she was fourteen? And she is how old now?"

"Seventy-seven," Lunzie confessed, and braced herself for a jibing remark. "An accident to my space transport forced me into cold sleep."

To her surprise, Teodor only nodded. "Ah. So the dates in this record are accurate. Another thing which we have in common, Lunzie. May I call you Lunzie? Such an unusual name."

"Certainly, citizen Janos."

"I am Tee. Teodor to my parents and my employer, only."

"Thank you, Tee."

"So, let us go over your questions, please, if you don't mind. I promise you, it is the last time."

With a deep sigh, Lunzie started from the top of her now-familiar recitation. "When I disappeared, Fiona was sent from Tau Ceti to my brother Edgard on MarsBase. She finished school there, and came here to study medicine. Her first employer was Dr. Clora, affiliated with Didomaki Hospital. She went into private practice and got married. According to transmissions found for me by Looking-GLASS, she applied to the FSP a few years after that. And that is the last I've been able to discover. Everything else about her is locked up in the databanks of the FSP, and no one will tell me anything."

Tee frowned sympathetically. "I will get information for you, Lunzie," he promised. "Is your communications code here? I'll notify you whenever I find something."

With greater hope than she had felt in weeks, Lunzie walked out into the warm air. She was in such good spirits she decided to go back to her quarters on foot. It was a long walk, but the day was fine and clear. Her parcels bumped forgotten against her back.

She checked the message board automatically on her way into the residence hall. Beneath the school's notices and invitations for the three roommates from the Gang was a small, frantically flashing message: "Lunzie, call Tee," and a code number. Lunzie hurried up to the apartment, tossed her parcels onto her bed, and flew over to the communications center. She danced impatiently from one foot to the other, waiting for the connection to go through.

"Tee, I got your message. What is it?" she demanded of the image on the comset breathlessly. "What is it? What have you found?"

"Nothing, nothing but you, lovely lady," Tee replied.

"What?" Lunzie shrieked, disbelievingly. She couldn't have heard him correctly. "Say that again? No, don't— What has this to do with my investigation?"

"Only my eagerness to know the querent better: you. It occurred to me only when you had gone, that I would enjoy escorting you to dinner this evening. But it was too late to ask. You had already departed. So I called and left a message. You do not mind?" he inquired, his voice a soothing purr.

One part of Lunzie felt extremely let down, but the rest of her was flattered by the attention. "I don't mind, I suppose, though you could have been less cryptic in your message."

"Ah, but the mystery made you react more quickly." Tee smiled wickedly. "I finish work very soon. Shall I come by for you?"

"It's a long way out here. I'm at the tail end of the '15' Transportation Line. Why don't we meet?"

"Why not? Where?" Tee asked.

"Where else?" Lunzie answered, hand over the cutoff control. "The Tri-D Forum."

In spite of his audacity, Tee proved otherwise to be a courteous and charming companion. He chose the restaurant, one of Astris's finest, and stated unequivocally that he would pay for both their meals, but he insisted that Lunzie choose from the menu for both of them.

Lunzie, fond of good food and wine, and weary of student synth-swill, went down the list with a critical eye. The selection was very good, and she was pleased by the variety, exclaiming over a few of her old favorites which the restaurant offered. To the human server's obvious approval, she selected a well-orchestrated dinner in every detail from appetizers to dessert. "I have a heirloom recipe from my great-granny for the potatoes Vesuvio. If their dish is anything like hers, this meal will be worth eating."

"But you must also choose wines," Tee offered, temptingly.

"Oh, I couldn't," Lunzie said. "This will already cost the wide blue sky."

"Then I shall." And he did, choosing a wine Lunzie loved, one which wouldn't be overpowered by the garlic in the main course; and finishing up for dessert with a fine vintage blue Altairian cordial, the price of which he would not let Lunzie see.

Lunzie enjoyed her meal wholeheartedly, both the food and the company. Because of their common interest in Tri-D, she and Tee were able to converse almost infinitely on a range of subjects, including galactic politics and trends. Their opinions were dissimilar, but to her relief, not mutually exclusive. Beyond the outrageous compliments he ˉpaid her throughout the meal, which Lunzie saw as camouflage fireworks for a sensitive nature that had been wounded in the past, Tee was otherwise an interesting and intelligent companion. They talked about cooking and compared various ethnic cuisines they had tried. Tee loved his food as much as she did, though his frame was the ectomorphic sort that would never wear excess weight for long. Lunzie looked down cautiously at the shimmering, teal tissue sheath that she had purchased that afternoon at Pomayla's urging. It was gorgeous, but outlined every curve. That wouldn't fit long if she indulged like this too frequently.

Tee was a man of expansive physical gestures. He waved his hands to underscore the importance of a point he was making, nearly to the destruction of the meals for the next table, being delivered at that moment by a server. Lunzie always noticed hands. His were long-boned but very broad in the palm, and the fingers were square at the tips. Capable hands. His thick dark brown hair fell often into his eyes, tangling in his eyelashes, which were shamefully long for a man's. Lunzie wished hers would look so good without enhancement. He was a handsome man. She wondered why it had taken her so long to notice that fact. It struck her too that it had been a long time since she'd been out for an evening with an admirer, not since she and Sion Mespil were courting. She rather missed the experience.

Tee caught her staring at him, and caught her hand up in his. "You haven't heard what I just said," he accused her lightly. He kissed her fingertips.

"No," she admitted. "I was thinking. Tee, what

did you mean when you said in the EEC office that we had something more in common?"

"Ah, so that's it. We have in common lost time. I don't know whether cryogenics is a boon to the galaxy at large or not. It is not to me. I almost rather that I had died, or remained awake, then being closed away from the world. At least I would know what went on in my absence, instead of finding it out in a single moment when I returned."

Lunzie nodded sympathetically. "How long?"

Tee grimaced dramatically. "Eleven years. When my spacecraft was becalmed because of fuel-source failure, I was the leading engineer on the FSP project to perfect laser technology in space drive navigation systems and FTL communications. On the very cutting edge, you will pardon the joke. Light beams to send information more quickly and accurately among components than ion impulse or electron could. When I awoke two years ago, the process was not only old, but obsolete! I was the most highly trained man in the FSP for a skill that was no longer needed. They offered to retire me at full salary plus my back pay, but I could not stand to feel useless. I wanted to work. It would take too long to retrain me for space technology as it has evolved—so fast!" His hands described the flight of spacecraft. "So I took any job they offered me as soon as I could. They said I wasn't over the trauma yet, so I couldn't have a space-borne post."

"It's for your own safety. It takes on the average of three to five years to recover," Lunzie pointed out, thinking of her own days of therapy on the Descartes Platform and thereafter. Through the University clinic, she still had psychologists running her through periodic tests to check her progress. "It will be even longer for me, because I have more to assimilate than you did. I'm an extreme case in point. My own medical knowledge is as archaic as trepanning to these new people. The researchers consider me fascinating because of my 'quaint notions.' It's lucky that bodies haven't changed radically. But, there are more subgroups than before. There's so much that it might have been better if I'd started from scratch."

"Yes, but you can still practice your craft! I can not. I worked in Supply for a year, pushing paper for replacement drive parts though I had no idea what they did. They called that an 'extension' of my previous job, but it was their way of keeping me safely out of trouble. The therapists pretended they were doing it for my sake. In the end, I transferred to Research, where I would be around people who did not pity me. Besides casework, I can also fix the laser computers. It saves a call to Maintenance when something breaks." Tee drummed moodily on the table. The diners next to them gave him a wary glance as they inserted their credit medallions into the table till and left.

Lunzie wisely remained silent. Introspection, personal evaluation, was an important part of the healing process. Muhlah knew she'd spent enough of her time doing just that. She just waited and watched Tee think, wondering what pictures were going through his mind. When the server approached, Lunzie caught his eye and signalled for more cordial to be poured. The ring of ceramic on crystal awoke Tee from his reverie. He reached over and pressed her fingers.

"Forgive me, lovely Lunzie. I invite you to dine with me, not to watch me sulk."

"Believe me, I understand completely. I don't always brood in private, myself. It's been so frustrating hearing nothing from the EEC that I tell everybody my troubles, hoping somebody will help me."

"You will have no trouble in future, not with Teodor Janos making the search on your behalf. You must

have guessed that assignment to a caseworker such
as I is only made if they cannot make you go away."

Lunzie nodded firmly. "I guessed it. Oh, how I
loathe bureaucrats. I'm proud of the stubborn streak
in my family. Fiona has it, too—I'm sorry. I didn't
mean to bring up business. I've had such a splendid
time with you."

"As have I." Tee consulted his sleeve chronome-
ter. "It grows late, and you have classes early tomorrow. I will escort you home in a private shuttle. No,
no. It is my pleasure. You may treat next time, if you
choose. Or apply your prodigious and discerning skills
to prepare some of the delightful-sounding recipes
you have hoarded in your family memory banks."

Lunzie was met at the door to the apartment by
Pomayla, Shof, and half the Gang, who, by the look
of things, had been studying together with the concerted assistance of processed carbohydrates and synthesized beer.

"Well, who was it, and what was he, she, or it
like?" Pomayla demanded.

"Who was who?"

"Tee, of course. We've been wondering all evening."

"How do you know about him?"

"I told you it'd be a he," Shof called out, taunt-
ingly, from his seat on the floor. He and Bordlin, a
Gurnsan student, were working on an engineering
project that had something to do with lasers. There
was a new burn mark in the wall over their heads.
"Ask Mr. Data, that's me." Bordlin shook his horned
head, and searched the ceiling with long-suffering
bovine eyes.

"You forgot to erase the message on the board
down in the foyer," Pomayla explained. "Everyone
read it as they came in. Our curiosity's been running
out of control."

"Let it run," Lunzie said loftily. "It's good for you
to wonder. I'm going to bed."

"True love!" Shof crowed as Lunzie closed her cubicle door on them. For once she did not have trouble relaxing into sleep. She remembered the gentle pressure of Tee's fingers on hers and smiled.

As Tee had promised, Lunzie began to get results from the EEC much more quickly with his help. Fiona's virology work for the FSP was largely classified. Her official rank was Civilian Specialist, and the grade had increased steadily over the years. Her pay records showed several bonuses for hazardous duty. She had worked for the EEC for several years before her marriage in positions of increasing responsibility. She took a furlough for eight years, and resumed field work afterward. Tee still hoped to track down her service record.

This quantity of news would have seemed small to her roommates, but Lunzie was overjoyed to have it. Her mood was lighter, and not only because the barrier between herself and her daughter was falling away. She was also seeing a lot more of Tee.

He changed his viewing time to coincide with hers. They sat together on the padded bench, drinking in the news of the day, saving up their observations to discuss later over synth-lunch. Tee was amused by Lunzie's economies, but acknowledged that the fees for remote retrieval of old documents and records were steep.

When Lunzie's classes or labs didn't interfere, they would meet for an evening meal. Tee's quarters were larger than hers, a quarter of a floor in an elderly former residence of higher-level civil servants. Besides the food synthesizer, there were actual cooking facilities. "An opulent conceit," Tee admitted, "but they work. When I have time, I like to create."

They tried to set aside one day a week for a real-meal, cooked with local ingredients. Lunzie

retraced her steps to the Astris combine farms she
had patronized decades before, and chose vegetables
from the roadside stands and pick-it-yourself crops.
Tee marveled at the healthy produce, far cheaper
than it was in the population centers. How clever
she was to know where to find such things, he told
her over and over, and so surprisingly close to the
campus!

"City boy," Lunzie teased him. A part of her that
had been neglected reasserted itself and began to
blossom again in the warmth of his devoted admiration. She was not unattractive, vanity forced her to
admit, and she started to take more pleasure in
caring for herself, choosing garments that were flattering to her figure instead of ones that just pre-
served modesty and protected her from atmospheric
exposure. Pomayla was delighted to have Lunzie join
her on restday shopping expeditions. Lunzie found
she was also rediscovering the simple pleasures which
gave life its texture.

After a good deal of friendly teasing and many
unsubtle hints from her young roommates, Lunzie
was persuaded to bring Tee back to the apartment to
meet them.

"You can't keep him out of the Gang's way for
long," Pomayla remarked. "He might as well join
now and face the music."

Though he was eager to please Lunzie, Tee was
reluctant to encounter her young suitemates. From
the moment he entered the apartment, he felt nervous, and wondered if he would lose too much face if
he decided to bolt.

"You live such a distance from town center I have
had too much time to worry," he complained, straight-
ening his tunic again as they swept upward in the
turbovator.

"Come now, they're only children. Be a man, my
son."

"You don't understand. I like youngsters. Ten years ago, I may have felt no discomfort, but . . . oh, you'll see. It has not happened to you yet."

Shof, Pomayla and Pomayla's boyfriend Laren were waiting for them in their common living room. The apartment was clean. They had done a commendable job in making the place look neat, but Lunzie was uncomfortably aware for the first time how scholastically plain the apartment was. Though she knew Tee would understand why she chose to live in such cheap quarters, she wished illogically that it looked more sophisticated.

Tee, bless him, reacted in exactly the right way to make her feel comfortable once more. "This looks like a place where things are done," he cried, stretching his arms out, feeling the atmosphere. "A good room to work." He gave them a wide grin, encompassing them all in its sunshine.

"You're never at a loss anywhere you go, are you?" she asked, a small, cynical smile tweaking up the corner of her mouth.

"I mean it," Tee replied. "Some quarters are merely to sleep in. Some, you can sleep and eat in. This, you can live in."

"Sort of," Shof said grudgingly. "But there's no storage space to speak of, and Krim knows, you can't bring a date here."

"It would be easier to get around in if you didn't have models hanging everywhere," Pomayla told him.

"I've been in worse on shipboard, believe me," Tee said. "In which every bunk belongs to three crew, who use it in turn for a shift apiece. No sleeping late. No lingering in the morning to get to know one another all over again." He glanced at Lunzie through his eyelashes with an exaggerated look of longing, and she laughed.

"My lad, you should simply have gotten to know

someone on the next shift, so then you could move on to her bunk."

Pomayla, who was shy about personal relations, promptly got up to serve drinks.

"Were you in the FSP?" Shof asked Tee.

"Only as a contractor. I helped to develop a new star navigations system. My specialty was computer-driven laser technology."

"Stellar, citizen," Shof said, enthusiastically. "Me, too. I built my first laser beam calculator out of spare parts when I was four." He held up his right hand. "Cauterized this index finger clean off. I've generally had bad luck with this finger. It's been regenerated twice now. But I've learned to use a laser director better since then."

"Laser director?" Tee asked. "You don't use a laser director to create the synapse links."

"I do."

"No wonder you burned off your finger, little man. Why didn't you simply recalculate the angles before trying to connect power?"

They began to argue research and technique, going immediately from lay explanation, which the other three could understand, into the most involved technical lingo. It sounded like gibberish to Lunzie and Pomayla, and probably did to Laren, who sat politely nodding and smiling whenever anyone met his eyes. Lunzie remembered that he was an economics major.

"So," asked Shof, stopping for breath, "what's the new system based on? Ion propulsion with laser memory's faulty; they've figured that out now. Gravity well drives are still science fiction. Laser technology's too delicate by itself to stand up against the new matter-antimatter drives."

"But why not?" Tee began, looking lost. "That was new when I was working for the FSP. The laser system was supposed to revolutionize space travel. It should have lasted for two hundred years."

"Yeah. Went in and out of fashion like plaid knickers," Shof said, deprecatingly. "Doppler shift, you know. Well, you've got to start somewhere."

"Somewhere?" Tee echoed, indignantly. "Our technology was the very newest, the most promising. . . ."

Shof spread out his hands and said reasonably, "I'm not saying that the current system wasn't based on LT. Where have you been for the last decade, Earth?"

Tee's face, once open and animated, had closed up into tight lines. His mouth twisted, fighting back some sour retort. His involuntary passage with cold sleep was still a sore point with him. Lunzie suddenly understood why he was reluctant to talk about his past experiences with anyone. The experiential gap between the people who experienced time at its normal pace and the cold sleepers was real and troubling to the sleepers. Tee felt caught out of time, and Shof didn't understand. "Peace!" Lunzie cried over Shof's exposition of modern intergalactic propulsion. "That's enough. I declare Hatha's peace of the watering hole. I will permit no more disputes in this place."

Shof opened his mouth to say something, but stopped. He stared at Tee, then looked to Lunzie for help. "Have I said something wrong?"

"Shof, you can behave yourself or make yourself scarce," Pomayla declared.

"What'd I do?" With a wounded expression, Shof withdrew to arrange dinner from the synthesizer. Pomayla and Laren went to the worktable, and peeled and cut up a selection of fresh vegetables to supplement the meal. Tee watched them work, looking lost.

Lunzie rose to her feet. "Now that we have a natural break in the conversation, I'll give Tee the tenth-credit tour." She twined her arm with Tee's and led him away.

Once the door to Lunzie's cubicle had shut behind them, Tee let his shoulders sag. "I am sorry. But you see? It might have been a hundred years. I have been left far behind. Everything I knew, all the complicated technology I developed, is now toys for children."

"I must apologize. I tossed you into the middle of it. You seemed to be holding your own very well," Lunzie said, contritely.

Tee shook his head, precipitating a fall of black hair into his eyes. "When a child can blithely reel off what a hundred of us worked on for eight years—for which some of us lost our lives!—and refute it, with logic, I feel old and stupid." Lunzie started a hand to smooth the unsettled forelock, but stopped to let him do it himself.

"I feel the same way, you know," she said. "Young people, much younger than I am, at any rate, who understand the new medical technology to a fare-thee-well, when I have to be shown where the on-off switch is! I should have realized that I'm not alone in what I'm going through. It was most inconsiderate of me." Lunzie kneaded the muscles at the back of Tee's neck with her strong fingers. Tee seized her hand and kissed it.

"Ah, but you have the healing touch." He glanced at the console set and smiled at the hologram prism with the image of a lovely young girl beaming out at him. "Fiona?"

"Yes." Lunzie stroked the edge of the hologram with pride.

"She is not very like you in coloring, but in character, ah!"

"What? You can see the stubborn streak from there?" Lunzie said mockingly.

"It runs right here, along your back." His fingers traced her spine, and she shivered delightedly. "Fiona is beautiful, just as you are. May I take this?" Tee asked, turning it in his hands and admiring the clarity of the portrait. "If I can feed an image to the computers, it may stir some memory bank that has not yet responded to my queries."

Lunzie felt a wrench at giving up her only physical tie to her daughter, but had to concede the logic. "All right," she agreed reluctantly.

"I promise you, nothing will happen to it, and much good may result."

She stood on tiptoe to kiss him. "I trust you. Are you ready to rejoin the others?"

Shof had clearly been chastised in Lunzie's absence. During dinner around the worktable, he questioned Tee respectfully about the details of his research. The others joined in, and the conversation turned to several subjects. Laren proved also to be a Tri-D viewer. Lunzie and he compared their impressions of fashion trends, amidst hilarious laughter from the other two males. Blushing red for making her opinions known, Pomayla tried to defend the fashion industry.

"Well, you practically support them," Shof said, wickedly, baiting her as he would a sister.

"What's wrong with garb that makes you look good?" she replied, taking up the challenge.

"If it isn't comfortable, why wear it?" Lunzie asked, reasonably, joining the fray on Shof's side.

"For the style—" Pomayla explained, desperately.

Lunzie raised an eyebrow humorously. " 'We must suffer to be beautiful'? And you call me old fashioned!"

"I don't know where they get the ideas for these new frocks," Laren said. After a quick glance at Pomayla, "No offense, sweetheart, but some of the fads are so weird."

"Do you really want to know?" Lunzie asked. "To stay in style for the rest of your life, never throw out any of your clothes. The latest style for next season—I saw it in the Tri-D—is the very same tunic I wore to my primary-school graduation. It probably came around once while I was in cold sleep, and here it is again. Completely new to you youngsters, and too youthful a fashion to be worn by anyone who can remember the last time it was in vogue."

"Can I look through your family holos?" Pomayla asked, conceding the battle with an impish gleam in her eye. "I want to see what's coming next year. I'll be seasons ahead of the whole Gang."

The remains of the meal went into the disposer, and Tee rose, stretching his arms over his head and producing a series of cracks down his spine. "Ah. That was just as I remember school food."

"Terrible, right?" Pomayla inquired, with a twinkle.

"Terrible. I hate to end the evening now, but I must go. As Lunzie said so truly, you are at the outer end of nowhere, and it will take me time to get home."

Lunzie ran for her textcubes. "I think I'll come in with you. My shift at the hospital begins in just four hours. Sanitary collection units won't wait. I might as well travel while I can still see. Perhaps I'll nap at your place."

Tee swept her a bow. "I should be glad for your company." He expanded the salute to include the others. "Thank you for a pleasant evening. Good night."

Pomayla and Laren called their goodnights to him from the worn freeform couch in the far corner of the room. Shof ran to catch up with them at the door. "Hey," he called softly, as they stepped into the turbovator foyer. "Good luck finding Lunzie's daughter, huh?"

Lunzie goggled at him. "Why, you imp. You know?"

Shof gave them his elfin smile. "Sure I know. I don't tell everything I find out." He winked at Lunzie as the door slid between them.

*   *   *

Lunzie's studies progressed well throughout the rest of the term. To their mutual satisfaction, she and the cardiology professor declared a truce. She toned down her open criticism of his bedside manner, and he overlooked what he termed her "bleeding heart," openly approving her grasp of his instruction. His personal evaluation of her at the end of term was flattering, for him, according to students who had had him before. Lunzie thought she had never seen a harsher dressing down ever committed to plas-sheet, but the grade noted below the diatribe showed that he was pleased with her.

The new term began. The Discipline course continued straight through vacation, since it was not a traditional format class. No grade was issued to the University computer for Discipline. Either a student kept up with the art, or he dropped out. It was still eating up a large part of Lunzie's day, which was now busier than ever.

Her new courses included supervised practical experience at the University Hospital. The practicum was worth twice the credits of other classes, but the hours involved were flexible according to need, and invariably ran long. Lunzie and her fellows followed a senior resident on his rounds for the first few weeks, observing his techniques of diagnosis and treatment, and then worked under him in the hospital clinic. Lunzie liked Dr. Root, a Human man of sixty honest Standard years, whose plump pink cheeks and broad hands always looked freshly scrubbed.

Many patients who came to the clinics were of species that Lunzie had seen before only in textbooks, and some of them only recently. Under the admiring gaze of his eight apprentices, Root removed from the nucleus of a five-foot protoplasmic entity a single chromosome the size of Lunzie's finger, altered and replaced it, with deft motions suggesting he did this kind of thing every day. Even before he finished sealing the purple cell wall, the creature was quivering.

"Conscious already?" Dr. Root transmitted through the voice-synthesizer the giant cell wore around the base of a long cilium.

". . . good . . . is good . . . divide now . . . good. . . ."

"No, absolutely not. You may not induce mitosis until we are sure that your nucleus can successfully replicate itself."

". . . rest . . . good. . . ."

Root wrinkled his nose cheerfully at Lunzie. "Nice when a patient takes a doctor's advice, isn't it?"

Whenever Root held clinic, his students did the preliminary examinations, and, if it was within their capabilities, the treatment as well. Like Lunzie, the others were advanced year students. Most would be taking internships next year in whichever of the University-approved hospitals and medical centers throughout the FSP would take them. Lunzie's own plan was to apply to the University Hospital each term for residency, until they took her, or the search for Fiona led off-planet at last. Her advisor reminded her that she didn't need to follow the curriculum as if she was a new student. Lunzie argued that she needed as much refreshment as she could get to regain her skills. The grueling pace of internship was the quickest way to be exposed to the most facets of new medicine.

The clinic's com-unit chirped during Dr. Root's demonstration of how to treat a suppurating wound on a shelled creature. The tortoiselike alien lay patiently on the examination table with probes hanging in the air around it and any number of tubes and scopes poked under the edge of its shell. With the help of a longhandled clamp and two self-motivated cautery units, Root was gently fitting a layer of new plas-skin over the freshly cleaned site, and watching his progress on a hovering Tri-D field. He handed the clamp over to one of the students. "Close up, please."

"Emergency code," Root announced mildly to the roomful of students after taking the call. "Construction workers from the spaceport. They are airlifting them in to the roof. Some nasty wounds, a lot of blood, patients likely to be in shock. To your stations, doctors."

Lunzie and her Brachian lab partner, Rik-ik-it, fled to treatment room C, scrubbed, and helped each other put on fresh surgical gear. They had just enough time to do a check on supplies and power before they heard the screaming.

"Muhlah, what are they?"

"I can scream louder than that," Rik scoffed.

"Don't," ordered Lunzie, listening. "Shh."

The door to their treatment room slid open, and two enormous men staggered in, one supporting the other. Heavyworlders. Lunzie looked up at them in dismay.

"Help me," Rik chittered, springing forward to help the more badly wounded man to the canted table. His tremendous strength supplemented that of the other heavyworlder, and together they got the man settled on the gurney. Lunzie started to move toward him, when the other man brushed her away, and assisted Rik in laying his friend face down onto the padded surface.

It was amazing that the prone heavyworlder had made it to the clinic on his feet. There was a tremendous tear through the muscles on his back. One calf was split down the middle, probably sliced by the same falling object. Blood was flowing and spurting from both wounds.

"What happened?" she demanded, pushing past the other two. She cut away the heavy cloth of the prone man's trouserleg and began cleaning

the wound with sterile cleanser. By main strength,
Rik tore open the slit in his tunic and began to
search the wound with a microscopic device. Lunzie
tossed the scraps of cloth to one side and put pressure on the pumping blood vessel. When the spurting stopped, she applied a quicksplint to it with an
electronically directed clamp. Its edges forced together under the flexible tubeform splint, the tear
would heal now by itself.

"Runway extension buckled, fell down on us," the
other man said, clutching his arm. "Sarn it, I knew
those struts were faulty. Trust Plasteel Corporation,
the crew boss told us. Gurn shit! The machines'll tell
us if any of the extrusions won't hold up. Uh-huh."

"I can handle this one now," Rik told Lunzie.

With a comprehending nod, Lunzie turned away
from the table to the other man. By the heavens, he
was tall! He ground his teeth together, rasping them
audibly. Lunzie knew that he was in tremendous
pain.

"Sit down," she said, quickly, swallowing her nervousness. Her stomach rolled. She knew she was
going to have to touch him, and she was afraid.
These angry giants seemed more than human to her:
larger, louder, more emphatic. They frightened her.
In the depths of her soul, she still associated heavyworlders with the loss of Fiona, and she was surprised how much it affected her. She had to remind
herself of her duty.

"It's my arm," the heavyworlder said, starting to
unfasten the front closure of his tunic. Lunzie quelled
her feelings and unsealed the magnetic seam running
the length of his sleeve. She eased the fabric down,
trying to avoid touching the swelling in the upper
arm, and helped him ease the sleeve down over the
injured limb. His hand, gigantic next to hers, clenched
and twitched as she undid the wrist fastening, and

the plas-canvas fabric flapped free against the man's ribs.

A quick glance told her that the right humerus was broken, and the shoulder was badly dislocated. "Let me give you something for the pain," Lunzie said, signalling for the hypo-arm. The servomechanism swung the multiple injector-head down to her, and the LEDs on its control glowed into life. "Why not?" she demanded when the heavyworlder shook his head.

"You're not gonna knock me out. I don't trust bonecrackers. I want to see what you do."

"As you wish," Lunzie said, adjusting the setting. "How about a local? It won't make you drowsy, but it will kill the pain."

"Yeah. All right." He stuck his arm out toward her suddenly, and Lunzie jumped back, startled. The heavyworlder frowned at her, lowering his eyebrows suspiciously.

Made more nervous by his disapproving scrutiny, Lunzie stammered as she spoke to the hypo-arm control. "A-analyze for allergies and in-incompatibilities. Local only, right upper arm and shoulder. Implement." The head moved purposefully forward and touched the man's skin. The air gauge hissed briefly, then the unit rotated and withdrew. Lunzie felt the arm tentatively, examining the break. That bone was going to be difficult to set through the thick layers of muscle.

"Get on with it, dammit!" the man roared.

"Does something else hurt?" Lunzie asked, jerking her hands away.

"No, but the way you mince around makes me crazy. Put a rocket in it, lady!"

Stung, Lunzie paused for a moment to gather the resources of Discipline deep within her, as much for strength enough to set the arm as for mental insulation from her feelings against the heavyworlder. She would not allow herself to react in an adverse fashion. Her breathing slowed down until it was even and slow. She was a doctor. Many people were afraid of doctors. It was not unnatural. He was traumatized because of the accident and the pain; no need to take his behavior personally. But Lunzie kept seeing the newsvideo of Phoenix, the bare hollow where the human camp used to be. . . .

The burst of adrenaline characteristic of Discipline raced through her system, blanketing her normal responses, shoring up her weaknesses, and strengthening her sinews far beyond their unenhanced capability. Her hands braced against the heavyworlder's bunched muscle, spread out, and grasped.

The heavyworlder screamed and flailed at her with his free hand, knocking her backwards against the wall. "Suffering burnout, let go! Dammit, get me a doctor who's gonna treat me like a human being, for Krim's sake!" he howled. He clenched his hand around the wounded shoulder, and sweat poured down his face, which was white with shock.

"Is there a problem here?" Rik-ik-it asked, peering shortsightedly down on Lunzie. His silver-pupilled eyes blinked quizzically as he helped her up.

Furiously, the heavyworlder angled his chin toward Lunzie. "This fem is a klondiking butcher. She's torn my arm apart!"

Still held in Discipline trance, Lunzie backed away. She hadn't been hurt. The man's anger held no terror for her as long as she held her feelings in check under the curtain of iron control. What had gone wrong? She reviewed her actions with the perfect recall at her command. Two quick twists, one front to back, the other, in a leftward arc. She knew, as if an ultrasonic image had been projected before her, that the shoulder was once again in place and that the broken bone had been realigned. Discipline also increased the sensitivity of her five senses.

Rik examined the arm carefully, then read the

indicators on the hypo-arm. "There is nothing wrong here," he said calmly. "The doctor has set your arm correctly. It will heal well now. It is just that the anesthetic had not yet taken effect." He glanced at the clock on the wall. "It should be starting to work right now."

"I should have checked the time factor," Lunzie chided herself later when she and Tee were alone together. "But all I could think of was fixing him up and getting him out of there. It was a stupid mistake, stupid and embarrassing." She waved her hands helplessly as she paced, unable to light anywhere for long. "Rik says that I'm overreacting. He thinks that I have a—phobia of heavyworlders, otherwise I would have remembered the time factor." Miserably, she programmed herself a cup of ersatz coffee from the food synthesizer. "Look. I'm reverting. Maybe I should get therapy. I was in Discipline trance; I might have torn the man's arm off." She swallowed the coffee and made a wry face.

"But you didn't," Tee said, sympathetically, guiding her to sit close to him on the wide couch in the center room of his quarters. She looked away as he clasped her hand in both of his. She couldn't stand the pity in his eyes.

"I should quit. Perhaps I can go into research, where I can keep away from any life larger than a microbe." Her mouth quivered, trying to hold up the corners of a feeble little grin, though she still stared at Tee's knees. "I never suffer fools gladly, especially when one of them is myself."

"That doesn't sound like my Lunzie. She who is taking hold with both hands in this new world. And she who persuades me not to be discouraged when small boys know more than I do about my hard-learned craft."

Her self-pity shot down, Lunzie had to smile. She met Tee's eyes for the first time. "That poor man kept shouting to me to hurry up, to fix his arm and be done with it. I knew he was scared of me because I am a doctor, but I was more scared of him! However Brobdignagian in dimension, he was just another human being! My daughter's father was involved in the genetic evolution of heavyworlders. I used to get intersystem mail from Sion, long after we parted, talking about the steps he and the other researchers were taking to better adapt their subjects to the high-grav worlds. I know a lot about their technical development, and nothing about their society. It's funny that humanity is the only species making fundamental changes on itself. Catch the Ryxi altering one feather of their makeup."

"Never. It must be our curiosity: what we can do with any raw material, including ourselves," Tee suggested. "You must not blame yourself so much. It is so pointless."

Lunzie wiped the corners of her eyes with a sleeve. "It isn't. I misused my training, and I can't forget that—mustn't forget it. I'm not used to thinking of myself as a bigot. I'm a throwback. I don't belong in this century."

"Ah, but you're wrong," Tee said, removing the ignored, half-empty cup from her hand and setting it down on the hovering disk at the end of the couch. "It was an accident and you are sorry. You don't rejoice in his pain. You are a good doctor, and a good person. For who else would have been so loving and patient with me as you have been? You have much you can teach these poor ignorant people of the future." Gently, his arms stole around her, and hugged her tightly. Between soft kisses, he whispered to her. "You belong here. You belong with me."

Lunzie wrapped her arms around his ribs and rested her head on his shoulder. She closed her eyes, feeling warm and wanted. The tension of the day melted out of her neck and shoulders like a shower of petals falling from an apple tree as his tiny kisses travelled up the side of her throat, touched her ear. Tee kneaded the muscles in her lower back with his strong fingers, and she sighed with pleasure. His hands encircled her waist, swept upward, still stroking, putting aside fastenings and folds of cloth until they touched bare skin. Lunzie followed suit, admiring the line of shadows that dappled the strong muscles of his shoulders. The springy band of dark hair across his chest pleased her with its silky texture.

One of Tee's hands drifted up to touch her chin. He raised her face. His deep-set, dark eyes were solemn and caring. "Stay with me always, Lunzie. I love you. Please stay." Tilting his head forward, he brushed his lips tenderly against hers, again and again.

"I will," she murmured, easing back with him into the deep cushions. "I'll stay as long as I can."

Chapter Five

The hologram of Fiona held pride of place on the hovering disk table in the main room of Lunzie's and Tee's shared living quarters. Lunzie glanced up at it from time to time while she studied patient records. Fiona's beaming, never-fading smile beckoned her mother. Find me, it said. Sunlight shone through the image, sending lights of ruby and crystal dancing along the soft white walls of the room. Lunzie was coming to the end of her second full year on Astris. It was difficult to keep her promise to Chief Wilkins to be patient when she felt she ought to be out in the galaxy, looking for her daughter. In spite of the time Lunzie devoted to her many other activities and Discipline exercises, she never failed to check in with Looking-GLASS and her other sources of information in hopes of finding a trace of Fiona. She was spending a lot of money, but it had been a long time since she had learned anything new. It was frustrating.

It had been several months since she and Tee decided to live together, which decision coincided almost perfectly with Pomayla's timid request that her steady boyfriend be allowed to move into the apartment with her. Pomayla was overly shy about normal behavior between consenting adult beings. There was no stigma in present-day culture against "sharing warmth," as it was called, nor had there been for centuries. Students—in fact, all citizens—who participated in an open sex lifestyle were responsible for ensuring they were disease- and vermin-free or honestly stating that there was a problem, so there was no risk, just joy. Lovers who lied about their conditions soon found that they were left strictly alone: the word spread, and no one would trust them. Medical students especially were aware of what horrible things could happen if care was not taken to stay "clean," so they were scrupulous about it. Otherwise, one of their own number would eventually rake them over the philosophical coals later on when treatment was sought. Lunzie liked Laren, so she ceded him her own bedroom without a qualm, and moved her few belongings to Tee's.

Tee was a considerate, even deferential, suitemate. He behaved from the first day as if he considered it a favor bestowed by Lunzie that she had chosen to move in with him. Without offering his opinions first, so as not to prejudice her to his choices, he begged her to look around the roomy apartment and decide if she felt anything ought to be moved or changed to make her comfort greater. Everything was to be done for her pleasure. Lunzie was a little overwhelmed by his enthusiasm; she was used to the laissez faire style of her roommates, or the privacy-craving nature characteristic of those who lived in space. Tee had few possessions of his own, except for a number of books on plaque and cube, and a great quantity of music disks. All of the furniture was secondhand, a commodity plentiful on a university world. Most of his belongings, he explained, had been divided up according to his previous will, automatically probated when he had remained out of touch with any FSP command post for ten years. It was a stupid policy, he argued, since one could be out of touch much longer than that in a large galaxy, and still be awake!

Careful to consider his feelings, and perhaps out of her naturally stubborn reaction to his insistence, Lunzie changed as little as possible in his quarters. She liked the spare decor. It helped her to concentrate more than the homey clutter of the student apartment did. When Tee complained that she was behaving like a visitor instead of a resident, she had taken him out shopping. They chose a two-dimensional painting by a university artist and a couple of handsome holograph prints that they both liked, and Lunzie purchased them, refusing to let Tee see the prices. Together, they arranged the pieces of art in the room where they spent the most time.

"Now that is Lunzie's touch," Tee had exclaimed, satisfied, admiring the way the color picked up the moon in the predominantly white room. "Now it is our home."

Lunzie put down the last datacube. She loved Tee's apartment. It was spacious, ostentatiously so for a single person's quarters, and it had wide window panels extending clear around two walls of the main room. Lunzie reached up for a tendon-crackling stretch that dragged the cuffs of her loose knit exercise pants up over her ankles, and dropped wide sweatshirt sleeves onto the top of her head, mussing her hair, and stalked over to open the casements to let the warm afternoon breezes through. The irising controls of the window panels were adjusted to let in the maximum sunlight on the soft white carpeting. At that time of the afternoon, both walls were full of light. A pot of fragrant herbal tea was warming on the element in the cooking area, which was visible through a doorway. The food synthesizer, a much better model than she'd had in the University-owned apartment, was disguised behind an ornamental panel in the cooking room wall, making it easy to ignore.

She and Tee still preferred cooking for one another
when they had time. Lunzie was becoming happily
spoiled by the small luxuries which were rarely available to students or spacefarers.

During this school term, Lunzie had been assigned
as Dr. Root's assistant in the walk-in clinic. After she
shamefacedly admitted having been upset by her
heavyworlder patient, and voiced her concerns about
its effect on her treatment to him, Root had counselled her and interviewed Rik-ik-it. It was his deter-
mination that there was nothing wrong with her that
a little more exposure to the subjects wouldn't dispel. He dismissed her fears that she was a xeno-
phobe. "An angry heavyworlder," he assured her,
"could easily intimidate a normal human. You may
fear one with impunity."

She was grateful that he hadn't seen it as a major
departure from normalcy, and vowed to keep a cooler
head in the future. So far, she hadn't had to test her
new resolve, as few heavyworlders made use of the
medical facility.

The University Hospital clinic treated all students
free of charge, and assessed only a nominal fee from
outsiders. Accident victims, too, like the heavyworlder
construction workers, were frequently brought directly to the University Hospital because the wait
time for treatment was usually shorter than it was at
the private facilities. Most of the Astris students
Lunzie saw were of human derivation, not because
non-humans were less interested in advanced education or were discriminated against, but because most
species were capable of passing on knowledge to
infants in utero or in ova, and only one University
education per subject was required per family tree.
Humans required education after birth, which some
other member races of the FSP, particularly the Seti
and the Weft, saw as a terrible waste of time. Lunzie
felt the crowing over race memory and other charac-

teristics to be a sort of inferiority complex in itself, and let the comments pass without reply. Race memory was only useful when it dealt with situations that one's ancestors had experienced before. She treated numerous Weft engineering students for dehydration, especially during their first semesters on Astris. Young Seti, on Astris to study interplanetary diplomacy, tended toward digestive ailments, and had to be trained as to which native Astrian foods to avoid.

It had been a slow day in the office. None of her case histories demanded immediate action, so she pushed them into a heap on the side of the couch and sat down with a cup of tea. There was time to relax a bit before she needed to report back to Dr. Root. He was a good and patient teacher, who only smiled at her need to circumvent the healing machines instead of chiding her for her ancient ideals. Lunzie felt confident again in her skills. She still fought to maintain personal interaction with the patient, but there was less and less for the healer to do. Lunzie sensed it was a mistake to learn to rely too heavily on mechanical aids. A healer was not just another technician, in her strongly maintained opinion. She was alone in her views.

The band of sunshine crept across the room and settled at her feet like a contented pet. Lunzie looked longingly across at her portable personal reader, which had been a thirty-sixth birthday gift from Tee, and the small rack of ancient classical book plaques she had purchased from used book stores. An unabridged *Works of Rudyard Kipling*, replacement for her own lost, much-loved copy, sat at the front of the book-rack, beckoning. Though there wasn't time to page through her favorites before she needed to go in to work, there was, coincidentally, just enough to perform her daily Discipline exercises. With a sigh, she put aside the empty cup and began limbering up.

"Duty before pleasure, Kip," Lunzie said, regretfully. "You'd understand that."

The tight Achilles tendons between her hips and heels had been stretched so well that she could bend over and lay her hands flat on the floor and relax her elbows without bowing her knees. Muscular stiffness melted away as she moved gracefully through the series of dancelike fighting positions. Lunzie was careful to avoid the computer console and the art pedestals as she sprang lightly around the room, sparring with an invisible opponent. Discipline taught control and enhancement of the capability of muscle and sinew. Each pose not only exercised her limbs, but left her feeling more energetic than when she began the drills. Under her conscious control, her footfalls made no sound. She was as silent as the black shadows limned on the light walls by the sun. She moved in balance, every motion a reaction, an answer to one that came before.

Holding her back beam-straight, she settled down into a meditation pose sitting on her crossed feet in front of the couch with the sunshine washing across her lap. She held her arms out before her, turned her hands palms up, and let them drop slowly to the floor on either side of her knees.

Lunzie closed her eyes, and drew in the wings of her consciousness, until she was aware only of her body, the muscles holding her back straight, the pressure of her buttocks into the arches of her feet, the heat of the sun on her legs, the rough-smooth rasp of the carpet on the tops of her hands and feet.

Tighter in. At the base of her sinuses, she tasted the last savor of the tea that she had swallowed, and felt the faint distension of her stomach around the warm liquid. Lunzie studied every muscle which worked to draw in breath and release it, felt the relief of each part of her body as fresh oxygen reached it, displacing tired, used carbon dioxide. The flesh of her cheeks and forehead hung heavily against her facial bones. She let her jaw relax.

She began to picture the organs and blood vessels of her body as passages, and sent her thought along them, checking their functions. All was well. Finally she allowed her consciousness to return to her center. It was time to travel inward toward the peace which was the Disciple's greatest source of strength and the goal toward which her soul strove.

Lunzie emerged from her trance state just in time to hear the whir of the turbovator as it stopped outside the door. Her body was relaxed and loose, her inner self calm. She looked up as Tee burst into the room, his good-natured face beaming.

"The best of news, my Lunzie! The very best! I have found your Fiona! She is alive!"

Lunzie's hands clenched where they lay on the ground, and her heart felt as if it had stopped beating. The calm dispersed in a wash of hope and fear and excitement. Could it be true? She wanted to share the joy she saw in his eyes, but she did not dare.

"Oh, Tee," she whispered, her throat suddenly tight. Her hands were shaking as she extended them to Tee, who fell to his knees in front of her. He clasped her wrists and kissed the tips of her fingers. "What have you found?" All of her anxieties came back in a rush. She could not yet allow herself to feel that it might be true.

Tee slipped a small ceramic information brick from his pocket and placed it in her palms. "It is all here. I have proof in *three dimensions*. Grade One Med Tech Fiona Mespil was retrieved off-planet by the EEC shortly before the colony vanished. She was needed urgently on another assignment," Tee explained. "It was an emergency, and the ship which picked her up was not FSP—a nearby merchant

voyager—so her name was not removed from the
rolls of poor Phoenix. She is alive!"

"Alive . . ." Lunzie made no attempt to hold back
the flood of joyful tears which spilled from her eyes.
Tee wiped them, then dabbed at his own bright
eyes. "Oh, Tee, thank you! I'm so happy."

"I am happy, too—for you. It is a secret I have
held many weeks now, waiting for a reply to my
inquiries. I couldn't be sure. I did not want to tor-
ture you with hope only to have bad news later on.
But now, I am glad to reveal all!"

"Two years I've waited. A few weeks more couldn't
hurt," Lunzie said, casting around for a handkerchief.
Tee plucked his out of his sleeve and offered it to
her. She wiped her eyes and nose, and blew loudly.
"Where is she, Tee?"

"Dr. Fiona has been working for five years on
Glamorgan, many light years out toward Vega, to
stem a plague virus that threatened the colony's survival. Her work there is done. She is en route to her
home on Alpha Centauri for a reunion with her family. It is a multiple-jump trip even with FTL capabilities, and will take her probably two years to arrive
home. I did not make contact with her directly." Tee
grinned his most implike grin, obviously saving the
best for last. "But your three grandchildren, five
great-grandchildren, and nine great-great-grandchil-
dren say they are delighted that they will get to meet
their illustrious ancestress. I have holograms of all of
them there in this cube."

Lunzie listened with growing excitement to his
recitation, and threw her arms around him as he
produced the cube with a flourish. "Oh! Grandchildren. I never thought of grandchildren. Let me see
them."

"This is downloaded from the post brick brought
from Alpha Centauri by the purser aboard the merchant ship *Prospero*," Tee explained as he tucked the

cube into the computer console reader. Lunzie scrambled up onto the couch and watched the platform with shining eyes as an image began to coalesce. "There is only sketchy family information on all of these. The message is short. I think your grandson Lars must be a tightwad. It is his voice narrating."

The holographic image of a black-haired human man in his early fifties appeared on the console platform. Lunzie leaned in to have a closer look. The image spoke. "Greetings, Lunzie. My name is Lars, Fiona's son. Since I don't know when this will reach you, I will give the names and Standard birthdates for all family members instead of the current date. First, myself. I'm the eldest of the family. I was born in 2801.

"Here is Mother, the last image I have of her before she blasted off last time." The voice was reproving. "She is very busy in her career, as I guess you know."

And before Lunzie was the image of a middle-aged woman. It was clearly a studio picture taken by a professional, sharp and clear. Her dark hair, stroked only here and there with a gentle brushing of silver, was piled up on top of her head in a plaited bun. Standing at her ease, she was dressed in a spotless uniform tunic which in contrast to her stance was formal and correct to the last crease. There were fine, crinkly lines at the corners of her eyes and underscoring her lashes, and smile lines had etched themselves deeply between her nose and the corners of her mouth, but the smile was the wonderful, happy grin that Lunzie remembered best. She closed her eyes, and for a moment was back on Tau Ceti in the sunshine, that last day before she left for the Descartes Platform.

"Oh, my baby," Lunzie murmured, overcome with longing and regret. She pressed her hand to her mouth as she looked from the holo of Fiona as a teenager to the image she saw now. "She's so different. I missed all her growing up."

"She is fine," Tee said, halting the playback. "She was happy, see? Wouldn't you like to see the rest of your family?"

Shortly, Lunzie nodded and opened her eyes. Tee passed his hand over the solenoid switch, and the image of Fiona disappeared. It was followed by a very slim young man in Fleet uniform. "My brother Dougal, born 2807," stated Lars's voice. "Unmarried, no attachments to speak of outside his career. He's not home much, as he is commissioned in the FSP Fleet as a captain. Sometimes transports Mother and her germ dogs from place to place. It's often the only time one of us gets to see her.

"My wife's camera shy, and won't stand still for an image." In the background, Lunzie could hear a high-pitched shriek. "Oh, Lars! Really!"

Lunzie grinned. "He has the family sense of humor anyway."

The image changed. "My daughter Dierdre, born 2825. Her husband Moykol, and their three girls. I call them the Fates. Here we have Rudi, born 2843, Capella, 2844, and Anthea Rose, 2845.

"My other girl, Georgia, 2828. One son, Gordon, 2846. Smart lad, if his own grandfather does have to say so.

"Melanie, daughter of Fiona, born Standard year 2803." This was a stunningly lovely woman with medium brown hair like Lunzie's own, and Fiona's jaw and eyes. She had a comfortably motherly figure, soft in outline without seeming overweight for her slender bones. She stood with one arm firmly around the waist of a very tall man with a sharp, narrow, hawklike face which looked incongruous under his mop of soft blond hair. "Husband, Dalton Ingrich."

"Their third son, Drew, 2827. Drew has two boys,

who are away at Centauri Institute of Technology. I don't have a current holo.

"Melanie's older boys Jai and Thad are identical twins, born 2821. Thad, and daughter Cassia, born 2842.

"This is Jai and his wife and two imps, Deram, 2842, and Lona, 2847."

There was an interruption of Lars's narration as the image of Melanie reappeared. She stepped forward in the holofield to speak, extending her hands welcomingly. "We'll be delighted to meet you, ancestress. Please come."

The image faded. Lunzie sat staring at the empty console-head as the computer whirred and expelled the datacube.

Lunzie let out her breath in a rush. "Well. A moment ago I was an orphan in the great galaxy. Now I'm the mother of a population explosion!" She shook her head is disbelief. "Do you know, I believe I've missed having a family to belong to."

"You must go," Tee said softly. He was watching her tenderly, careful not to touch her before she needed him to.

"Why didn't they tell me where she is?" Lunzie asked. Tee didn't have to ask which "she."

"They can't. They don't know. Because her assignments deal with planet-decimating disease, who knows when a curiosity seeker might land, perhaps to get a story to sell to Tri-D."

Lunzie recalled the holo-story about Phoenix. "That is so true. He might spread the plague farther than his story might ever reach. But it is just so frustrating!"

"Well, you will see her now. She will arrive home from the distant edge of the galaxy within two years." Tee looked pleased with himself. "You can be there waiting for her, to celebrate your reunion, and her new appointment, which was made public. That is how I found her at last, I confess, though it was because I was looking that I noticed the articles of commission. For long and meritorious service to the FSP, Dr. Fiona is appointed Surgeon General of the Eridani system. A great honor."

"Did you notice? A couple of the children look just like her." Lunzie chuckled. "One or two of them look like me. Not that these looks bear repeating."

"You insult yourself, my Lunzie. You are beautiful." Tee smiled warmly at her. "Your face is not what cosmetic models have, but what they wish they had."

Lunzie wasn't listening. "To think that all this . . . this frustration could have been avoided, if Phoenix could simply have transmitted word that Fiona'd left when she did. It was the one blocked path I couldn't find my way around, no matter what I did. The planet pirates are responsible for that, for two, almost three years I've spent—in anger, never knowing if I was hunting for a . . . a ghost. I think—I think if I had someone I knew was a pirate on my examination table with a bullet near his heart that only I could remove. . . . Well, I might just forget my Hippocratic oath." Lunzie set her jaw, furiously contemplating revenge.

"But you wouldn't," Tee said, firmly, squeezing her hand. "I know you."

"I wouldn't," she agreed, resignedly, letting the hot images fade. "But I'd have to wrangle it out with the devil. And I'll never forget the sorrow or the frustration. Or the loneliness." She shot Tee a look of gratitude and love. "Though I'm not alone now."

Tee persisted. "But you will go, of course? To Alpha Centauri."

"It would cost a planetary ransom!"

"What is money? You have spent money only seeking Fiona over the last many months, even though you are well off. You have saved every hundredth credit else. What else is it for?"

Lunzie bit her lip and stared at a corner of the room, thinking. She was almost afraid to see Fiona after all this time, because what would she say to her? All the time when she'd been searching for her, she played many scenes in her mind, of happy, tearful reconciliations. But now it was a reality: she was going to see Fiona again. What would the real one say to her? Fiona had told her when she left that she feared her mother would never come back. Once resentment faded, she must long ago have given up hope, believing her mother dead. Lunzie worried about the hurt she had caused Fiona. She imagined an angry Fiona, her jaw locked and nose red as they had been the last morning on Tau Ceti. Lunzie blanched defensively. It wasn't her fault that the space carrier had met with an accident, but did she have to leave Fiona at all? She could have taken a less distant post, one that was less dangerous though it paid less. But, no: for all her self-doubts and newly acquired hindsight, she had to admit that at the time she left Tau Ceti, the job with Descartes seemed the best possible path for her to take. She couldn't have foreseen what would happen.

She missed Fiona, but for her the separation had only been a matter of a few years. She tried to imagine how it would feel if it had been most of a lifetime, as it had for her daughter. She'd be a stranger after all these years. They'd have to become acquainted all over again. Would she like the new Fiona? Would Fiona like her, with the experience of her years behind her? She would just have to wait and see.

"Lunzie?" Tee's soft voice brought her back to herself. When she blinked the dryness from her eyes, she found Tee watching her with his dark eyes full of concern.

"What are you thinking of, my Lunzie? You are always so controlled. I would prefer it if you cry, or laugh, or shout. Your private thoughts are too private. I can never tell what it is you're thinking. Have I not brought you good news?"

She took a deep breath, and then hesitated. "What—what if she doesn't want to see me? After all these years, she probably hates me."

"She will love you, and forgive you. It was not your fault. You began to search for her as soon as it was possible to do so," he stated reasonably.

Lunzie sighed. "I should never have left her."

Tee grabbed both of her arms and turned her so that he could look into her eyes. "You did the right thing. You needed to support your child. You wanted to make her very comfortable, instead of merely to subsist. She was left in the best of care. Blame the fates. Blame whatever you must, but not yourself. Now. Are you going? Will you meet with your daughter and your grandchildren?"

Lunzie nodded at last. "I'm going. I have to."

"Good. Then this is a celebration!" He swept back to the parcel he had carried home with him, and removed from it a bottle of rare Cetian wine and a pair of long-stemmed glasses. "It is my triumph and yours, and I want you to drink to it with me. You should at least look like you want to celebrate."

"But I do," Lunzie protested.

"Then wash that worried look from your face and come with me!" Switching the glasses to the hand that held the wine, Tee bent over, and with one effort, threw Lunzie across his shoulders. Lunzie shrieked like a schoolgirl as he carried her into their bedchamber and dumped her onto the double-width bed.

"I can't! Root is expecting me." She flipped over and looked at the digital clock in the headboard. "Oh, Muhlah, now I'm late!" She started to get up, but he forestalled her.

"I will take care of that." Tee stalked out. The com-unit chimed as he made a connection. Lunzie had to stifle a giggle as he asked for Dr. Root and solemnly requested that she be allowed to miss a shift. ". . . for a family emergency," he said, in a sepulchral voice that made her bury a hoot of laughter in the bedclothes.

"There," Tee said, as he returned, shucking his tunic off into a corner of the room and kicking off his boots. "You are clear and on green, and he sends his concern and regards."

"I don't know why I'm letting you do that. I shouldn't play hooky," Lunzie chided, a little ashamed of herself. "I usually take my responsibilities more seriously than that."

"Could you honestly have stood and taken blood pressures with this knowledge dancing in your brain?" Tee asked, incredulously. "Fiona is found!"

"Well, no . . ."

"Then enjoy it," Tee encouraged her. "Allow me." He knelt before her and grabbed one of her feet, and started to ease the exercise pants down her leg. When her legs were free, he started a trail of kisses beginning at her toes and skimming gently upward along her bare skin. His hands reached around to squeeze and caress her thighs and buttocks, and upward, thumbs stroking the hollows inside her hipbones, as his lips reached her belly. His warm breath sent tingles of excitement racing through her loins. Lunzie lay back on the bed, sighing with pleasure. Her hands played with Tee's hair, running the backs of her nails gently through his hair and along the delicate lines of his ears. She closed her eyes and allowed the pleasure to carry her, moaning softly, until the waves of ecstasy ebbed.

He raised his head and crept further up, poised, hovering over her. Lunzie opened her eyes to smile at him, and met an impish glance.

"Oh, no, you don't," she warned, as he descended,

pinioning her, and dipping his tongue into her navel to tickle. "Agh! Unfair!"

He captured her arms as they flailed frantically at his head. "Now, now. All is fair in love, my Lunzie, and I love you."

"Then come up here and fight like a man, damn you." Lunzie freed her hands and pulled at his shoulders. Tee crawled up and settled on his hip beside her. She undid the magnetic seams of his trousers as he lifted himself up, and threw them into the corner after his tunic.

He was already fully aroused. Lunzie stroked him gently with her fingertips as they melted together along the lengths of their bodies for a deep kiss. He bent to run his tongue around the tips of her breasts, cupping them, and spreading his fingers to run his hands down her rib cage. Their hands joined, intertwined, parted, trailing along the other's arm to draw sensual patterns on the skin of throat and chest and belly. Tee rolled onto his back, taking Lunzie on top of him so he could caress her. She spread her palms along his chest, messaging the flesh with her fingers, and reached behind her to brace against the long, hard muscles of his thighs. She arched up, straddling him, moving so that their bodies joined and rocked together in a rhythm of increasing tempo.

At last, Tee dragged her torso down, and they locked their arms around one another, kissing ears and neck and parted lips as passion overcame them.

Lunzie held tightly to Tee until her heart slowed down to its normal pace. She rubbed her cheek against his jaw, and felt the answering pressure of his arms around her shoulders. Through the joy at having found the object of her search, she was sad at the thought of having to leave Tee. Not only was there a physical compatibility, but they were comfortable with one another. She and Tee were familiar with one another's likes and desires and feelings, like two

people who had been together all their lives. She
was torn between completing a quest she had set
herself years ago, and staying with a man who
loved her. If there was only a way that he could
come with her—He wasn't denying her her chance
to rebuild her life after her experiences with cold
sleep; she mustn't deny him his. He had worked too
hard and had lost so much. Lunzie felt guilty at even
thinking of asking him to come with her. But she
loved him too, and knew how much she was going to
miss him.

She shifted to take her weight off his arm, and
rolled into a hard obstruction in the tangled folds of
the coverlet. Curiously, she spread out the edge of
the cloth and uncovered the bottle of wine.

"Ah, yes. Cetus, 2755. Your year of birth, I believe. The vintage is only fit to drink after eighty
years or more."

"Where are the glasses?" Lunzie asked. "This worthy wine deserves crystal."

"We will share from the bottle," answered Tee,
gathering Lunzie close again. "I am not leaving this
spot until I get up from here to cook you a marvelous
celebratory dinner, for which I bought all the ingredients on the way home."

He fell back among the pillows, tracing the lines of
her jaw with one finger. Lunzie lay dreamily enjoying the sensation. Abruptly, a thought struck her.
"You know," she said, raising herself on one elbow,
"maybe I should travel to Alpha as a staff doctor.
That way I could save a good part of the spacefare."

Tee pretended to be shocked. "At this moment
you can think of money? Woman, you have no soul,
no romance."

Lunzie narrowed one eye at him. "Oh, yes, I
have." She sighed. "Tee, I'll miss you so. It might be
years before I come back."

"I will be here, awaiting you with all my heart,"

he said. "I love you, did you not know that?" He opened the bottle and offered her the first sip. Then he drank, and leaned over to give her a wine-flavored kiss.

They made love again, but slowly and with more care. To Lunzie, every movement was now more precious and important. She was committing to memory the feeling of Tee's gentle touch along her body, the growing urgency of his caresses, his hot strength meeting hers.

"I'm sorry we didn't meet under other circumstances," Lunzie said, sadly, when they lay quietly together afterward. The wine was gone.

"I have no regrets. If you didn't need the EEC, we would not have met. I bless Fiona for having driven you into my arms. When you come back, we can make it permanent," Tee offered. "And more. I would love to help you raise a child of ours. Or two."

"Do you know, I always meant to have more children. Just now, the thought seems ludicrous, since my only child is in her seventh decade. I'm still young enough."

"There will be time enough, if you come back to me."

"I will," Lunzie said. "Just as soon as things are settled with Fiona, I'll come back. Dr. Root said that he'd sponsor me as a resident—that is, if he'll still speak to me after my subterfuge to get a night off!"

"If he knew the truth, he'd forgive you. Shall I make us some supper?"

"No. I'm too comfortable to move. Hold me."

Tee drew Lunzie's head onto his chest, and the two of them relaxed together. As Lunzie started to drop off to sleep, the com-unit began chuckling quietly to itself. She sat up to answer it.

"Ignore it until morning," Tee said, pulling her back into bed. "Remember, you have a family emergency. I have asked for travel brochures from all the

cruise lines and merchant ships which will pass between Astris and Alpha Centauri over the next six
months. We can look over them all in the morning. I
do not see you off gladly, but I want you to go safely.
We will choose the best of them all, for you."

Lunzie glanced at the growing heap of plastic fold-
ers sliding out of the printer, and wondered how
she'd ever begin to sort through the mass. "Just the
soonest. That will be good enough for me."

Tee shook his head. "None are good enough for
you. But the sooner you go, the sooner you may
return. Two years or three, they will seem as that
many hundred until we meet again. But think about
it in the morning. For once, for one night, there is
only we two alone in the galaxy."

Lunzie fell asleep with the sound of Tee's heartbeat under her cheek, and felt content.

In the morning, they sat on the floor among a
litter of holographic travel advertisements, sorting
them into three categories: Unsuitable, Inexpensive,
and Short Voyage.

The Unsuitable ones Tee immediately stuffed into
the printer's return slot, where the emulsion would
be wiped and the plastic melted down so it could be
reused in future facsimile transmissions. Glamorous
holographs, usually taken of the dining room, the
entertainment complex, or the shopping arcades of
each line's vessels, hung in the air, as Tee and Lunzie
compared price, comfort, and schedule. Lunzie looked
most closely at the ones which they designated Inexpensive, while Tee paged through those promising
Short Voyages.

Of the sixty or so brochures still under consideration, Tee's favorite was the *Destiny Calls*, a compound liner from the Destiny Cruise Lines.

"It is the fastest of all. It makes only three ports of
call between here and Alpha Centauri over five
months."

Lunzie took one look at the fine print on the plas-sheet under the hologram and blanched. "It's too expensive! Look at those prices. Even the least expensive inside cabin is a year's pay."

"They feed, house, and entertain you for five months," Tee said, reasonably. "Not a bad return after taxes."

"No, it won't do. How about the Caravan Voyages' *Cymbeline*? It's much cheaper." Lunzie pointed to another brochure decorated with more modest photography. "I don't need all those amenities the *Destiny Calls* has. Look, they offer you free the services of a personal psychotherapist, and your choice of a massage mattress or a trained masseuse. Ridiculous!"

"But they are so slow," Tee complained. "You did not want to wait for a merchant to make orbit because of all the stops he would make on the way; you do not want this. If you would pretend that money does not matter for just a moment, it would horrify your efficient soul to find that the *Cymbeline* takes thirteen months to take you where the *Destiny Calls* does in five. And it will not be as comfortable. Come now, think," he said in a wheedling tone. "What about your idea to work your way there on the voyage? Then the question of expense will not come up."

Lunzie was attracted by the idea of travelling on a compound liner, which had quarters for methane- and water-breathers, as well as ordinary oxygen-nitrogen breathers. "Well. . . ."

Tee could tell by her face she was more than half persuaded already. "If you are taking a luxury cruise, why not the best? You will meet many interesting people, eat wonderful food, and have a very good time. Do not even think how much I will be missing you."

She laughed ruefully. "Well, all right then. Let's call them and see if they have room for me."

Tee called the com-unit code for the Destiny Line to inquire for package deals on travels. While he was chatting with a salesclerk, he asked very casually if they needed a ship's medical officer for human passengers.

To Lunzie's delight and relief, they responded with alacrity that they did. Their previous officer had gone ashore at the ship's last port of call, and they hadn't had time to arrange for a replacement. Tee instantly transmitted a copy of Lunzie's credentials and references, which were forwarded to the personnel department. She was asked to come in that day for interviews with the cruise office, the captain of the ship and the chief medical officer by FTL comlink, which Lunzie felt went rather well. She was hired. The ship would make orbit around Astris Alexandria in less than a month to pick her up.

Chapter Six

"Please, gentlebeings, pay attention. This information may save your life one day."

There was a general groan throughout the opulent dining room as the human steward went through his often-recited lecture on space safety and evacuation plans. He pointed out the emergency exits which led to the lifeboats moored inside vacuum hatches along the port and starboard sides of the luxury space liner *Destiny Calls*. Holographic displays to his right and left demonstrated how the emergency atmosphere equipment was to be used by the numerous humanoid and non-humanoid races who were aboard the *Destiny*.

None of the lavishly dressed diners in the Early Seating for Oxygen-Breathers seemed to be watching him except for a clutch of frightened-looking humanoid bipeds with huge eyes and pale gray skin whom Lunzie recognized from her staff briefing as Stribans. Most were far more interested in the moving holographic centerpieces of their tables, which displayed such wonders as bouquets of flowers maturing in minutes from bud to bloom, a black-and-silver-clad being doing magic tricks, or, as at Lunzie's table, a sculptor chipping away with hammer and chisel at an alabaster statue. The steward raised his voice to be heard over the murmuring, but the murmuring just got louder. She had to admit that the young man projected well, and he had a pleasant voice, but the talk was the same, word for word, that was given on every ship that lifted, and any frequent traveller could have recited it along with him. He finished with an ironic "Thank you for your attention."

"Well, thank the stars that's over!" stated Retired Admiral Coromell, in a voice loud enough for the steward to hear. There were titters from several of the surrounding tables. "Nobody listens to the dam-fool things anyway. Only time you can get 'em to-gether is at mealtimes. Captive audience. The ones who seek out the information on their own are the ones who ought to survive anyway. Those nitwits who wait for somebody to save them are as good as dead anyhow." He turned back to his neglected ap-petizer and took a spoonful of sliced fruit and sweetened grains. The young man gathered up his demonstration gear and retired to a table at the back of the room, looking harassed. "Where was I?" the old man demanded.

Lunzie put down her spoon and leaned over to shout at him. "You were in the middle of the engage-ment with the Green Force from the Antari civil war."

"So I was. No need to raise your voice." At great length and corresponding volume, the Admiral re-lated his adventure to the seven fellow passengers at his table. Coromell was a large man who must have been powerfully built in his youth. His curly hair, though crisp white, was still thick. Pedantically, he tended to repeat the statistics of each maneuver two or three times to make sure the others understood them, whether or not they were interested in his narrative. He finished his story with a great flourish for his victory, just in time for the service of the soup course, which arrived at that moment.

Lunzie was surprised to see just how much of the service was handled by individual beings, instead of by servomechanisms and food-synth hatches in the middle of the tables. Clearly, the cruise directors wanted to emphasize how special each facet of their preparations was, down to the ingredients of each course. Even if the ingredients were synthesized out of sight in the kitchen, personal service made the customers think the meals were being prepared from imported spices and produce gathered from exotic ports of call all over the galaxy. In fact, Lunzie had toured the storerooms when she first came aboard, and was more impressed than her tablemates that morel mushrooms were served as the centerpiece in the salad course, since she alone knew that they were real.

The diverse and ornamental menu was a microcosm of the ship itself. The variety of accommodation available on the huge vessel was broad, extending from tiny economy class cabins deep inside the ship, along narrow corridors, to entire suites of elegant chambers which had broad portholes looking out into space, and were served by elaborate Tri-D entertainment facilities and had their own staffs of servitors.

Lunzie found the decor in her personal cabin fantastic, all the more so because she was only a crew member, one of several physicians on board the *Destiny*. It was explained to her by the purser that guests might need her services when she was not on a duty shift. The illusion of endless opulence was not to be spoiled at any price, even to the cost of maintaining the doctors in a luxury surrounding, lest the rich passengers glimpse any evidence of economy. This way was cheaper than dealing with the consequences of their potential distress. Lunzie was surprised to discover that the entertainment system in her quarters was as fancy as the ones in the first-class cabins. There was a wet bar filled with genuine vintage distillations, as well as a drink synthesizer.

The computer outlet in the adjoining infirmary was preprogrammed with a constantly updating medical profile of all crew members and guests. Though she was unlikely to serve a non-humanoid guest, she was provided with a complete set of environment suits in her size, appropriate to each of the habitats provided for methane-breathers, water-breathers, or ultra cold- or hot-loving species, and language translators for each.

Dr. Root would have loved the infirmary. It had every single gadget she had seen listed in the medical supplies catalog. Her own bod bird and gimmick-kit were superfluous among the array of gadgets, so she left them in her suitcase in the cabin locker. She was filled with admiration for the state-of-the-art chemistry lab, which she shared with the other eight medical officers. The *Destiny* had remained in orbit for six days around Astris after taking on Lunzie and fifteen other crew, so she had had plenty of time to study the profiles of her fellow employees and guests. The files made fascinating reading. The cruise line was taking no chances on emergencies in transit, and their health questionnaires were comprehensive. As soon as a new passenger came aboard, a full profile was netted to each doctor's personal computer console.

Lunzie turned to Baraki Don, the Admiral's personal aide, a handsome man in his seventh or eighth decade whose silver hair waved above surprisingly bright blue eyes and black eyebrows. "I'm not suggesting that I should do the procedure, but shouldn't he have his inner ear rebuilt? Shouting at his listeners is usually a sign that his own hearing is failing. I believe the Admiral's file mentioned that he's over a hundred Standard years old."

Don waved away the suggestion with a look of long suffering. "Age has nothing to do with it. He's always bellowed like that. You could hear him clear down in engineering without an intercom from the bridge."

"What an old bore," one of their tablemates said, in a rare moment when the Admiral was occupied with his food. She was a Human woman with black-and green-streaked hair styled into a huge puff, and clad in a fantastic silver dress that clung to her frame.

Lunzie merely smiled. "It's fascinating what the Admiral has seen in his career."

"If any of it is true," the woman said with a sniff. She took a taste of fruit and made a face. "Ugh, how awful."

"But you've only to look at all the medals on his tunic front. I'm sure that they aren't all for good conduct and keeping his gear in order," Lunzie said and gave vent to a wicked impulse. "What's the green metal one with the double star for, Admiral?"

The Admiral aimed his keen blue gaze at Lunzie, who was all polite attention. The green-haired woman groaned unbelievingly. Coromell smiled, touching the tiny decoration in the triple line of his chest.

"Young lady, that might interest you as you're a medical specialist. I commanded a scout team ordered to deliver serum to Denby XI. Seems an explorer was grounded there, and they started one by one to come down with a joint ailment that was crippling them. Most of 'em were too weak to move when we got there. Our scientists found that trace elements were present in the dust that they were bringing in on their atmosphere suits that irritated the connective tissue, caused fever and swelling, and eventually, death. Particles were so small they sort of fell right through the skin. We, too, had a couple cases of the itch before it was all cleaned up. Nobody was that sick, but they gave us all medals. That also reminds me of the Casper mission . . ."

The woman turned her eyes to the ceiling in disgust and took a sniff from the carved perfume bottle at her wrist. A heady wave of scent rolled across the table, and the other patrons coughed. Lunzie gave her a pitying look. There must be something about privilege and wealth that made one bored with life. And Coromell had lived such an amazing one. If only half of what he said was true, he was a hero many times over.

The black-coated chief server appeared at the head of the dining hall and tapped a tiny silver bell with a porcelain clapper. "Gentlebeings, honored passengers, the dessert!"

"Hey, what?" The announcement interrupted Coromell in full spate, to the relief of some of the others at the table. He waited as a server helped him to a plate of dainty cakes, and took a tentative bite. He leveled his fork at the dessert and boomed happily at his aide. "See here, Don, these are delicious."

"They have Gurnsan pastry chefs in the kitchen." Lunzie smiled at him as she took a forkful of a luscious cream pastry. He was more interesting than anyone she'd ever met or had seen on Tri-D. She realized that he was just a few years older than she was. Perhaps he had read Kipling or Service in his youth.

"Well, well, very satisfactory, I must say. Beats the black hole out of Fleet food, doesn't it, Don?"

"Yes, indeed, Admiral."

"Well, well. Well, well," the Admiral murmured to himself between bites, as their tablemates finished their meals and left.

"I should go, too," Lunzie said, excusing herself and preparing to rise. "I've got to hold after-dinner office hours."

The Admiral looked up from his plate and the corners of his eyes crinkled up wisely at her. "Tell me, young doctor. Were you listening because you were interested, or just to humor an old man? I noticed that green-haired female popinjay myself."

"I truly enjoyed hearing your experiences, Admiral," Lunzie said sincerely. "I come from a long line of Fleet career officers."

Coromell was pleased. "Do you! You must join us later. We always have a liqueur in the holo-room during second shift. You can tell us about your family."

"I'd be honored." Lunzie smiled, and hurried away.

"That's nasty," Lunzie said, peeling away the pantsleg of a human engineer and probing at the bruised flesh above and below the knee. She poked an experimental finger at the side of the patella and frowned.

"Agh!" grunted the engineer, squirming away. "That hurt."

"It isn't dislocated, Perkin," Lunzie assured him, lowering the sonic viewscreen over the leg. "Let's see now." On the screen, the bone and tendons stood out among a dark mass of muscle. Tiny lines, veins and arteries throbbed as blood pulsed along them. Near the knee, the veins swelled and melded with one another, distended abnormally. "But if you think it's pretty now, wait a day or so. There's quite a bit of intramuscular bleeding. You didn't do that in an ordinary fall—the bone's bruised, too. How did it happen?" Lunzie reached under the screen to turn his leg for a different view, and curiously watched the muscles twist on the backs of her skeletal hands. This was state-of-the-art equipment.

"Off the record, Doctor?" Perkin asked hesitantly, looking around the examination room.

Lunzie looked around too, then stared at the man's face, trying to discern what was making him so nervous. "It shouldn't be, but if that's the only way you'll tell me . . ."

The man let go a deep sigh of relief. "Off the record, then. I got my leg pinched in a storage hatch door. It shut on me without warning. The thing is six meters tall and almost fifteen centimeters thick. There should have been a klaxon and flashing lights. Nothing."

"Who disconnected them?" Lunzie asked, suddenly and irrationally worried about heavyworlders. Perhaps there was a plot afoot to attack the Admiral.

"No one had to, Doctor. Don't you know about the Destiny Cruise Line? It's owned by the Paraden Company."

Lunzie shook her head. "I don't know anything about them, to be honest. I think I've heard the name before, but that's all. I'm a temporary employee, until we pull into orbit around Alpha Centauri, four months from now. Why, what's wrong with the Paraden Company?"

The engineer curled his lip. "I sure hope this room hasn't got listening devices. The Paraden Company keeps their craft in space as long as it possibly can without drydocking them. Minor maintenance gets done, but major things get put off until someone complains. And that someone always gets fired."

"That sounds horribly unfair." Lunzie was shocked.

"Not to mention hazardous to living beings, Lunzie. Well, whistle-blowing has never been a safe practice. They're Parchandris, the family who owns the company, and they want to squeeze every hundredth credit out of their assets. The Destiny Line is just a tiny part of their holdings."

Lunzie had heard of the Parchandri. They had a reputation for miserliness. "Are you suggesting that this starship isn't spaceworthy?" she asked nervously. Now *she* was looking for listening devices.

Perkin sighed. "It probably is. It most likely is. But it's long overdue for service. It should have stayed back on Alpha the last time we were there. The portmaster was reluctant to let us break orbit. That's been bad for morale, I can tell you. We old-timers don't usually tell the new crew our troubles—

we're afraid that either they're company spies working for Lady Paraden, or they'll be too frightened to stay on board."

"Well, if anything goes wrong, you'll be sure to warn me, won't you?" She noticed that his face suddenly wore a shuttered look. "Oh, please," she appealed to him. "I'm not a spy. I'm on my way to see my daughter. We haven't seen each other since she was a youngster. I don't want anything to get in the way of that. I've already been in one space accident."

"Now, now," Perkin said soothingly. "Lightning doesn't strike twice in the same place."

"Unless you're a lightning rod!"

Perkin relaxed, a little ashamed for having distrusted her. "I'll keep you informed, Lunzie. You may count on it. But what about my leg here?"

She pointed to the discoloration on his skin. "Well then, except for the aurora borealis, and no one need know about that but you and your roommate, there will be nothing to draw attention to your er, mishap," Lunzie said, resealing his magnetic seams. "There's no permanent damage of any kind. The leg will be stiff for a while until the hematoma subsides, and there might be some pain. If the pain gets too bad, take the analgesic which I'm programming into your cabin synthesizer, but no more than once a shift."

"Make me high, will it?" the engineer asked, pushing himself off the table with extra care for his sore leg.

"A little. But more importantly, it will stop up your bowels better than an oatmeal-and-banana sandwich," Lunzie answered, her eyes dancing merrily. "I never prescribe that mix for young Seti. They have enough problems with human-dominated menus as it is."

Perkin chuckled. "So they do. I had one working for me once. He was always suffering. The cooks

grew senna for him. Didn't know much about him
other than that. They're the most private species I've
ever known."

"If you like, I'll also give you a liniment to rub in
your leg following a good hot soak."

"Thank you, Lunzie." Perkin accepted the plastic
packet Lunzie handed him and slipped out the door
past the next patient waiting to see the doctor.

After that day, Lunzie began to notice things about
the ship which weren't quite right. It was hard to tell
under all the ornamentation, but the clues were
there for eyes paying attention. Perkin was right
about the lack of maintenance on ship's systems.
There was a persistent leak in the decks around the
methane environment, which made various passengers complain of the smell in the hallway near the
fitness center. Perkin and the other engineers shrugged
as they put one more temporary seal on the cracks,
and promised to keep the problem under control
until they made the next port with repair facilities,
months away at Alpha Centauri.

Lunzie began to worry whether there was a chance
that the ship might fail somewhere en route to Alpha
Centauri. The odds of meeting with a space accident
twice in a lifetime were in the millions, but it still
niggled at her. It couldn't happen to her again, could
it? She hoped Perkin was exaggerating his concerns.
With an uncomfortable feeling that ill fate was just
past the next benchmark, Lunzie started listening
more intently to the evacuation instructions. True to
her word, she didn't mention Perkin's confidences to
anyone else, but she kept her eyes open.

Seating arrangements in the dining room had been
changed over the course of the last month. Lunzie,
Admiral Coromell, and Baraki Don had been given
seats at the Captain's table, presided over at the
early seating by the First Mate. This was a distinguished woman of color who was probably of an age

with Commander Don. First Mate Sharu was very small of stature. The top of her head was on a level with Lunzie's chin. Sharu wore a snugly cut long evening dress of the same regimental purple as her uniform. Her military bearing suggested that she had been in the service before coming to Destiny Cruise Lines. The ornate gold braid at the wrist of the single sleeve showed her rank, and hid a small, powerful communicator, which she employed to keep in touch with the ship's bridge during the meal. The other arm, which bore a brilliantly cut diamond bangle, was bare to the shoulder. To Lunzie's delight, Sharu, too, loved a good yarn, so Coromell had a responsive audience for his tales.

Not that he appeared to appreciate it. He was still grouchy at times, and occasionally snapped at them for humoring an old man. After a while, Lunzie stopped protesting her innocence and turned the tables on him.

"Maybe I am just humoring you," she told Coromell airily, who stopped in full harangue and glared at her in surprise. "I've gone to school lectures where there was more of a dialogue than you allow. We have opinions, too. Once in a while I'd like to voice one."

"Heh, heh, heh! Methinks I do protest too much, eh?" Coromell chortled approvingly. "That's Shakespeare, for all you beings too young to have read any. Well, well. Perhaps I'm at the age when I'm at the mercy of my environment, in a world for which I have insufficient say any more, and I don't like it. Rather like those poor heavyworlder creatures, wouldn't you say?"

Lunzie perked up immediately at the phrase. "What about the heavyworlders, Admiral?"

"Had a few serving under me in my last command. When was that, eight, ten years ago, Don?"

"Fourteen, Admiral."

Coromell thrust his jaw out and counted the years on the ceiling. "So it was. Damn those desk jobs. They make you lose all track of intervening time. Heavyworlders! Bad idea, that. Shouldn't adapt people to worlds. You should adapt worlds to people. What God intended, after all!"

"Terraforming takes too long, Admiral," Sharu put in, reasonably. "The worlds the heavyworlders live on are good for human habitation, except for the gravity. They were created to adapt to that."

"Yes, created! Created a minority, that's what they did," the Admiral sputtered. "We have enough trouble in politics with partisanship anyway. Just when you have all the subgroups there are already getting used to each other, you throw in another one, and start the whole mess over. You've got people screaming about that Phoenix disaster, saying that the heavyworlders were dancing on the graves of the lightweights who were there before 'em, but you can bet they paid a hefty finder's fee to whoever helped them make landfall—probably a goodly percentage of their export income to boot."

"I've heard that planet pirates destroyed the first settlement," Lunzie said, angrily remembering the anguished two years she had spent believing that Fiona had been one of the dead on Phoenix.

"Doctor, you may believe it. Probably they cut off Phoenix's communications with the outside first, destroying their support system, traders and so on. Soon as a planet's population can't take care of itself, the rights go to the next group who can. My ship got the mayday from a merchant ship being chased by a pirate outside of the Eridani system. They had been damaged pretty heavily, but they were still hauling ions when we came on the scene. My communications officer kept up chatter with their bridge for three weeks until we could come to the rescue. Lose your spirit, lose the war, that's what I say!"

"Did you capture the pirate?" Lunzie asked eagerly, leaning forward.

The Admiral shook his head regretfully. "Sunspots, no. That'd have been a pretty star on my bow if we had. We engaged them as they streaked after the merchant ship, exchanging fire. That poor little merchant begged heaven's blessings down on us, and scooted! The pirate had no choice. He couldn't turn his back on me again. My ship was holed, but no lives were lost. The pirate wasn't so lucky. I saw hull plates and other debris shoot away from the body of his ship, and the frayed edges curled, imploded! Must have been an atmosphered chamber, which meant crew. I hope to heaven it didn't mean prisoners.

"Whatever they had in their engines, ours was better. We chased them outside the system into the radiation belt, we chased them past comets. Finally, my gunner struck their port engine. They spiralled in circles for a couple of turns, and got back on a steady course, but my gunner hit them again. Dead in the water. As soon as we relayed to them that we were going to board them with a prize crew, they blew themselves up!" The Admiral held out his hands before him, cupping air. "I had them like this, so close! No captain has ever succeeded in capturing a planet pirate. But I flatter myself, that if I couldn't, no man can."

"You do flatter yourself, Admiral," Sharu remarked flippantly. "But most likely, you're right."

Lunzie still joined the Admiral and his aide in the holo-room during the evenings after she held infirmary call. Coromell had two favorite holos he requested in the alcove in which he and Don spent the hours before turning in. The first was the bridge of his flagship, the *Federation*. The second appeared when Lunzie suspected that Coromell was in a pensive mood. It was a roaring fireplace with a broad tiled hearth and an ornamented copper hood set in a stone-and-brick wall.

The quality hologram system was equipped with temperature and olfactory controls as well as visual display. She could smell the burning hardwoods and feel the heat of the flames as she took a seat in the third of the deep, cushiony armchairs furnished in the alcove. Don stood up as she approached, and signalled a server to bring her a drink. As she suspected, Coromell sat bent with one elbow on his knee and a balloon glass in the other hand, staring into the dance of shadows and lights and listening to the soft music playing in the background. He hadn't noticed her arrive. Lunzie waited a little while, watching him. He looked pensive and rather sad.

"What are you thinking of, Admiral?" Lunzie asked in a soft voice.

"Hm? Oh, Doctor. Nothing. Nothing of importance. Just thinking of my son. He's in the service. Means to go far, too, and see if he doesn't."

"You miss him," she suggested, intuitively sensing that the old man wanted to talk.

"Dammit, I do. He's a fine young man. You're about his age, I'd say. You . . . you don't have any children, do you?"

"Just one; a daughter. I'm meeting her on Alpha Centauri."

"A little girl, eh? You look so young." Coromell coughed self-deprecatingly. "Of course, at my age, everyone looks young."

"Admiral, I'm closer to your age than to your son's." Lunzie shrugged. "It's in the ship's records; you could find out if you wanted. I've been through cold sleep. My little girl will be seventy-eight on her next birthday."

"You don't say? Well, well, that's why you understand all the ancient history I've been spouting. You've been there. We should talk about old times." The

Admiral shot her a look of lonely appeal which touched Lunzie's heart. "There are so few left who remember. I'd consider it a personal favor."

"Admiral, I'd be doing it out of blatant self-interest. I've only been in this century two years."

"Hmph! I feel as though I've been on this ship that long. Where are we bound for?"

"Sybaris Planet. It's a luxury spa. . . ."

"I know what it is," Coromell interrupted her impatiently. "Another dumping ground for the useless rich. Phah! When I get to be that helpless you can arrange for my eulogy."

Lunzie smiled. The server bowed next to her, presenting a deep balloon glass like the one the Admiral had, washed a scant half inch across the bottom with a rich, ruddy amber liquid. It was an excellent rare brandy. Delicate vapors wafted out of the glass headily as the liquid warmed in the heat from the fire. Lunzie took a very small sip and felt that heat travel down her throat. She closed her eyes.

"Like it?" Coromell rumbled.

"Very nice. I don't usually indulge in anything this strong."

"Hmph. Truth is, neither do I. Never drank on duty." Coromell cupped the glass in his big hand and swirled the brandy gently under his nose before tipping it up to drink. "But today I felt a little self-indulgent."

Lunzie became aware suddenly that the background music had changed. Under the lull of the music was a discreet jingling that could have been mistaken for a technical fault by anyone but a member of the crew. To the crew, it meant impending disaster. Lunzie set down her glass and looked around the shadows.

"Chibor!" She hailed a mate of Perkin's staff who was passing through the immense chamber. She looked up at the sound of her voice and waved.

"I was looking for you, Lunzie. Perkin told me . . ."

"Yes! The alarm. What is it? You can speak in front of the Admiral. He doesn't scare easily."

Coromell straightened up, and set aside his glass. "No, indeed. What's in the wind?"

Chibor signalled for a more discreet tone and leaned toward her. "You know about the engine trouble we've been having. It was giving off some weird harmonics, so we had to turn it off and drop out of warp early. There's no way to get back into warp for a while until it's been tuned, and we jumped right into the path of an ion storm. It's moving toward us pretty fast. The navigator accidentally let us drift into its perimeters, and it's playing merry hell with the antimatter drives. We're heading behind the gas giant in the system to shield us until it passes."

"Will that work?" Lunzie asked, her eyes huge and worried. She fought down the clutch of fear in her guts.

"May do," Coromell answered calmly, interrupting Chibor. "May not."

"We're preparing to go to emergency systems. Perkin said you'd want to know." Chibor nodded and rushed away. Lunzie watched her go. No one else noticed her enter or leave the holo-room. They were involved in their own pursuits.

"I'd better go up and see what is going on," Lunzie said. "Excuse me, Admiral."

The gas giant of Carson's System was as huge and as spectacular as promised. The rapidly rotating planet had a solid core deep inside an envelope of swirling gases thousands of miles thick. A few of her fellow passengers had gathered on the ship's gallery to view it through the thick quartz port.

The captain of the *Destiny Calls* increased the ship's velocity to match the planet's two-hour period of rotation and followed a landmark in the gas layer, the starting point of a pair of horizontal black stripes, around to the sunward side of the planet, where they stood off, and held a position behind the planet's protective bulk. The green-and-yellow giant was just short of being a star, lacking only a small increase in mass or primary ignition. The planet's orbit was much closer to the system's sun than was common with most gas giants, and the sun itself burned an actinic white on the ship's screens. Telemetry warned of lashing arms of magnetic disturbance that kicked outward from the gaseous surface. This was the only formed planet in this system, and ships passing by were required to use it when aligning for their final jump through the sparsely starred region to Sybaris. Still the planet's rapid rotation and the massive magnetic field it generated meant that here gases and radiation churned constantly, even on its dark side. Lunzie suspected they were closer to the planet, which filled half the viewport, than was normal, but said nothing. Other passengers, the more well-travelled looking ones, seemed concerned as well. The captain appeared a few minutes later, a forced smile belying his attempts to calm his passengers' fears.

"Gentlebeings," Captain Wynline said, wryly, watching the giant's surface spin beneath them. "Due to technical considerations, we were forced to drop out of warp at this point. But as a result, we are able to offer you a fabulous view seen by only a few since it was discovered: Carson's Giant. This gas giant should have been a second sun, making this system a binary without planets, but it never ignited, thereby leaving us with a galactic wonder, for study and speculation. Oh . . . and don't anybody drop a match."

The passengers watching the huge globe revolve chuckled and whispered among themselves.

The *Destiny* waited behind the gas giant's rapidly spinning globe until they were sure that the particu-

larly violent ion storm had swirled past and moved
entirely out of the ecliptic. The first edges of the
storm, which an unmanned monitor had warned them
of the instant they had entered normal space, filled
the dark sky around the giant with a dancing aurora.

"Captain!" Telemetry Officer Hord entered the
gallery and stood next to the captain. "Another major
solar flare on the sun's surface! That'll play havoc
with the planet's magnetic field," he offered softly,
and then paused, watching to see how the captain
reacted. The chief officer didn't seem overly concerned. "This will combine with the effects of the ion
storm, sir," he added, when no response was forthcoming.

"I'm aware of the ramifications, Hord," the captain
assured him and tripped his collar mike. He spoke
decisively in a low voice. Lunzie noticed the change
in his hearty tone and moved closer to listen. The
captain observed her, but saw only another crew
member, and continued with his commands. "Helm,
try to maneuver us away from the worst of this. Use
whatever drives are ready and tuned. Telemetry, tell
us when the storm's passed by enough to venture out
again. I don't like this a bit. Computer systems, get
the ceramic brick hard copies of our programming
out of mothballs. Just in case. Inform Engineering.
What's the period for magnetic disturbance reaching
us from the sun, Hord?"

"Nine hours, sir. But the flame disturbances are
coming pretty close together. I estimate that some
are coming toward us already. There's no way to tell,
too much noise to get anything meaningful from the
monitor." Both officers looked worried now. The
com-unit on the captain's collar bleeped. "Engineering here, Captain. We're getting magnetic interference in the drives. The antimatter bottle is becoming
unstable. I'm bringing in portable units to step it
up."

The captain wiped his forehead. "So it's begun. We can't depend on the containment systems. Prepare to evacuate the ship. Sound the alarms, but don't launch. Gentlebeings!" Everyone on the gallery looked up expectantly. "There has been a development. Will you please return immediately to your quarters, and wait for an announcement. Now, please."

As soon as the gallery cleared, the captain ordered the Communications Officer to make the announcement over shipwide comsystems. When Lunzie turned toward the gallery's door to go back to the holochamber, everything went dark, as the ship abruptly went onto battery. The emergency lights glowed red for a brief instant in the corners and around the hatchway.

"What the hell was that?" the captain demanded as the full lights came back on.

"Overload, probably from the solar flares," Hord snapped out, monitoring his readouts on his portable remote unit. "We'll lose the computer memory if that happens again. Watch out, here it goes!"

Lunzie dashed back toward her cabin through flickering lights. Interstellar travel is safer than taking a bath, less accidents per million, she repeated the often-advertised claim to reassure herself. No one was ever in two incidents, not in this modern age. Every vessel, even one as old as the *Destiny*, was double-checked and had triple back-ups on every circuit.

"Attention please," announced the calm voice of the Communications Officer, cutting through the incidental music and all the video and Tri-D programs. "Attention. Please leave your present locations immediately and make your way to the lifeboat stations. Please leave your present locations and make your way to the lifeboat stations. This is not a drill. Do not use the turbovators as they may not continue to function. Repeat, do not use the turbovators."

The voice was interrupted occasionally by crackling, and faded out entirely at one point.

"What was that?" A passenger noticed Lunzie's uniform and grabbed her arm. "I saw the lights go down. There's something wrong, isn't there?"

"Please, sir. Go to the lifeboat stations right now. Do you remember your team number?"

"Five B. Yes, it was Five B." The man's eyes went huge. "Do you mean there's a real emergency?"

Lunzie shuddered. "I hope not, sir. Please, go. They'll tell you what's going on when you're in your place. Hurry!" She turned around and ran with him to the dining hall level.

The message continued to repeat over the loudspeakers.

The corridor filled instantly with hundreds of humanoids, hurrying in all directions. Some seemed to have forgotten not only which stations they were assigned to, but where the dining hall was. Emergency chase lights were intermittent, but they provided a directional beacon for the terrified passengers to follow. There were cries and groans as the passengers tried to speculate on what was happening.

The crowd huddled in the gigantic holo-room near the metal double doors to the dining room, milling about, directionless, babbling among themselves in fear. The holo-room was the largest open space on the level, and could be used for illusions to entertain thousands of people. At one end of the room, several dozen humans, unaware that anything was going on around them, were fending off holographic bandits with realistic-looking swords. In a cave just next to the doors in the dining room, a knot of costumed cavedwellers huddled together over a stick fire. At that moment, the illusion projectors in the alcoves shut off, eliciting loud protests from viewers as their varied fantasies disappeared, leaving the room a bare, ghost-gray shell with a few pieces of real furniture here and there. The costumed figures stood up, looking around for ship personnel to fix the problem, and saw the crowds bearing down on them into the newly opened space. They panicked and broke for the exits. More passengers appeared, trying to shove past them into the dining hall, yelling. Fights began among them. Into the midst of this came the child-caretakers with their charges. The head of child care, a thin Human male, spoke through a portable loudspeaker, paging each parent one at a time to come and retrieve its offspring.

"Listen up!" Coromell appeared from his alcove with Don behind him. "Listen!" His deep voice cut across the screaming and the mechanical whine of overtaxed life support systems. "Now listen! Everyone calm down. Calm down, I say! You all ignored the emergency procedures in the dining hall. Those of you who know what to do, proceed to your stations, NOW! Those of you who don't know what to do, pipe down so you can hear instructions over the loudspeakers. Move it! That is all!"

"The doors are shut! We can't get through!" a large Human woman wailed.

"Just hold your water! Look! They're opening right now."

The engineers appeared in a widening gap between the huge double metal blast doors between the holo-room and the oxygen-breathers' dining hall. The crowd, considerably quieter, rushed through, grabbing oxygen equipment from crew lined up on either side of the doors. Stewards directed them to the irised-open hatchways of the escape capsules and ordered them to sit down.

Coromell, with Don's help, continued to direct the flow of traffic, pushing water-breathers in bubble-suits and frantically shapechanging Weft passengers toward the access stairway to the water environment.

"Attention, please, this is the captain," the chief

officer's voice boomed over the public address system. "Please proceed calmly to your assigned evacuation pod. This will be a temporary measure. Please follow the instructions of the crew. Thank you."

In the midst of the screaming and shouting, Lunzie heard frantic cries for help. She forced her way through the press of beings to a little girl who had tripped and fallen, and was unable to get up again. She had nearly been trampled. Her face was bruised and she was crying. Shouting words of comfort, Lunzie picked her up high and handed her over the heads of the crowd to her shrieking mother. Don escorted the woman and child into the dining room and saw them onto a capsule. As the escape vehicles filled, the hatches irised closed, and the pods were sealed. It was an abrupt change from the leisurely pace of the luxury liner, and most people were not making the transition well. Lunzie hurried back and forth throughout the huge chamber with an emergency medical kit from a hatch hidden behind an ornate tapestry. She splinted the limbs of trampled victims long enough to get them through the door and slapped bandages on cuts and scrapes suffered by passengers who had had to climb out of the turbovators through accessways in the ceiling. She dispensed mild sedatives for passengers who were clearly on the edge of hysteria.

"Just enough to calm you," she explained, keeping a placid smile on her face though she too was terrified. "Everything is going to be all right. This is standard procedure." Space accident! This could not be happening to her again.

"My jewelry!" a blue-haired Human woman screamed as she was dragged toward the dining hall by a young man in formal clothing. "All of it is still in my cabin. We must go back!" She pulled her hand out of the young man's grip and made to dash back toward the cabins.

"Stop her!" the man shouted. "Lady Cholder, no!"

The woman was borne back toward him on the wave of panicked passengers, but still struggled to move upstream. "I can't leave my jewelry!"

Lunzie seized her arm as soon as it was within reach and pressed the hypo to it. The woman moved her lips, trying to speak, but she collapsed between Lunzie and the young man. He looked quizzically from Lady Cholder to Lunzie.

"She'll sleep for about an hour. The sedative has no permanent effects. By then, you'll be well into space. The distress beacon is already broadcasting," Lunzie explained. "Just try to keep calm."

"Thanks," the young man said, sincerely, picking up Lady Cholder in his arms and hurrying toward an escape capsule.

Lunzie heard rumbling and tearing behind her. She spun.

"There it goes again!" Two ship's engineers leaped toward the double doors, which were sliding closed on the hysterical crowd. The lights went out again. Along the ceiling the lines of red emergency lights came on, bathing them all in shadow.

"Cut off that switch!" Perkin shouted at one of his assistants, pointing to the open control box next to the doorway. "It's only supposed to do that when the hull is breached."

"All the programming's messed up, Perkin!" The other engineer pushed and pulled at the levers on the control panel, trying to read the screen in the reduced light. "We'll have to try and keep it open manually."

"We've only got minutes. Get between 'em!" Perkin leaped between the heavy metal doors, now rolling closed, and tried to force one of them back. His men started to force their way through the crowd to help him, but they couldn't reach him before he screamed.

"I'm being crushed! Help!" The doors had closed with him between them.

Lunzie was galvanized by his cries. Mustering the strength of Discipline, she shoved her way through the crowd. Perkin's face was screwed up with pain as he tried to get out from between the doors which were threatening to cut him in half lengthwise. The adrenaline rush hit her just as she reached the front of the line. She and the other engineers took hold of the doors and pulled.

Slowly, grudgingly, the metal blast doors rolled back along their tracks. The crowd, now more frantic than before, rushed into the dining hall around Perkin, who was nearly collapsing. As soon as the doors had been braced open with chucks blocking the tracks, Lunzie rushed to catch Perkin and help him out of the way. He was almost unable to walk, and outweighed her by fifty percent, but in her Discipline trance, Lunzie could carry him easily.

She pulled open his tunic and examined his chest, hissing sympathetically at what she saw. Her fingers confirmed what her heightened perception detected: his left rib cage was crushed, endangering the lung. If she worked quickly, she could free the ribs before that lung collapsed.

"Lunzie! Where are you going?" the voice of Coromell demanded as she hurried to the access stairway leading to the upper decks.

"I've got to get some quick-cast from my office. Perkin will die if I don't brace those ribs."

"Admiral! We'd better go, too," Don shouted, urging him toward the doors.

Coromell pushed his aide's hands away. "Not a chance! I won't be shoved into one of those tiny life preservers with a hundred hysterical grand dames wailing for their money! They need all hands to keep this hulk from spinning into that planet. We can save lives. I may be old, but I can still do my part. The captain hasn't given the evacuation order yet." Suddenly he felt at his chest, and took a deep, painful breath. The color rushed out of his face. "Dammit, not now! Where's my medication?" With shaking fingers, he undid his collar.

Don led him to a couch at the side of the room. "Sit here, sir. I'll find the doctor."

"Don't plague her, Don," Coromell snapped, as Don pushed him down into the seat. "She's busy. There's nothing wrong with me. I'm only old."

Lunzie flew up the steps. As she rounded the first landing, she found herself in the way of another crowd of frantic passengers running down, heading to the dining hall from their cabins. She tried to catch the stair rail, but was knocked off her feet and shoved underfoot. Lunzie grabbed at the legs of the passing humans, trying to pull herself to her feet, but they shook her off. Still possessed of her Discipline strength she forced her way to the wall and walked her hands upward until she was standing up. Keeping to the wall, Lunzie focused on staying balanced and pushed through the mob, paying no attention to the protests of the people in her way. Another herd of humans barreled past her, trying to climb over one another in their panic to get to safety. She knew she was as terrified as they were, but between Discipline and duty, she didn't—wouldn't—feel it.

The next level was practically deserted. The emergency hatch to the methane environment, normally sealed, had drifted open, dissipating the nauseating atmosphere through the rest of the ship. The rescue capsules on that level were gone. Gagging and choking on the stench, Lunzie ran to her office.

The power in this section had gone on and off several times. Hatchways held in place by magnetic seals had lost their cohesiveness and fallen to the ground, denting walls and floors. Lunzie dodged past them and physically pushed open the door to the infirmary.

With the corridors clearing, she could see that there were other victims of the tragedy. With Perkin's ribs correctly strapped and braced, he was out of danger. She left him on the soft couch to rest. Tirelessly, she sought out other injured members of the crew.

"Here, Lunzie!" Don waved her over to the dark corner where the Admiral lay unconscious. "It's his heart."

As soon as she saw the old man's pinched face, Lunzie gasped. Even in the red light she could tell his skin was going from pasty to blue-tinged white. She dropped to her knees and dug through the medical bag for a hypospray, which she pressed against Coromell's arm. She and Don waited anxiously as she peered at her scanner for his vital signs to improve. The Admiral suddenly stirred and groaned, waving them away with an impatient hand.

"I'm going to give him a vitamin shot with iron," Lunzie said, reaching for a different vial. "He must rest!"

"Can't rest when people are in danger," muttered Coromell.

"You're retired, sir," Don said patiently. "I'll help you walk."

"You'd better get to the capsules," First Mate Sharu called to them.

"Not going in the capsules," Coromell wheezed.

"I'll stay and help, Sharu," Lunzie shouted back.

Sharu nodded gratefully, and signalled for the remaining capsules to close their doors. "Captain," she told her wrist communicator, "you may give the order."

"What can we do?" Don asked, as they helped the Admiral toward the stairs. "This situation will only worsen his condition. He'll want to help!"

"Let's get him to one of the cryogenic chambers.

I'll give him a sedative, and he and the other critically injured crew can cold-sleep it until we're rescued." Lunzie half carried the old man toward the infirmary ward, worrying whether he would survive long enough to be given the cryogenic drug.

There was another tremor in the ship's hull, and all the lights went off. This time they stayed off for several seconds. Only the corner emergency beacons came on in the great holo-room.

"That's it, then," Chibor groaned. "No more drives. Those lights are on batteries."

A crewman battered at the side of the control screen next to the doors. "The function computers are wiped. The programs'll all have to be loaded again from ceramic. It'll take. months, years to get the whole ship running again. We could lose everything, power, life support. . . ."

"Concentrate on one section at a time, Nais, so we have partial environment to live in," Sharu ordered. "I suggest the hydroponics sections. For now there's plenty of fresh air for the few of us left. Set up mechancial circulation fans to keep it moving. Rig a mayday beacon."

"Telemetry said that we're too close to the planet. No one will be able to see us," Nais argued pugnaciously. His nerves were obviously frayed. "We're not supposed to be here anyway. The giant is only our landmark in this system. We're millions of kiloms from our proper jump mark."

"Don't you want to be found?" Sharu shot back, grabbing his shoulder and shaking him. "Check with Captain Wynline, see what he wants to do. He's up on the bridge."

"Yes, Sharu," Nais gasped and dashed toward the accessway.

"It'll be dangerous here until we regain systems stabilization," Sharu said to Lunzie, who had just returned to the holo-room. "Can I help in any way?"

"Get me a battery-powered light down here, and I can keep going." Lunzie was grateful that she hadn't become totally dependent on all the toys of modern medical technology. What would those fellow physicians of hers from Astris Alexandria do now without their electronic scalpels?

She was still working on the burst of adrenaline evoked from her Discipline training. When it wore off, she'd be almost helpless. Until then, she intended to help the wounded.

There was a sound like a muffled explosion behind her. Lunzie stood up to see what it was in the dimness. Only half visible in the gloom, the metal blast doors rolled slowly, inexorably closed on the empty dining hall.

"There go the chucks! The doors are closing!" Chibor cried. "Look out!"

A sharp-cornered weight hit Lunzie full in the chest, knocking her backwards. She slammed against the wall and slid down it to the floor, unconscious, over the body of her patient. Chibor ran to her, mopping the blood from Lunzie's cut lip, and felt for a pulse.

Sharu appeared a few minutes later, sweeping the beam of a powerful hand-held searchlight before her. "Lunzie, will this do? Lunzie?"

"Over here, Sharu," Chibor called, a formless shape in the red spotlights.

The First Mate ran toward the voice. "Krim!" She sighed. "Dammit. Put her in the cold-sleep chamber with Admiral Coromell. We'll get medical attention for her as soon as somebody rescues us. Meantime, she'll be safe in cold sleep. Then let's get back to work."

BOOK THREE

Chapter Seven

Lunzie opened her eyes and immediately closed them again to shut out a bright sharp light that was shining down on her.

"Sorry about that, Doctor," a dry, practical male voice said. "I was checking your pupils when you revived all of a sudden. Here"—a cloth was laid across the hand shielding her eyes—"open them gradually so you can get used to the ambient light. It isn't too strong."

"The door chuck hit me in the chest," Lunzie said, remembering. "It must have broken some ribs, but then I hit the back of my head, and . . . I guess I was knocked unconscious." With her free hand, she felt cautiously down the length of her rib cage. "That's funny. They don't feel cracked or constricted. Am I under local anesthetic?"

"Lunzie?" another voice asked tentatively. "How are you feeling?"

"Tee?" Lunzie snatched the cloth from her face and sat up, suddenly woozy from the change in blood pressure. Strong arms caught and steadied her. She squinted through the glaring light until the two faces became clear. The man on the left was a short, powerfully built stranger, a medical officer wearing Fleet insignia of rank. The other was Tee. He took her hand between both of his and kissed it. She hugged him, babbling in her astonishment.

"What are you doing here? We're ten light years out from Astris. Wait, where am I now?" Lunzie recovered herself suddenly and glanced around at the examination room, whose walls bore a burnished stainless steel finish. "This isn't the infirmary."

The stranger answered her. "You're on the Fleet vessel *Ban Sidhe*. There was a space wreck. Do you remember? You were injured and put into cold sleep."

Lunzie's face went very pale. She looked to Tee for confirmation. He nodded quietly. She noticed that his face was a little more lined than it was when she had last seen him, and his skin was pale. The changes shocked and worried her. "How long?"

"Ten point three years, Doctor," the Fleet medic said crisply. "Your First Mate was debriefed just a little while ago. She and the captain spent the whole time awake, manning the beacon. We very nearly missed the ship. It's about sixteen percent lower into the Carson's Giant's atmosphere than it was when they sent out the mayday and released the escape pods. The orbit is decaying. Looked like a piece of debris. Destiny decided it doesn't want to retrieve the hulk. In about fifty more years, it'll fall into the methane. Too bad. It's a pretty fine ship."

"No!" Lunzie breathed.

The medic was cheerful. "Just a little down time. It happens to about a fifth of Fleet personnel at one time in their careers. You should feel just fine. What's the matter?" He closed a firm, professional hand around her wrist.

"It's the second time it's happened to me," Lunzie sagged. "I didn't think it could happen to me again. Two space wrecks in one lifetime. Muhlah!"

"Twice? Good grief, you've had an excess of bad luck." He released her hand and quickly ran a scan-

ner in front of her chest. "Normal. You've recovered
quickly. You must be very strong, Doctor."

"You need exercise and food," Tee said. "Can I
take her away, Harris? Good. Walk with me through
the ship. We have recovered all forty-seven of the
crew who stayed behind, and two passengers. It is
because of one of them that we were able to come
looking for you."

"What? Who stayed on board with us?"

"Admiral Coromell. Come. Walk with me to the
mess hall, and I'll tell you.

"It was after you had been gone two years that I
began to worry about you," Tee explained, dispensing a much-needed pepper to Lunzie. They programmed meals from the synthesizer and sat down at
a table near the wall in the big room. The walls here
were white. Lunzie noticed that the navy vessel ran
to two styles of decoration in its common rooms,
burnished steel or flat ceramic white. She hoped the
bunkrooms were more inviting. Tedium caused its
own kinds of space sickness. "I knew something was
wrong, but I didn't know what it could be. You had
only written to me once. I found out from the AT&T
operator that it was the only communication charged
to your access code number in all that time."

Lunzie was feeling more lively after drinking the
mild stimulant. "How did you do that? Astris Tele-
communication and Transmission is notoriously un-
cooperative in giving out information like that."

Tee smiled, his dark eyes warm. "Shof and I became friends after you left. He and Pomayla knew
how lonely I was without you, as they were. I taught
him much about the practical application of laser
technology, and in exchange he gave me insight to
computer tricks he and his friends nosed out. He was
very pleased to learn from me. I think he made some
points with his technology teacher, being able to
give detailed reports on the earliest prototypes of the

system. Oh, he wanted me to let you know that he graduated with honors." He sighed. "That was eight years ago, of course. He gave me a ticket for the graduation. I went with the rest of the Gang who were still at the University, and we had a party later on, where your name was toasted in good wine. I did miss you so much."

Lunzie noticed the slight emphasis on "did," but let it pass. There seemed to be a distance between them, but that was to be expected, after all the time that had passed. Ten years didn't pack the same shock value as sixty-two, but at least she could picture the passage of that interval of time. "I'm happy to hear about Shof. Thank you for letting me know. But how did you get here?"

"It was the video you sent me, and the fact that you sent no more, which made me go looking for answers. You seemed to be very happy. You told of many things which you had observed on the ship already. The cabin in which you were living was the daydream of a rich man. The other physicians were good people, and all dedicated professionals. You had just delivered a baby to a dolphin couple underwater in the salt-water environment. You missed me. That was all. If you had meant to tell me that you had found someone else, and it was all over between us, you would have sent a second message. You were sometimes very mysterious, my Lunzie, but never less than polite."

"Well," Lunzie said, taking a forkful of potatoes gratinee, "I do hate being cubbyholed like that, but you're right. So my manners saved my life? Whew, this meal is a shock after the *Destiny*'s cooking. It isn't bad, you understand."

"Not bad, just uninteresting. How I miss the apartment's cooking facilities!" Tee looked ceilingward. "So long as I live, I will never be entirely happy with synth-swill. Fresh vegetables are issued sparingly to us from the hydroponics pod up top. I never know when I will next see something that was actually grown, not formed from carbohydrate molecules."

"To us?" It registered with Lunzie for the first time that Tee was dressed in a uniform. "Are you stationed on the *Ban Sidhe*, Tee?"

"I am temporarily, yes, but that comes at the end of the story, not the beginning. Let me tell you what happened:

"I was not informed when the space liner first went missing. Whenever I asked the cruise line why I was not receiving messages from you, I was told that interstellar mail was slow, and perhaps you were too busy to send any. That I could accept for a time. It could take a long while for a message brick to reach Astris from Alpha. But surely, after more than two years, I should have heard from you about your meeting with Fiona. Even," Tee added self-consciously, "if it was no more than a thank you to me as your caseworker."

"Surely, if anyone does, you had a right to a full narration of our reunion. I owe you much more than that. Oh, I have missed you, Tee. Great heavens!" Lunzie clutched her head. "Another ten years gone! They were expecting me—Fiona might have had to leave again for Eridani! I must get to touch with Lars."

Tee patted her hand. "I have already sent a communication to him. You should hear back very soon."

"Thank you." Lunzie rubbed her eyes. "My head isn't very clear yet. I probably did have a concussion when they put me in the freezer. I should have your doctor scan my skull."

"Would you like another pepper?" Tee asked solicitously.

"Oh, no. No, thank you. One of those is always enough. So the cruise line said everything was fine, and it was just the post which was going astray. I smell a very nasty rat."

Tee disposed of their trays and brought a steaming carafe of herb tea to the table. "Yes. So did I, but I had no proof. I believed them until I saw on the Tri-D that *Destiny Calls* was supposed to have been lost in an ion storm. The Destiny Line had recovered the passengers, who were sent out in escape capsules. Some of them gave interviews to Tri-D. Even after that, I still hadn't heard from you. Then, I began to move planets and moons to find out what had happened. Like you with Fiona, I ran into the one block in my path. No one knew what had happened after the *Destiny Calls* left its first stop after Astris. The Destiny Line was eager to help, they said, but never did I get any real answers from them. I insisted that they pay for a search to recover the vessel. I told them that you must still be aboard."

"In fact I was. There were a lot of crew wounded when everything began to fall apart, and I couldn't leave them." Tee was nodding. "You know about it already?" Lunzie asked.

"The First Mate had kept a handwritten log on plas-sheets from the moment the power failed, then kept files in a word processing program as soon as the terminals were reprogrammed. When we reached the *Destiny*, they had the most vital systems up and running, but the interface between engineering and the drives had been destroyed. I examined it myself. Even to me, the system was primitive."

"How did the Destiny Line get a military vessel involved in looking for a commercial liner?" Lunzie asked curiously, blowing on her cup to cool the tea.

"They didn't. I felt there was something false about the assurances they gave out that the search was progressing well. Using some of my own contacts—plus a few of Shof's tricks—I discovered that the Paraden Company had put in claims on the insurance on the *Destiny Calls*, using the testimony of recovered passengers to prove that the ship had met with an accident. The search was no more than a token, to satisfy the claims adjuster! The company had already written off the lives of the people still on board, you among them. I was angry. I went to the offices myself, on the other side of Astris, to break bones and windows until they should make the search real. I stayed there all day, growling at everyone who walked into the office to book cruises. I'm sure I drove away dozens of potential passengers. They wanted to have me removed because I was hurting business, but I told them I would not go. If they called for a peace officer, I would tell the whole story in my statement, and it would be all over the streets— and that would hurt their business far more!

"I was not the only one who had the idea to confront them personally. I met Commander Coromell there the next morning."

"Commander Coromell. The Admiral's son! I had no idea he was on Astris."

"It was the nearest Destiny Lines office when he got the news. He and I occupied seats at opposite ends of the reception room, waiting silently for one of the company lackeys to tell us more lies. Around midday, we began to converse and compare notes. Our missing persons were on the same ship. The day passed and it was clear that the Destiny Lines manager would not see us. We joined forces, and decided to start a legal action against the company.

"It was too late, you see. They had already been paid by the insurance company, and were uninterested in expending the cost of a search vessel. They were willing to pay the maximum their policy allowed for loss of life to each of us, but no more. Coromell was upset. He used political clout, based on his father's heroic service record, and his own reputation, to urge the Fleet to get involved. They commissioned the *Ban Sidhe* to make the search.

Admiral Coromell is a great hero, and they did not like the idea of losing him."

"Bravo to that. You should hear some of his stories. How did you get aboard her? I thought you were still restricted from outer-space posts."

"More clout. Commander Coromell is a very influential man, in a family with a long, distinguished history in the FSP Fleet. He reopened my service file, and arranged for my commission. Commander Coromell gave me a chance to get back into space. It is the chance I was dreaming of, but I thought out of my reach for so much longer. I am very grateful to him."

"So am I. I never hoped to see you so soon," Lunzie said, touching Tee's hand.

"It isn't so soon," Tee answered sadly. "We made many jumps through this system, following the route *Destiny Calls* should have taken. It was my friend Naomi who noticed the magnesium flare near the dark side of Carson's Giant, and led us to investigate the planet. You should not have been there," Tee chided.

Lunzie raised an outraged eyebrow at him. "We were running from an ion storm, as I think you know," she retorted. "It was a calculated risk. If we'd jumped to this system only a little earlier or a little later, we wouldn't have been in the storm's path."

"It was the worst of bad luck, but you are safe now," Tee said, gently, rising to his feet and extending a hand to her. "Come, let's reunite you with the rest of the *Destiny's* crew."

"Well, she's as good as scrap. Without a program dump from another Destiny Lines mainframe, we can't get the hulk to tell us all the places where it hurts, let alone fix them," Engineer Perkin explained, ruefully.

"Do rights of salvage apply?" One of the younger

Fleet officers spoke up, then looked ashamed of himself as everyone turned to look at him. "Sorry. Don't mean to sound greedy."

"Hell, Destiny Lines had already abandoned us for dead," First Mate Sharu said, waving the gaffe away. "Take whatever you want, but please leave us our personal belongings. We've also laid claim to the insured valuables left behind by some of our passengers."

"I . . . I was thinking of fresh foodstuffs," the lieutenant stammered. "That's all."

"Oh," Sharu grinned. "The hydroponic section is alive and well, Lieutenant. There's enough growing there to feed thousands. The grapefruits are just ripe. So are the ompoyas, cacceri leaf, groatberries, marshpeas, yellow grapes, artichokes, five kinds of tomatoes, about a hundred kinds of herbs, and more things ripening every day. We ate well in exile. Help yourselves."

The younger officers at the table cheered and one threw his hat in the air. The older officers just smiled.

"We'll take advantage of your kindly offer, First Mate," the Fleet captain said, smiling on her genially. "Like any vessel whose primary aim is never to carry unnecessary loads, our hydro section is limited to what is considered vital for healthy organisms, and no more."

"Captain Aelock, we owe you much more than a puny load of groceries. I'm sure when Captain Wynline comes back from the *Destiny*'s hulk with your men, he'll tell you the same. He may even help you strip equipment out personally. To say he's bitter about our abandonment is a pitiful understatement. Ah, Lunzie! Feeling better?" Sharu smiled as Lunzie and Tee entered, and gestured to the medic to sit by her.

"I'm fine, thanks."

"It seems we owe our rescue to the persuasiveness of Ensign Janos, is that correct?"

"In part," Tee said, modestly. "It is actually Commander Coromell that we all must thank."

"I'm grateful to everyone. I've set aside some of the salvage goods for both of you. Lunzie, do you fancy Lady Cholder's jewels? It's a poor bonus for losing ten years, but they're yours. I would say they're worth something between half a million and a million credits."

"Thank you, Sharu, that's more than generous. Am I the last awake?" Lunzie asked.

"No. The Commander's father and his father's aide were the last," Aelock answered. "I've asked them to join us here when they've finished in the Communications Center."

"I should have been consulted," Lunzie said, with some asperity. "The Admiral has a heart condition."

"We had that information from his son," Aelock said apologetically. "Besides, his health records are in the Fleet computer banks."

"Ah, there you are, Doctor," the senior Coromell said in a booming voice, striding into the room, followed by his aide. "If there is ever anything that I or my descendants can do for you, consider it a sacred trust. This young lady saved my life, Captain. I just told my son so." Lunzie blushed. The Admiral smiled on her and continued. "He's very grateful that I'm alive, but no more so than I. He spent a lot of air time ticking off his old man for heroics, and then said he'd probably have done the same thing himself. I'm to meet him on Tau Ceti. I'll take responsibility if anyone asks why the transmission on a secure channel was so lengthy."

"I have discretion in this matter, Admiral, but thank you," Aelock said graciously. "Now, what is to be done with all of you? Since Destiny Lines seems to have washed its hands of you. At least temporarily, that is. I shall be preferring charges in FSP court against them for reckless abandonment of a space vessel."

"With your permission," Sharu asked, "may I com-

municate with the head office? Since I have managed
to live in spite of their efforts, I may be able to
shame them into paying for our retrieval and continuing travel to our destination from wherever you
may drop us off."

Captain Aelock nodded. "Of course."

"Oh, and Doctor, there was a transmission for you
on the FTL link, too," the Admiral told her when
the meeting broke up. "You might want to take it in
private." It was the softest voice she'd ever heard
him use.

"Thank you, Admiral." Lunzie was puzzled by his
uncommon solicitousness. He smiled and marched
off down the corridor with Captain Aelock, with Don
and Aelock's officers trailing behind.

"Come," Tee said. "It is easy to find. You should
begin to learn the layout of the ship." They stood
outside the meeting room in a corridor about two
and a half meters wide. "This is the main thorough-
fare of the ship. It runs from the bridge straight back
to the access to engineering. It was considered un-
wise," he added humorously, "to have the engineering section directly behind the bridge. An explosion
there would send a fireball straight through the control panels directing the ship."

"I can't argue with that logic," Lunzie agreed.

"I will give you the full tour later. For now, let's
see what Lars has to say."

There was a small commotion when Tee led Lunzie
into the Communications Center.

"So, this is the lady who launched a thousand
rescuers, eh?" winked a Human officer, twirling the
ends of his black mustache.

"This is Lunzie, Stawrt," Tee acknowledged,
uncomfortably.

"A pleasure," Lunzie said, shaking hands around.
There were three officers on duty, the communica-

tions chief, Stawrt, and two Wefts, Ensigns Huli and
Vaer. Huli, instead of wearing the standard humanoid form so widely used by Wefts in the presence of
humans, had extruded eight or ten tentaclelike arms
with two fingers each, with which he played the
complicated board before him.

Huli tapped her with one of the attenuated digits
on his fifth hand. "You would like to view your
message? Would you care to step into that privacy
booth?" Another hand snaked over to point at a door
on an interior wall.

"Tee, would you come and listen, too?" Lunzie
asked quietly, suddenly uneasy.

The privacy booth was a very small compartment
with thick beige soundproofing on all walls, floor and
ceiling. Any words spoken seemed to be swallowed
up by the pierced panels. In the center of the room
was a standard holofield projector, with chairs arranged around it. Lunzie took a chair, and Tee settled down beside her. She half expected him to take
her hand but he didn't touch her. In fact, except for
when she'd practically fainted into his arms when she
woke up, he hadn't touched her at all.

"Press this red button to start," Tee said, pointing
to a small keypad on the arm of her chair. "The black
stops transmission, the yellow freezes the action in
place, and the blue restarts the transmission from
the beginning."

Lunzie touched the red button, feeling very nervous.

In the holofield, the image of Lars appeared. He,
like Tee, had aged slightly. His hair was thinner, he
was getting thicker around the middle, and the pursed
lines at the side of his mouth were deeper.

"Ancestress," Lars began, bowing. "I'm happy to
hear that you have been recovered safely. When you
didn't arrive on schedule, we were very concerned.
Ensign Janos was kind enough to tell me the whole
story.

"I am very sorry to tell you that Mother isn't here any more. She arrived, as scheduled, two years after we heard from you." The dour face smiled at his memories. "She was so delighted when we sent a message to her that you were expected. Ancestress, she waited eighteen months more for you. Since we had not heard further from you, we were forced to conclude that you had changed your mind. I know now that was an erroneous judgment. I am sorry. You will still be more than welcome if you come to Alpha Centauri. My grandchildren have been nagging me to make sure I remember to extend the invitation. Well, consider it extended.

"Before she left for Eridani, she recorded the following holo for you." Lars hastily blinked out, to be replaced by a larger image of Fiona's head and shoulders, which meant that the recording had been made on a communications console. Now, more clearly than before, Lunzie could see the resemblance in the older Fiona to the child. Age had only softened the beautiful lines of her face, not marred them. The hooded eyes were full of experience and confidence and a deep, welling grief that tore at Lunzie's heart. Her eyes filled with tears as Fiona began to speak.

"Lunzie, I guess that you aren't coming. What made you change your mind?

"I wanted to see you. Truly, I did. I resented like hell having you go away from me when I was a girl. I mean, I understood why you went, but it didn't make it any easier. Uncle Edgard came to get me after the shipwreck, and took me to MarsBase. It was nice. I roomed with cousins Yonata and Immethy, his two daughters. I worried so much about you, but then time went by, and I had to stop worrying, and get on with my life. You know by now I went into medicine," the image grinned, and Lunzie smiled back. "The family vocation. I worked hard at it, got good grades, and I think I earned the respect of my

professors. I would have given anything to hear you
tell me you were proud of me. In the end, I had to
be proud of myself." Fiona seemed to be having
trouble getting the words out. Her eyes were bright
with tears, too.

"I was proud of you, baby," Lunzie whispered,
her mouth dry. "Muhlah, I wish you knew that."

"I got to be pretty good at what I did," Fiona
continued. "I joined the EEC and racked up a re-
spectable service record. Your mother's brother
Jermold hired me; I think he's still working the same
desk job in Personnel, even at his advanced age. I've
been all over the galaxy in the service, though I've
seen mostly new colony worlds in their worst possible condition—suffering from disease epidemics!—but
I have had a great time, and I loved it. They think
they're rewarding me by assigning me to a desk job.

"Lunzie, there are a thousand things I want to tell
you, all the things I thought about when you went
away. Most of them were the resentful mutterings of
a child. I won't trouble you with those. Some were
beautiful things that I discovered that I wanted so to
share with you. I wish you could have met Garmol,
my husband. You and he would have gotten along so
well, though we've always had itchy feet, and he was
the original ground-bounder. But the most important
thing I wanted to let you know is that I love you. I
always did, and always will.

"I have to leave for Eridani now, and assume the
duties of my office as Surgeon General. I've made
them wait for me as long as I've dared, but now I
must go.

"Lunzie . . ." Fiona's voice became very hoarse,
and she stopped to swallow. She cleared her throat
and raised her chin decisively, the image of her eyes
meeting Lunzie's across the light years. "Mother,
goodbye."

Lunzie was quiet for a long time, staring at the

empty holofield long after the image faded. She shut
her eyes with a deep-chested sigh, and shook her
head. She turned to Tee, almost blindly, lost in her
own thoughts.

"What should I do now?"

He had been studying her. She could tell that he,
too, was moved by Fiona's message, but his expression changed immediately.

"What should you do?" Tee repeated quizzically.
"I am not in charge of your life. You must decide."

Lunzie rubbed her temples. "For the first time in
my life, I haven't got an immediate goal to work
toward. I've left school. Fiona's given up on me.
Who could blame her? But it leaves me adrift."

Tee's face softened. "I'm sorry. You must feel
terrible."

Lunzie wrinkled her forehead, thinking deeply. "I
should, you know. But I don't. I'm grieved, certainly, but I don't feel as devastated as I . . . think
that I should."

"You should go and see your grandchildren. Did
you hear? They want to see you."

"Tee, how will I get there now?" Lunzie asked in a
small voice. "Where is the *Ban Sidhe* dropping us?"

"We are waiting for orders. As soon as I know, you
will know."

Captain Aelock had already received the *Ban Sidhe*'s
flight orders, and was happy to share the details with
Lunzie. "We've been transferred to the Central Sector for the duration, Lunzie. Partly because of the
Admiral's influence but also because it is convenient
to our mission, we're going to Alpha Centauri, then
toward Sol. Would you mind if we set you down
there? It'll be our first port of call."

Lunzie's eyes shone with gratitude. "Thank you,
sir. It takes a great load off my mind. I must admit
I've been worrying about it."

"Worry no longer. The Admiral was quite insistent that you should have whatever you needed. He's very impressed with your skill, claims you saved his life. You can assist our medical officers while we're en route. 'No idle hands' is our motto."

"So I've heard."

"With all the *Destiny* refugees aboard, things will be somewhat cramped, but I have discretion with regard to officers. You and Sharu will share a cabin in officer country. If there are any problems," Aelock smiled down on her paternally, "my door is always open."

"I was never so glad in my life to see anything as this destroyer popping out of warp just as we rounded the dark side of the planet," Sharu said, sipping fresh juice the next morning at mess with a tableful of the *Ban Sidhe*'s junior officers. Lunzie sat between the First Mate and Captain Wynline. Tee was on duty that shift. "We had a magnesium bonfire all ready to go behind the quartz observation desk port. I lit it and jumped back, and it roared up into silver flames like a nova. The ship was sunk into the gravity well of the planet and was following its orbit instead of staying stationary. Because Carson's Giant spins so fast, our window of opportunity was very small. Our signal had to be dramatic."

"Magnesium?" declared Ensign Riaman. "No wonder that deck was slagged. It was probably red hot for hours afterward."

"It was. I got burns on my arms and face. They're only just healing now," Sharu said, displaying her wrists. "See?"

"It was worth it," Captain Wynline said positively. "It worked, didn't it? You saw it."

"We certainly did," added Lieutenant Naomi, a blond woman in her early thirties. "A tiny spark on the planet's surface where nothing should have been. You were lucky."

"Oh, I know," Sharu acknowledged. "There has never been a prettier sight than that of your ship homing in on us. We have seen so many ships go by without seeing us. We did everything but jump up and down and wave our arms to get their attention. We were very lucky that you were looking the right way at the right time."

"We could have been planet pirates," Ensign Tob suggested.

He was shouted down by his fellows. "Shut up, Tob." "Who'd be stupid enough to mistake us for them?" "It'd be an insult to the Fleet."

"You were wounded when the ship was first evacuated," Ensign Riaman asked Lunzie, who was spreading jam on a slice of toast. "Was it a shock to wake up and find you had been in cold sleep?"

"Not really. I've been in cold sleep before," Lunzie explained.

"Really? For what? An experiment? An operation?" Riaman asked eagerly. "My aunt was put in cryosleep for two years until a replacement for a bum heart valve could be grown. My family has a rare antibody system. She couldn't take a transplant."

"No, nothing like that," Lunzie said. "My family is disgustingly ordinary when it comes to organ or antibody compatibility. I was in another space wreck once, on the way to take a job on a mining platform for the Descartes Company."

To her surprise, the young ensign goggled at her and hastily went back to his meal. She looked around at the others seated at the table. A couple of them stared at her, and quickly looked away. The rest were paying deep attention to their breakfasts. Dismayed and confused, she bent to her meal.

"Jonah," she heard someone whisper. "She must be a Jonah." Out of the corner of her eye, Lunzie tried to spot the speaker. Jonah? What was that?

"Lunzie," Sharu said, speaking to break the si-

lence. "Our personal belongings are being brought
aboard in the next few hours. Would you care to
come with me and help me sort out the valuables
that were left in the purser's safe? We'll package up
what we aren't claiming for shipment to their owners
when we make orbit again."

"Of course, Sharu. I'll go get freshened up, and
wait for you." Hoping she didn't sound as uncomfortable as she felt, Lunzie blotted her lips with her
napkin and hurried toward the door.

"Bad luck comes in threes," a voice said behind
her as she went out of the door, but when she
turned, no one was looking at her.

"It's my fault. I should have warned you to keep
quiet about the other wreck," Sharu apologized when
she and Lunzie were alone. Before them were dozens of sealed boxes from the purser's strongroom and
a hundred empty security cartons for shipping. "I've
been in the Fleet so I remember what it was like.
One space accident is within the realm of possibility.
Two looks like disastrously bad luck. No one's more
superstitious than a sailor."

"Sharu, what is a Jonah?"

"You heard that? Jonah was a character in the Old
Earth Bible. Whenever he sailed on a ship, it ran
into technical difficulties. Some sank. Some were
becalmed. One of the sailors decided Jonah had offended Yahweh, their God, so he was being visited
with bad luck that was endangering the whole ship.
They threw him overboard into the sea to save themselves. He was swallowed by a sea leviathan."

"Ulp!" Lunzie swallowed nervously, pouring a string
of priceless glow pearls into a bubblepack envelope.
"But they wouldn't throw me overboard? Space me?"

"I doubt it," Sharu frowned as she sorted jewelry.
"But they won't go out of their way to rub elbows
with you, either. Don't mention it again, and maybe
it'll pass."

Lunzie put the bubblepack into a carton and sealed it, labeling the carton Fragile—Do Not Expose To Extremes of Temperature, which made her think of Illin Romsey, the Descartes crystal miner who rescued her, and the Thek that accompanied him. She hadn't thought of that Thek in months. It was still a mystery to Lunzie why a Thek should take an interest in her.

"Of course, Sharu. I never knowingly stick my head into a lion's mouth. You can't tell when it might sneeze."

Among the jewels and other fragile valuables, she found her translucent hologram of Fiona. Lunzie was shocked to find that she was now used to the image of the grown woman Fiona, and this dear, smiling child was a stranger, a long-ago memory. With deliberate care, she sealed it in a bubblepack and put it aside.

Three days later, Lunzie waited outside the bridge until the silver door slid noiselessly aside into its niche. Captain Aelock had left word for her in her cabin that he wished to speak with her. Before she stepped over the threshold, she heard her name, and stopped.

". . . She'll bring bad luck to the ship, sir. We ought to put her planetside long before Alpha Centauri. We might never make it if we don't." The voice was Ensign Riaman's. The young officer had been ignoring her pointedly at mealtimes and muttering behind her back when they passed in the corridors.

"Nonsense," Captain Aelock snapped. It sounded as though this was the end of a lengthy argument, and his patience had been worn thin. "Besides, we've got orders, and we will obey them. You don't have to associate with her if she makes you nervous, but for myself I find her charming company. Is that all?"

"Yes, sir," Riaman replied in a submissive murmur that did nothing to disguise his resentment.

"Dismiss, then."

Riaman threw the captain a snappy salute, but by then Aelock had already turned back toward the viewscreen. Smarting from the reproach, the ensign marched off the bridge past Lunzie, who had decided that she'd rather be obvious than be caught eavesdropping. When their eyes met, he turned scarlet to his collar, and shot out of the room as if he'd been launched. Lunzie straightened her shoulders defiantly and approached the captain. He met her with a friendly smile, and offered her a seat near the command chair in the rear center of the bridge.

"This Jonah nonsense is a lot of spacedust, of course," Aelock told Lunzie firmly. "You're to pay no attention to it."

"I understand, sir," Lunzie said. The captain appeared to be embarrassed that she had been affected by the opinion of one of his officers, so she gave him a sincere smile to put him at his ease. He nodded.

"We've been out on maneuvers trying to catch up with planet pirates, and they still haven't come down from the adrenaline high. After a while we were seeing radar shadows behind every asteroid. It was time we had a more pedestrian assignment. Perhaps even a little shore leave," Aelock sighed, shrugging toward the door by which the ensign had just left, "though Alpha Centauri wouldn't be my first choice. It's a little too industrialized for my tastes. I like to visit the nature preserves of Earth myself, but my lads consider it tame."

"Have the pirates struck again?" Lunzie asked, horrified. "The last raid I heard of was on Phoenix. I once thought my daughter had been killed by the raiders."

"What, Doctor Fiona?" Aelock demanded, smiling, watching Lunzie's mouth drop open. "It may surprise you to know, Dr. Mespil, that we had the pleasure of hosting the lady and her dog act fifteen

Standard years ago. As charming as yourself, I must say. I can see the family resemblance."

"The galaxy is shrinking," Lunzie said, shaking her head. "This is too much of a coincidence."

"Not at all, when you consider that she and I serve the same segment of the FSP population. We're both needed chiefly by the new colonies that are just past the threshold of viability, and hence under FSP protection. The emergency medical staff like her use our ships because we're the only kind of vehicle that can convey help there quickly enough."

"Such as against planet pirates?"

Aelock looked troubled. "Well, it's been very quiet lately. Too quiet. There hasn't been a peep out of them in months—almost a year since the last incident. I think they're planning another strike, but I haven't a clue where. By the time we reach Alpha, I'm expecting to hear from one of my contacts, a friend of a friend of a friend of a supplier who sells to the pirates. We still don't know who they are, or who is providing them with bases and repair facilities, drydocks and that kind of thing. I'm hoping that I can make a breakthrough before someone follows the line of inquiry back to me. People who stick their noses into the pirates' business frequently end up dead."

Lunzie gulped, thinking of Jonahs and the airlock. The captain seemed to divine her thoughts and chuckled.

"Ignore the finger-crossers among my crew. They're good souls, and they'll make you comfortable while you're aboard. We'll have you safe and sound, breathing smoggy Alpha Centauri air before you know it."

Chapter Eight

She didn't have time to worry about her new label of Jonah on the brief trip to Alpha Centauri. A number of the crew from the *Destiny Calls* broke out in raging symptoms of space traumatic stress. There was a lot of fighting and name-calling among them, which the ship's chief medical officer diagnosed as pure reaction to danger. In order to prevent violence, Dr. Harris assigned Lunzie to organize therapy for them. On her records, he had noticed the mention of Lunzie's training in treating space-induced mental disorders and put the patients' care in her hands.

"Now that it's all over, they're remembering to react," Harris noted, privately to Lunzie, during a briefing. "Not uncommon after great efforts. I won't interfere in the sessions. I'll just be an observer. They know and trust you, whereas they would not open up well to me. Perhaps I can pick up pointers on technique from you."

Lunzie held mass encounter sessions with the *Destiny* crew. Nearly all the survivors attended the daily meetings, where they discussed their feelings of anxiety and resentment toward the company with a good deal of fire. Lunzie listened more than she talked, making notes, and throwing in a question or a

statement when the conversation lagged or went off
on a tangent; and observed which employees might
need private or more extensive therapy.

Lunzie found that the group therapy sessions did
her as much good as they did for the other crew
members. Her own anxieties and concerns were ad-
dressed and discussed thoroughly. To her relief, no
one seemed to lose respect for her as a therapist
when she talked about her feelings. They sympathized with her, and they appreciated that she cared
about their mental well-being, not clinically distant,
but as one of them.

The mainframe and drives engineers were the most
stressed out, but the worst afflicted with paranoid
disorders were the service staff. They complained of
helplessness throughout the time they'd spent awake
helping to clean up the *Destiny Calls*, since they
could do nothing to better the situation for themselves or anyone else. For the mental health of the
crew at large, Captain Wynline had ordered stressed
employees to be put into cold sleep. In order to
continue working efficiently on the systems which
would preserve their lives, the technicians had to be
shielded from additional tension.

"But there we were on the job, and all of a sudden, we'd been rescued while we were asleep," Voor,
one of the Gurnsan cooks, complained in her gentle
voice. "There was no time for us to get used to the
new circumstances."

"No interval of adjustment, do you mean?" Lunzie
asked.

"That's right," a human chef put in. "To be knocked
out and stored like unwanted baggage—it isn't the
way to treat sentient beings."

Perkin and the other heads of Engineering de-
fended the captain's actions.

"Not at all. For the sake of general peace of mind,
hysteria had to be stifled," Perkin insisted. "I wouldn't

have been able to concentrate. At least cryo-sleep isn't fatal."

"It might as well have been! Life and death—my life and death—taken out of my hands."

Lunzie pounced on that remark. "It sounds like you don't resent the cold sleep as much as you do the order to take it."

"Well . . ." The chef pondered the suggestion. "I suppose if the captain had asked for volunteers, I probably would have offered. I like to get along."

Captain Wynline cleared his throat. "In that case, Koberly, I apologize. I'm only human, and I was under a good deal of strain, too. I ask for your forgiveness."

There was a general outburst of protest. Many of the others shouted Koberly down, but a few agreed pugnaciously that Wynline owed them an apology.

"Does that satisfy you, Koberly?" Lunzie asked, encouragingly.

The chef shrugged and looked down at the floor. "I guess so. Next time, let me volunteer first, huh?"

Wynline nodded gravely. "You have my word."

"Now, what's this about our not getting paid for our down time?" Chibor asked the captain.

Wynline was almost automatically on the defensive. "I'm sorry to have to tell you this, but since the ship was treated as lost, the Paraden Company feels that the employees aboard her were needlessly risking their lives. Only the crew who were picked up with the escape pods were given compensatory pay. Our employment was terminated on the day the insurance company paid off the *Destiny Calls*."

There was a loud outcry over that. "They can't do that to us!" Koberly protested. "We should be getting ten years back pay!"

"Where's justice when you need it?"

Dr. Harris cleared his throat. "The captain is planning to press charges against the Paraden Company to recover the cost of the deepspace search. You can all sign on as co-plaintiffs against them. We'll give statements to the court recorder when we reach Alpha Centauri."

Lunzie and a handful of the *Destiny's* crew watched from a remote video pickup in the rec room as the *Ban Sidhe* pulled into a stable orbit around Alpha Centauri. It was the first time that she'd been this close to the center of the settled galaxy. The infrared view of the night side of the planet showed almost continuous heat trace across all the land masses and even some under the seas, indicating population centers. She'd never seen such a crowded planet in her life. And somewhere down on that world was her family. Lunzie couldn't wait to meet them.

Two unimaginably long shifts later, she received permission to go dirtside in the landing shuttle. She took a small duffle with some of her clothes and toiletries and Fiona's hologram. After checking her new short haircut hastily in the lavatory mirror, she hurried to the airlock. Some of the *Destiny's* kitchen staff were already waiting there for the shuttle, surrounded by all of their belongings.

"I'm staying," Koberly declared, "until I can get the Tribunal to hear my case against Destiny Lines. Those unsanctioned progeny of a human union won't get away with shoving me into a freezer for ten years, and then cheating me out of my rights."

"I'm just staying," said Voor, clasping her utensil case to her astounding double bosom. "There are always plenty of jobs on settled worlds for good cooks. I plan to apply to the biggest and best hotels in Alpha City. They'd be eager to snap up a pastry chef who can cook for ten thousand on short notice."

Koberly shook his head pityingly at the Gurnsan's complacent attitude. "Don't be dumb. You're an artist, cowgirl. You shouldn't apply for a job just because you're fast, or because you supply your own milk. Let 'em give you an audition. Once they taste your desserts they will give you anything to keep you from leaving their establishment without saying yes. Anything."

"You're too kind," Voor protested gently, shaking her broad head.

"I agree with him," Lunzie put in sincerely. "Perhaps you should hold an auction and sell your services to the highest bidder."

"If you like, I will handle the business arrangements for you," said a voice behind Lunzie. "May I join you while you wait? It is my turn to go on shore leave as well." It was Tee, glowing like a nova in his white dress uniform. Lunzie and the others greeted him warmly.

"Delighted, Ensign," Voor said. "You saved my life. I will always be happy to see you."

"I haven't seen much of you the last few days," Lunzie told him, hoping it didn't sound like a reproach.

Tee grinned, showing his white teeth. "But I have seen you! Playing the therapy sessions like a master conductor. I have stood in the back of the chamber listening, as first one speaks up, then another speaks up, and you solve all their problems. You are so wise."

Lunzie laughed. "In this case the complaint was easy to diagnose. I'm a sufferer, too."

Behind the burnished steel door came a hissing, and the booming of metal on metal. Around the edge of the doorway, red lights began flashing, and a siren whooped. Lunzie and the others automatically jumped back, alarmed.

"It is only the airlock in use," Tee explained apologetically. "If there had been an actual emergency, we would be too close to it to be safe anyway."

With a hiss, the door slid back, and the shuttle

pilot appeared inside the hollow chamber, and gestured the passengers inside. "Ten hundred hours. Is
everyone ready?"

"Yes!" The pilot dived aside as his cargo rushed
past him eagerly.

"Unrecirculated air!" Lunzie stepped out of the
spaceport in Alpha City and felt the caress of a
natural wind for the first time since leaving Astris.
She held her face up to the sun and took a deep
breath of air. And expelled it immediately in a fit of
coughing.

"Wha—what's the matter with the air?" she asked,
sniffing cautiously and wrinkling her nose at the odor.
It was laden with chemical fumes and the smell of
spoiling vegetation. She looked up at the sky and saw
the sun ringed with a grayish haze that shimmered
over the surrounding city.

"Some good news, and some bad news, Doctor
Lunzie," a Fleet ensign explained. "The good news
is it's natural, and it hasn't been reoxygenated by
machines a million times. The bad news is what the
humans who live on Alpha have been throwing into
it for thousands of years. Airborne garbage."

"Ough! How could they do this to themselves?
The very air they breathe!" Lunzie moaned, dabbing
her streaming eyes with a handkerchief.

Tee picked up her bags and hailed a groundcar. "It
shouldn't be as bad further from the spaceport. Come
on." He hurried her down the concrete ramp and
into the sealed car.

"Where are you going?" Lunzie demanded when
she could speak. She blew her nose loudly into the
handkerchief.

"With you. I would not miss your family reunion
for the world. I have an invitation from Melanie."

"What is your destination?" the robotic voice of
the groundcar demanded. "With or without travel
guide?"

Tee reeled off an address. "What do you think, Lunzie? Do you want it to tell you about the sights we pass?"

Lunzie peered through the windows at the unending panorama of gray buildings, gray streets, and gray air. The only color was the clothing of the few pedestrians they passed. "I don't think so. It all looks the same, for kilometers in every direction, and it's so gloomy. I just want to get there and meet them. I wonder how they've all changed in ten years. Do you suppose there are new babies?"

"Why not? No travel guide," Tee ordered.

"Acknowledged."

Tee chatted brightly with her as they sailed along the superhighways toward Melanie's. Once they had disembarked from the *Ban Sidhe*, he was his old self, expansive and affectionate. Lunzie decided that it must be the military atmosphere of the Fleet ship which squashed his usually sunny nature. She was relieved that he was feeling better.

It was twilight when they finally arrived. The groundcar disgorged them in suburban Shaygo, only two hundred kilometers from Alpha City. Lunzie couldn't tell by watching when one city left off and the second one began. They had obviously grown together over the years. There was no open space, no parks, no havens for vegetation, just intertwining thoroughfares with thousands of similar podlike groundcars hurtling along them. The trail of air transports penned on the gray sky in white between the tall buildings. Lunzie found the sight depressing.

The house, one of an attached row, sat at the top of a small yard with trees on either side of the walk leading to the door. A twinkling bunch of tiny lights next to the door read "Ingrich." Except for the gardens, every house was identical. Melanie's was a riot of colorful flowers and tall herbs spilling out of their beds on the trim lawn, a burst of individuality on a street of bland repetition.

"Muhlah, I'd hate to come home drunk," Lunzie said, looking up and down the endless row. The other side of the street was the same. Three floors of curtained windows stared blankly down on them.

"The robot taxi would get you safely home," Tee assured her.

She heard noises coming from inside the house as they approached, and the door irised open suddenly. A plump woman with soft brown hair bustled out and seized each of them by the hand. Lunzie recognized her instantly. It was her granddaughter.

"You are Lunzie, aren't you?" The woman beamed. "I'm Melanie. Welcome, welcome, at last! And Citizen Janos. I'm so glad to see you at last."

"Tee," Tee insisted, accepting a hug in his turn.

"How wonderful to meet you at last," Lunzie exclaimed. "I'm grateful you wanted to extend the invitation to me, after I stood you up last time."

"Oh, of course. We wanted to meet you. Come in. Everyone has been waiting for you." Melanie wrapped an arm warmly around Lunzie's waist and led her inside. Tee trailed behind, looking amused. "Mother was so disappointed that you didn't come to our last reunion. But when we heard about the accident, we were devastated that she had left with the wrong impression. I sent a message to Eridani to let her know what happened and that you're all right, but it's so far away she may still be on her way there. I just have no idea! Only the gods of chaos know when the message will reach her. There's been a lot of service interruptions lately. And no explanation from the company!"

She led them into a well-lit room with white walls and carpets, decorated with colorful wall hangings in good artistic taste, and set about with cushiony furniture. In the middle of one wall was an electronic hearth, and in the middle of the other was a Tri-D viewing platform, surrounded by teenaged children watching a sports event. Lunzie noticed that the holographic image was purer and sharper than anything she'd ever seen before. There had obviously been strides made in image projection since she went into cold sleep.

Two slightly built men with dark, curly hair, identical twins, and two women, all of early middle age, who had been chatting when Lunzie entered, rose from their seats and came forward.

"Oh, what a lovely home you have," Lunzie said, looking around approvingly. "Is this your mate?"

The tall man sprawled on a couch set aside his personal reader and stood up to offer them a hand. "Now and forever. Dalton is my name. How do you do, ancestress?"

"Very well, thank you," she said, shaking hands. Dalton had a firm, smooth grip, but not at all bonecrushing, as she feared it might be after noticing the prominent tendons on his wrists. "But please, call me Lunzie."

"I'll tell everyone your wishes, but Lars might not comply. He can be very stuffy and proper."

"I communicated with them as soon as you let us know you were here. They'll arrive in a little while," Melanie said busily, urging them into the middle of the common room. "Now, may I get you anything before I show you where you're going to stay? Something to drink?"

"Juice would be welcome. The air is . . . rather thick if you're not used to it," Lunzie said, diplomatically.

"Mmm. There was a smog alert today. I should have said something when you communicated with us. But we're all used to it." Melanie hurried away.

"Just like her to forget the rest of the introductions," Dalton said indulgently as his mate left the room. He embraced Lunzie, and waved a hand at the others in the room. "Everyone! This is Lunzie, here at last!" The children watching the Tri-D stood up to greet her. Lunzie smiled at them in turn, trying to identify them from the ten-year-old holos. She could account for all but two. Dalton explained, "Not all of this crowd is ours, but we get the grandchildren a lot because our house is the largest. Lunzie, please meet my sons Jai and Thad, and their mates, Ionia and Chirli." The women, one with short red tresses and one with shining pale blond hair, smiled at her. "Drew is still at work, but he'll be joining us for dinner."

The twins shook hands gravely. "You look more like a sister to us than what? A great-grandmother?" one of them said.

"You'll have to forgive us if we occasionally slip up and don't show the respect due your age," the other said playfully.

"I'll understand," Lunzie said, hugging them, and pulling the two women closer to include them in the embrace. The children pressed in to take their turns. There were nine of them, four girls and five boys. Lunzie could see resemblances to herself or Fiona in all of them. She was so overwhelmed with joy, she was nearly bursting inside.

"How old are you?" asked the youngest child, a boy who seemed to be eleven or twelve Standard years of age.

"Pedder, that's not a polite question," Jai's red-headed wife said sternly.

"Drew's youngest," Dalton explained in his deep voice over the heads of the throng clustered around her.

"Sorry, Aunt Ionia. I 'pologize," the boy muttered in a sulky voice.

"I'm not offended," Lunzie insisted, winning the boy's admiration immediately. "I was born in 2755, if that's what you mean."

"Wo-ow," Pedder said, impressed. "That's old. I mean, you don't look like it."

"Brend and Corrin," Dalton pointed, "are Pedder's older brothers, and possessed, I hope, of more tact, or at least less curiosity. The eldest, Evan, isn't here. He's at work. Dierdre's youngest, Anthea, is at school."

"Oh, I'm delighted to meet you all," Lunzie said happily. "I've been replaying the holos over and over again." She squeezed Brend's hand and ruffled Corrin's hair. The boys blushed red, and drew back to let the other cousins through.

"I'm Capella," said an attractive girl with black hair styled in fantastic waves and loops all over her head. In Lunzie's opinion, the girl wore too much makeup, and the LED-studded earrings on her earlobes were almost blinding.

"You've changed since the last picture I saw of you," Lunzie said diplomatically.

"Oh, really," Capella giggled. "It has to be ten years, right? I was just a microsquirt then." Tee, standing behind Capella, smiled widely and raised his eyes heavenward. Lunzie returned his grin.

Pedder became distracted by the Tri-D program, where it appeared that one team was about to drive a bright scarlet ball into a net past the other team's defense. "Give it to 'em good, Centauri! Plasmic!"

A slim young woman with long hair in a ribbon-bound plait rose from the other side of the viewing field and made her way awkwardly over to Lunzie, holding out a hand. She was several months pregnant. "How do you do, Lunzie? I'm Rudi."

Lunzie greeted her warmly. "Lars's first grand-daughter. I'm delighted to meet you. When is the baby due?"

"Oh, not soon enough," Rudi smiled. "Two and a half months. Since it'll be the first great-grandchild, everyone's helping me count the days. This is Gordon. He's shy, but he'll get over it, since you're family." Lars's only grandson was a stocky boy of eighteen whose short, spiky mouse-brown hair stuck straight out all over his fair scalp.

Lunzie took his hand and drew him toward her to give him a kiss on the cheek. "I'm pleased to meet you, Gordon." The boy reddened and withdrew his hand, grinning self-consciously.

With the last goal, the game appeared to be over. Dalton leaned across the crowd and turned off the Tri-D field under the disappointed noses of the boys. "Enough! No more holovision. We have guests."

Cassia and Deram, cousins born within two days of each other, claimed the seats on either side of Lunzie, as she was settled down into the deep couch with a tall glass of fruit juice.

"It almost makes us twins, you see, just like our fathers," stated Deram proudly. In fact, he and Cassia did look as remarkably alike as a young man and woman could.

"We've always been best friends, from birth onward," Cassia added.

"Ugh!" Lona, Deram's younger sister, a lanky seventeen, settled at their feet, and shook back her long, straight black hair. "How phony. Lie, why don't you? You fight like Tokme birds all the time."

"Lona, that's not nice to say," Cassia chided, looking nervously at Lunzie, but the teenager regarded her with unrepentant scorn.

Of all the grandchildren, Lona looked the·most like Fiona. Lunzie found herself drawn to the girl over the course of the evening, feeling as though she was talking to her own long-lost daughter. It became a point of contention among the other cousins, who felt that Lona should fairly share the attention of the prized new relative.

Lunzie overheard the whispered arguments and realized that she was near to starting off a family war.

She neatly changed the subject, directing her conversation to each cousin in turn. Everyone was smiling in satisfaction when the adults arrived.

Lars greeted her and Tee with great ceremony. "Five generations in the same house!" he exclaimed to the assembled. "Ancestress Lunzie, we are very pleased to have you among us. Welcome!"

Lars was a stocky man who had inherited Fiona's jaw and a smaller version of her eyes, which wore a familiar obdurate expression that Lunzie recognized as a family trait. His hair was thinning, and Lunzie estimated that he would enter into his eighth decade completely bald. His wife, Dierdre, was fashionably thin, but with a scrawny neck. She had not changed much since the first holo Lunzie had seen. Drew, Melanie's third son, was a stockier version of his cheerful older brothers. He greeted Lunzie with a smacking kiss on the cheek.

"We've also got a surprise for you," Lars added, standing aside from the doorway to let one more man in. "Our brother Dougal arrived home for shore leave only last week."

Dougal was handsome. He had inherited all of Fiona's good looks plus a gene or two from Lunzie's maternal grandfather, who had also been tall and slim with broad shoulders. His coloring was similar to Lunzie's: medium brown hair and green-hazel eyes, and he had her short, straight nose. His Fleet uniform was a pristine white, like Tee's, but it bore more wrist braid, and there was a line of medals on his left breast.

"Welcome, Lunzie. Fiona told me a lot about you. I hope this is the beginning of a long visit, and the first of many more."

Lunzie glanced back at Tee, who shrugged. "Well, I don't know. There're a few matters I might have to take care of. But I'll stay as long as I can."

"Good!" Dougal wrapped her up in an embrace

that made her squeak. "I've been looking forward to exchanging stories with you."

Lars started to reproach his brother, when Melanie stepped between them.

"Dinner, boys." She gave them a look which Lunzie could only describe as significant, and led the way to the dining room.

"Melanie, I must say, you've inherited my mother's cooking arm. That was absolutely delicious," Lunzie said. She and Tee sat across from each other on either side of Dalton at one end of the long table. Lars sat at the other end and nodded paternally over the wine. "What spice was that in the carrot mousse? And the celeriac and herb soup was just delightful."

Melanie glowed at Lunzie's praise. "I usually say the recipes are a family secret but I couldn't keep them from you, could I?"

"I hope not. Truly, I'd love to take a look at your recipe file. I can offer some of my inventions in return."

"Take her up on the offer," Tee put in, gesturing with his spoon. "Do not let her change her mind, Melanie. Lunzie is a superb cook. As for me, I have been eating synthetic Fleet food for many years now, and this is like a divine blessing."

"I know what you mean, brother," Dougal said, noisily scraping the last of the spiced cheese and bean dish out onto his plate. "Depending on how long a ship is in space, the crew forget first the love they left behind them, then fresh air, then food. Between crises, I dream about good meals, especially my sister's cooking."

"Thank you, Dougal," Melanie acknowledged prettily. "It's always nice to have you home."

"I made dessert," Lona answered, getting up to clear the plates. "Is anyone ready for it yet?"

Pedder and his brothers chorused, "Yes," and sat

up straight hopefully, but their mother shook her head at them. They sighed deeply, and relaxed back into their seats.

"We'll have dessert in the common room, shall we, Lona?" Melanie suggested, getting up to clear away the dishes.

"All right. Good idea," Lona agreed. "That way I can display everything artistically."

"Aw, who cares?" Corrin said rudely, pushing back. "It all gets chewed up and swallowed anyway."

"Fall into a black hole!" Lona swung at him with an empty casserole dish, but he evaded her, and fled into the common room. Lona threw a sneer after him and continued stacking plates. Lunzie automatically got up and began helping to clear away.

"Oh, no, Lunzie," Lars reproved her. "Please. You're a guest. Come with me and sit down. Let the hosts clean up. I've been waiting to hear about your adventures." He tucked Lunzie's arm under his own and propelled her into the common room.

"Dessert!" Lona called, pushing a hover-tray into the middle of the room.

The supports of the cart hung six inches above the carpet until Lona hit a control, when it lowered itself gently to the ground.

"There." Melanie hurried around the tray, setting serving utensils and stacks of napkins along the sides. "It's beautiful, darling."

Rescued from Lars's relentless interrogation, Lunzie immediately stood up to inspect the contents of the tray. Lona had prepared tiny fruit tarts in a rainbow of colors. They were arranged in a spray which was half-curled around three dishes of rich creams. "Good heavens, what gracious bounty. It looks like Carmen Miranda's hat!"

"Who?" Melanie asked blankly.

"Why, uh . . ." Lunzie had to stop herself from saying *someone your age would surely remember*

Carmen Miranda. "Oh, ancient history. A woman who became famous for wearing fruit on her head. She was in the old two-D pictures that Fiona and I used to watch together."

"That's dumb," opined Pedder. "Wearing fruit on your head."

"Oh, we don't watch two-D. Flatscreen pictures don't have enough life in them," Melanie explained. "I prefer holovision every time."

"There are some great classics in two-D. I always felt it was like reading a book with pictures substituted for words," Lunzie said. "Especially the very ancient monochrome two-Ds. Easy once you get used to it."

"Oh, I see. Well, I don't read much, either. I don't have time for it," Melanie laughed lightly. "I have such a busy schedule. Here, everyone gather around, and I'll serve. Lunzie, you must try this green fruit. The toppings are sweet apricot, sour cherry, and chocolate. Lona made the pastry cream herself. It is marvelous."

The dessert was indeed delicious, and the boys made sure that leftovers wouldn't be a problem. They were looking for more when the empty cart was driven back to the food preparation room. Lona was given a round of applause by her happily sated cousins.

"Truly artistic, in every sense of the word," Dougal praised her. "That will fuel food dreams for me for the entire next tour. You're getting to be as good a cook as your grandmother."

Lona preened, looking pleased. "Thanks, Uncle Dougal."

"Oh, don't call me a grandmother," Melanie pleaded, brushing at invisible crumbs on her skirt. "It makes me feel so old."

"And think of how it would make Lunzie feel," Lars said, with more truth than tact. Lunzie shot him a sharp look, but he seemed oblivious.

"How are things at the factory?" Drew asked Lars, settling back with a glass of wine.

"Oh, the same, the same. We've got a contingent from Alien Council for Liberty and Unity protesting before the gates right now."

"The ACLU?" Drew echoed, shocked. "Can they close you down?"

"They can try. But we'll demonstrate substantial losses far beyond accounts receivable for the products, and all they can do is accept what we offer."

"What are they protesting?" Lunzie asked, alarmed.

Lars waved it away as unimportant. "They're representing the Ssli we fired last month from the underwater hydraulics assembly line. Unsuitable for the job."

"But the Ssli are a marine race. Why, what makes them unsuitable?"

"You wouldn't understand. They're too different. They don't mix well with the other employees. And there's problems in providing them with insurance. We have to buy a rider for every mobile tank they bring onto the premises to live in. And that's another thing: they live right on the factory grounds. We almost lost our insurance because of them."

"Well, they can not commute from the sea every day," Tee quipped.

"So they say." Lars dismissed the Ssli with a frown, entirely missing Tee's sarcasm. "We'll settle the matter within a few days. If they don't leave, we'll have to shut the line down entirely anyway. There's other work they can do. We've offered to extend our placement service to them."

"Oh, I see," Lunzie said, heavily. "Very generous of you." It was not so much that she thought the company should drive itself into bankruptcy for the sake of equity as that Lars seemed quite oblivious to the moral dimension of the situation.

Lars leveled a benevolent eye at her. "Why, ancestress, how good of you to say so."

Melanie and Lars's wife beamed at her approval, also entirely missing her cynical emphasis.

"Is it considered backwards to read books nowadays?" Lunzie asked Tee later when they were alone in the guest room. "I've only been on the Platform and Astris since I came out of cold sleep the first time. I haven't any idea what society at large has been doing."

"Has that been bothering you?" Tee asked, as he pulled his tunic over his head. "No. Reading has not gone out of fashion in the last number of years, nor in the years you were awake before, nor in the ones while you slept in the asteroid belt. Your relatives do not wish to expose themselves to deep thought, lest they be affected by it."

Lunzie pulled off her boots and dropped them on the floor. "What do you think of them?"

"Your relatives? Very nice. A trifle pretentious, very conservative, I would say. Conservative in every way except that they seem to have put us together in this guest room, instead of at opposite ends of the house. I'm glad they did, though. I would find it cold and lonely with only those dreary moralizers."

"Me, too. I don't know whether to say I'm delighted with them or disappointed. They show so little spirit. Everything they do has such petty motives. Shallow. Born dirtsiders, all of them."

"Except the girl, I think," Tee said, meditatively, sitting down on a fluffy seat next to the bed.

"Oh, yes, Lona. I apologize to her from afar for lumping her with the rest of these . . . these closedminded warts on a log. She's the only one with any gumption. And I hope she shows sense and gets out of here as soon as she can."

"So should we." Tee moved over behind Lunzie and began to rub her neck.

Lunzie sighed and relaxed her spine, leaning back against his crossed legs. He circled an arm around her shoulders and kissed her hair while his other hand kneaded the muscles in her back. "I don't think I can be polite for very long. We should stay a couple of days, and then let's find an excuse to go."

"As you wish," Tee offered quietly, feeling the tense cords in her back relax. "I would not mind escaping from here, either."

Lunzie tiptoed down the ramp from the sleeping rooms into the common room and the dining room. There was no sound except the far-off humming of the air-recirculation system. "Hello?" she called softly. "Melanie?"

Lona popped up the ramp from the lower level of the house. "Nope, just me. Good morning!"

"Good morning. Shouldn't you be in school?" Lunzie asked, smiling at the girl's eagerness. Lona was both pretty and lively, she looked like a throwback to Lunzie's own family, instead of a member of Melanie's conservative Alphan brood.

"No classes today," Lona explained, plumping down beside her on the couch. "I'm in a communications technology discipline, remember? Our courses are every other day, alternating with work experience either at a factory or a broadcast facility. I've got the day off."

"Good," Lunzie said, looking around. "I was wondering where everyone was."

"I'm your reception committee. Melanie's just gone shopping, and Dalton normally works at home, but he's got a meeting this morning. Where's Tee?"

"Still asleep. His circadian rhythm is set for a duty shift that begins later on."

Lona shook her head. "Please. Don't bother giving me the details. I flunked biology. I'm majoring in communications engineering. Oh, Melanie left you

something to look at." Lona produced a package
sealed in a black plastic pouch. Curious, Lunzie pulled
open the wrapping, and discovered a plastic case with
her name printed on the lid.

"They're Fiona's. She left them behind when she
went away," Lona explained, peering over Lunzie's
shoulder as Lunzie opened the box. It was full of
two-D and three-D images on wafers.

"It's all of her baby pictures," Lunzie breathed,
"and mine, too. Oh, I thought these were lost!" She
picked up one, and then another, exclaiming over
them happily.

"Not lost. Melanie said that Fiona brought all of
that stuff to MarsBase with her. We don't know who
most of these people are. Would you mind identify-
ing them?"

"They're your ancestors, and some friends of ours
from long ago. Sit down and I'll show you. Oh,
Muhlah, look at that! That's me at four years of age."
Lunzie peered at a small two-D image, as they sat
down on the couch with the box on their knees.

"Your hair stuck out just like Gordon's does," Lona
pointed out, snickering.

"His looks better," Lunzie put that picture back in
the box and took out the next one. "This is my
mother. She was a doctor, too. She was born in
England on Old Earth, as true a *sassenach* as ever
wandered the Yorkshire Dales."

"What's a sassenach?" Lona asked, peering at the
image of the petite fair-haired woman.

"An old dialect word for a contentious Englishman.
Mother was what you'd call strong-minded. She introduced me to the works of Rudyard Kipling, who
has always been my favorite author."

"Did you ever get to meet him?"

Lunzie laughed. "Oh, no, child. Let's see, what is
this year?"

" 'Sixty-four."

"Well, then, next year will be the thousandth anniversary of his birth."

Lona was impressed. "Oh. Very ancient."

"Don't let that put you off reading him," Lunzie cautioned her. "He's too good to miss out on all your life. Kipling was a wise man, and a fine writer. He wrote adventures and children's stories and poetry, but what I loved most of all was his keen way of looking at a situation and seeing the truth of it."

"I'll look for some of Kipling in the library," Lona promised. "Who's this man?" she asked, pointing.

"This is my father. He was a teacher."

"They look nice. I wish I could have known them, like I'm getting to know you."

Lunzie put an arm around Lona. "You'd have liked them. And they would have been crazy about you."

They went through the box of pictures. Lunzie lingered over pictures of Fiona as a small child, and studied the images of the girl as she grew to womanhood. There were pictures of Fiona's late mate and all the babies. Even as an infant, Lars had a solemn, self-important expression, which made them both giggle. Lona turned out the bottom compartment of the box and held out Lunzie's university diploma.

"Why is your name Lunzie Mespil, instead of just Lunzie?" Lona asked, reading the ornate characters on the plastic-coated parchment.

"What's wrong with Mespil?" Lunzie wanted to know.

Lona turned up her lips scornfully. "Surnames are barbaric. They let people judge you by your ancestry or your profession, instead of by your behavior."

"Do you want the true answer, or the one your uncle Lars would prefer?"

Lona grinned wickedly. She obviously shared Lunzie's opinion of Lars as a pompous old fogy. "What's the truth?"

"The truth is that when I was a student, I contracted to a term marriage with Sion Mespil. He was an angelically handsome charmer attending medical school at the same time I was. I loved him dearly, and I think he felt the same about me. We didn't want a permanent marriage at that time because neither of us knew where we would end up after school. I was in the mental sciences, and he was in genetics and reproductive sciences. We might go to opposite ends of the galaxy—and in fact, we did. If we had stayed together, of course, we might have made it permanent. I kept his last name and gave it to our baby, Fiona, to help her avoid marrying one of her half-brothers at some time in the future." Lunzie chuckled. "I swear Sion was majoring in gynecology just so he could deliver his own offspring. With the exception of the time we were married, I've never see a man with such an active love life in all my days."

"Didn't you want him to help raise Fiona?" Lona asked.

"I felt perfectly capable of taking care of her on my own. I loved her dearly, and truth be told, Sion Mespil was far better at the engendering of children than the raising. He was just as happy to leave it to me. Besides, my specialty required that I travel a lot. I couldn't ask him to keep up with us as we moved. It would be hard enough on Fiona."

Lona was taking in Lunzie's story through every pore, as if it was a Tri-D adventure. "Did you ever hear from him again after medical school?" she demanded.

"Oh, yes, of course," Lunzie assured her, smiling. "Fiona was his child. He sent us ten K of data or so every time he heard of a message batch being compiled for our system. We did the same. Of course, I had to edit his letters for Fiona. I don't think at her age it was good for her to hear details of her father's sex life, but his genetics work was interesting. He did

work on the heavyworld mutation, you know. I think
he influenced her to go into medicine as much as I
did."

"Is that him?" Lona pointed to one of the men in
Lunzie's medical school graduation picture. "He's
handsome."

"No. That one." Lunzie cupped her hand behind
Sion's holo, to make it stand out. "He had the face of
a benevolent spirit, but his heart was as black as his
hair. The galaxy's worst practical joker, bar none. He
played a nasty trick with a cadaver once in Anatomy
. . . um, never mind." Lunzie recoiled from the
memory.

"Tell me!" Lona begged.

"That story is too sick to tell anyone. I'm surprised
I remember it."

"Please!"

Remembering the nauseating details more and more
clearly, Lunzie held firm. "No, not that one. I've got
lots of others I could tell you. When do you have to
go home?"

Lona waved a dismissive hand. "No one expects
me home. I'm always hanging around here. They're
used to it. Melanie and Dalton are the only interesting people. The other cousins are so dull, and as for
the parents . . ." Lona let the sentence trail off,
rolling her eyes expressively.

"That's not very tolerant of you. They *are* your
family," Lunzie observed in a neutral voice, though
she privately agreed with Lona.

"They may be family to you, but they're just relatives to me. Whenever I talk about taking a job
off-planet, you would think I was going to commit
piracy and a public indecency! What an uproar. No
one from our family ever goes into space, except
Uncle Dougal. He doesn't listen to Uncle Lars's
rules."

Lunzie nodded wisely. "You've got the family complaint. Itchy feet. Well, you don't have to stay in one place if you don't want to. Otherwise, it'll drive you mad. You live your own life." Lunzie punctuated her sentence with jabs in the air, ignoring the intrusive conscience which told her she was meddling in affairs that didn't concern her.

"Why did you leave Fiona?" Lona asked suddenly, laying a hand on her arm. "I've always wondered. I think that's why everyone else is allergic to relatives going out into space. They never come back."

It was the question that had lain unspoken between her and the others all the last evening. Unsurprised at Lona's honest assessment of her family situation, Lunzie stopped to think.

"I have wished and wished again that I hadn't done it," she answered after a time, squeezing the girl's fingers. "I couldn't take her with me. Life on a Platform or any beginning colony is dangerous. But they pay desperation wages for good, qualified employees and we needed money. I had never intended to be gone longer than five years at the outside."

"I've heard the pay is good. I'm going to join a mining colony as soon as I've graduated," Lona said, accepting Lunzie's words with a sharp nod. "My boyfriend is a biotechnologist with a specialty in botany. The original green thumb, if you'll forgive such an archaic expression. What am I saying?" Lona went wide-eyed in mock shame and Lunzie laughed. "Well, I can fix nearly anything. We'd qualify easily. They say you can get rich in a new colony. If you survive. Fiona used to say it was a half-and-half chance." Lona wrinkled her nose as she sorted the pictures and put them away. "Of course, there's the Oh-Two money. Neither of us has a credit to our names."

Lunzie considered deeply for a few minutes before she spoke. "Lona, I think you should do what you want to do. I'll give you the money."

"Oh, I couldn't ask it," Lona gasped. "It's too much money. A good stake would be hundreds of thousands of credits." But her eyes held a lively spark of hope.

Lunzie noticed it. She was suddenly aware of the generations which lay between them. She had slept through so many that this girl, who could have been her own daughter, was her granddaughter's granddaughter. She peered closely at Lona, noticing the resemblance between her and Fiona. This child was the same age Fiona would have been if all had gone well on Descartes, and she had returned on time. "If that's the only thing standing in your way, if you're independent enough to ignore family opinion and unwanted advice, that's good enough for me. It won't beggar me, I promise you. Far from it. I got sixty years back pay from Descartes, and I hardly know what to do with it. Do me the favor of accepting this gift—er, loan, to pass on to future generations."

"Well, if it means that much to you . . ." Lona began solemnly. Unable to maintain the formal expressions for another moment more, she broke into laughter, and Lunzie joined in.

"Your parents will undoubtedly tell me to mind my own business," Lunzie sighed, "and they'd be within their rights. I'm no better than a stranger to all of you."

"What if they do?" Lona declared defiantly. "I'm legally an adult. They can't live my life for me. It's a bargain, Lunzie. I accept. I promise to pass it on at least one more generation. And thank you. I'll never, never forget it."

"A cheery good morning!" Tee said, as he clumped down the ramp into the common room toward them. He kissed Lunzie and bowed over Lona's hand. "I heard laughter. Everyone is in a good mood today? Is there any hope of breakfast? If you show me the food synthesizer, I will serve myself."

"Not a chance!" Lona scolded him. "Melanie would have my eyelashes if I gave you synth food in her house. Come on, I'll cook something for you."

Lona's parents were not pleased that their remote ancestress was taking a personal interest in their daughter's future. "You shouldn't encourage instability like that," Jai complained. "She wants to go gallivanting off, without a thought for the future."

"There's nothing unstable about wanting to take a job in space," Lunzie retorted. "That's the basic of galactic enterprise."

"Well, we won't hear of it. And with the greatest of respect, Lunzie, let us raise our child our way, please?"

Lunzie simmered silently at the reproval, but Lona gave her the thumbs up behind her father's back. Evidently, the girl was not going to mention Lunzie's gift. Neither would she. It would be a surprise to all of them when she left one day, but Lunzie refused to feel guilty. It wasn't as though the signs weren't pointed out to them.

After three days more, Lunzie had had enough of her descendents. She announced at dinner that night that she would be leaving.

"I thought you would stay," Melanie wailed. "We've got plenty of room, Lunzie. Don't go. We've hardly had a chance to get acquainted. Stay at least a few more days."

"Oh, I can't, Melanie. Tee's got to get back to the *Ban Sidhe*, and so do I. I do appreciate your offer, though," Lunzie assured her. "I promise to visit whenever I'm in the vicinity. Thank you so much for your hospitality. I'll carry the memories of your family with me always."

Chapter Nine

As they rode back into Alpha City in a robot groundcar the next morning, Tee patted Lunzie on the hand. "Let us not go back to the ship just yet. Shall we do some sightseeing? I was talking to Dougal. He says there is a fine museum of antiquities here, with controlled atmosphere. And it is connected to a large shopping mall. We could make an afternoon of it."

Lunzie came back from the far reaches and smiled. She had been staring out the window at the gray expanse of city and thinking. "I'd love it. Walking might help clear my head."

"What is cluttering it?" Tee asked, lightly. "I thought we had left the clutter behind."

"I've been examining my life. My original goal, when I woke up the first time, to find Fiona and make sure she was happy and well, was really accomplished long ago, even before I set out for Alpha Centauri. I think I came here just to see Fiona again, to ask her to forgive me. Well, that was for me, not for her. She's moved on and made a life—quite a successful one—without me. It's time I learned to let go of her. There are three generations more already, whose upbringing is so different from mine we have nothing to say to one another."

200

"They are shallow. You have met interesting people of this generation," Tee pointed out.

"Yes, but it's a sorry note when it's your own descendents you're disappointed in," Lunzie said ruefully. "But I don't know where to go next."

"Why don't we brainstorm while we walk?" Tee pleaded. "I am getting cramped sitting in this car. Museum of Galactic History, please," he ordered the groundcar's robot brain.

"Acknowledged," said the mechanical voice. "Working." The groundcar slowed down and made a sharp right off the highway onto a small side street.

"You could join the service," Tee suggested as they strolled through the cool halls of the museum past rows of plexiglas cases. "They have treated me very well."

"I'm not sure I want to do that. I know my family has a history in the Fleet, but I'm not sure I could stand being under orders all the time, or staying in just one place. I'm too independent."

Tee shrugged. "It's your life."

"If it *is* my life, why can't I spend two years running without someone throwing me into deepsleep?" She sighed, stepping closer to the wall to let a herd of shouting children run by. "Oh, I wish we could go back to Astris, Tee. We were so happy there. Your beautiful apartment, and our collection of book plaques. Coming home evenings and seeing who could get to the food-prep area first." Lunzie smiled up at him fondly. "Just before I left, we were talking about children of our own."

Tee squinted into the distance, avoiding her eyes. "It was so long ago, Lunzie. I gave up that apartment when I left Astris. I have been on the *Ban Sidhe* for more than six years. You remember it well because for you it has been only months. For me, it is the beloved past." His tone made that clear.

Lunzie felt very sad. "You're happy being back in

space again, aren't you? You came to rescue me, but it's more than that now. I couldn't ask you to give it up."

"I have my career, yes," Tee agreed softly. "But there is also something else." He paused. "You've met Naomi, yes?"

"Yes, I've met Naomi. She treats me with great respect," Lunzie said aggrievedly. "It drives me half mad, and I haven't been able to break her of it. What about her?" she asked, guessing the answer before he spoke.

Tee glanced at her, and gazed down at the floor, abashed.

"I am responsible for the respect she holds for you. I have talked much of you in the years I've been on board. How can she fail to have a high opinion of you? She is the chief telemetry officer on the *Ban Sidhe*. The commander let me go on the rescue mission on the condition that I signed on to work. He would allow no idle hands, for who knew how long it would take to find the ship and rescue all aboard her? Naomi took me as her apprentice. I learned quickly, I worked hard, and I came to be expert at my job. I found also that I care for her. Captain Aelock offered me a permanent commission if I wish to stay, and I do. I never want to go back to a planet-bound job. Naomi confesses that she cares for me, too, so there is a double attraction. We both mean to spend the rest of our careers in space." He stopped walking and took both of her hands between his. "Lunzie, I feel terrible. I feel as though I have betrayed you by falling in love with someone else before I could see you, but the emotion is strong." He shrugged expressively. "It has been ten years, Lunzie."

She watched him sadly, feeling another part of her life crumble into dust. "I know." She forced herself to smile. "I should have understood that. I don't blame you, my dear, and I couldn't expect you to remain celibate so long. I'm grateful you stayed with me as long as you did."

Tee was still upset. "I am sorry. I wish I could be more supporting."

Lunzie inhaled and let out a deep breath. She was aching to reach out to him. "Thank you, Tee, but you've done all that I really needed, you know. You were by me when I woke up, and you let me talk my head off just so I could reorient myself in time. And if I hadn't had someone to talk to while I was in Melanie's house, I think I would have jetted through the roof! But that's over, now. It's all over, now," Lunzie said, bitterly. "Time has run past me and I never saw it go by. I thought that ten years of cold sleep would have been easier to accept than sixty, but it's worse. My family is gone and you've moved on. I accept that, I really do. Let's go back to the ship before I decide to let them put me in one of those glass cases as an antiquarian object of curiosity."

They arrived just in time for Tee to resume his usual duty shift, and Lunzie went back to her compartment to move the rest of her things down to the BOQ at the base down on Alpha. No matter what she let Tee believe, she had lost a lot of the underpinnings of her self-esteem in the last few days, and it hurt.

Sharu wasn't here, so Lunzie allowed herself fifteen minutes for a good cry, and then sat up to reassess her situation. Self-pity was all very well, but it wouldn't keep her busy or put oxygen in the air tanks. The shuttle was empty except for her and the pilot. Thankfully, he didn't feel like talking. Lunzie was able to be alone with her thoughts.

The base consisted of perfectly even rows of huge, boxlike buildings that all looked exactly alike to Lunzie. A human officer jogging by with a handful of document cubes was able to direct her to the Bachelor Officers' Quarters, where the stranded employees of the Destiny Lines would stay until after they gave their statements to the court. When she reached the BOQ, she took her bags to quarters assigned for her use, and left them there. The nearest computer facilities, she was told, were in the recreation hall.

Using an unoccupied console in the rec room, she called up the current want ads network and began to page through suitable entry headings.

By the middle of the afternoon, Lunzie was feeling much better. She was resolute that she would no longer depend on another single person for her happiness. She added a "reminder" into her daily Discipline meditation to help increase her confidence. The wounds of loss would hurt for a while. That was natural. But in time, they would heal and leave little trace.

She realized all of a sudden that she had had nothing to eat since morning, and now it was nearly time for the evening meal. Her bout of introspection, not to mention the taxing Discipline workout, had left her feeling hollow in the middle. Surely the serving hatches in the mess hall would be open by now. She went back to her quarters, put on fresh garments and pulled on boots to go check.

"Lunzie! The very person. Lunzie, may I speak to you?" Captain Aelock hurried up to her as she stepped out into the main corridor of the building.

"Of course, Captain. I was just on the way to get myself some supper. Would you care to sit with me?"

"Well, er," he smiled a trifle sheepishly, "supper was exactly what I had planned to offer you, but not here. I was hoping to have a chance to chat with you before the *Ban Sidhe* departed. I am very grateful for the help you've given Dr. Harris since you came aboard. In fact, he is reluctant to let you go. So am I.

I don't suppose I can persuade you to join us? We could use more level-headed personnel with your qualifications."

Aelock would be a fine commander to serve under. Lunzie almost opened her mouth to say yes, but remembered Tee and Naomi. "I'm sorry, Captain, but no, thank you."

The captain looked genuinely disappointed. "Ah, well. At any rate, I had in mind to offer you a farewell dinner here on Alpha. I know some splendid local places."

Lunzie was flattered. "That's very kind of you, Captain, but I was only doing my job. A cliche, but still true."

"I would still find it pleasant to stand you a meal, but I must admit that I have a more pressing reason to ask you to dine with me tonight." The captain pulled her around a corner as a handful of crew members walked by along the corridor.

"You have my entire attention," Lunzie assured him, returning the friendly but curious gazes shot toward her by the passing officers.

Aelock tucked her arm under his and started walking in the opposite direction. "I remember when I mentioned planet pirates to you, you were very interested. Am I wrong?"

"No. You said that one of the reasons you were here was to get information as to their whereabouts." Lunzie kept her voice low. "I have very personal reasons for wanting to see them stopped. Personal motives for vengeance, in fact. How can I help?"

"I suspect that one operation might be based out of Alpha's own spaceport, but I haven't got proof!" Lunzie looked shocked and Aelock nodded sadly. "One of my, er, snitches sent me a place and a time when he will contact me, to give me that information. Have dinner with me at that place. If I'm seen dining alone, they'll know something is up. My contact is already under observation, and in terror of his life. You're not in the Fleet computers; you'll look like a local date. That may throw off the pirates' spies. Will you come?"

"Willingly," she said firmly. "And able to do anything to stop the pirates. How shall I dress?"

Aelock glanced over the casual trousers and tunic and polymer exercise boots Lunzie was wearing.

"You'll do just as you are, Lunzie. The food is quite good, but this restaurant is rather on the informal side. It isn't where I should like to entertain you, you may be sure, but my contact won't be entirely out of place there."

"No complaint from me, Captain, so long as supper's soon," Lunzie told him. "I'm starving."

The host of Colchie's Cabana seated Lunzie and Aelock in the shadow of an artificial cliff. The restaurant, a moderately priced supper club, had overdone itself in displaying a tropical motif. All the fruit drinks, sweet or not, had kebabs of fresh fruit skewered on little plastic swords floating in them. Lunzie nibbled on the fruit and took handfuls of salty nut snacks from the baskets in the center of their table to cut the sugary taste.

Lunzie examined the holo-menu with pleasure. The array of dishes on offer was extensive and appetizing. In spite of the kitschy decor and the gaudy costumes of the human help, the food being served to other diners smelled wonderful. Lunzie hoped the rumbling in her stomach wasn't audible. The restaurant was packed with locals chatting while live music added to the clamor.

"Have you had a good look at the corner band?" Lunzie asked, unable to restrain a giggle as she leaned toward Aelock, hiding her face behind the plas-sheet menu. "The percussionist seems to be playing a tree-stump with two handfuls of broccoli! That does, of course, fit in with the general decor very well."

"I know," Aelock said with an apologetic shudder. "Let me reassure you that the food is an improvement on the ambience. Well cooked and, with some exceptions, spiced with restraint."

Despite the casual clothes he was wearing, the captain's bearing still marked him for what he was, making him stand out from the rest of the clientele. Lunzie had a moment's anxiety over that, but surely off-duty officers might dine here without causing great comment.

"That's a relief," Lunzie replied drily, watching the facial contortions of a diner who had just taken a bite of a dish with a very red sauce.

The man gulped water and hurriedly reached for his bowl of rice. Aelock followed her eyes and smiled.

"Probably not a regular, or too daring for his stomach's good. The menu tells you which dishes are hot and which aren't. And ask if you want the milder ones. He's obviously overestimated his tolerance for Chiki peppers."

"Will you have more drinks, or will you order?" A humanoid server stood over them, bowing deferentially, keypad in hand. His costume consisted of a colorful knee-length tunic over baggy trousers with a soft silk cape draped over one shoulder. On his head was a loose turban pinned at the center with a huge jeweled clip. He turned a pleasant expression of inquiry toward Lunzie who managed to keep her countenance. The man had large, liquid black eyes but his face was a chalky white with colorless lips, a jarring lack in the frame of his gaudy uniform. Except for the vivid eyes, the doubtless perfectly healthy alien looked like a human cadaver. Diners here had to have strong stomachs for more than the food.

"I'm ready," Lunzie announced. "Shall I begin? I'd like the mushroom samosas, salad with house dressing, and special number five."

"That one's hot, Lunzie. Are you sure you'd like to

try it?" Aelock asked. "It has a lot of tiny red and green capsica peppers. They're nearly rocket fuel."

"Oh, yes. Good heavens, I used to *grow* LED peppers."

"Good, just checking. I'll have the tomato and cheese salad, and number nine."

"Thank you, gracious citizens," the server said, bowing himself away from the table.

Lunzie and Aelock fed the menus back into the dispenser slots.

"You know, I'm surprised at the amount of sentient labor on Alpha," Lunzie observed as the human server stopped to take drink orders from another table. "There were live tourguides at the museum this morning, and the customs service is only half-automated turnstiles at the spaceport."

"Alpha Centauri has an enormous population, all of whom need jobs," Aelock explained. "It is mostly human. This was one of the first of Earth's outposts, considered a human Homeworld. The non-humanoid population is larger than the entire census of most colonies, but on Alpha, it is still a very small minority. In the outlying cities, most children grow up never having seen an outworlder."

"Sounds like an open field for prejudice," Lunzie remarked, remembering Lars.

"Yes, I'm afraid so. With the huge numbers of people in the workforce, and the finite number of jobs, there's bound to be strife between the immigrants and the natives. That's why I joined the Fleet. There was no guarantee of advancement here for me."

Lunzie nodded. "I understand. So they created a labor-intensive system, using cheap labor instead of mechanicals. You'd be overqualified for ninety percent of the jobs and probably unwilling to do the ones which promise advancement. Who is the person we're waiting for?" she asked in an undertone as a loud party rolled in through the restaurant doors.

Aelock quickly glanced at the other diners to make sure they hadn't been overheard. "Please. He's an old friend of mine. We were at primary school together. May we talk of something else?"

Lunzie complied immediately, remembering that secrecy was the reason she was here. "Do you read Kipling?"

"I do now," Aelock replied with a quick grin of appreciation. "When we had him in primary school literature, I didn't think much of Citizen Kipling. Then, when I came back fresh from my first military engagement in defense of my homeworld, and the half-educated fools here treated me with no more respect than if I'd been a groundcar, I found one of his passages described my situation rather well: 'It's Tommy this, an' Tommy that, an' 'Chuck him out, the brute!'"

"Mmm," said Lunzie, thoughtfully, watching the bitterness on Aelock's face. "Not a prophet in your own land, I would guess."

"Far from it."

"I've been fervently reciting 'If' like a mantra today, particularly the lines 'If you can meet with Triumph and Disaster, And treat those two impostors just the same . . .' " Lunzie quoted with a sigh. "I hate it when Rudy is so apt."

The relative merits of the author's poetry versus his prose occupied them until the appetizers arrived. The server whisked his billowing cape to one side to reveal the chilled metal bowl containing the captain's salad and the steaming odwood plate bearing Lunzie's appetizer.

"This is delicious," she exclaimed after a taste, and smiled up at the waiting server.

"We are proud to serve," the man declared, bowing, and swirled away.

"Flamboyant, aren't they?" Lunzie grinned.

"I think everyone in a service job needs to be a little exhibitionist," the captain said, amused.

He took a forkful of salad, and nodded approvingly. Lunzie smelled fresh herbs in the dressing. Another gaudily dressed employee with burning eyes appeared at their table and bowed.

"Citizen A-el-ock?" The captain looked up from his dish.

"Yes?"

"There is a communication for you, sir. The caller claimed urgency. Will you follow me?"

"Yes. Will you excuse me, my dear?" Aelock asked gallantly, standing up.

Lunzie simpered at him, using a little of the ambient flamboyance in her role of evening companion. "Hurry back." She waggled her fingers coyly after him.

The darkeyed employee glanced back at her, and ran a pale tan tongue over his lips. Lunzie was offended at his open scrutiny, hoping that he wasn't going to make a pest of himself while Aelock was away. She didn't want to attract attention to them by defending herself from harassment. To her relief, he turned away, and led the captain to the back of the restaurant.

Alone briefly, Lunzie felt it perfectly in character to glance at the other diners in the restaurant, wondering which of them, if any, could be the mysterious contact. She didn't notice anyone getting up to follow Aelock out, but of course the snitch would have been careful to leave a sufficient interval before having him summoned. She also didn't notice anyone surreptitiously watching their table, or her.

She was a minor player in a very dangerous game in which the opponents were ruthless. Lunzie tried not to worry, tried to concentrate on the excellence of her appetizer. One life more or less was nothing to the pirates who slaughtered millions carelessly. But if the captain's part was suspected, his life would be forfeit. When Aelock reappeared at last through the hanging vegetation, she looked a question at him. He nodded guardedly, inclining his head imperceptibly. She relaxed.

"I was thinking of ordering another drink with the entree. Will you join me?"

"A splendid notion. My throat is unaccountably dry," Aelock agreed. "Such good company on such a fine evening calls for a little indulgence." He pushed the service button on the edge of the table. He had been successful.

Lunzie controlled a surge of curiosity as discretion overcame stupidity. It was far wiser to wait until they were safely back on the base.

"By the way, what do you plan to do next, now that you're no longer employed by Destiny Cruise Lines?" Aelock asked. "Most of the others are already on their way to other jobs. That is, the ones who aren't staying here to sue the Paraden Company."

Lunzie smiled brightly. "In fact, I've just been checking some leads through the library computer," she said and summarized her afternoon's activities. "I do know that I absolutely do not want to stay on this planet—for all the reasons you gave, and more, but especially the pollution. I have this constant urge to irrigate my eyes."

Aelock plucked a large clean handkerchief out of his pocket and deposited it before Lunzie. "I understand completely. I'm a native, so I'm immune, but the unlucky visitor has the same reaction. Tell me, did you enjoy working as a commercial ship's medic?"

"Oh, yes. I could get to like that sort of a life very easily. I was very well treated. I was assigned a luxury cabin, all perks, far beyond this humble person's usual means. Not to mention a laboratory out of my dreams, plus a full medical library," Lunzie replied enthusiastically. "I got the chance to copy out some tests on neurological disorders that I had never seen before in all my research. Interesting people, too. I enjoyed meeting the Admiral, and most of the others I encountered during those two months. I wouldn't mind another stint of that at all. Temporary positions pay better than permanent employ."

Aelock grinned and there was something more lurking in his eyes that made Lunzie wonder if this was just casual conversation.

"Hear, hear. See the galaxy. And you wouldn't have to stay with a company long if you don't care for the way they treat you."

"Just so long as I don't get tossed into deepsleep again. I'm so out of date now that if I go down again, no one will be able to understand me when I speak. I'd have to be completely retrained, or take a menial position mixing medicines."

"It's against all the odds to happen again, Lunzie," Aelock assured her.

"The odds are exactly the same for me as anybody else," Lunzie said darkly—"and bad things come in threes," she added suddenly as she remembered the whispers in the Officers' Mess.

The captain shook his head wryly. "Good things should come in threes, too."

"Gracious citizens, the main course."

Their server appeared before them, touching his forehead in salute. Lunzie and Aelock looked up at him expectantly. Apparently not entirely familiar with his waiter's uniform, the server swirled aside his huge cape with one hand as, with the other, he started to draw a small weapon that had been concealed in his broad sash.

But Aelock was *fast*. "Needlegun!" he snarled as he threw his arm across the table to knock Lunzie to the floor and then dove out of the other side of their seat in a ground-hugging roll.

Startled, the pale-faced humanoid completed his draw too late and the silent dart struck the back of the seat where Aelock had been a split second before. With a roar and a flash of flame, the booth blew up. The ridiculous cloak swirling behind him, the server turned and ran.

The frightened patrons around them leaped out of their seats, screaming. With remarkable agility, the captain sprang to his feet and pursued the pasty-faced man toward the back of the restaurant. There was a concerted rush for the door by terrified diners and the musicians. Smoke and bits of debris filled the room.

Summoning Discipline, Lunzie burst out from under the shadow of the false cliff where Aelock's push had landed her, intending to follow Aelock and help him stop his would-be assassin. As she gained her feet, someone behind her threw one arm around her neck and squeezed, grabbing for her wrist with the other hand. Lunzie strained to see her assailant. It was the other pale-faced employee, his eyes glittering as he pressed in on her windpipe.

She tried to get her arms free, but the silk folds of his costume restricted her. Polymer boots weren't very suitable for stomping insteps so she opted for raking her heel down the man's shins and ramming the sole down onto the tendons joining foot and ankle. With a growl of pain, he gripped her throat tighter.

Lunzie promptly shot an elbow backward into his midsection, and was rewarded by an *oof*! His grip loosened slightly and she turned in his grasp, freeing her wrist. Growling, he tightened his arms to crush her. She jabbed for the pressure points on the rib cage under his arms with her thumbs, and brought a knee up between his legs, on the chance that whatever this humanoid's heritage, it hadn't robbed her of a sensitive point of attack.

It hadn't. As he folded, Lunzie delivered a solid chop to the back of his neck with her stiffened hand. He collapsed in a heap, and she ran for the door of the restaurant, shouting for a peace officer.

The local authorities had been alerted to the fire and disturbance in Colchie's. A host of uniformed officers had arrived in a groundvan, and were collecting reports from the frightened, coughing patrons milling on the street.

"An assassin," Lunzie explained excitedly to the officer who followed her back into the smoke-filled building. "He attacked me but I managed to disable him. His partner tried to shoot my dinner companion with a needlegun."

"A needlegun?" the officer reported in disbelief. "Are you sure what you saw? Those are illegal on this planet."

"A most sensible measure," Lunzie replied grimly. "But that's what blew up our booth. There, he's getting up again! Stop him!"

She pointed at the gaily costumed being, who was slowly climbing to his feet. In a couple of strides, the peace officer had caught up with Lunzie's attacker and seized him by the arm. The assassin snarled and squirmed loose, brandishing a shimmering blade—then folded yet again as the officer's stunner discharged into his sternum. The limp assassin was carried off by a pair of officers who had just arrived to back up their colleague.

"Citizen," the first one said to her, "I'll need a report from you."

While Lunzie was giving her report to the peace officer, Captain Aelock came out the front of the restaurant with the other assassin in an armlock. The captain's tunic was torn, and his thick gray hair was disheveled. She noticed blood on his face and streaking down one sleeve.

The assassin joined his quiescent partner in the

groundvan while the captain took the report officer aside and made a private explanation.

"I see, sir," the Alphan said, respectfully, giving a half salute. "We'll contact FSP Fleet Command if we need any further details from you."

"We may leave, then?"

"Of course, sir. Thank you for your assistance."

Aelock gave him a preoccupied nod and hurried Lunzie away. He looked shaken and unhappy.

"What else happened?" she demanded.

"We've got to get out of here. Those two probably weren't alone."

Lunzie lengthened her stride. "That's not all that's bothering you."

"My contact is dead. I found him in the alley behind the building when I chased that man. Dammit, how did they get on to me? The whole affair has been top secret, need-to-know only. It means—and I hate to imagine how—the pirates must have spies within the top echelons of the service."

"What?" Lunzie exclaimed.

"There's been no one else who could have known. I reported my contact with my poor dead friend only to my superiors—and I have told no one else. It must mean Aidkisagi is involved," Aelock muttered almost to himself in a preoccupied undertone.

They turned another corner onto an empty street. Lunzie glanced behind them nervously. Yellow city lights reflected off the smooth surfaces of the building facades and the sidewalk as if they were two mirrors set at right angles. Each of them had two bright-edged shadows wavering along behind them which made Lunzie feel as if they were being followed. Aelock set a bruising pace for a spacer. They heard no footfalls behind them.

When he was sure that they had not been followed, Aelock stopped in the middle of a small public park where he had a 360 degree field of vision. The low shrubs twenty yards away offered no cover.

"Lunzie, it's more imperative than ever that I get a message to Commander Coromell on Tau Ceti. He's Chief Investigator for Fleet Intelligence. He must know about this matter."

"Why not give it to the Admiral? He told me he was going to visit his son."

In the half shadow of the park, Aelock's grimace looked malevolent rather than regretful. "He would have been ideal but he left this morning." Aelock gazed down hopefully at Lunzie and took hold of her wrists. "I can't trust this message to any ordinary form of transmission, but it must get to Coromell. It is vital. Would you carry it?"

"Me?" Lunzie felt her throat tighten. "How?"

"Do exactly what you were going to do. Take a position as medical officer. Only make it a berth on a fast ship, anything that is going directly to Tau Ceti as soon as possible. Tomorrow, if you can. Alpha is one of the busiest spaceports in the galaxy. Freighters and merchants leave hourly. I'll make sure you have impeccable references even if they won't connect you with me. Will you do it?"

Lunzie hesitated for a heartbeat in which she remembered the devastated landscape of Phoenix, and the triple-column list of the dead colonists.

"You bet I will!"

The look of intense relief on Aelock's face was reward in itself. From a small pocket in the front of his tunic, he took a tiny ceramic tube and put it in her hands. "Take this message brick to Coromell and say: 'It's Ambrosia.' Got it? Even if you lose this, remember the phrase."

Lunzie hefted the cube, no bigger than her thumbnail. " 'It's Ambrosia,' " she repeated carefully. "All right. I'll find a ship tomorrow morning." She tucked the ceramic into her right boot.

Aelock gripped her shoulders gratefully. "Thank you. One more thing. Under no circumstances should you try to play that cube. It can only be placed into a reader with the authorized codes."

"It'll blank?" she asked.

Aelock smiled at her naivete. "It will explode. That's a high-security brick. The powerful explosive it contains would level the building if the wrong sort of reader's laser touches it. Do you understand?"

"Oh, after tonight, I believe you, even if this whole evening has been like something from Tri-D." She grinned reassuringly at him.

"Good. Now, don't go back to the BOQ. They must not realize that you're with me. It could mean your life if they think you are connected with the Fleet. They killed my friend, a harmless fellow, a welder in the shipyard. His family had been at Phoenix. Couldn't hurt a fly, but they killed him." Aelock shuddered at the memory. "I won't tell you how. I've seen many forms of death, but that sort of savagery . . ."

Lunzie felt the Discipline boost wearing off and she'd little reserve of strength. "I won't risk it then, but what about my things?"

"I'll have them sent to you. Take a groundcar. Go to the Alpha Meridian Hotel and get a room. Here's my credit seal."

"I've got plenty of credits, thank you. That's no problem."

Aelock saw a groundcar, its 'empty' light flashing, and hailed it. "That one ought to be safe, coming from the west. Someone will bring your things to the hotel. It will be someone you know. Don't let anyone else in." He opened the car hatch and helped her in. He leaned over her before closing the car. "We won't meet again, Lunzie. But thank you, from the bottom of my heart. You're saving lives."

Then he slipped away into shadow as yellow streetlights washed across the rounded windows of the rolling groundcar. Lunzie buckled herself in and gave her destination to the robot-brain.

The Alpha Meridian reminded Lunzie of the *Destiny Calls*. In the main lobby, there were golden cherubs and other benevolent spirits on the ceiling holding up sconces of vapor-lights. Ornate pillars with a leaf motif, also in gold, marched through the room like fantastic trees. A human server met her at the door and escorted her to the registration desk. No mention was made of her casual clothing, though she appeared a mendicant in comparison to the expensively dressed patrons taking a late evening morsel in cushiony armchairs around the lobby.

The receptionist, who Lunzie suspected was a shapechanging Weft because of the utter perfection of her human form, impassively checked Lunzie's credit code. As the confirmation appeared, her demeanor instantly altered. "Of course we can accommodate you, Citizen Doctor Lunzie. Do you require a suite? We have a most appealing one available on the four-hundredth-floor penthouse level."

"No, thank you," Lunzie replied, amused. "Not for one night. If I were staying a week or more, certainly I would need a suite. My garment cases will follow by messenger."

"As you wish, Citizen Doctor." The receptionist lifted a discreet eyebrow, and a bellhop appeared at Lunzie's side. "One-oh-seven-twelve, for the Citizen Doctor Lunzie." The bellhop bowed and escorted her toward the bank of turbovators.

Her room was on a corridor lined with velvety dark red carpet, and smelled pleasantly musky and old. The Meridian was a member of a grand hotel chain of the old style, reputed to have brought Earth-culture hostelry to the stars. The bellhop turned on the lights and waited discreetly at the door until Lunzie had stepped in, then withdrew on silent feet. In her nervous state, she flew to the door and opened it, to make sure he had really gone. The bellhop, waiting at the turboshaft for the 'vator to come back, threw her a curious glance. She ducked back into her room and locked the door behind her.

"I must calm down," Lunzie said out loud. "No one followed me. No one knows where I am."

She paced the small room, staying clear of the curtained window, which provided her with a view of a tiny park and an enormous industrial complex. The bedroom was panelled in a dark, smooth-grained wood with discreet carvings along the edges near the ceiling and floor. The canopied bed was deep and soft, covered with a thick, velvety spread in maroon edged with gold trim that matched the smooth carpeting. It was a room designed for comfort and sleep but Lunzie was too nervous to enjoy it. She wanted to use the com-unit and call the ship to see if Aelock had made it back safely. A stupid urge and dangerous for both of them. Shaking, Lunzie sat down on the end of the bed and clenched her hands in her lap.

Someone would be coming by later with her clothing and possessions. Until that someone came, she couldn't sleep though her body craved rest after the draining of Discipline. The hotel provided a reader and small library in every room. Hers was next to the bed on a wooden shelf that protruded from the wall. She was far too restless to read, the events of the evening on constant replay in her mind. Even if the two assailants had been captured, that didn't mean they had been alone, or that their capture would go unremarked. That left a bath to fill in the time and that at least was a constructive act, helping to draw tension out of her body and ready it for the sleep she so badly needed.

While the scented water was splashing into the tub, Lunzie kept imagining she heard the sound of knocking on her door and kept running out to answer it.

"This is ridiculous," she told herself forcefully. "I can take care of myself. They would scarcely draw attention to themselves by leveling the hotel because I'm in it. I must relax. I will."

Her clothes were dirty and sweat-stained and there was a large blot of sauce on the underside of one forearm. She tossed them in the refresher unit, and listened to them swirl while she lay in the warm bath water.

The bathroom was supplied with every luxury. Mechanical beauty aids offered themselves to her in the bath. A facial cone lowered itself to her face and hovered, humming discreetly. "No, thank you," Lunzie said. It rose out of her way and disappeared into a hatch in the marble-tiled ceiling. A dental kit appeared next. "Yes, please." She allowed it to clean her teeth and gums. More mechanisms descended and were refused: a manicure/pedicure kit, a tonsor, a skin exfoliant. Lunzie accepted a shampoo and rinse with scalp massage from the hairdressing unit, and then got out of the tub to a warmed towel and robe, presented by another mechanical conveyance.

It was close to midnight by then and Lunzie found that she was hungry. Her entree at Colchie's had turned out to be an assassin with a needlegun. She considered summoning a meal from room service but she was loath to, picturing chalky-faced waiters in silk capes streaming into the tiny room with guns hidden in their sashes. She'd been hungrier than this before. Wearing the robe, Lunzie climbed into bed to wait for the messenger with her bags.

Most of the book plaques on the shelf were bestsellers of the romance-and-intrigue variety. Lunzie found a pleasant whodunnit in the stack and put it into the reader. Pulling the reader's supporting arm over the bed, Lunzie lay back, trying to involve herself in the ratiocinations of Toli Alopa, a Weft detective who could shapechange to follow a suspect without fear of being spotted.

Somewhere in the middle of a chase scene, Lunzie fell into a fitful dream of pasty-faced waiters who called her Jonah and chased her through the *Destiny Calls*, finally pitching her out of the space liner in full warp drive. The airlock alarm chimed insistently that the hatch was open. There was danger. Lunzie awoke suddenly, seeing the shadow of an arm over her face. She screamed.

"Lunzie!" Tee's voice called through the door and the door signal rang again. "Are you all right?"

"Just a moment!" Fully awake now, Lunzie saw that the arm was just the reader unit, faithfully turning pages in the book plaque. She swept it aside and hurried to the door.

"I'm alone," Tee assured her, slipping in and sealing the locks behind him. He gave her a quick embrace before she realized that he was wearing civilian clothes. "Here are your bags. I think I have everything of yours. Sharu helped me pack them."

"Oh, Tee, I am so glad to see you. Did the captain tell you what happened?"

"He did. What an ordeal, my Lunzie!" Tee exclaimed.

"What was the scream I heard?"

"An overactive imagination, nothing more," Lunzie said, self-deprecatingly. She was ashamed that Tee had heard her panic.

"The captain suggested that you would trust me to bring your possessions. Of course, you might not want to see me . . ." He let the sentence trail off.

"Nonsense, Tee, I will always trust you. And your coming means that the captain got safely back. That's an incredible relief."

Tee grinned. "And I've got orders to continue to confuddle whoever it is that sends assassins after my good friends. When I leave here, I am going to the

local Tri-D Forum and watch the news until dawn.
Then I am going to an employment agency to job
hunt." Tee held up a finger as Lunzie's mouth opened
and closed. "Part of the blind. I go back to the ship
when you are safely out of the way and no connection can be made between us. Now, is there anything else I can do for you?"

"Yes indeed," Lunzie said. "I never got past the
appetizer and I haven't eaten since you and I had
breakfast this morning. I don't dare trust room service, but I am positively ravenous. If the wooden
walls didn't have preservative varnishes rubbed into
them, I'd eat them."

"Say no more," Tee said, "though this establishment would suffer terrible mortification if they knew
you'd gone for a carryout meal when the delights of
their very fancy kitchens are at your beck and call."
He kissed her hand and slipped out of the room
again.

In a short time, he reappeared with an armful of
small bags.

"Here is a salad, cheese, dessert, and a cold bean-
curd dish. The fruit is for tomorrow morning if you
still feel insecure eating in public restaurants."

Lunzie accepted the parcels gratefully and set them
aside on the bedtable. "Thank you, Tee. I owe you
so much. Give my best to Naomi. I hope you and
she will be very happy. I want you to be."

"We are," Tee smiled, with one of his characteristic wideflung gestures. "I promise you. Until we
meet again." He wrapped his arms around her and
kissed her. "I always will love you, my Lunzie."

"And I, you." Lunzie hugged him to her heart
with all her might, and then she let him go. "Goodbye, Tee."

When she let him out and locked the door, Lunzie
sorted through her duffelbags. At the bottom of one,
she found the holo of Fiona wrapped securely in

bubblepack. Loosening an edge of the pack, she took the message cube out of her boot. At the bottom of the bubblepack were two small cubes that Lunzie cherished, containing the transmissions sent her by her daughter's family to Astris and the *Ban Sidhe*. One more anonymous cube would attract no attention. Unless, of course, someone tried to read it in an unauthorized reader. She hoped she wouldn't be in the same vicinity when that happened. She could wish they'd used a less drastic protection scheme; what if an "innocent" snoop were to get his hands on it? She would have to be *very* careful. *Hmm . . .* she mused. Maybe that was the point.

Lunzie tried to go to sleep, but she was wide awake again. She put on the video system and scrolled through the Remote Shopping Network for a while. One of the offerings was a security alarm with a powerful siren and flashing strobe light for travellers to attach to the doors of hotel rooms for greater protection. Lunzie bought one by credit, extracting a promise from the RSN representative by comlink that it would be delivered to the hotel in the morning. The parcel was waiting for her at the desk when she came down early the next day to check out. She hugged it to her as she rode down to the spaceport to find a berth on an express freighter to Tau Ceti.

Chapter Ten

Two weeks later, Lunzie disembarked from the freighter *Nova Mirage* in the spaceport at Tau Ceti and stared as she walked along the corridors to the customs area. The change after seventy-five years was dramatic, even for that lapse of time on a colony world. The corrugated plastic hangars had been replaced by dozens of formed stone buildings that, had Lunzie not known better, she would have believed grew right out of the ground.

She felt an element of shock when she stepped outside. The unpaved roads had been widened and coated with a porous, self-draining polyester surface compound. Most of the buildings she remembered were gone, replaced by structures twice as large. She had seen the Tau Ceti colony in its infancy. It was now in full bloom. She was a little sad that the unspoiled beauty had been violated although the additions had been done with taste and color, adding to, rather than detracting from their surroundings. Tau Ceti was still a healthy, comfortable place, unlike the gray dullness of Alpha Centauri. The cool air she inhaled tasted sweet and natural after two weeks of ship air, and a week's worth of pollution before that. The sun was warm on her face.

Lunzie appreciated the irony of carrying the same

duffelbags over her shoulder today that she had lugged so many decades before when she had left Fiona there on Tau Ceti. They'd all showed remarkably little visible wear. Well, all that was behind her. She was beginning her life afresh. Pay voucher in hand, she sought *Nova Mirage*'s office to collect her wages and ask for directions.

The trip hadn't been restful but it had been fast and non-threatening. The *Nova Mirage*, an FTL medium-haul freighter, was carrying plumbing supplies and industrial chemicals to Tau Ceti. Halfway there, some of the crew had begun to complain of a hacking cough and displayed symptoms that Lunzie recognized as a form of silicosis. An investigation showed that one of the gigantic tubs in the storage hold containing powdered carbon crystals had cracked. This wouldn't have mattered except that the tub was located next to an accidentally opened intake to the ventilation system; the fumes had leaked all over the ship. Except for being short fifty kilos on the order, all was well. It was merely an accident, with no evidence of sabotage. A week's worth of exposure posed no permanent damage to the sufferers, but it was unpleasant while it lasted.

Lunzie had had the security alarm on her infirmary door during her sleep shift. It hadn't let out so much as a peep the entire voyage. The hologram and its attendant cubes remained undisturbed at the bottom of her duffelbag. None of the crew had sensed that their friendly ship's medic was anything out of the ordinary. And now she was on her way to deliver it and her message to their destination.

"I'd like to see Commander Coromell, please," Lunzie requested at Fleet Central Command. "My name is Lunzie."

"Admiral Coromell is in a meeting, Lunzie. Can you wait?" the receptionist asked politely, gesturing to a padded bench against the wall of the sparsely furnished, white-painted room. "You must have been travelling, Citizen. He's had a promotion recently. Not a Lieutenant Commander any more."

"Admiralties seem to run in his family," Lunzie remarked. "And I'll be careful to give him his correct rank, Ensign. Thank you."

In a short time, a uniformed aide appeared to escort her to the office of the newly appointed Admiral Coromell.

"There she is," a familiar voice boomed as she stepped into the room. "I told you there couldn't be two Lunzies. Uncommon name. Uncommon woman to go with it." Retired Admiral Coromell stood up from a chair before the honeywood desk in the square office and took her hand. "How do you do, Doctor? It's a pleasure to see you, though I'm surprised to see you so soon."

Lunzie greeted him with pleasure. "I'm happy to see you looking so well, sir. I hadn't had a chance to give you a final checkup before they told me you'd gone."

The old man smiled. "Well, well. But you surely didn't chase me all the way here to listen to my heart, did you? I've never met a more conscientious doctor." He did look better than he had when Lunzie saw him last, recently recovered from cold sleep, but she longed to run a scanner over him. She didn't like the look of his skin tone. The deep lines of his face had sunken, and something about his eyes worried her. He was over a hundred years old which shouldn't be a worry when human beings averaged 120 Standard years. Still, he had been through additional strain lately that had no doubt affected his constitution. His outlook was good, and that ought to help him prolong his life.

"I think she came to see me, Father."

The man behind the desk rose and came around to offer her a hand in welcome. His hair was thick and curly like his father's, but it was honey brown instead of white. Under pale brown brows, his eyes, of the same piercing blue as the senior Coromell's, bore into her as if they would read her thoughts. Lunzie felt a little overwhelmed by the intensity.

He was so tall that she had to crane her head back to maintain eye contact with him.

"You certainly do tend to inspire loyalty, Lunzie," the Admiral's son said in a gentle version of his father's boom. He was a very attractive man, exuding a powerful personality which Lunzie recognized as well suited to a position of authority in the Intelligence Service. "Your friend Teodor Janos was prepared to turn the galaxy inside out to find you. He certainly is proficient at computerized research. If it were not for him, I wouldn't have had half the evidence I needed to convince the Fleet to commission a ship for the search, even with my own father one of the missing. It's nice to finally meet you. How do you do?"

"Very well, Admiral," Lunzie replied, flattered. "Er, I'm sorry. That's going to become confusing, since both of you have the same name, and the same rank."

The old man beamed at both of them. "Isn't he a fine fellow? When I went away, he was just a lad with his new captain's bars. I arrived two days ago and they were making him an admiral. I couldn't be more proud."

The young admiral smiled down at her. "As far as I'm concerned, there's only one Admiral Coromell," and he gestured to his father. "Between us, Lunzie, my name will be sufficient."

Lunzie was dismayed with herself as she returned his smile. Hadn't she just vowed not to let anyone affect her so strongly? With the painful breakup with Tee so fresh in her mind? Certainly Coromell was handsome and she couldn't deny the charm nor the intelligence she sensed behind it. How dare she melt? She had only just met the man. Abruptly, she recovered herself and recalled her mission.

"I've got a message for you, er, Coromell. From Captain Aelock of the *Ban Sidhe*."

"Yes? I've only just spoken with him via secure-channel FTL comlink. He said nothing about sending you or a message."

Lunzie launched into an explanation, describing the aborted dinner date, the murder of Aelock's contact and the attempted murder of the two of them. "He gave me this cube," she finished, holding out the ceramic block, "and told me to tell you, 'It's Ambrosia.' "

"Great heavens," Coromell said, amazed, taking the block from her. "How in the galaxy did you get it here without incident?"

The old Admiral let out a hearty laugh. "The same way she travelled with me, I'll wager," he suggested, shrewdly. "As an anonymous doctor on a nondescript vessel. Am I not correct? You needn't look so surprised, my dear. I was once head of Fleet Intelligence myself. It was an obvious ploy."

Coromell shook his head, wonderingly. "I could use you in our operations on a regular basis, Lunzie."

"It wasn't my idea. Aelock suggested it," Lunzie protested.

"Ah, yes, but he didn't carry it out. You did. And no one suspected that you were a courier with top secret information in your rucksack—this!" Coromell shook the cube. He spun and punched a control on the panel atop his desk. "Ensign, please tell Cryptography I want them standing by."

"Aye, aye, sir," the receptionist's voice filtered out of a hidden speaker.

"We'll get on this right away. Thank you, Lunzie." Coromell ushered her and his father out. "I'm sorry, but I've got to keep this information among as few ears as possible."

"Well, well," said the Admiral to an equally surprised Lunzie as they found themselves in the corridor. "May I offer you some lunch, my dear? What d'you say? We can talk about old times. I saw the most curious thing the other day, something I haven't seen in years: a Carmen Miranda film. In two-D."

Lunzie passed a few pleasant days in Tau Ceti, visiting places she'd known when she stayed there. It was still an attractive place. A shame, on the whole, that there hadn't been a job here for her seventy-four years ago. The weather was pleasant and sunny, except for a brief rainshower early in the afternoon. By the hemispheric calendar, it was the beginning of spring. The medical center in which she worked had expanded, adding on a nursing school and a fine hospital. None of the people she'd known were still there. Flatteringly enough, the administrator looked up her records and offered her a position in the psychoneurology department.

"Since Tau Ceti became the administrative center for the FSP, we've seen a large influx of cases of space-induced trauma," he explained. "Nearly a third of Fleet personnel end up in cryogenic sleep for one reason or another. With your history and training, you would be the de facto expert on cold sleep. We would be delighted if you would join the staff."

Tempted, Lunzie promised she'd think it over.

She also interviewed with the shipping companies who were based on Tau Ceti for another position as a ship's medic. To her dismay, a few of them took one look at the notation in her records indicating that she'd been in two space wrecks and instantly showed her the door. Others were more cordial and less superstitious. Those promised to let her know the next time they had need of her services. Three who had ships leaving within the next month were willing to sign her on.

She spent some time with old Admiral Coromell, talking about old times. She also found it affected her profoundly to be in a familiar venue in which no one remembered many of the events that she did. To her, less than four years had passed since she had left Fiona there. The Admiral was the only other one who recalled events of that era and he shared her feelings of isolation.

Two weeks later, Coromell himself stopped by to see her at the guest house where she had taken a room.

"Sorry to have booted you and Father out of the office the other day," he apologized, with an engaging smile. "That information required immediate attention. I've been working on nothing else since then."

"My feelings weren't hurt," Lunzie assured him. "I was just incredibly relieved that I'd got it to you. Aelock had impressed its important on me. Several ways." The assassin's grim face flashed before her eyes again.

Coromell smiled more easily now. "Lunzie, you're a tolerant soul! To cross a galaxy with an urgent message and find the recipient is brusque to the point of rudeness. May I make amends now that all the flap is over and show you around? Or, perhaps, it's more to the point that you show me around. I know you'd been here when Tau Ceti was just started."

"I would enjoy that very much. When?"

"Today? With the nights I've been putting in, they won't begrudge me an afternoon off. That's why I came over." He held open the door and the sunlight streamed in. "It's too nice a day, even for Tau Ceti, to waste stuck indoors."

They spent the day in the nature preserve which had been Fiona's favorite haunt. The imported trees, saplings when she left, were mature giants now, casting cool shade over the river path. Following her memory, Lunzie led Coromell to her and Fiona's favorite place. The brief midday showers had soaked the ground and a heady smell of humus filled the air. In the crowns of the trees, they could hear the twitter of birdsong celebrating the lovely weather. Lunzie and Coromell ducked under the heavy boughs and clambered up the slope to a stone overhang. At one time in the planet's geologic history, stone strata had met and collided, shifting one of them upward toward the surface so that a ledge projected out over the river.

"It's good for sitting and thinking, and feeding the birds, if you happen to have any scraps of bread with you," Lunzie said, half lying on the great slab of sun-warmed stone to peer down into the water at small shadows chasing each other down the stream. "Or the fishoids."

Coromell patted his pockets. "Sorry. No bread. Perhaps next time."

"It's just as well. We'd be overrun with supplicants."

He laughed, and settled next to her to watch the dappled water dance over the rocks. "I needed this. It's been very hectic of late and I get to spend so little time in planetary atmosphere. My father has talked of no one else but you since he got here. He married late in life and doesn't want me to make the same mistake. He's lonely," Coromell added, wistfully. "He's been working on throwing us together."

"I wouldn't mind that," Lunzie said, turning her head to smile at him. Coromell was an attractive man. He had to be on the far side of forty-five but he had a youthful skin and, out of his official surroundings, he displayed more enthusiasm than she supposed careworn or rank-conscious admirals usually did.

"Well, I wouldn't either. I won't lie to you," he

replied carefully. "But be warned, I can't offer much in the way of commitments. I'm a career man. The Fleet is my life and I love it. Anything else would run second place."

Lunzie shrugged, pulling pieces of moss off the rock and dropping them into the water to watch the ripples. "And I'm a wanderer, probably by nature as well as experience. If I hadn't had a daughter, I'd never have been trying to earn Oh-Two money to join a colony. I enjoy travelling to new places, learning new things, and meeting new people. It would certainly be best not to make lifetime commitments. Nor very good for your reputation to have a time-lagged medic who's suspected of being a Jonah appearing on your arm at Fleet functions."

Coromell made a disgusted noise. "That doesn't matter a raking shard to me. Father told me about the chatter going on behind your back on the *Ban Sidhe*. I should put those fools on report for making your journey harder with such asinine superstitious babbling."

Lunzie laid a hand on his arm. "No, don't. If they need shared fears and experiences as a crutch to help them handle daily crisis, leave it to them. They'll grow out of it." She smiled reassuringly, and he slumped back with a hand shielding his eyes from the sun.

"As you wish. But we can still enjoy each other as long as we're together, no?"

"Oh, yes."

"I'm glad. Sure I can't persuade you to join up?" Coromell asked in a half-humorous tone. "It'll improve your reputation considerably to be a part of Fleet Intelligence. You could go places, meet new people and see new things while gathering information for us."

"What? Is that a condition for seeing you?" Lunzie

asked in mock outrage. "I have to join the navy?"
She raised an eyebrow.

"No. But if that's the only way I can get you to join
up, maybe I'll have the regulations altered," he chuckled wryly. "Do stay on Tau Ceti for a while. I'm
stationed here, flying a desk on this operation. I
hope to persuade you to change your mind about the
service. You could be a true asset to the Fleet. Stay
for a while, please."

Lunzie hesitated, considering. "I wouldn't feel right
hanging around waiting for you to get off work every
day. I'd be useless."

Coromell cleared his throat. "Didn't you speak to
the Medical Center about a job? You could be employed there, until you decide what to do. They,
um, called me to ask if your services were available.
They seem to think you're Fleet personnel already.
You have other unsuspected valuable traits. You listen to my father, who would be so happy to spend
time with you. At his age, there are so few people he
can talk to." Coromell looked wistfully hopeful, an
expression at odds with both uniform and occupation.

Her last protests evaporated. How well she understood old Admiral Coromell's dilemma. "All right.
None of the current prospects at the spaceport appeal to me. But that's not why I'm staying. I'm
enjoying myself."

"I like you, Dr. Lunzie."

"I like you, too, Admiral Coromell." She squeezed
his hand, and they sat together quietly for a while,
simply enjoying the brook's quiet murmur and the
sound of birdsong in the warmth of the afternoon.

Thereafter, they spent time together whenever
possible. Coromell's favorite idea of a relaxing afternoon was a stroll or a few hours listening to music or
watching a classical event on Tri-D. They shared
their music and literature libraries, and discussed
their favorites. Lunzie enjoyed being with him. He

was frequently tense when they met, but relaxed quickly once he had put the day behind him. Their relationship was different from the one she had had with Tee. Coromell expected her to offer opinions, and held to his own even if they differed. He was perfectly polite, as was appropriate to an officer and a gentleman, but he could be very stubborn. Even when they got into a knock-down-drag-out argument, Lunzie found it refreshing after Tee's selfless deferral to her tastes. Coromell trusted her with his honest views, and expected the same in return.

Coromell's schedule was irregular. When pirates had been sighted, he would be swamped with reports that had to be analyzed to the last detail. He had other duties which had not yet been reassigned to an officer of lesser rank that could keep him at the complex for four or five shifts on end. Lunzie, not wishing to take a permanent job yet, found herself with time on her hands that not even her Discipline training could use up.

Coromell knew that she had passed through the Adept stage of Discipline. At his urging, and with his personal recommendation to the group master, she joined a classified course in advanced Discipline taught in a gymnasium deep in the FSP complex.

There were two or three other pupils in the meditation sessions, but no names were ever exchanged, so she had no idea who they were. Her guess that they were upper echelon officers in the Fleet or senior diplomats was never verified or disproved. The master instructed them in fascinating types of mind control that built on early techniques accessible even to the first-level students. Using Discipline to heighten the senses to listen and follow the development of a subject's trance state, one could plant detailed posthypnotic suggestions. The shortened form of trance induction was amazing in its simplicity.

"This would be a terrific help in field surgery,"

Lunzie pointed out at the end of one private session. "I could persuade a patient to ignore poor physical conditions and remain calm."

"Your patient would still have to trust you. A strong will can counteract any attempt at suggestion, as you know, as can panic," the master warned her, gazing into her eyes. "Do not consider this a weapon, but rather a tool. The Council of Adepts would not be pleased. You are not merely a student-probationer any more."

Lunzie opened her mouth to protest that she would never do such a thing, but closed it again. He must have known of cases in which students had tried to rely upon this single technique to control an enemy, only to fail, perhaps at the cost of their lives. Then she smiled. Perhaps the technique worked too well and she had to learn to apply it correctly and with a fine discrimination for its use.

One delightful change which had occurred while she was in her second bout of cold sleep was that coffee had had a renaissance. On a fine afternoon following her workout, Lunzie came back from the spaceport and programmed a pot of coffee from the synth unit. The formula the synthesizers poured out had no caffeine, but it smelled oily and rich and wonderful, and tasted just like she remembered the real brew. There was even real coffee available occasionally in the food shops, an expensive treat in which, with her credit balance of back pay, she could afford to revel. She wondered if Satia Somileaux back on the Descartes Platform would ever try any.

The message light on her com-unit was blinking. Lunzie wandered over to it with a hot cup in her hands and hit the recall control. Coromell's face appeared on the screen.

"I'm sorry to ask on such short notice, Lunzie, but do you have a formal outfit? I'm expected to appear at a Delegate's Ball tonight at 2000 hours and your company would make it considerably less tedious an affair. I will be in the office until 1700 hours, awaiting your reply." The image blinked off.

"Gack, it's 1630 now!"

Bolting her coffee, Lunzie flew for her cases and rummaged through them for the teal-tissue sheath. The frock was easily compressed and didn't take up much room, so it was difficult to find. Yes, it was there, and it was clean and in good condition, needing only a quick wrinkle-proofing. She communicated immediately with Coromell's office that she would be free to come and hastened to set the clothes-freshener to Touch Up. She tossed the sweat-stained workout clothes in a corner and dashed through the sonic cleanser.

"Much more modest than I remembered." Approvingly, she noted her reflection in the mirror, making a final twirl. She smoothed down the sides of the thin fabric which shimmered in the evening sunlight coming through her window, allowing herself to admire the trim curves of her body. "You wouldn't think I was interested in this man, with the fuss I'm making to look good for him, would you?"

Lunzie fastened on her favorite necklace, a simple copper-and-gold choker that complemented the color of her dress and picked up becoming highlights in her hair and eyes.

Coromell arrived for her at 1945, looking correct and somewhat uncomfortable in his dark blue dress uniform. He gave Lunzie an approving once-over as he presented her with a corsage of white camellias. "Earth flowers. One of our botanists grows them as a hobby. How very pretty you look. Most becoming, that shimmery blue thing. I've never seen that style before," he said as he escorted her out to his chauffered groundcar. "Is it the lastest fashion?"

Lunzie chuckled. "I'll tell you a secret: it's a ten-year-old frock from halfway across the galaxy. It's surely the latest vogue somewhere."

The party had not yet begun when they arrived at the Ryxi Embassy, one of an identical row of three-story stone buildings set aside for the diplomatic corps of each major race in the FSP. Lunzie was amused to observe the resemblance between the embassies and the BOQ barracks on the Fleet bases. A flock of the excitable two-meter-tall avians stood at the entrance greeting their guests, flanked by a host of silent Ryxi wearing the crossed sashes of honor guards.

"Great ones for standing on their dignities, the Ryxi," Coromell said in an aside as they waited in turn to pass inside. "Excited they forget everything, and I shouldn't like to tangle with an enraged birdling."

A storklike Ryxi stepped forward to bow jerkily to Coromell. "Admirrral, a pleasurre," he trilled. The Ryxi normally spoke very fast. They expected others to comprehend them but occasionally, as on this festive evening, they slowed their speech to gracious comprehensibility.

Coromell bowed. "How nice to see you, Ambassador Chrrr. May I present my companion, Dr. Lunzie?"

Chrrr bowed like a glass barometer. "Welcome among the flock, Doctorrrr. Please make yourrrself frrreee of the Embassy of the Rrryxi."

"You're very kind," Lunzie nodded, beating back a temptation to roll the one *r* like a Scotsman.

With their stiff legs, Ryxi preferred to stand unless sitting was absolutely necessary. For the convenience of humans, Seti, Weft, and the dozen or so other species represented that night, their great hall had been provided with plenty of varied seats for their comrades of inferior race.

"That's what they consider us," Coromell murmured as they moved into the hall, "or any race that hasn't a flight capability."

"Where do they rank Thek?"

"They ignore them whenever possible." Coromell chuckled. "The Ryxi don't think it's worth the time it takes to listen."

An elderly Seti, who was the personal ambassador from the Seti of Fomalhaut, held court from the U-shaped backless chair which accommodated his reptilian tail. He made a pleasant face at her as she was introduced to him.

"Sso, you were graduated from Astriss Alexandria," he hissed. "As was I. Classs of 2784."

"Ah, you were four years behind me," Lunzie calculated. "Do you remember Chancellor Graystone?"

"I do. A fine administrator, for a Human. How curious, elder one, that you do not appear of such advanced years as your knowledge suggests," the Seti remarked politely. Seti were very private individuals. In Lunzie's experience, this was the closest that one had ever come to asking a personal question.

"Why, thank you, honored Ambassador. How kind of you to notice," Lunzie said, bowing away as Coromell swept her on to the next introduction.

"I'm surprised there aren't any Thek here," Lunzie commented as they acknowledged other acquaintances of Coromell's.

He cleared his throat. "The Thek aren't very popular right now among some members of the FSP. Even though the ordinary Ryxi never seem to care what anyone else thinks, the diplomatic corps are sensitive to public feeling."

"That makes them unusual?" Lunzie asked.

"You have no idea," Coromell said dryly.

"Why, Admiral, how nice to see you. And who is your charming companion?"

Lunzie turned to smile politely at the speaker and took an abrupt step back. A dark-haired female

heavyworlder with overhanging brow ridges was glaring down at her. But she had not spoken. Seated in
front of the huge female in an elegant padded armchair was a slight human male with large, glowing
black eyes. He was apparently quite used to having the
massive woman hovering protectively behind him.
Lunzie recovered herself and nodded courteously to
the man in the chair.

"Ienois, this is Lunzie," Coromell said. "Lunzie,
Ienois is the head of the well-known Parchandri mer-
chant family whose trade is most important to Tau
Ceti."

"This humble soul is overwhelmed by such com-
plements from the noble Admiral." The little man
inclined his head politely. "And delighted to meet
you."

"The pleasure is mine," Lunzie responded as com-
posedly as she could. It would never do to display
her distrust and surprise. She knew the reputation of
the Parchandris. Something about Ienois made her
dislike him on the spot. Not to mention his taste in
companions.

Ienois indicated the heavyworlder woman behind
him. "My diplomatic aide, Quinada." She bowed and
straightened up again without ever taking her eyes
off Lunzie. "We haven't had the pleasure of seeing
you before, Lunzie. Are you a resident of Tau Ceti?"

"No. I've only just arrived from Alpha Centauri,"
she answered politely. Coromell had assured her
there was no reason to hide her origins beyond the
dictates of simple good taste.

"Alpha Centauri? How interesting," intoned the
Parchandri.

"My daughter's family lives in Shaygo," Lunzie
replied civilly. "I had never met them and they
invited me to a family reunion."

"Ah! How irreplaceable is family. In our business,
we trust family first and others a most regrettably

distant second. Fortunately, ours is a very large family. Alpha Centauri is a marvelously large world with so many amenities and wonders. You must have found it hard to leave."

"Not very," Lunzie returned drily, "since the atmosphere's so polluted it's not fit to breathe."

"Not fit to breathe? Not fit?" The Parchandri bent forward in an unexpected fit of laughter. "That's very good. But, Lunzie," and he had suddenly sobered, "surely the air of a planet is more breathable than that of a ship?"

Lunzie remembered suddenly the engineer Perkin's warning about the owners of the Destiny Cruise Lines. They were a Parchandri merchant family called Paraden. She didn't know if Ienois was a Paraden but preferred not to provoke him or arouse his curiosity. What if he was one of the defendants in the case against Destiny Cruise Lines? Coromell might need this man's good will.

"Lunzie was shipwrecked on her way to Alpha Centauri," Coromell said, completely surprising Lunzie with this remark delivered in the manner of keeping a conversation going.

"I see. How dreadful." The Parchandri's large eyes gleamed as if it were not dreadful to him at all and, in some twisted way, she became more interesting to him. That was a weird perversion. "Were you long in that state?" the Parchandri pressed her. "Or were your engineers able to make repairs to your vessel? It is quite a frightening thing to be at the mercy of your machines in deep space. You appear to have survived the calamity without trauma. Commendable fortitude. Do tell this lowly one all!" His eyes glittered with anticipation.

Lunzie shrugged, not at all willing to gratify this strange man. Coromell would not have placed her in jeopardy if this Ienois was a Paraden and possibly

one of the defendants in the case against Destiny
Cruise Lines.

"There's not much to tell, really. We were towed
in by a military ship who happened to pass by the
site of the wreck."

"How fortuitous a rescue." Ienois's eyes glittered.
His . . . minder—no matter if he called her a diplomatic aide, she was a bodyguard if ever Lunzie had
seen one—never wavered in the stare she favored
Lunzie. "Stranded in space, landed on Alpha Centauri
and now you're here. How brave you are."

"Not at all," Lunzie said, wishing they could move
away from this vile man and his glowering "aide" but
Coromell's hand on her elbow imperceptibly restrained
her. Strange that he failed to notice that she had
given no details about her ship. Did Ienois already
"know"? "Travel is a fact of life these days. Ships and
rumors traverse the galaxy with equal speed."

Ienois ignored her flippancy. "Admiral," he turned
to Coromell, "have you tried the refreshments yet? I
do believe that the Ryxi have brought in a genuine
Terran wine for our pleasure. From Frans, I am
told."

"France," Coromell corrected him with a bow. "A
province in the northern hemisphere of Earth."

"Ah, yes. This is one world to which I have not yet
been. The Ryxi have truly provided a splendid repast
for their guests. Raw nuts and seeds are not much to
my liking, but there are sweet cream delicacies that
would serve to delight those far above my humble
station. And the cheeses! Pure ambrosia." The
Parchandri kissed the back of his hand.

In spite of her shield of will, Lunzie flinched involuntarily. Ambrosia. It was a coincidence that the
Parchandri should use that word. Having carried and
cherished it like an unborn child for the better part
of three months, Lunzie was sensitive to its use. She
caught both men looking at her. Coromell hadn't

reacted. He knew the significance of the word, but what of the merchant? Ienois was studying her curiously.

"Is the temperature not comfortable for you, Doctor?" Ienois asked in a sympathetic tone. "In my opinion, the Ryxi keep the room very warm, but I am accustomed to my home which is in a mountainous region. Much cooler than here." He beckoned upward to his gigantic bodyguard. They whispered together shortly, then Quinada left the room. Ienois shrugged. "I require a lighter jacket or I will stifle before I am able to give my greetings to my hosts."

Ienois drew the conversation on to subjects of common interest on which he held forth charmingly, but Lunzie was sure that he was watching her. There was a secretive air about the little merchant which had nothing to do with pleasant surprises. She found him sinister as well as perverted and wished she and Coromell could leave. Lunzie was made uncomfortable by Ienois's scrutiny, and tried not to meet his eyes.

Finally, Coromell seemed to notice Lunzie's signals to move on. "Forgive me, Ienois. The Weftian ambassador from Parok is here. I must speak to him. Will you excuse us?"

Ienois extended a moist hand to both of them. Lunzie gave it a hearty squeeze in spite of her revulsion and was rewarded by a tiny moue of amusement. "Can we count on seeing the two of you at our little party in five days time?" the merchant asked. "The Parchandri wish to reignite the flame of our regard in the hearts of our treasured friends and valued customers. Will you brighten our lives by attending?"

"Yes, of course," Coromell said graciously. "Thank you for extending the invitation."

The Parchandri was on his feet now, bowing elaborately. "Thank you. You restore face to this humble one." He made a deep obeisance and sat down.

"Must we go to the party of the unscrupulous Parchandri?" Lunzie asked in an undertone as they moved away.

Coromell seemed surprised. "We do have to maintain good relations. Why not?"

"That unscrup makes me think he'd sell his mother for ten shares of Progressive Galactic."

"He probably would. But come anyway. These dos are very dull without company."

"There's something about him that makes me very nervous. He said 'ambrosia.' Did you see him stare at me when I reacted? He couldn't have failed to notice it."

"He used the word in an acceptable context, Lunzie. You're just sensitive to it. Not surprising after all you've been through. Ienois is too indolent to be involved in anything as energetic as business." Coromell drew her arm through his and led her toward the next ambassador.

"She lied," Quinada muttered to her employer as she bowed to present a lighter dress tunic. "I checked with the main office. According to our reports from Alpha Centauri covering those dates, no disabled vessel was towed in. However, numerous beings of civilian garb were observed disembarking from a military cruiser, the *Ban Sidhe*. One matches her description. That places her on Alpha at the correct time, and with a false covering story."

"Inconclusive," Ienois said lightly, watching Lunzie and Coromell chatting with the Weftian ambassador and another merchant lord. "I could not make a sale with so weak a provenance. I need more."

"There is more. The man in the restaurant to whom the dead spy reported had a female companion, whose description also matches our admiral's lady in blue."

"Ah. Then there is no doubt." Ienois continued to smile at anyone who glanced his way, though his eyes remained coldly half-lidded. "Our friends' plans may have to be . . . altered." He pressed his lips together. "Kill her. But not here. There is no need to provoke an interplanetary incident over so simple a matter as the death of a spy. But see to it that she troubles us no further."

"As your will dictates." Quinada withdrew.

A live band in one corner struck up dance music. Lunzie listened longingly to the lively beat while Coromell exchanged endless stories with another officer and the representative from a colony which had just attained protected status. Coromell turned to ask her a question and found that her attention was focused on the dance floor. He caught her eye and made a formal bow.

"May I have the honor?" he asked and, excusing himself to his friends, swept her out among the swirling couples. He was an excellent dancer. Lunzie found it easy to follow his lead and let her body move to the beat of the music.

"Forgive me for boring you," Coromell apologized, as they sidestepped between two couples. "These parties are stamped out of a mold. It's a boon when I find any friends attending with whom I can chat."

"Oh, you're not boring me," Lunzie assured him. "I hope I wasn't looking bored. That would be unforgivable."

"It won't be too much longer before we may leave," Coromell promised. "I'm weary myself. The tradition is for the hosts giving the party to toast the guests with many compliments, and for the guests to return the honors. It should happen any time now."

The dance music ended, and the elderly Ryxi made

his way to the front of the room with a beaker in one
wingclaw. He raised the beaker to the assembled. At
his signal, Lunzie and the others hastened to the
refreshment table. Coromell poured them both glasses
of French wine.

When everyone was ready, the ambassador began
to speak in his mellow tenor cheep. "To our honored
guests! Long life! To our fellow members of the
Federated Sentient Planets! Long life! To my old
friend the Speaker for the Weft!"

Coromell sighed and leaned toward Lunzie. "This
is going to take a long time. Your patience and
forbearance are appreciated."

Lunzie stifled a giggle and raised her glass to the
Ryxi.

"I can't wear the same dress to two diplomatic
functions in a row," Lunzie explained to Coromell
over lunch the next day. "I'm going shopping for a
second gown."

When she had arrived on Tau Ceti, Lunzie had
marked down in her mind the new shopping center
that adjoined the spaceport. Originally the site had
been a field used for large-vehicle repair and construction of housing modules, half hidden by a hill of
mounded dirt suitable for sliding down by the local
children.

The hill was still there, landscaped and clipped to
the most stringent gardening standard. Behind it lay
a beautifully constructed arcade of dark red brick and
the local soft gray stone. In spite of the conservative
appearance, the high atrium rang with the laughter
of children, five generations descended from the ones
Fiona had once played with. Lunzie overheard animated conversations echoing through the corridors
as she strolled.

Most of the stores were devoted to oxygen-breathers,
though at the ground level there were specialty shops

with airlock hatches instead of doors to serve customers whose atmosphere differed from the norm. Lunzie
window-shopped along one level and wound her way
up the ramp to the next, mentally measuring dresses
and outfits for herself. The variety for sale was im-
pressive, perhaps too impressively large. She doubted
whether there were three stores here which would
have anything to suit her. Some of the fashions were
very extreme. She stood back to peruse the show
windows.

In the lexan panes, she caught a glimpse of something very large moving toward her from the left.
Lunzie looked up. A party of heavyworld humans
was stumping down the walkway, angling to get past
her. She recognized the somber male at the head of
the group as the representative from Diplo, whom
Coromell had pointed out to her at the Ryxi party.
They took up so much of the ramp walking two
abreast that Lunzie scooted into Finzer's Fashions
until they passed.

"How may I assist you, Citizen?" A human male
two-thirds of Lunzie's height with elegantly frilled
ears approached her, bowing and smiling. "I am
Finzer, the proprietor of this fine outlet."

Lunzie glanced out into the atrium. The party was
gone, all except for one female who had stopped to
look into one shop window across the corridor. And
she wasn't one of the Diplo cortege. It was the
Parchandri's bodyguard, Quinada. The heavyworld
female turned, and her dark eyes met Lunzie's with
a stupid, heavy gaze. Lunzie smiled at her, hoping a
polite response was in order. Quinada stared back
expressionlessly for a moment before walking away.
Puzzled, Lunzie glanced back at the shopkeeper,
who was still waiting by her side.

"I'm looking for evening wear," she told Finzer.
"Do you have something classic in a size ten?"

Finzer produced a classic dress in dusty rose pink

with a bodice that hugged Lunzie's rib cage and a full evening skirt that swirled around her feet.

Two evenings later, she held the folds of the dress bunched up on her lap as she and Coromell rode toward the Parchandri's residence.

"I'm not imagining it, Coromell," Lunzie said firmly. "Quinada's been everywhere that I've gone these past two days. Every time I turned around, she was there. She's following me."

"Coincidence," Coromell said blithely. "The area in which the Tau Ceti diplomatic set circulate is surprisingly small. You and Quinada had smiliar errands this week, that's all."

"That's not all. She stares at me, with a look I can only describe as hungry. I don't trust that perverse unscrup she works for any further than I could toss him. Didn't you see how his eyes glittered when I said I'd been spacewrecked? He's got nasty tastes in amusement."

"You're making too much of coincidence," Coromell offered gently. "Certainly you're safe from perversion here in Tau Ceti. Kidnapping is a serious breach of diplomatic immunity, one a man of Ienois's status and family position would hardly risk. As for that aide of his, you told me yourself that you have a deep-seated fear of heavyworlders."

"I do not have a persecution complex," Lunzie said in dead earnest. "Putting aside my deep-seated fear, once I got to thinking that Quinada might be following me, I tried to lose her. Tell me why she was in four different provisions stores without buying a thing! Or three different beauty salons! Not only that, she was waiting outside the FSP complex when I finished my Discipline lessons."

Coromell was thoughtful. "You're convinced, aren't you?"

"I am. And I think it probably has to do with ambrosia, even if you won't enlighten me on that score." Coromell smiled slightly at the reference but said nothing, which further annoyed her in her circumstances. Ambrosia must be a classified matter at the highest level, and she was only the envelope which had delivered the letter, not entitled to know more. Stubbornly, she continued. "I don't think Ienois's reference was as casual as you do, despite his unassailable diplomatic status. In any event, I find his aide's surveillance sinister."

"On a personal level, there's not much I can do to discourage that, Lunzie. However," and he cocked his head at her, a sly gleam in his eyes, "enlist in Fleet Intelligence and you have the service to protect you."

Lunzie cast a long searching look at his handsome face to dispel the unworthy thought that popped into her head. "To what ends *would* you go, Admiral Coromell, to get me into Fleet Intelligence?"

"I do want you in FI—you'd be a great asset, and frankly it would be wonderful having you around— but not at any cost. I can't compromise Fleet regulations, not that you'd want me to, and I can't give you any special consideration, not that you'd accept it anyway. The most important thing of all, Lunzie, is that you're willing to join. Even if I could press you into service, that's not the kind of recruit we want. I do know that you'd be ten times better as an operative than someone like Quinada . . . if you do decide to volunteer."

Lunzie hesitated, then nodded. "All right. I'm in."

Coromell smiled and squeezed her arm. "Good. I'll see to your credentials tomorrow morning. There will be a follow-up interview, but I have most of the details of your life on disk already. I hope you won't regret it. I don't think you will."

"I'm feeling more secure already," Lunzie said, sincerely.

"Good timing. We've arrived."

The Parchandri mansion lay on the outskirts of the main Tau Ceti settlement. Ienois and a group of Parchandri were waiting on the steps to greet their guests in the deepening twilight. Pots to either side of the wide doors swirled heavily scented and colored smoke into the air. Two servants met each vehicle as it pulled up. One opened the door as the other ascertained who was inside and announced the names to the hosts. Lunzie caught a passing glimpse of burning dark eyes in pasty-white faces and gulped. The unexpected appearance of representatives of the same race as the assassins in the Alpha Centauri restaurant was unsettling to say the least. The burning eyes, however, held no flicker of recognition. But then, why should they? She was getting overly sensitive to too many coincidences.

Ienois greeted them warmly, introducing Coromell to members of his family. Each was dressed in garb of such understated elegance Lunzie found herself trying to estimate the value of their clothes. If her guess was correct, each Parchandri was wearing more than the value of the clothes on the entire party of diplomats. As the evening weather was fine, drinks were circulated under the portico by liveried servants.

"Admiral Coromell! And Lunzzie, how very niccce to sssee you again," said the Seti Ambassador, wending his way ponderously up the front stairs from the welcoming committee. "Admiral, I had hoped to sssee you a few days ago, but I missssed my opportunity."

Knowing a hint for privacy when she heard one, Lunzie excused herself. "I'll just find the ladies' lounge," she told Coromell, placing her drink on the tray of a passing servant.

Asking directions from one of the Parchandri ladies, Lunzie made her way into the building. Ienois had given her no more than a disinterested "Good evening," which reassured her. Maybe her assumption was only part of her heightened awareness since

that disastrous evening with Aelock. She was pleased
to have escaped his attention. Rumors she had heard
since the Ryxi party confirmed her feelings about his
proclivities and the reality was worse than she had
imagined. Discounting half of what she'd heard, he
was still far too sophisticated in his perversities.

Lunzie found herself in the Great Hall, a high-
ceilinged chamber in an old-fashioned, elegant style.
The ladies' lounge for humanoids was at the end of a
pink marble corridor just to the right of the double
winding staircase with gold-plated pillars which spiralled to the three upper floors. Several other corridors, all darkened, led away from the Hall on this
level.

"How beautiful! They certainly do know how to
live," Lunzie murmured. Her voice rang in the big,
empty room. The lights were low, but there was
enough illumination at the far end of the corridor for
her to see another woman emerging from a swinging
door. "Ah. There it is."

Lunzie readjusted her makeup in the mirror once
more, straightened the skirt of her dress, and then
sat down with a thump on the couch provided under
the corner-mounted sconces which illuminated the
room. No one else was making use of the facilities,
so she was quite alone. There was only so much
time she could waste in the ladies' room. It was
a shame she didn't know any of the other diplomats
present. She hoped that Coromell had nearly finished
his negotiations with the Seti.

Well, she couldn't stay hidden in the lounge for
the entire evening. She would have to circulate.
Sighing, she pushed open the lounge door to return
to the party. There, on the other side, was Quinada,
massively blocking the hallway. Startled, Lunzie stood
aside to let her by, intending to squeeze out and
return to Coromell. The heavyworlder female filled
the doorway and came on. Lunzie backed a few paces

and stepped to the left, angling to pass as soon as the door was clear. Quinada wrapped a burly hand around her upper arm and steered her, protesting, back into the lounge.

"Here you are," she said, bearing the lightweight woman back into a corner of the room. "I've been waiting for you."

"You have?" Lunzie asked in polite surprise. She braced herself and looked for a way around the heavyworlder's massive frame. "Why?"

Quinada's heavy brow ridges lowered sullenly over her eyes. "My employer wants you disposed of. I must follow his orders. I don't really want to, but I serve him."

Lunzie trembled. So her intuitions hadn't erred. Ienois suspected her. But to order her death on the strength of a recognized word? The heavyworlder pressed her back against the wall and eyed her smugly. Quinada could crush her to death by just bearing down.

Mastering her fear, Lunzie gazed into the other's eyes. "You don't want to kill me?" she asked simply, hoping she didn't sound as if she was begging. That could arouse the sadistic side of the big female's nature. Quinada was the type who would enjoy hurting her. And Lunzie needed just a little more time to muster Discipline. She had already made a tactical mistake, allowing herself to be put at a significant physical disadvantage. Quinada and her master must have been hoping for the opportunity. Quinada had seen her emerging from the FSP complex. Could they possibly know that she was an Adept?

"No, I don't want to kill you," Quinada cooed in a lighter voice, charged with implications which alarmed Lunzie considerably more. "Not if I don't have to. If you weren't my enemy, I wouldn't have to kill you at all."

"I'm not your enemy," Lunzie said soothingly.

"No? You smiled at me."

"I was trying to be friendly," Lunzie replied, disliking the intent and appraising fashion in which Quinada was staring at her.

"I wasn't sure. In this city all the diplomats smile, in deference to the lightweights. Their smiles are phony."

"Well, I'm not a diplomat. When I smile, it's genuine. I'm not paid to practice diplomacy." Lunzie rapidly assessed her chances of talking her way out of this tight spot. If she used Discipline but didn't kill the heavyworlder, her secret would be out. The next attempt on her life wouldn't be face to face. But if she used Discipline to kill, her ability would be revealed when Medical examination would show that a small female's hands had delivered the death blows. And then she'd have an Adept tribunal to face.

"Good," Quinada said, narrowing her eyes to glinting lights under her thick brow ridges, and leaning closer. Lunzie could feel the heat of the big female's skin almost against her own. "That pleases me. I want you to be friendly with me. My employer doesn't like you but if we are friends, I can't treat you like an enemy, can I? That's such a pretty gown." Quinada stroked the fabric covering Lunzie's shoulder with the back of one thick finger. "I saw you when you bought it. It suits you so well, brings out your coloring. You attract me. We don't have to stay at this dull party. Come away with me now. Perhaps we can share warmth."

Lunzie was frightened, but now she had a tremendous urge to laugh. The heavyworlder was offering to trade Lunzie's life for her favors! This scene would have been uproariously funny if it hadn't been in deadly earnest. If she managed to live through it, she could look back on it and laugh.

"Come with me, we'll be friends, and I'll forget my instructions," Quinada offered, purring. Her stare had turned proprietary. Lunzie tried not to squirm with disgust.

Masking her revulsion at Quinada's touch, Lunzie thought that even with the heavyworlder's promised protection, she was likely to wind up dead. Ienois was the sort of man whose orders were followed. How could Quinada fake her death? She had to get away, to warn Coromell. She found herself measuring her words carefully, injecting them with sufficient promise to seem compliant.

"Not now. The Admiral will be waiting for me. I'll give him the slip and meet you later." Lunzie forced herself to give Quinada's arm a soft caress, though her hand felt slimy as she completed the gesture. "It's important to keep up appearances. You know that."

"A secret meeting," Quinada smiled, her lips twisting to one side. "Very well. It adds excitement. When?"

"When the toasting is over," Lunzie promised. "They'll miss me if I'm not there to salute your master. But then I can meet you wherever you say."

"That's true," Quinada agreed, backing away from her. "That is the custom. And your disappearance would be marked."

Lunzie nodded encouragingly and stepped toward the door. Before she had taken a second one, Quinada seized her bare arm and slapped her smartly across the cheek. Lunzie's head snapped back on her neck, and she stared wide-eyed at the heavyworlder, who gripped her with steely fingertips, and then let go. Lunzie staggered back and leaned against the wall to steady herself.

"Where do we meet? You haven't said that. If you are lying, I will kill you." Quinada's voice was caressing and chilled Lunzie to the bone.

"But we meet here," she said as if that had been a foregone conclusion. "It's the safest place. As soon as the toasting is done, I'll come back here and wait for you. That conceited Admiral will think I wish to make myself pretty for him. See you then, Quinada, but I've been gone a long time. I must get back." With a dazzling smile, Lunzie ducked under her arm and out the door.

Whether Quinada would have followed or not became academic, for a group of five chattering humans were coming down the corridor towards the ladies' room, providing a safeguard.

When Lunzie found Coromell and his ambassador, the Seti was expressing his gratitude to Coromell. He bowed to Lunzie as he turned away. Lunzie managed an appropriate response even as she pulled the admiral to one side behind the smoking incense pots.

"I must talk to you," she hissed, casting around to see if Quinada had followed her. To her relief, the heavyworld woman was nowhere in sight.

"Where have you been?" he asked, then clucked his tongue in concern. "What happened? You've bruised your arm. And there's another mark on your cheek."

"Darling Quinada, the Parchandri's aide," Lunzie whispered, letting the revulsion she felt color her words with bitter sarcasm, "followed me to the ladies' lounge and jumped me there." She took some satisfaction in the shock on Coromell's face which he quickly controlled. "She's under his orders to kill me! She didn't only because I tentatively accepted an exchange for my life I have no intention of granting. I'm Fleet now, Coromell. Protect me. Get me out of here! Now!"

BOOK FOUR

Chapter Eleven

She went into hiding in a Fleet-owned safe house while Coromell arranged for a shuttle to take her off-planet. Except for the Discipline Master and Admiral Coromell Senior, there was no one to regret her abrupt departure—except perhaps Quinada. But Lunzie did want the Adept to realize that she had been unavoidably called away. That was Discipline courtesy. Her studies in the special course had progressed to a point where she didn't need direct instruction although she had hoped to obtain permission to teach what she had learned. As it was, the powerful new techniques would take her years to perfect.

The next day a shuttle made a rendezvous in space with the Exploration and Evaluation Corps *ARCT-10*, a multi-generation, multi-environmental vessel that carried numerous exploration scouts and shuttlecraft. Lunzie was transferred aboard. Her files were edited so that her enlistment in Fleet Intelligence had been excised and a false employment record with the Tau Ceti medical center inserted. She was an ordinary doctor, joining the complement of the *ARCT-10* to explore and document new planets for colonization.

"There are thousands of beings aboard," Coromell had assured her. "You'll just be one of several hundred human specialists who sign on for three-year stints with the EEC. No one will have any reason to look twice at you. Once you're settled in, you can be another remote sensor on that vessel for me. Keep an ear open."

"You mean, I'm not entirely safe on board?"

"Far safer than on Tau Ceti," he replied encouragingly. "Blend in but don't call attention to yourself. You should be fine. You've got me slightly paranoid for your sake now." He ran restless fingers through his hair and gave her an exasperated look. "Think safe and you'll be safe! Just be cautious."

"I'm totally reassured!"

Once her shuttle matched velocity with the *ARCT-10*, it circled around the back of the long stern to the docking bay. The ship was built with a series of cylinders arranged in a ring with arcs joining each segment. Along the dorsal edge of the ship, Lunzie could see a partially shaded quartz dome which probably contained the hydroponics section. The drives, below and astern of the docking bay, could easily have swallowed the tiny shuttle up without a burp. The five exhaust cones arranged in a ring, rimed with a film of ice crystals, were almost a hundred feet across. The *ARCT-10* was reputed to be 250 years old. It had an air of majestic dignity, instead of creaking old age. It was the oldest of the original EEC generation ships still in space.

There was a Thek waiting in the docking bay as the shuttle doors cracked open. The meter-high specimen waited while Lunzie greeted the deck officer, then neatly blocked her path when she started to leave the deck without acknowledging it.

"I beg your pardon," she said, stopping short, and waited for the translator slung around the Thek's peak to slow her words down enough for it to understand.

"Ttttooooooooooooooorrrrrr," it drawled.

Tor. "Your name?" she asked. Talking with a Thek

was like playing the child's party game of Twenty Questions, but there was no guarantee she would get twenty answers. Theks did not like to use unnecessary verbiage when a syllable or two would do.

"Yyyyyeeeeessssss." Good, that was short and easy. This must be a relatively young Thek. There was more. Lunzie braced herself to comprehend Tor's voice.

"Llllllluuunnnnnnnnn . . . . . . zzzzzzzzzziiiiiieeeeeee . . . . sssssaaaaaaaaffffffeeeee . . . . . . hhhhhhhheeee eeerrrrrrrreeeeee."

Well, bless Coromell. She'd no idea he had Thek confederates aboard the *ARCT-10*. If he'd only thought to mention it, she'd have been more reassured.

"Thank you, Tor," she said. Although come to think on it, she wondered how much help a Thek could provide, flattering though such an offer was from such a source. Even the Thek who had pointed out her escape capsule to Illin Romsey hadn't been able to tow her in on its own. A thought struck her. Theks had no real defining characteristics, but this one was the same size as that Thek. "By any chance, were you the one—no, that's too long—Tor . . . rescued me . . . Descartes?"

A short rumble, sounding like an abbreviated version of his previous "yes," issued from the depths of the silicoid cone. Now this is one for the books, Lunzie thought, much heartened. Then Tor moved aside as an officer entered the landing bay with a hand out for Lunzie and it settled down into anonymous immobility.

"Doctor, welcome aboard," the tall man said. He had the attenuated fingers, limbs and long face that marked him as one of the ship-born, a human who had spent his whole life in space. The lighter gravity frequently allowed humans to grow taller on slenderer, wider-spaced bones than the planet-born. They also proved immune to the calcium attrition that planet-born space travellers experienced on long journeys. As she shook his hand, Lunzie had an uncomfortable feeling of déjà vu. Except for eyes that were green, not brown, the young man fit perfectly the genotype of the banned colony-clones that she'd investigated as a member of the investigative panel on Astris seventy years ago as a medical student. "I'm Lieutenant Sanborn. We had your records just two hours ago. It'll be good to have someone with your trauma specialty on board. Spacebound paranoia is one of the worst things we have to deal with. Walking wounded, you know. You have general training as well?"

"I can sew up wounds and deliver babies, if that's what you mean," Lunzie said drily.

Sanborn threw back his head and laughed. He seemed to be a likeable young man. She felt bad about teasing him. "I shouldn't have asked for a two-byte resume. Sorry. Let me show you to the visitors' quarters. You're in luck. There's an individual sleeping cubicle available in the visitor's section." He held out a hand for her bags and hoisted them over his shoulder. "This way, please, Lunzie."

Her compartment was tiny and spare, but just big enough to be comfortable. Lunzie put her things away in the drop-down ceiling locker before she followed Sanborn to the common room to get acquainted with her shipmates. The common room doubled as a light-use recreation center.

"The last third of each shift is reserved for conversation only so we don't have to worry about a game of grav-ball bouncing over our heads," Sanborn explained as he introduced Lunzie around. The common rooms in the humanoid oxygen-breathers' section were set with free-form furniture that managed to comfortably accommodate the smallest Weft or the largest heavyworlder.

"Welcome aboard," said the man in blue coveralls who was lounging with his seat tipped backwards against the wall. He had a smooth, dark brown skin and large, mild eyes.

A sallow-faced young man dressed in a pale green lab tunic sat nearby with his elbows braced on the back of his chair and glanced up at her expressionlessly. "I'm Coe. Join us. Do you play chess?" the dark man asked.

"Later perhaps, eh?" Sanborn intervened before she could answer. "I've got to get Lunzie to Orientation."

"Any time," Coe replied, waving.

His companion swept another look and met Lunzie's eyes, and said something to Coe. Lunzie thought she heard her name and the word "ambrosia."

Panic gripped her insides. Oh, no! she thought. Have I left one bad situation for a worse one? I'm trapped aboard this vessel with someone who knows about ambrosia!

"Who's that young man with Coe?" she asked Sanborn, forcing her voice to stay calm.

"Oh, that's Chacal. He's a communications tech. Not much of a conversationalist for a com-tech. Coe is the only one who can stand him. Keeps to himself when he's not on duty."

That would be appropriate if he was an agent for the Parchandri, or the planet pirates. Lunzie wondered to which, if either, Chacal might be attached. She wished she could speak to Coromell, but he was out of reach. Lunzie was on her own, for good or ill. What was the meaning of "ambrosia," anyway? Or was she simply exhibiting symptoms of spacebound paranoia, as Sanborn put it?

The ARCT-10 was so huge that it was easy to forget that she was travelling through space instead of living on a planet. It was designed to be entirely self-sufficient, not needing to make contact with a planet for years. Sanborn took Lunzie to the Administration offices by way of the life support dome where fresh vegetables, fruit, and grain were grown for carbohydrates to feed the synthesizers and to supplement the otherwise boring synth diet as well as refreshing the oxygen in the atmosphere. Lunzie admired the section, which was twice as big as the hydroponics plant aboard the *Destiny Calls*, though by no means stocked with the same exotic varieties.

One section of the ship was the multi-generation hive, where the Ship-born and Ship-bred lived, apart from the "Visitors' habitation." She quickly discovered that there was an unspoken rivalry between the two groups. The Ship-born were snobbish about the Visitors' difficulty adapting to almost all-synth food and the cramped living conditions on board. The Visitors, who were often part of the ship's complement for years on end, couldn't understand why the Ship-born were so proud of living under such limited conditions, like laboratory animals who were reduced to minimum needs. It was obvious to each group that its way was better. Mostly the rivalry was good-natured.

Since the Visitors on the ship were mission scientists or colonists awaiting transport to FSP sanctioned colonies, few crossed the boundary to socialize between groups. The matter was temporary, as far as the Visitors were concerned. On average, Visitors lasted about three years on the *ARCT*. When they could no longer stand the conditions, they quit.

The Ship-born felt they could ignore anyone for three years if they wanted to. In the million-light-year vision of the generation ships, that was just an eyeblink. Fortunately for more gregarious souls like Lunzie who joined the EEC, the boundaries were less than a formality.

Several of the major FSP races had groups aboard the *ARCT-10* in both habitations. Heavyworlders occupied specially pressurized units designed to duplicate the gravity and harsh weather conditions of their native worlds. The Ryxi needed more square meters per being than the other groups did. Many Visitors were resentful of the seemingly spacious quarters the Ryxi occupied, though the Ship-born understood that it was the minimum the Ryxi could stand.

Theks skimmed smoothly through the corridors like mountains receding in the distance with no extraneous movement. They ranged in size from Tor's one meter to a seven-meter specimen who lived in the hydroponics section and who spoke so slowly that it took a week to produce a comprehensible word. A small complement of Brachians worked aboard ship. Lunzie recognized their long-armed silhouettes immediately in their low-light habitation. A family of the marine race of Ssli occupied their only environment in the Ship-born hive. Those Ssli had resolved to devote their entire line to serving the EEC, and the *ARCT-10* was grateful for their expertise in chemistry and energy research.

As on the Descartes mining platform, there was an effort made to draw the inhabitants of the ship together as a community, rather than passengers on a vessel intended only for research and exploration. There was an emphasis on family involvement, in which praise was given not only to the child which got good grades, but for the family which supported and encouraged a child's success. Individual accomplishment was not ignored, but acknowledged in the context of the community. But Lunzie never sensed a heavy administrative hand ensuring that all were equally treated. Departments were given autonomy in their fields. The EEC administration only stepped in when necessary to ease understanding between them. Denizens of the ship were encouraged to sort out matters for themselves. Lunzie admired the system. It fostered achievement in an atmosphere of cooperation.

When she wasn't researching or working an infirmary shift, Lunzie spent time in the common room getting to know her shipmates, and her ship. The

ARCT-10 had been in space a hundred and fifty
Earth-Standard years. Some of the Ship-born were
descended from families who had been aboard since
its commissioning. One day, Lunzie became part of a
lively discussion group that held court in the middle
of the floor, suspending the normal polarization of
Visitors to one end of the room and Ship-born to the
other.

"But how can you stand the food?" Varian asked
Grabone, rolling over on her free-form cushion to
face him. Varian was a tall Xenobiologist Visitor. "It's
been recycled through the pipes, too, for seven
generations."

"Not at all," Grabone replied. "We use fresh carbohydrates for food. The recyclate is used for other
purposes, such as fertilizer and plas-sheeting. We're
completely self-sufficient." The Ship-born engineer's
shock of red hair helped to express his outrage.
"How can you question a system with less than four
percent breakdown over a hundred years?"

"But there's something lacking in the aesthetics,"
Lunzie said, entering the discussion. "I've never been
able to stand synthesizer food myself. It's the memory of real food, not the actual stuff."

"If your cooks just didn't make synth food so boring!" Varian said in disgust. "It'd be almost palatable
if it had some recognizable taste. I'll bet, Grabone,
that you've never *had* real food. Not even the vegetables they grow on the upper deck."

"Why take chances?" demanded Grabone, leaning
back defiantly on the floor and crossing his ankles.
"You could poison yourself with unhygienically grown
foodstuffs. You know the synth food is safe, and
nourishing."

"Have you ever even tried naturally grown food?"
Varian demanded.

"Can't tell the difference if I have. I've never been
off the *ARCT-10*," Grabone admitted. "I'm a drives

engineer. There's no reason for me to have to make planetfall on, I might point out, potentially hazardous missions. Risk your own neck. Leave mine alone."

"Life can be hazardous to your health," Lunzie said cheerfully to Varian beside her. She liked the lively, curly-haired girl who was unable to sit still for more than a few minutes. They did Discipline exercises together in the early shift. Lunzie could tell that Varian's training was of the most basic, though it would seem advanced to anyone who was not an Adept. "How are you chosen to go on planetside missions?" she asked Varian. "Do I have to put my name in the duty roster?"

"Oh, no," Varian replied. "Nothing that organized. Each mission requires such different skills that the first person off the queue might not be qualified. Details of a mission's personnel needs are posted days before the actual drop. If you're interested, you inform Comm Center and you're listed as available. A mission leader then picks the complement. Some missions are planned at FSP Center. Some develop out of circumstances. Let me explain. The *ARCT-10*'s job is to keep tabs on all the Exploration and Evaluation vessels in our sector and support them with ground teams when necessary. So you really never know what's or who's going to be needed. The *ARCT* also keeps checking in on message beacons previously set in this sector by initial EEC scouts. They strip off messages whenever we're in line of sight and send reports back to FSP Center. If a recon or an emergency team are needed, *ARCT* supplies it. So really," and Varian shrugged, "you can gain a lot of xeno experience in a three year stint."

"And that's what you're after?" Lunzie said.

"You bet! That's what'll get me a good dirtside job." Then her vivacious face changed and she lowered her voice. "There may be a very good one coming up. I've a friend in Com and he said for me to keep my ears open."

"Then you're not at all nervous about the scuttle-butt I've been hearing?"

"Which one?" asked Varian scornfully.

"The one about planting colonists without their permission?"

"That old one." Grabone was openly derisive. "Rumors sometimes start themselves, you know. I'll excuse you this time, Lunzie, since I know you're not long on board. You wouldn't know how many times that one's oozed through the deckplates."

"That's reassuring," Lunzie said. "It seems so unlike an official EEC position."

"It's a lot of space dust," Grabone went on. "You got that from the heavyworlders, didn't you? Their favorite paranoia. They think we'll strand them the first chance we get. Well, it isn't true."

"No, actually, it wasn't the heavyworlders," Lunzie said slowly; she'd kept well away from any of that group. "It was one of the visiting scientists who wants only to finish his duty and go home on time. I gather he's expecting a grandchild."

"For one thing," Grabone went on to prove the rumor fallacious, "*ARCT-10* can't plant anyone. Colonies take years of planning. It's hard enough to find the right mix of people who want to settle on a certain world, and live together in peace, not to say cooperation. You wouldn't believe the filework that has to go out to EEC before a colony is approved."

"Well, planting would be a quicker, if illicit, way to get more colonies started," Varian suggested. "There are some found that don't meet minimum requirements but if people were planted, they'd learn to cope."

"Doesn't anyone planetside practice birth control?" Lunzie asked, with a vivid memory of the crowds on Alpha Centauri. "Having dozens of offspring without a thought for environment or a reasonable standard of living for future citizens."

"Even a mathematical expansion of the population, one child per adult," Varian pointed out, "would soon deplete currently available resources, let alone a geometric increase. Judicious planting could reduce some of the pressure. Not that I advocate it, mind you."

One of the lights of the duty panel flickered. Involuntarily everyone in the room glanced at the blue medical light. Lunzie clambered to her feet. "I can respond."

She flipped on the switch at the panel. "Lunzie."

"Accident at interface A-10. One crew member down, several others injured."

Lunzie mentally plotted the fastest path to the scene of the accident and hit the comswitch again.

"Acknowledged," she said. "I'm on my way." She waved farewell to Grabone and Varian.

The interfaces were one of the most sensitive and carefully watched parts of the multi-environmental system aboard the ARCT-10. Whereas normal bulkheads were accustomed to the pressure of a single atmosphere, the interfaces had to stand between two different atmospheric zones, sometimes of vastly different pressure levels which might also vary according to program. A-10 stood between the normal-weight human environment and the heavyworlders' gravity zone. Had this happened in her first few weeks aboard, she'd have become hopelessly lost. Now she knew the scheme which named decks and section by location and personnel, she knew she wasn't far from A-10 and found her way there without trouble.

Dozens of other crew members were on the move through the corridors in the A Section. At the point at which A-10 had been breached, frigid wind of the same temperature as the ambient on Diplo was pouring through into the warmer lightweight zone. Clutching her medical bag to her chest, Lunzie passed through a hastily erected baffle chamber that cut off the icy winds from the rest of the deck and would act as a temporary barrier while the heavy gravity was restored. Beyond the broken wall, heavyworlders who had been in their exercise room were picking up weights and bodybuilding equipment made suddenly light by the drop in gravity. Workers of every configuration hurried in and out of the chambers, clearing away debris, tying down torn circuits and redirecting pipes whose broken ends pumped sewage and water across the floor. Lunzie made a wide circle around two workers who were cutting out the ragged remains of the damaged panel with an arc torch.

"Doctor, quickly!" An officer in the black uniform of environmental sciences motioned urgently where she knelt by the far wall. "Orlig's twitching even if he is unconscious. He was checking the wall when it blew."

Lunzie hurried over, ignoring the stench of sewage and the odor of burned flesh. Stretched out on the deck at the woman's side was a gigantic heavyworlder wearing a jumpsuit and protective goggles. He had been severely gashed by flying metal and a tremendous hematoma colored the side of his face. Though his eyes were closed, he was thrashing wildy and muttering. Lunzie's hands flew to her belt pouch for her bod bird.

"I don't dare give him a sedative until I know if there's neural damage, Truna," Lunzie explained.

"You do what you have to do. Other heavyworlders incurred only heavy bruises when the wall popped and they were blown against the bulkhead toward light gravity. They walked away. No one else was on this side of the wall. Orlig took the full blast. Poor beast." The environment tech got up and began shouting orders at the mob of workers, leaving Lunzie alone with her patient.

Orlig was one of the largest specimens of his subgroup that Lunzie had ever seen. Her outstretched hand covered only his palm and third phalange of his fingers. She had no idea what she would do if he went out of control.

"Fardling lightweights," he snarled, thrashing. Lunzie jumped back out of range as his swinging arm just missed her and smashed onto the deck. "Set me up to die! I'll kill them!" The arm swept up, fingers curved like claws, ripping at the air, and smashed down again, shaking the deck. "All of them!"

Nervous but equally determined not to let her fear of heavyworlders keep her from treating one in desperate need of her skills, Lunzie approached to take a bod bird reading. According to that, Orlig was bleeding internally. He had to be sedated and treated before he hemorrhaged to death.

She couldn't fix his arm while he was banging it around like that. The bod bird was inconclusive on the point of neural trauma. She would have to take her chances. She programmed a hefty dose of sedative and applied the hypogun to the nearest fleshy part of the thrashing man. Orlig levered himself up when he felt the injection hiss against his upper arm and snarled bare-toothed at Lunzie. The drug took speedy effect and his arms collapsed under him. He fell to the deck with a bang.

Still shaking, Lunzie began debriding his wounds and slapping patches of synthskin on them. Shards of metal had been driven into his flesh through the heavy fabric of the jumpsuit. The goggles had spared his eyes though the plasglas lens were cracked. What with flying debris and the force of the explosion, the man was lucky to be alive. She tried to think which ship's system could have blown like that.

Unbelievably, Orlig started moving again. How could he move? She'd given him enough sedative to sleep six shifts. Lunzie worked faster. She must unseal the upper half of his jumpsuit to repair his wounds. The fabric was so heavy she got mired in the folds of it. Then in a restless gesture, he jerked his arm and sent Lunzie stumbling across the room.

Lunzie crawled back to him and gathered her equipment together in her lap. She programmed the hypo for another massive dose of sedative and held it to the heavyworlder's arm. Just as she was about to push the button, Orlig's small eyes opened and focused on hers. His gigantic hand closed around her hand and wrist, immobilizing her but not hurting her.

He'll kill me! Lunzie thought nervously. She drew in a breath to yell for help from the struggling engineers at the broken wall.

"Who are you?" he demanded, bringing the other fist up under her face.

Lunzie kept her voice low out of fear. "My name is Lunzie. I'm a doctor."

Orlig's eyes narrowed, but the fist dropped. "Lunzie? Do you know a Thek?"

He's raving, Lunzie thought. "Orlig, please lie back. You were badly injured. I can't treat you if you keep thrashing about. Let go of my hand." Sometimes a firm no-nonsense voice reassured a nervous patient.

His fist grabbed her up by the neck of her tunic. "Do you know a Thek?"

"Yes. Tor."

Subtly the heavyworlder's attitude altered. He swiveled his head around to glare at the bustling crowd of workers and technicians, and wrinkled his nose at the sewage, now being mopped up.

"Then get me out of here. Someplace no one would expect to find me." With that he let her go and sagged to the floor.

Lunzie shouted for a gurney and waited by Orlig until it came. She sent an emergency crewman back for a grav lift so that she could manage the gurney herself in spite of Orlig's mass. He snarled when the crewman came a centimeter closer to him than necessary. He had to be in considerable pain with those wounds. She wondered just why he was braving it out. Without any help he somehow rolled his mangled body onto the gurney.

"Get me out of here," he muttered, eyes glittering with pain and an underlying fear that he permitted her to glimpse.

Operating the anti-grav lift, she guided the gurney out of the interface area, through one hatch, running along beside her patient and up a freight turbovator.

"Anybody following?" he demanded urgently, gripping her hand in his huge fingers.

"No, no one. Not even a rat."

He grunted. "Hurry it up."

"This was all your idea." But then she saw what she was looking for, one of the small first-aid stations that were located on every deck and section, usually for routine medichecks, contagion isolation quarters, or treatments that didn't require stays in the main infirmary.

Once the door slid shut behind them, Orlig grinned up at her.

"Krims, but you lightweights are easy to scare." He surveyed the room with a searching glance as Lunzie positioned the gurney by the soft-topped examination table which doubled as a hospital bed when the sides were raised. He raised a hand as Lunzie started toward him with the hypo. "No, no more sedatives. I'm practically unconscious now."

Lunzie stared at him. "I thought you must be immune to it."

Orlig grimaced. "I had to use pain to stay awake. Someone rigged that wall to fall on me. They want me dead."

With a sigh, Lunzie recognized the classic symp-

toms of agoraphobic paranoia. She put away the
hypospray and held up the flesh-knitter.

"Well, I'm a doctor and as I've never seen you
before, I have no urge to kill you." Yet, she thought.
"And since you heavyworlders are such big machismo
types, I'll sew you into one piece again in front of
your eyes. Does that relieve your mind?"

"Coromell didn't say you'd be so dumb, Doctor."

Lunzie nearly dropped the piece of equipment in
her hands. "Coromell?" she repeated. "First you want
to know my Thek acquaintances, now you're throwing the Admiralty at me. Just who are you?"

"I work for him, too. And I've got some information that he's got to have. This isn't the first attempt
on my life. I've been trying to figure out a legitimate
reason to contact you. But I had to be careful. Couldn't
have suspicion fall on you . . ."

"Like a wall fell on you?" Lunzie put in.

"Yeah, but it's working out just right, isn't it? I
can't risk this information getting lost." He groaned.
"I tried to get in touch with Tor. I think that's where
I blew it. Us heavyworlders don't generally seek out
Theks." He winced. "All right, I think I'll accept a
local anesthetic now you're playing tinkertoy with
my ribs. It feels like meteors were shot through it.
What's it look like?"

Lunzie peered at his chest and ran the bod bird
over it. "Like you got meteors shot through it. I
might be able to reach Tor without anyone suspect-
ing me. I don't know why, but it likes me."

"Few are as lucky. But you've got to find the right
Thek without asking for it by name. That's the hard
part. They all look alike at the size they fit on the
ARCT. Look . . ." Orlig's voice was weaker now as
shock began to seep through his formidable physical
stamina. He fumbled in his left ear, tilting his head.
"Fardles. You got something like tweezers? That wall
must've knocked it down inside."

"What am I looking for?"

"A message brick." He turned his head so she had the best angle for the search.

"You might have irreparably damaged your hearing," she said, disapprovingly as she finally retrieved the cube.

"It fit. It was safe," Orlig replied, unpenitent. "If you can't get to Tor, wait until Zebara gets back. You can tell him to check out AidkisagI VIII, the Seti of Fomalhaut. The cube gives him the rest of the pertinent details."

"The Seti of . . . their head of government?" Lunzie's voice rose in pitch to a surprised squeak.

"Shh! Keep it down!" Orlig hissed. "Whoever rigged that wall to blow may be looking for me now he knows he failed to kill me."

"Who?"

Orlig rolled his eyes at her naivete.

"Sorry."

"Wise up, gal, or you can end up like me. And you couldn't stand a wall falling on you." His voice was now a thin trickle of sound.

She tucked the cube into her soft ship boot. "Tor or Zebara. Count on me. Now, I stop being courier and start being medic."

Just as she finished and had him plas-skinned, his eyes sagged shut. The sedative and shock were finally overwhelming him.

"You're safe now," Lunzie murmured. "I'll pull the food synthesizer within your reach so you don't have to get up if you're hungry or thirsty. I'll lock the room so that no one can get in. And I'll knock if I want to come in."

Orlig nodded sleepily. "Use a password. Say 'ambrosia.' That way I'll know if it's you or someone you sent."

"That particular word keeps getting me in trouble. I'll use 'whisky' instead."

As soon as she sealed the infirmary door, Lunzie immediately went back to her compartment to change out of her bloodstained clothes. She kept the cube in her boot but decided to attach her Fleet ID disk against her skin under her clothes. It was safer to keep it on her person than to risk someone finding it among her possessions. Orlig's "accident" brought a resurgence of her paranoia. Too many odd things happened to couriers of messages to Coromell.

"How's the patient?" Truna called to her as Lunzie returned to the common room. The technician and her assistants were sitting slumped over a table with steaming mugs in their hands.

"As well as can be expected for a man who's been knocked about by a bulkhead blowing out on him," Lunzie answered, programming a cup of coffee for herself. "How'd repairs go?"

"We got the wall temporarily put together again. It's going to take at least a few days to recreate the components needed to replace the damaged systems. Those circuits got truly fried!" Truna said, taking a deep drink from her mug. The woman's eyes were puffy and rimmed with red.

"What caused the explosion?" Lunzie asked, settling down at the table with the others. As soon as she sat, she realized how sore her muscles were from dealing with Orlig and his injuries.

"I was about to ask you. Could Orlig tell what happened?"

"Not really," Lunzie nodded. "He was too shocked to be lucid. Though come to think of it, he rabbited on about the chem lab. Could something have been flushed away that shouldn't be and detonated in the pipe?"

"Well, the waste pipes sure were blown into a black hole," Truna agreed. "I'll check with the biochemistry section on the ninth level. They use that disposal system. Thanks for the suggestion."

"Will Orlig recover?" a crewman asked.

"Oh, I expect so," Lunzie replied offhandedly. "Even heavyworlder physiques get bent out of shape from time to time. He'll be sore a while."

Lunzie sat with Truna and her crew for a short time, chatting and encouraging them to share their experiences with her. All the time she was apparently listening, she was wondering how she could get to Tor or how long it would be before "someone" discovered that Orlig wasn't in the infirmary. Then her thoughts would revolve back to the astonishing information that a Seti of Fomalhaut was involved in planetary piracy. That news would rock a few foundations. That was what Orlig had implied. Well, Seti were known to take gambles. The stakes would be very high, if the Phoenix affair had been any guide.

In the back of her mind, she ran scenarios on how to track down Tor. First she'd have to find out where the Theks were quartered. She couldn't just list it all on the *ARCT* e-mail channel.

"I must check up on my patient," she told the environment engineers she'd dined with. "I left him alone to sleep, but he's probably stirring again."

"Good idea," Truna said. "Tell him I hope he heals soon."

She took a circuitous route to Orlig but saw no one obviously following her.

"It's Lunzie," she announced in a low voice, tapping on the infirmary door with her knuckles. "Um, oh, whisky."

The door slid back noiselessly on its track. Orlig was behind it, clutching his injured ribs tenderly in one arm. "I wondered how long it was gonna be before you came back. I haven't been able to relax. Even with that sleep-stuff you shot into me I tossed and turned."

Lunzie pushed him into a chair so she could check the pupils of his eyes. "Sorry. That happens sometimes in shock cases. The sedative acts as an upper instead of a downer. Let me try you on calcium and L-tryptophane. It's an amino acid which the body does not produce for itself. Those should help you sleep. You don't have any sensitivities to mineral supplements, do you?"

"You sure don't know much about heavyworlders, do you? I have to pop mineral supplements all the time to keep my bones from crumbling in your puny gravity." Orlig produced a handful of uncoated vitamin tablets from a singed belt pouch and poured them into her palm.

Lunzie analyzed one with the tracer. "Iron, copper, zinc, calcium, magnesium, boron. Good. And I'll see to it that the amino acid is added to your food for the next few days. It will help you to relax and sleep naturally."

"Look, while you were gone, I thought of something to get the bugger that's after me. You can noise it about that I was critically injured and may not live," Orlig suggested grimly. "Maybe I can trick my assassins into the open. Let them think they have another chance at me while I'm weak."

"That's not only dangerous but plain stupid," Lunzie replied but he gave her such a formidable look, she shrugged in resignation. "You're healing but your injuries were severe. You may think you're smart but right now you've little stamina to get into a fight. Give yourself a chance to regain your strength. Then you can be moved to the infirmary—and at least have assistance near at hand when you try a damfool scheme like that."

"I'll handle this my own way," Orlig said brusquely. "Out. I want to go to sleep." He sat down on the examination bed and swung his legs up, ignoring her.

Irritated by his dismissal, Lunzie left. The door shut behind her, with the double hiss that meant the seals were being put on.

What they had both forgotten was that Lunzie was the medic on record attending that accident. The CMO asked for a report on the status of the victim. Lunzie filled out the requisite forms but asked the CMO to keep it secure.

"The man's suffering from a mild paranoia."

"Don't think I'd blame him with a wall blowing out like that. Those heavyworlder vendettas are costly."

"I've put him in one of the small treatment rooms. He felt safer there, but I'm trying to get him to transfer to the infirmary. He'd be safer from retaliation here."

Her next visit was brief, too. Orlig was improving so much that he had a raging case of cabin fever, and exploded at Lunzie.

"Why haven't you passed that brick on to Tor? What in the comet's tail are you waiting for?"

"I suppose I should just list it on the Bulletin Board that Lunzie Mespil, medic, wishes to speak with Thek Tor?" Lunzie snapped back tartly. "You told me not to draw attention to myself so I'm not."

"I risked my life for that information. You lightweights think you're so smart—well, think up a plausible reason but pass that information on."

"When circumstances permit!"

That began a screaming argument in which, to her surprise, Lunzie managed to hold her own. In retaliation, Orlig threw a few very personal insults at her that questioned her parentage and personal habits, and showed an intimate knowledge of the details of her life. Had Coromell actually given him access to her file? Shocked and offended, she marched out, vowing that it would be a warm and sunny day midspace before she'd go back.

Three more shifts passed. Lunzie felt guilty for having lost her temper with Orlig. He was as much under strain as she was, and it was wrong to indulge in a petty fit of temper at his expense. She returned to the infirmary and tapped on the door.

"Orlig? It's Lunzie. Oh, whisky! Orlig? Let me in."

She tapped at the doorplate and the door swung partly in. It was neither locked nor sealed. Startled, Lunzie leaned cautiously forward to investigate. The chamber was dark inside, reeking with a peculiar, heavy smell. She passed her hand over the panel for lights, and jumped back, gasping at what she saw.

There had been a fight. Most of the furniture was smashed or bent, and there were smears of blood on the walls. The sink had been torn out of the wall and stuffed halfway into the disposer unit. The equipment cabinets were smashed open, with their contents strewn throughout the chamber. Still attached to the wall, the shattered hand dryer sputtered fitfully to itself, dropping hot sparks.

Orlig lay sprawled on the floor. Guiltily Lunzie thought for a moment that internal bleeding had begun again. The cause of death was all too evident. Orlig had been strangled. His face was darkened with extravasated blood, and his eyes bulged. She had seen death before, even violent death. But not ruthless murder.

The marks of opposable digits were livid on the dead man's windpipe. Someone with incredible strength had thrown Orlig all over the room before pressing him to the ground and wringing his neck. Lunzie felt weak.

Only another heavyworlder could have done that to Orlig. And she'd thought that he was the biggest one on the ARCT-10. So who? And what did that person know or suspect about her? She checked the door to see how the killer had forced its way. But there was no sign of a forced entry. The seals were unsecured. Orlig had let his assailant into the room himself. Had the killer followed her, undetected, and overheard her use the agreed password? Or had

Orlig overestimated his own returning strength and cunning? Sometimes being a lightweight was an advantage—you found it easier to recognize physical limitations.

If the murderer should decide to eliminate Orlig's medic on the possibility that the dead man had passed on his knowledge, she was once again in jeopardy from heavyworlders. How long had Orlig been dead? How much more "safety" did she have left?

"I've got to get off this ship. Just finding Tor and passing on that brick are not going to be the answer. But how?"

First she had to report the death to the CMO, who was appalled by the murder but not terribly surprised.

"These guys are temperamental, you know. Strangest things set off personal vendettas." But the CMO could and did slam a security lock on the details.

Since the CMO didn't ask more details from her, Lunzie ventured none. Enough people had seen Orlig manhandle her after the accident so that she would seem an unlikely recipient of any confidences. But she wouldn't rest easy on that assumption. She continued to feel vulnerable. To her own surprise, she felt more anger than fright.

She did take the precaution of attaching her personal alarm to the door of her cubicle at night. She was cautious enough to stay in a group at all times.

"They wanted me to find him, that's clear," Lunzie mused blackly as she went about her duties the next day. "Otherwise, they'd have stuffed the body into the disposer and let the recycling systems have it. His absence might even have passed without any notice. Maybe I should grumble about patients who discharge themselves without medic permission." She doubted that would do any good and scanned the updates on mission personnel with an anxious eye. Surely she could wangle the medic's spot on the next one. Even if she had to pull out her FI ID.

Chapter Twelve

"It's Ambrosia," was her greeting from those in the common room the next morning. She recoiled in shock. "It's Ambrosia!" people were chorusing joyfully. "It really is Ambrosia."

Lunzie was stunned to hear the dangerous statement delivered in a chant, taken up by every new arrival.

"What's Ambrosia?" she demanded of Nafti, one of the scientists. He grabbed her hands and danced her around the room in his enthusiasm. She calmed him down long enough to get an explanation.

"Ambrosia's a brand-new colonizable, human-desirable planet," Nafti told her, his homely face wreathed in idiotic delight. "An EEC Team's on its way in. The comlinks are oozing news about the most glorious find in decades. The team's called it Ambrosia. Believe it or not, an E-class planet, with a 3-to-1 nitrogen/oxygen atmosphere and .96 Earth gravity."

Everyone was clamoring to hear more details but the captain of the EEC Team was wisely keeping the specifics to himself until the *ARCT-10* labs verified the findings. Rumors ranged to the implausible and unlikely but most accounts agreed that Ambrosia's parameters made it the most Earthlike planet ever discovered by the EEC.

Lunzie wasn't sure of her reaction to the news: relief that "It's Ambrosia" was now public information, or confusion. The phrase that had already cost lives and severely altered hers might have nothing at all to do with the new planet. It could be a ridiculous coincidence. And it could very well mean that the new planet might be the next target for the planetary pirates. Only how could a planet, which was now known to the thousands of folk on board the ARCT-10, get pirated out from under the noses of legitimate FSP interests by, if the past was any indication, even the most violent means?

The arrival of the Team meant more than good news to her. Zebara was the captain. A lot easier to find than that one Thek named Tor. She asked one of the communications techs to add her name to the queue to speak to Captain Zebara when he arrived. A moment's private conversation with him and she'd have kept faith with Orlig.

Like most of her plans lately, that one had to be aborted. When Captain Zebara arrived on board, he was all but mobbed by the people on the ARCT-10 who wanted to be first to learn the details of Ambrosia. Lunzie heard he'd had to be locked in the day officer's wardroom to protect him. Shortly afterward, an announcement was made by the exec officer that Zebara would speak to the entire ship from the oxygen-breathers' common room. With a shipwide and translated broadcast, everyone could share Zebara's news.

Lunzie waited with Coe amid a buzzingly eager audience packing the common room. There was a small flurry as the Team Captain entered the room. Lunzie peered around her neighbors, saw a head of fuzzy blond hair, and belatedly realized that the man towered a good foot above most of those in the surrounding crowd.

"He's a heavyworlder," she said, disbelievingly.

"Zebara's an okay guy," Grabone said, hearing the

hostility in Lunzie's tone. "He's different. Friendly. Doesn't have the chip on his shoulder that most of the heavyworlders wear."

"He's also not from Diplo," added Coe. "He was raised on one of the heavyworld colonies which had a reasonably normal climate. I'd never thought climate had that much effect on folks, but he's nowhere near as bad as the Diplos."

Lunzie did not voice her doubts but Coe saw her skeptical expression.

"C'mon, Lunzie, he's a fine fellow. I'll introduce you later," Coe offered. "Zebara and I are old buddies."

"Thanks, Coe," Lunzie murmured politely. Zebara had a very catholic selection of friends if both Orlig and Coe were numbered among them.

"Wait, he's starting to speak."

Zebara was a good orator. He had a trick of smiling just before he let go of a piece of particularly encouraging data. His audience soon caught on and was almost holding its breath, waiting for the next grin. For a heavyworlder, whose features tended to be rough, Zebara was the exception, with a narrow face, a beaky, high-bridged nose and sharp blue eyes.

Lunzie decided that his composure was assumed. He was as excited as his listeners were about his subject.

"Ambrosia! Nectar of the gods! Air you want to drink as well as smell. Only it doesn't smell. It's there, light in the lungs, buoyant about you. This planet is fourth position out from a class-M sun, with a blue sky stretched over six small landmasses that cover only about a third of the surface. The rest is water! Sweet water. Hydrogen dioxide!" There was a cheer from the assembled as Zebara took a flask from his pouch and held it aloft. "There are of course trace elements," he added, "but nothing toxic in either the mineral content or the oceanic flora. No free cya-

nides. Two small moons far out and one large one
close in, so there are some spectacular tides. There's
a certain amount of vulcanism, but that only makes
the place interesting. Ambrosia has no indigenous
sentient life-forms."

"Are you sure?" one of the heavyworlder men in
the audience shouted out.

Sentience was the final test of a planet; the EEC
prohibited colonization of a planet which already had
an evolving intelligent species. "Brock, we've spent
two years there and nothing we tested had an intelligence reading that showed up on any of the sociolog-
ical scales. One of the insectoids, which we call
mason beetles, have a complicated hive society but
EV's are more interested in the chemical they se-
crete while hunting. It can melt solid rock. There's a
very friendly species which my xenobiologist calls
kittisnakes but they don't even have very much animal intelligence. There're a lot of pretty avians"—a
squawk of alarm rose from the Ryxi scattered throughout the crowded chamber—"but no intelligent bird
life." The squawks changed to coos. They were jeal-
ous of their position as the only sentient avians in the
FSP.

Zebara threw the meeting open for questions, and
a clamorous chorus of voices attempted to shout one
another down.

"Well, this will take hours," Coe sighed. "Let's
leave him a message and see him next shift."

"No," Lunzie said. "Let's stay and listen for a while.
Then we'll go down and wait for him by the captain's
cabin. I'm sure he'll go there next, to give the administrators a private debriefing."

Coe looked at her admiringly. "For someone who
hasn't been with the EEC long, you sure figured out
the process quickly."

Lunzie grinned. "Bureaucracy works the same way
everywhere. Once he's thrown enough to the lower

echelons to keep 'em happy, he'll be sequestered with the brass until he satisfies their curiosity."

They timed the approach perfectly, catching the heavyworlder as he emerged from the turbovator near the administrative offices.

"You came back in style from this one, didn't you, Zeb!"

"Coe! Good to see you." Zebara and the brown-skinned man exchanged friendly embraces. The big man reached down to pat the smaller one familiarly on the head. "I've got to talk to the bitty big bosses right now. Wait for me?"

"Sure. Oh, Zebara, this is Dr. Lunzie Mespil. She asked especially to meet you."

"Charmed, Citizen." Cold blue eyes turned to her.

Intimidated, Lunzie felt a chill go up her backbone. Nevertheless, she had a promise to keep. She thrust a hand at the heavyworlder who engulfed it in polite reaction. He felt the Fleet ID disk that she had palmed to him.

"Congratulations on your discovery, Captain. I had a patient recently who told me to see you as soon as you got back."

"As soon as the brass finish with me, Lunzie Mespil," he said, keenly searching her face. "That I promise you. Now if you'll excuse me . . . Lunzie Mespil." He gave her one more long look as he palmed the panel and let himself in.

"Well, he got your name right at least," Coe said, a bit sourly.

"Who can ignore the brass when it calls? I'll catch him later. Thanks for the intro, Coe."

"My pleasure," Coe answered, watching her face in puzzlement.

She left Coe there, right in the passageway, and went back to her cubicle to wait for a response from Zebara. The disk alone was tacit command for a private meeting. Why hadn't she anticipated that he might be a heavyworlder? Because you don't like heavyworlders, stupid, not after that Quinada woman. Maybe she should find Tor. She trusted Theks. Though why she did, she couldn't have said. They weren't even humanoid. Just the nearest thing we have to visible gods, that's all. Well, she was committed now, handshake, cryptic comments and all.

The passageway along which her space lay was almost empty, unusual for that time of day but she hardly noticed, except that no eyebrows or feather crests went up when she kicked a wall in frustration.

Both Coe and Grabone spoke well of Zebara, and they hadn't of any of the other heavyworlders. That said something for the man. If he's at all loyal to the EEC—but if he doesn't get back to me as soon as he's finished debriefing, I'm finding me a Thek named Tor.

Then something Zebara had said bobbed up in her thoughts. Zebara had been on Ambrosia for two years. Her first courier job had been less than a year ago, with Ambrosia the important feature. Had Zebara had an informant on his scout ship?

With such uncomfortable thoughts galling her, Lunzie let herself into her room and changed into a uniform tunic for her infirmary shift. She tossed the off-duty tunic into the synthesizer hatch, to be broken down into component fibers and rewoven, without the dirt. The cool, efficient function of the machine made her recall Orlig's body on the infirmary floor. Why had his killer left the body there? What had he expected her to do when she found it? Maybe she ought to have followed her initial impulse and run screaming from the little chamber, alerting everyone in earshot that she had found a murder victim. Maybe that would have been smarter. Maybe she'd outsmarted herself?

The communications panel chimed, breaking into

her morbid reflections. It let out a click as an audio
pickup was engaged somewhere on the ship.

"Lunzie," said the CMO's voice, "please respond."

She leaned over to slap the panel. "Lunzie here,
Carlo."

"Where are you? There's a Brachian in the early
stages of labor. She's literally climbing the walls.
Someone said you were good with the species."

"Who said that?" Lunzie asked, surprised. She
couldn't recall mentioning her gynecological experiences with anyone on the *ARCT-10*.

"I don't know." That didn't surprise her, for the
Chief was notoriously bad at remembering names.
"But if you are, I need you asap."

"I'm on my way, sir," she answered, fastening the
neck of the tunic. Anyone would be a more capable
midwife for a Brachian than the Chief.

Lunzie slipped into the empty corridor. Her quick
footsteps echoed loudly back to her in the long empty
metal corridor even though she was wearing soft-
soled boots. Where was everyone? She had neighbors on both sides who had small children. Probably
all were still in the common room, rehashing Zebara's
talk. There wasn't a spare sound within earshot, just
the *swish-thump swish-thump* of her step. Curious,
she altered her pace to hear the difference in the
noise she made. There was a T-intersection just ahead.
It would pick up the echoes splendidly. Abruptly,
she lengthened her stride and the swish grew shorter
and faltered. That wasn't an echo of her own step.
There was someone behind her, carefully matching
her.

She spun to see a human male, half a head taller
than she, about ten paces behind her. He was a
burly man, with brassy brown hair and a wide, ape-
like jaw.

"Who are you?" she demanded.

The man only grinned at her and moved to close

the distance between them, his hands menacingly outstretched. Lunzie backed away from him, then turned and ran toward the intersecting corridor. Letting out a piercing whistle, the man dashed after her.

He couldn't be Orlig's killer, she thought. He wasn't big enough to have strangled the heavyworlder. But he was big enough to kill her if she wasn't careful. She initiated the Discipline routine, though running was not the recommended starting position. She needed some time. Lunzie thought hard to remember if either corridor ended in a dead end. Yes, the right-hand way led to a thick metal door that housed a supplementary power station. She veered left. As she rounded the corner, a gaudily colored female Ryxi appeared, stalking toward her.

"Help me," Lunzie panted, indicating the man behind her. "He intends me harm."

The Ryxi didn't say anything. Instead, she jumped back against a bulkhead and stuck out a long, skinny leg. Lunzie tried to hurdle it but the Ryxi merely raised her foot. Lunzie fell headlong, skidding on the metal floor into the wall.

Who would have expected the avian to be a human's accomplice? She'd been well and truly ambushed. Her vision swimming from her skid into the hard bulkhead at the end of her spin, she walked her hands up the wall, trying to regain her feet. Before she was fully upright, strong hands grabbed her from behind.

Automatically, Lunzie kicked backwards, but her blow was without real force. She got a rabbit punch in the back of her neck for her pains. Her head swam and her knees sagged momentarily under her. Discipline! Where were all those Adept tricks she'd so carefully practiced?

"Watch it, Birra, she thinks she's tough."

The man's voice was gloating as they turned her around, keeping a tight grip on her upper arms.

Dazed, Lunzie struggled. She tried again for Discipline but her head was too fuzzy. The Ryxi was very tall for her species and the muscle masses at the tops of her stalky legs were thick and well corded. She lifted one long-toed foot and wrapped it around Lunzie's leg, picking it up off the ground. Lunzie, leaning her weight on her assailant's arms, kicked at the Ryxi, trying to free herself.

She began to scream loudly, hoping to attract the attention of anyone living on the corridor. Where was everyone?

"Shut up, space dust," the man growled. He hit her in the stomach, knocking the air out of her.

That shut off Lunzie's cries for help but left one of her arms free. She deliberately let herself fall backwards to the deck, twisting out of the Ryxi's grip. She scissored a kick upward at the Ryxi's thin leg and felt her boot jar against its bone. With a squawk of pain, Birra jerked away, clutching her knee. The man dove forward and kicked out at Lunzie's ribs. Clumsily, Lunzie rolled away.

"Kill herrr," the Ryxi chirred angrily, hopping forward on one foot. "Kill her, Knorrrradel, she has hurrt me."

The man kicked again at Lunzie who found that she had trapped herself against the bulkhead. The Ryxi raked her clawed foot down Lunzie's shoulder and attempted to close the long toes around the human woman's throat. Lunzie curled her knees up close to protect her belly and chest and tried to wrench apart the knobby toes with both hands. It was getting harder to breathe and the talons were as tough as tree roots under her useless fingers. Lunzie felt the bruised patch on the side of her head beginning to throb. A black haze was seeping into her vision from that side. She knew she was about to lose consciousness. The man laughed viciously and kicked her in the side again and brought his foot down against her upraised left arm. The bone snapped audibly in the empty corridor. Lunzie screamed out what little air remained in her lungs.

He raised his foot again—and to her relief and amazement, the surge of adrenaline evoked by fear and pain awoke Discipline.

Ruthlessly ignoring the break in her forearm, she grasped the Ryxi's toes in her hands. With the strength of Discipline she pulled them apart and up, and twisted the leg toward the avian's other limb. Ryxi had notoriously bad knees. They only bent forward and outward, not inward. The Ryxi, caught off balance, opened her claw wide, searching for purchase. The creature fell against the man, knocking him off balance before she collapsed in a heap of swearing, colorful feathers to the deck.

In one smooth move, the human doctor was on her feet, *en garde*, two meters from her would-be assassins. Her mind was alert now as, her chest heaving like a bellow, she coolly summed up her opponents. The Ryxi was more adaptable; she had already proved that by countering Lunzie's moves, but Lunzie knew the avian body's weak point and there wasn't room enough in this corridor for the avian to fly. Though the human was more powerful than Lunzie, he wasn't a methodical fighter.

Lunzie's recovery surprised Knoradel. That gave her her first advantage. She didn't want to kill them unless as a last resort. If she could disable them, knock them unconscious or lock them up, she could get to safety. Curling her good hand to stiffen the edge, Lunzie feinted forward at the man. Automatically, rather than consciously, his hands balled into fists. He danced backward, one leg forward, and one back. So he'd had some martial arts training—but not the polish of Discipline.

Lunzie had the edge on him. Her left hand, deprived of muscle tension because of the snapped bone, was beginning to curl into a claw. She curved the other hand so it looked as though she had two good ones. She had to get away from her assailants before the adrenaline wore off and she would again feel the pain. As long as it looked as if the broken bone hadn't affected her at all, Knoradel would be disconcerted.

The Ryxi was also on her feet again. Lunzie had to take care of the man before dealing with the wily avian and her long reach. He was sweating. His ambush plan had gone wrong and he hadn't the brains or experience to adapt. Lunzie feinted left, then right, then a double left, which made Knoradel unconsciously step in front of his cohort to counter Lunzie's moves. When he was just far enough in front of the avian to block her attack, Lunzie spun backwards in a swift roundhouse kick. It took the man squarely under the chin and flung him against the wall. His head snapped back, connecting with the metal bulkhead with a hearty *boom*! He slid down to the floor, his eyes rolling back in his head. If Lunzie could dispatch the Ryxi quickly, Knoradel wouldn't be able to chase her.

But Birra stepped swiftly into the fray as soon as her partner was out of her path. She was relying on her clawed feet and the heavy expanse of her wings with their clawed joints as weapons, keeping the delicate three-fingered manipulative extremity at the tips of her wings folded out of danger. Lunzie fought to grab at one of those hands, knowing that Birra would be thrown off guard to protect them.

"You wingless mutant," Birra hissed shrilly, raking at Lunzie's belly with one claw. It tore her tunic from the midriff to the hem as Lunzie jumped back out of the way. She countered immediately with a sweep kick at the avian's bony knees. As the avian moved to guard herself, Lunzie grabbed the fold of a wing that flapped above her head, threw an arm across Birra's body, and flipped her.

Automatically, the wings opened out to save the Ryxi. Birra shrieked as her hands rammed against the walls of the narrow corridors. Her wingspan was too great. Swiftly, she folded her pinions again, with the single deadly claws at their center joints arching over her shoulders at Lunzie. She pecked at the medic with her sharp beak. Lunzie drew up her crossed hands to block the blow and knocked the avian's head up and back.

"Fardles, I really hate to do this to you," she said apologetically. With both hands balled into fists, she smashed them in under Birra's wings against the avian's exposed rib cage. Wincing, she felt the delicate bones snap.

The Ryxi shrieked, her voice carrying into higher and higher registers as she clawed and flapped blindly at Lunzie.

"You're still ambulatory," Lunzie said, moving backward and countering the attack. "If you get to a medic right away he can set those bones so you don't puncture a lung. Let me go, or I'll be forced to keep you here until it's too late."

"Horrible biped! You lie!" Birra cradled one wounded side, then the other. She was gasping, beak open.

"I'm not lying. You know I'm a doctor. You knew that when you were sent to attack me," Lunzie threw back. "Who told you to attack me?"

The Ryxi gasped with fury, and clenched both wings against her midsection. "I die." Her round black eyes were starting to become glassy and she rocked back and forth.

"No!" Lunzie shouted. "You daft bird."

The Ryxi was going into shock. She was no longer a danger to Lunzie but she might put herself into a lethal coma.

Disgusted to be caught by the moral dilemma, Lunzie limped to the nearest communications panel and hit the blue stud.

"Emergency, level 11. Code Urgent. Emergency involving a Ryxi. Rib cage injury, going into shock. Emergency." Lunzie turned away from the panel. "Someone will be here in minutes. I meant to inflict no lasting damage on you but I'm not staying around in case the person who gave you your orders shows up first. You will keep my name out of an investigation, won't you? Good luck."

The Ryxi rocked back and forth rhythmically, ignoring Lunzie as she slipped through the access hatch to the stairs at the end of the corridor.

Impatiently Lunzie tapped out the sequence of the officers' lounge. She couldn't go there, even with an overlarge smock covering the shreds of her blood-stained uniform. But she prayed to all the gods that govern that Zebara was available. The adrenaline of Discipline was wearing off and she would soon be caught by the post-Discipline enervation. She had to hand over the cube asap.

"Officers' lounge." To her infinite relief she recognized Lieutenant Sanborn's bright tenor voice.

"Is Captain Zebara here?" she asked, trying to sound medium casual. "It's Lunzie Mespil. Something's come up and I need a word with him."

"Yes, he just came in from the brass meeting. Having a drink and he needs it, Lunzie. Is this really urgent?"

"Let him judge. Just tell him I'm standing by, would you, Lieutenant?" She wanted to add, "like a good boy and go do as mother asks" but she didn't.

"Right you are," Sanborn replied obligingly.

She fidgeted, blotting blood from the wound on her temple. The flesh was awfully tender: she'd shortly have a massive hematoma and there weren't many ways to conceal that obvious a bruise. What was taking Sanborn so long? The lounge wasn't that big.

"Zebara." He announced himself in a deep voice that made the intercom rattle. "I'd just placed a call to your quarters. Where are you?"

"Hiding, Captain, and I need to see you as soon as possible." She heard him sigh. Well, he might as well get all the bad news at once. "First they dropped a wall on Orlig, then they strangled him while I had him stashed in a nice out-of-the-way treatment room. I've just had an encounter with a life-seeking duet and I'd like to transfer the incriminating evidence before my demise."

"Where are you?" he repeated.

She gave him the deck, section and corridor.

"How well do you know this vessel?"

"As well as most. Medics need to get places in a hurry."

"Then I suggest you get yourself to Scout Bay 5 by the best way and wait for me. I certainly have a good reason to return to my ship. Over and out."

His crisp voice steadied her. In the first place it had none of the soggy mushmouth tones that most heavyworlders seemed to project. His suggestion was sensible, keeping her out of the way of anyone likely to see her, and surely the scout ship would be the last place "they" would expect her to go.

She took the emergency shafts down to the flight decks, assisted by the half-gee force at which they were kept. She got the wrong bay the first time she emerged into the main access corridors, but they were empty so she continued on to Five. He entered from the main turbovator and didn't so much as slow his stride as he caught her by the arm. He pulled out a small com-unit and mumbled into it as he half carried her up the ramp into the not-so-small scout ship.

"You got rightly messed up if your face is any

indication," he said, pausing in the airlock to examine her. He twitched away the large coat and his eyebrows rose. "So they got Orlig. What have you got?"

"One of those neat little message bricks which had better go forward to its destination with all possible speed."

"There's usually a phrase to go with a brick?" He arched an eyebrow in query. It gave him a decidedly satanic look.

"I'm paranoid at the moment. I keep thinking people are trying to kill me." Her facetiousness brought a slight smile to his face.

"We'll get your message off and then maybe you'll trust this heavyworlder. Come!"

He took her hand and led her through the narrow corridors of the scout vessel to the command deck. A centimeter less on each side and the ceiling, Lunzie thought, and he wouldn't fit. Then he handed her into a small communications booth, slid the panel shut and went on into the bridge. She sat down dazed while he spoke briefly to the heavyworlder woman on duty. She instantly swung around with a grin to Lunzie and made rapid passes over her comboard.

"This is a secure channel," she said, her voice coming through a speaker in the wall. "Just insert the brick in the appropriate slot in front of you. They're usually constructed to set the coding frequency. I'm shutting down in here." She pulled off her earpiece and held up both hands. For a heavyworlder, she had a very friendly grin.

Lunzie fumbled with the brick but finally got it into the slot which closed over it like some weird alien ingesting sustenance. There was no indication that anything was happening. Abruptly the slot opened, spitting the little brick out. As she watched, the thing dissolved. It didn't steam or smolder or melt. It just dissolved and she was looking at a small pile of black dust.

She sent the communications officer the finger-thumb *O* of completion and sagged back with a deep sigh of relief. Zebara rose from his seat next to the com-tech and came around the doorway into the tiny chamber where Lunzie was seated.

"Mission completed in the usual pile of dust, I see," he said and swept it off onto the floor. Then he took a handful of mineral tablets from his pocket and popped a couple into his mouth.

Lunzie looked up at him limply. "I thank Muhlah!"

"And now we're going to do something about you." He sounded ominous.

Lunzie tensed in a moment of sheer panic which had no basis whatsoever except that Zebara was pounding on the quartz window with one massive palm.

"Flor, tell Bringan to get up here on the double. You look like hell, Lunzie Mespil. Sit tight for the medic."

Lunzie forced herself to relax when she noticed Zebara regarding her with some amusement.

"So what do we do about you?" he asked rhetorically. "Even on a ship as huge as the *ARCT-10*, you can't really be safely hidden. You escaped once but you are unquestionably in jeopardy." She wished he would sit down instead of looming over her. "Did you get a look at your assailants?"

"A Ryxi female named Birra and a human male she called Knoradel." She rattled off physical descriptions. "The Ryxi has a crushed rib cage. I left a few marks on the man."

"They shouldn't be too hard to apprehend," Zebara said and depressed a toggle on the board. She heard him giving the descriptions to the Ship Provost. "You won't object to remaining here until they have been detained? No? Sensible of you." He regarded her for a long moment and then grinned, looking more like a predatory fish than an amused human. "In fact, it would be even more sensible if you didn't go back to the *ARCT-10* at all."

"In deep space there aren't many alternatives," Lunzie remarked, feeling the weakness of post-Discipline seeping through her.

"I can think of one." He looked at her expectantly and, when she didn't respond, gave a disappointed sigh. "You can come back to Ambrosia with us."

"Ambrosia?" Lunzie wasn't certain that the planet appealed to her at all.

"An excellent solution since you're already involved up to your lightweight neck in Ambrosian affairs. Highly appropriate. Assassins won't get another chance at terminating your life on any ship I command. I'll clear your reappointment with the *ARCT-10* authorities."

Lunzie was really surprised. Somehow, she had not expected such positive cooperation and solicitousness from this heavyworlder. "Why?"

"You're in considerable danger. Partly because you gave unstinting assistance to another heavyworlder. I was well acquainted with Orlig. My people are beneficiaries of your risk as much as yours are. Do you have any objections?"

"No," Lunzie decided. "It'll be a great relief to be able to sleep safely again." She was beginning to feel weightless, a sure sign that adrenaline exhaustion was taking hold.

Zebara grinned his shark's-tooth smile again, and crunched another tablet. "If Orlig's murder and the attempt on your life are an indication, and I believe they are, then Ambrosia may be in even more danger than I thought it was. Orlig was keeping his ears open for me on the *ARCT*, which was receiving and transmitting my reports. So we'd already had an indication that this plum would fall into the wrong paws. You confirm that. I came back to ask for mili-

tary support to meet us there to stave off a possible
pirate takeover until a colony can be legitimately
installed with the appropriate fanfare. Relax, Lunzie
Mespil."

"Thank you," Lunzie called faintly after him, the
weight of her own indecision and insecurity sliding
off her sagging shoulders now that someone believed
her. She let her head roll back against the cushioned
chair.

Soon, she became aware that someone was in the
tiny cubicle with her.

"Ah, you're awake. Don't move too quickly. I'm
setting your arm." A thickset man with red-blond
hair cut short knelt at her side. "I'm Doctor Bringan.
Normally I'm just the xenobiologist but I'm not averse
to using my talents on *known* species. I run the
checkups and bandage scratches for the crew. Understand you're signing on as medical officer." Very
gently, he pulled her wrist and forearm in opposite
directions. The curled fingers slowly straightened
out. "That'll be a relief," he added with a welcoming
smile. "I might just put the wrong bits together and
that could prove awkward for someone."

"Um, yes," Lunzie agreed, watching him carefully. Mercifully the arm was numb. He must have
given her a nerve block. "Wait, I didn't hear the
bones mesh yet."

"I'm just testing to see if any of the ligatures were
torn. No. All's well." Bringan waved a small diagnostic unit over her arm. "You were lucky you were
wearing a tight sleeve. The swelling would have
been much worse left unchecked."

"So I see," Lunzie said, eyeing the reddish wash
along the skin of her arm which marked subcutane-
ous bleeding. It would soon surface as a fading rainbow of colors as the blood dispersed. She poked at
the flesh with an experimental finger and, with curious detachment, felt it give.

Bringan put the DU in his belt pouch and gave a deft twist to her arm. Lunzie heard the ulna and radius grate slightly as they settled into place.

"I'm going to put you in a non-confining brace to hold your bones steady. Won't interfere with movement and you can wash the arm, cautiously. Everything will be tender once the nerve block wears off." He flexed her fingers back and forth. "You should have normal range of motion in a few hours." Then he gave a snort of a chuckle and eyed her. "I should be telling you!"

She managed a weak, but grateful, smile. "Bringan, are we going to Ambrosia?"

The doctor raised surprised blond brows at her. "Oh, yes indeed we are. Myself, I can't wait to get back. Why, I intend to put in to settle here when I retire. I've never seen such a perfect planet."

"I mean, are we going soon?" She stressed the last word.

"That's what I meant." He gave her a searching look. "Zebara has told me nothing about you, or why you arrive looking like the survivor of a corridor war, but he logged you on FTL. So I can enjoy a few shrewd guesses, most of which include planet pirates." He winked at her. "Which gives the most excellent of reasons for burning tubes back there. The FSP needs witnesses on hand. Or maybe that's your role on our roster."

"I'll witness, believe you me, I'll witness," Lunzie said with all the fervor left in her depleted body.

Bringan chuckled as he gathered up his gear. "If we're delayed in any way, by any agency, I think Zebara would probably tank himself up and swim back shipless. He's allergic to the mention of pirates. And bloody piracy's turning epidemic. It seems to me that every time a real plum turns up in the last century, the pirates are there to wrest it away from the legitimate finders. With a sophisticated violence that makes alien creatures seem like housecats."

"Bringan," Lunzie asked again, tentatively, "what's Zebara like?"

"Do you mean, is he your usual prototype heavy-worlder chauvinist? No. He's a good leader, and good friend. I've known him for thirty years. You'll appreciate his fair treatment, but watch out for the grin. That means trouble."

Lunzie cocked an eyebrow at Bringan. "You mean the shark-face he puts on? I've already seen it."

"Ho, ho! I hope it wasn't meant for you!" The doctor bunched himself onto his feet. "There, you're in good shape. Come with me, and we'll see about a bunk for you. You need to rest and let those injuries start to heal."

"When do we cast off the *ARCT-10*?" Lunzie asked. She followed Bringan, not too wobbly on her strength-less legs. Had the Ryxi received help before her lungs collapsed?

"As soon as Zebara is back on board."

On the way to that bunk, Lunzie got the briefest of introductions to the rest of the scout crew. Besides Flor, the Ship-born communications tech who doubled as historian, and Bringan, the xeobiologist, there were seven more. Dondara and Pollili, a mated pair, were heavyworlders from Diplo. Pollili was the telemetry officer, and Dondara was a geologist. Unlike most of their number who served for a few missions and then retired to their cold, bleak homeworlds, Pollili and Dondara had served with Zebara's Explorers Team for eight years, and had every intention of continuing in that posting. They spent one to two months a year in intensive exercise in the heavyworld environment aboard the *ARCT-10* to maintain their muscle tone. The other five EX Team members were human. Scarran, tan-skinned and nearsighted, was a systems technologist. Vir, offshoot of a golden-

complected breed with heavily lidded eyes, was an
environmental specialist who shared security duties
with Dondara. Elessa, charming but not strictly pretty,
held the double duties of synthesizer tech and botanist. Timmins was a chemist. Wendell, the pilot, had
gone over to the *ARCT-10* with Zebara.

Everyone's specialties overlapped somewhat so the
necessarily small crew of the scout had a measure of
redundancy of talent in case of emergency. The little
ship was compactly built but amazingly not cramped
in its design. Hydroponic racks of edible plants
were arrayed anywhere there was space, and the
extra light made the rooms seem more cheerful and
inviting. Bringan explained the ship was capable of
running on its own power indefinitely in sublight, or
making a single warp jump between short sprints
before recharging.

Ambrosia was a long jump out toward the edge of
explored space. The scout could never be certain of
finding edible food on any planet it explored and its
crew needed to be able to provide their own carbohydrates for the synthesizers.

Lunzie's bunk was in the same alcove as Elessa's.
She lay on the padding with her arm strapped across
her chest, staring at the bunkshelf above her. Bringan
had ordered her to rest but she couldn't close her
eyes. She was grateful to be safe but somehow it
rankled her that her rescuer should prove to be a
heavyworlder. Zebara seemed all right. She couldn't
repress the suspicion that he might just be waiting
until they got into deep space to toss her out the
airlock. That didn't compute—not with a mixed-species
crew all of whom were impressively loyal to him.

Abruptly the last adrenaline that had been but-
tressing her drained away. "Well, I ought to be truly
grateful," she chided herself. "And he's got a very
good press from his crew. That Quinada! I was getting used to heavyworlders when I had to run into

someone like her! I suppose there's a bad chip in every board."

Still vaguely uneasy, Lunzie let herself drift off to sleep.

She awoke with a start to see Zebara staring down at her. It took her a moment to remember where she was.

"We're under way," he announced without preamble. "I've had you made an official member of my crew. No one else tried to pressure the little bosses to get on this cruise, so either your attackers have given up the job or . . . there are nasty plans for all of us."

"You're so comforting," Lunzie remarked drolly, determined to modify her attitude, at least toward a heavyworlder named Zebara. "How long have I been asleep?"

The heavyworld captain turned his palms upward. "How'd I know? We've been under way about five hours. Bringan told me to let you rest and I have, but now I need to talk to you. Do you feel strong enough?"

Lunzie tested her muscles and drew herself into a sitting position. Her arm was sore but she could move her fingers now. Bringan's cast held it immobile without putting pressure on the bruised muscles of her forearm. The rest of her body felt battered, but she already felt better for having had some rest.

"Talk? Yes, I'm up to talking."

"Come to my quarters. We can speak privately there."

"I was half expecting to be approached on the ARCT-10," Zebara said, pouring two glasses of Sverulan brandy. His quarters were close to spacious; that is to say, the room was eight paces wide by ten, instead of four. Zebara had a computer desk equipped with a device Lunzie recognized as a private memory storage. His records would not be accessible to anyone else on the ship or on the ship's communication network. "The exact location of Ambrosia is known only to myself and my crew and, regrettably, the administrators aboard the *ARCT*." He showed his teeth. "I trust my crew. I suspect there's an unpluggable leak aboard the *ARCT*."

"A leak leading right to the EEC Administration?" Lunzie was beginning to see the pieces of the minor puzzle which involved her coming together. The whole was part of a much larger puzzle.

"That's a gamble I have to take. If the pirates beat us back to Ambrosia, that means the information on Ambrosia's exact location is being transmitted to them right now. I want Fleet protection, yes, but I'm also interested in luring the pirates out into the open. They might just catch the spy within the Administration chambers this time." Zebara wrinkled his nose.

"The spy might be too high up in the echelons to find, impossible to trace—above suspicion." As the Seti of Fomalhaut would assuredly be. Hastily Lunzie took a sip of her drink and felt the warmth of the liquor in her belly. Zebara had splendid taste in intoxicants. She said slowly, "In the past the heavy-worlders appear to have been the chief beneficiaries of this sort of piracy. Is it at all possible that the FSP will believe that YOU let them know where to find the planet?" Now the feral grin was aimed at her. Lunzie felt a chill trace the line of her spine. "Mind you," she added hastily, "I'm acting devil's advocate but if *I* can suspect collusion, others might certainly do so, if only to divert suspicion."

"A possible interpretation, I grant you. Let me say in my own defense I dislike the idea that my people are beholden in any way to mass murderers." He drained his glass and poured each of them a second tot deep enough to bathe in, Lunzie thought. He must have a truly spectacular tolerance. Nevertheless she took a deep draught of the brandy, to thaw her spine, of course.

"I feel obliged to explain that I thought for quite a few years that I had lost my daughter to pirates during the Phoenix incident," she said. "The first thing anyone knew, the legitimate colony was gone and heavyworlders had moved in. I harbored a very deep resentment that they were living on that bright and shiny new planet while I grieved for my daughter. It's affected my good judgment somewhat ever since." Lunzie swallowed. "I apologize for indulging myself with such a shockingly biased generalization. It's the pirates I should hate, and I do."

Zebara smiled wryly. "I appreciate your candor and your explanation. Biased generalizations are not confined to your subgroup. I resent lightweights as a group for constantly putting my people in subordinate and inferior positions, where we're assigned the worst of the picking, or have to work under lightweights in a mixed group. In my view, there has been no true equality in the distribution of colonizable planets. Many of us, especially groups from Diplo, felt that Phoenix should have been assigned to us in the first place. One of our unassailable skills is mine engineering and production. The gen in my community was that the heavy people who landed on Phoenix had paid significant bribes to a merchant broker who assured them that the planet was virgin and vacant. They were cheated," Zebara added heatedly. "They were promised transuranics, but the planet had been stripped before they got there. It was no more than a place to live, with little a struggling colony could use as barter in the galactic community."

"Then somebody made double profits out of Phoenix. Triple, if you count the goods and machinery that the original settlers brought with them." The brandy had relaxed Lunzie sufficiently so that she had no compunction about refilling her glass. "Do you know the Parchandri?"

Zebara waved a dismissive hand. "Profiteers, every last blinking one of them, and they've a wide family. Weaklings, most of the Parchandri, even by lightweight standards, but they're far too spineless to kill with the ferocity the pirates exhibit."

The Seti could be ruthless but Lunzie couldn't quite cast them in the role which, unfortunately, did fit heavyworlders. "Then who are they? Human renegades? Captain Aelock felt that they were based out of Alpha Centauri."

"Aelock's a canny man but I'd be surprised if the Centauris were actively involved. They've acquired too much veneer, too civilized, too cautious by half." An opinion with which Lunzie privately concurred. "Centauris think only of profit. Every person, every machine, is a cog in the credit machine."

Lunzie took a sip of the warm brown liquor and stared at her reflection in the depths of the glass. "A point well taken. My daughter's descendants all live on that world. I have never met such a pitiful load of stick-in-the-mud, bigoted, shortsighted mules in my life. I was appalled because my daughter herself had plenty of motivation. She's a real achiever. Not afraid to take chances . . ."

"Like her mother," Zebara added. Lunzie looked up at the heavyworld captain in surprise. He was looking at her kindly, without a trace of sarcasm or condescension.

"Why, thank you, Captain. Only I fret that none of her children, bar one, are unhappy living in a technological slum, polluted and hemmed in by mediocrity and duplication."

"Complacency and ignorance," Zebara suggested, pouring more brandy. "A very good way to keep a large population so tractable the society lacks rebellion."

"But they've no space, mental or physical, to grow

in and they don't realize what they're missing. It even grieves me that they're so happy in their ignorance. But I got out of Alpha Centauri as fast as I could, and not just because my life was at risk. Trouble with moving around like that, I keep losing the people I love, one by one." Lunzie halted, appalled by her maundering. "I am sorry. It's this brandy. Or is it sodium pentathol? I certainly didn't intend to download my personal problems on you."

The captain shook his head. "It sounds to me as though you'd had no one to talk to for a long time. Mind you," he went on, musing aloud, "such unquestioning cogs can turn a huge and complex wheel. The pirates are not just one ship, nor even just a full squadron. The vessels have to be ordered, provisioned, staffed with specially trained personnel"—he ignored Lunzie's involuntary shudder at what would constitute training—"and that means considerable administrative ability, not just privileged information."

Lunzie regarded him thoughtfully. He sounded as paranoid as she was, mistrusting everyone and everything. "It all gets so unsortably sordidly convoluted!" Her consonants were suffering from the brandy. "I'm not sure I can cope with all this."

Zebara chuckled. "I think you've been coping extremely well, Citizen Doctor Mespil. You're still alive!"

"A hundred and nine and a half years alive!" Oh, she was feeling the brandy. "But I'm learning. I'm learning. I'm especially learning," and she waggled an admonishing finger at him, "I'm gradually learning to accept each person as an individual, and not as just a representative of their subgroup or species. Each one is individual to his, her, itself and can't be lumped in with his, her or its peer group. My Discipline Master would be proud of me now, I think. I've learned the lesson he was doing his damnedest to impart to me." She took the last swallow of Sverulan brandy and fixed her eyes on his impassive face. "So,

Captain, we're on our way to Ambrosia. What do you think we'll find there?"

"All we may find is the kittisnakes chasing each other up trees. We will be ready for any surprises." The captain stood up and extended an arm to Lunzie as she struggled her way out of the deep armchair. "Can you get back to your bunk all right?"

"Captain Zebara, Mespils have been known for centuries to hold their liquor. Dam' fine brandy. Thank you, Captain, for that and the listening ear."

Chapter Thirteen

The scout ship slowed to sublight speed and came out of its warp at the edge of the disk of a star system. Lunzie was strapped in the fourth seat on the bridge, watching as the stars spread out from a single point before them and filled the sky. Only a single yellow-white star hung directly ahead of the ship.

"There she is, Captain," Pilot Wendell said with deep satisfaction. "Ambrosia's star."

Zebara nodded solemnly and made a few notes in the electronic log. "Any energy traces in range?" the heavyworlder asked.

"No, sir."

"Is Ambrosia itself visible from this position?" Lunzie asked eagerly.

"No, Doctor, not yet. According to system calculations, she's around behind the sun. We'll drop below the plane of the ecliptic and come up on her. There's an asteroid belt we don't like to pass through if we can help it."

"Why do you call Ambrosia 'she'?"

Wendell smiled over his shoulder at her. "Because she's beautiful as a goddess. You'll see."

"Any traces?" Zebara asked again, as they began the upward sweep into the ecliptic toward a blue-white disk.

"No, sir," Wendell repeated.

"Once we drop into atmosphere, we're vulnerable," Zebara reminded him. "Our sensors won't read as clearly. The pirates could get the drop on us."

"I know, Captain." The pilot looked nervous, but he turned up a helpless palm. "I don't have any readings that shouldn't be out there."

"Sir, why are we returning without military backup if you expect pirates to attack?" Lunzie asked, gently, hoping that the question wasn't out of line. "This scout has no defensive armament."

Zebara scowled. "I don't want anyone intruding on Ambrosia. It's our province," he said, waving an arm through the air to indicate the crew. "If we aren't here to back up our claim, someone else—someone who didn't spend years searching—Krims," Zebara said, banging a palm on the console. He passed a hand across his forehead, wiping away imaginary moisture. "I should be enjoying this ride. I suppose I'm too protective of our discovery. See, Lunzie, there's the source of all our pain and pleasure. Ambrosia."

The blue-white disk took on more definition as it swam toward them. Lunzie held her breath. Ambrosia did indeed look like the holos she had seen on Earth. Patterns of water-vapor clouds scudded across the surface. She could pick out four of the six small continents, hazy gray-green in the midst of the shimmering blue seas. A rakishly tilted icecap decorated the south pole of the planet. A swift-moving body separated itself from the cloud layer and disappeared around the planet's edge. The smallest moon, one of three. "The big satellite is behind the planet," Wendell explained. "It's a full moon on nightside this day. Look, there's the second little one, appearing on the left." A tiny jewel, ablaze with the star's light, peeked around Ambrosia's side.

"She is beautiful," Lunzie breathed, taking it all in.

"Prepare for orbit and descent," Zebara ordered. "We'll set down. A ship this small is a sitting target in orbit. Planetside, we'll have a chance to run a few more experiments while we wait for backup."

"Aye, sir."

"Just after midday local time," Wendell had assured them as he set the scout down on a low plateau covered with thick, furry-leaved vegetation. EEC regulations required that an Evaluation Team locate at least five potential landing sites on a planet intended for colonization. The astrogation chart showed no fewer than ten, one in the chief island of a major archipelago in the southern sea, one on each small continent and more on the larger ones.

As the hatchway opened, Lunzie could hear the scuttling and scurrying of tiny animals fleeing the noisy intrusion. A breeze of fresh, sweet air curled inside invitingly. With force-shield belts on, Dondara and Vir did the perimeter search so that no indigenous life would be shut inside the protective shield when it was switched on. They gave the go-ahead, and Pollili activated the controls. A loud, shrill humming arose, and dropped almost immediately into a range inaudible to human ears.

If the view from space was lovely, the surface of Ambrosia looked like an artist's rendition of the perfect planet. The air was crisp and fresh, with just a tantalizing scent of exotic flora in the distance. The colors ranged from vivid primaries to delicate pastels and they all looked clean.

Lunzie stepped out of the shuttle into the rich sunlight of dayside. The sky was a pale blue and the cumulus clouds were a pure, soft white. From the hilltop, the scout commanded a panoramic view of an ancient deciduous forest. The treetops were every shade of green imaginable, interspersed every so often with one whose foliage was a brilliant rose pink. Smaller saplings grew on the edge of the plateau, clinging at an absurd angle as if fearful to make the plunge.

Off to the left, an egg-shaped lake glistened in the sun. Lunzie could just pick out the silver ribbons of the two rivers which fed it. One wound down across the breast of the very hill she stood on. Lunzie rested in the sun close to the ship as the other crew members spread out nearby on the slope of the hill and took readings. Under her feet was a thick blue-green grassoid whose stems had a circular cross section.

"More like reeds than grass, but it's the dominant cover plant," Elessa explained. "It doesn't grow to more than six inches in height, which is decent of it. We don't have to slog through thickets of the stuff, unlike other planets I could name. You have to push it over to sit on it or it sticks you full of holes. See that tree with the pink leaves? The fruit is edible, really succulent, but eat only the ones whose rinds have turned entirely brown. We got the tip from the local avians who wait in hordes for the fruit to ripen. The unripe ones give you a fierce bellyache. Oh, look. I don't have a sample of that flower." Carefully, she uprooted a tiny star-shaped flower with a forked tool from among the grassoids and transferred it to a plastic vial. "They have a single deep taproot instead of a spread of small roots, which makes them easy to harvest. It's the stiff stem that keeps them upright, like the grassoid. You could denude this whole hillside with a tweezers."

A hovering oval shadow suddenly covered Lunzie and the botanist where they knelt.

"You ought to see more than a single meadow, Doctor," Dondara scolded her from above, appearing from the rear of the ship in a two-man sled. "You're enjoying a rare privilege. Not twelve intelligent life-forms have seen this landscape before. Come on," he beckoned her into the sled. "I've got some readings to take. You can come with me."

Reminding herself of her drink-taken vow to trust individuals of any subgroup, Lunzie levered herself to her feet and climbed in after him. Elessa looked up as she went by and seemed about to say something to her, but changed her mind. Lunzie looked questioningly at the botanist but the girl shot her a "What can I tell you?" expression. Lunzie had confided her distrust to the botanist during the long flight here and Elessa only reiterated the statement that Zebara and those on the scout were truly in a class all their own.

The medic wondered as she and Dondara passed through the force-shield and flew over the meadow. The terrain was dramatically different less than half a mile from the grassy landing site. Beyond the breast of the knobby hill which bounded the lake on its other side, the land began to change. The foliage was thinner here, reduced from lush forestry to a thin cover of marsh plants. Water flowed over worn shelves of rock, stained with red-brown iron oxide and tumbled into teeming pools. Nodules of pyrite in the rock faces glittered under the midday sun. Lunzie caught the occasional gleam of a marine creature in the shallow pools near a broad sweep of rapids that swept and foamed around massive boulders. In the distance, more forest covered the bases of rough, bare mountain peaks.

"Quite a division here; this could be another world entirely," Lunzie announced, delighted, twisting around in her seat to get the best view.

Dondara activated his force-belt and signalled to her to do the same as he set the sled down.

"This is a different continental plate from the landing site," Dondara explained, splashing through a pool.

Lunzie skirted it to follow him. He pointed out geological features which supported his theory, including an upthrust face of sedimentary rock that was a rust-streaked gray which contrasted with the sparkling granite of the hilly expanse of the continent. With unexpected courtesy, he helped her up onto a well-worn boulder pocked with small pools.

"This was once a piece with the landmass across the ocean northeast of here, got slid over a spreading center over a few million years. This plate is more brittle. But it's got its own interesting life-forms. Come here." He gestured her over to a tubular hollow in the rock.

Lunzie peered at the hole. It was so smooth that it could have been drilled by a laser. "What's down there?"

"A very shy sort of warm-water crustacean. It'll only come out when the sky is overcast. If you stand over the hole, it'll think it is cloudy." Curious, Lunzie leaned down. "Look closely and be patient."

Dondara moved back and sat down on a dry shelf nearby. "You've got to turn off your force-belt, or it won't come out. The frequency annoys them."

As soon as she had deactivated the belt, she could see movement deep in the hollow. Lunzie knelt closer and spread her shadow over the opening. She heard a soft clattering noise, a distant but distinct rattle of porcelain. Suddenly, she was hit in the face by a fountaining stream of warm water. Lunzie jumped back, sputtering. The water played down the front of her tunic and then ceased.

"What on Earth was that?" she demanded, wiping her face.

Dondara roared with laughter, making the stones ring. He rolled back and forth on his stone perch, banging a hand against the rock in his merriment.

"Just a shy Ambrosian stone crab!" he chortled, enjoying the look on her face. "They do that every time something blocks their lair. Ambrosia has baptized you! You're one of us now, Lunzie!"

Once she recovered from the surprise, Lunzie realized that she had fallen for one of the oldest jokes in the database. She joined in Dondara's laughter.

"How many of the others did you sting with your 'shy rock crustacean'?" she asked suspiciously.

The heavyworlder was pleased. "Everyone but Zebara. He smelled vermin, and refused to come close enough." Dondara grinned. "You're not mad?"

"Why? But you can be sure I won't get caught a second time. Here on Ambrosia or anywhere else," Lunzie promised him. She was also obscurely pleased that she had been set up. She'd passed a subtle test. She was also soaking and the air was chilly, weak lightweight that she was. She flicked some of the excess off her hands and shirt.

"You really got a dose. Must have roused the granddaddy. If I don't offend your lightweight sensibilities, you better get yourself back to the scout. Take the sled." She was beginning to feel that such solicitude was only to be expected from one of Zebara's crew. "I've got to take some temperature readings in the hot springs upstream. The exercise will do me good. I've got my communicator." With a hearty wave, the big humanoid waded off upstream.

Lunzie activated the sled's power pack to fly back up the hill to the ship. Just about halfway there, she began to assimilate the full implications of that little encounter. Dondara had treated her to the "baptism" as he had probably done everyone else on the scout . . . enjoying his little joke. She had taken no umbrage and begged no quarter. But he had been considerate without being patronizing, recognizing certain lightweight problems rarely encountered by heavyworlders—like a propensity for catching chills.

"Will such minor wonders never cease?" she said to herself, ruffling her slowly drying hair.

"What happened to you?" Vir called as she came into view.

"Dondara had me baptized Ambrosian style," Lunzie shouted back, holding out the front of her clammy wet tunic with her good hand.

As she came upon Elessa, she saw that the botanist was grinning. "You knew he was going to do that."

"I'm sorry," the girl giggled. "I almost stopped you; he's such an awful practical joker. To make amends, I found you a kittisnake to examine. Aren't they adorable? And so friendly." She held up a small handful of black fur.

"Hang on to it for me," Lunzie called.

She set the sled down behind the scout. Elessa met her halfway and wound the length of animal around her hands.

"This is one of the most plentiful life-forms on Ambrosia," the botanist explained, "oddly enough omnivorous. They're really Bringan's province but they so love the attention that they're irresistible."

The kittisnake had a small round face, with a round nose and round ears which peered out of its sleek, back-combed fur. It had no limbs, but it was apparent where the thicker body joined the more slender tail. Two bright green eyes with round black pupils opened suddenly and regarded Lunzie expressionlessly. It opened its mouth, revealing two rows of needles, and aspirated a breathy hiss.

"It likes you," Elessa declared, interpreting a response which Lunzie had misjudged. "Pet it. It won't bite you."

It certainly seemed to enjoy the caress, twisting itself into pretzel knots as Lunzie ran her hands down its length. She grinned up at the botanist.

"Responsive, aren't they? Good ambassadors for a flourishing tourist trade on Ambrosia."

While Lunzie was making friends with the kittisnake, a light breeze sprang up. She suddenly decided she needed a warmer tunic over her injured arm. Though the bones had already been knit together by Bringan,

the swollen tissue had yet to subside. Lunzie felt her
flesh was starting to creep.

"Excuse me, will you?" she asked the botanist.

She squeezed past Zebara, poised in the open
hatchway of the scout. He greeted the doctor, raising
an eyebrow at her wet hair and clothes.

"Dondara took you to see the snark, huh?"

"A granddaddy snark to judge by the volume of
baptismal waters." She grinned up at the heavyworlder.

"Haven't you raised Fleet yet, Flor?" the captain
asked, turning back from the hatchway toward the
semicircular pilot's compartment. The communications station occupied another quarter arc of the
circle facing the rear of the ship between the telemetry station and the corridor.

"Aye, aye, sir," called the communications tech.
"I'm just stripping the message from the beacon
now. They acknowledge your request and have des-
patched the *Zaid-Dayan.*"

"The who? That's a new designation on me," Zebara
growled. Lunzie caught the note of suspicion in his
voice.

"Be glad, sir. Brand-new commission, on its maiden
voyage," Flor said apologetically. "Heavy cruiser,
ZD-43, the Registry says, with lots of new hardware
and armament."

"What? I don't want to have to wet-nurse an unin-
tegrated lot of lightweight lubbers . . ." Zebara sighed,
pushing back into the communications booth and
looking over Flor's shoulder.

Lunzie slipped in behind him. "Isn't telemetry
showing a trace?" she said, noticing the blip on the
current sweep of the unit.

"Is that the ZD-43 arriving now? Wait, there's an
echo. I see two blips." Zebara eased her aside with
one huge hand and inserted himself into the telemetry officer's chair. "Oh-oh! Pollili!" he roared. His
voice echoed out onto the hillside. The broad-faced

blond woman appeared on the breast of the slope below the shuttle and hurried up it at double time. "Interpret this trace for me," Zebara ordered. "Is this an FSP vessel of any kind? Specifically a new cruiser?"

Pollili took the seat next to Flor as her captain moved aside. She peered at the controls and toggled a computer analysis. "No way. It's not FSP. Irregular engine trace, overpowered for its size. I'd say it's an intruder."

"A pirate?" Lunzie heard herself ask.

"Two, to be precise." Zebara's expression was ferocious. "They must have been hanging in the asteroid belt or dodging us around the sun. How close are they to making orbit?"

"An hour, maybe more. I get traces of big energy weapons, too," Pollili said, pointing to a readout on her screen. "One of 'em is leaking so much it's as much a danger to the ship carrying it as it is to us. An academic point, to be sure, since we're unarmed."

"Will they land?" Lunzie asked, alarmed.

"I doubt it. If we can see them, they can see us. They know someone is down here, but they don't know who or what," Zebara said.

"Forgive me for pointing out a minor difficulty, sir," Flor said in a remarkably level, even droll tone, "but they can dispose of us from space. The ZD-43 is at least three days behind us," she added, her healthy color beginning to pale. "Once they realize we're alone here, they'll kill us. Is there nothing we can do?"

Zebara smiled, showing all of his teeth.

What was it Bringan had said? When he grins like a shark, watch out?

"We bluff. Flor, send another message to the *Zaid-Dayan*. Tell them that we've got two pirates circling Ambrosia. Tell them to take any shortcuts they can. Force multiple jumps. If they don't hurry, we'll be just a scorch mark and crater on the landscape. We're going to stall the inevitable just as long as we can."

"How?" Lunzie demanded, wishing she felt as confident as Zebara sounded.

"That, Doctor, is what we must figure out. Flor, have you sent that? Good. Now get on the general communicator channel and get the crew back here for a conference.

"I want your most positive thinking on how we can keep those pirates off planet," Zebara began once the crew had assembled in the messroom.

"Those blips couldn't possibly be anything else, could they?" Bringan asked after clearing his throat.

Zebara gave a short bark of laughter. "They haven't answered hails and their profile doesn't match anything in our records. And it's not good neighborliness they're leaking. Think, my friends. Think hard. How do we stall them?"

"No black box, huh?" asked Vir, a thin human with straight black hair and a bleak expression.

Flor shook her head. "Those would be a long time disconnected." No legitimate ship would put out into space without the black box interface between control systems and engines which transmitted automatic identification signals. To disconnect it disabled the drives. Unscrupulous engineers had been known to jury-rig components, but such a ship would never be allowed in an FSP-sanctioned port.

Zebara smashed his fist into a palm. "Stop denying the problem. Think. We've got to stall them long enough to let the *Zaid-Dayan* reach Ambrosian space."

No one spoke for a long moment. No one even exchanged glances in the tense atmosphere of the wardroom.

"What if we take off? Can't we outrun them?" Vir demanded to Wendell, the pilot.

"Not a chance," Wendell said sadly. "My engines don't have the kick to push us far enough out of their range to make a warp jump. They'd catch us halfway there."

"So we're stuck on this planet while the predators line us up in their sights," Dondara growled, scrubbing his dusty hair with his hands. He had taken only thirty minutes to run the distance from the pools after he'd received Flor's mayday recall. Lunzie was full of admiration for the heavyworlder's stamina.

Scarran cleared his throat. His perpetually redshot brown eyes made him look choleric or sleepy and he had a naturally mild personality.

"What about a violent disease of some sort? We're all dead and dying of it. Highly contagious. Can't find an antidote," he suggested in a self-deprecating voice.

"No, that wouldn't work," Pollili scoffed, drawing her brows together. "Even assuming they're of a species with enough in common with ours to catch it, they'd blow our ship off the face of the planet to wipe out the contagion and then land where they pleased."

"What about natural disaster?" asked Elessa, collecting nods from Flor and Scarran. "Unstable tectonics? An earthquake! A volcano about to blow? They'd have sacrificed scanning potential to some sort of weaponry."

"Possibly," Pollili drawled. "Even the simplest telemetry systems warn you if you're going to put down on a shifting surface. And live volcanoes show up as hot spots on infrared."

"What about a hostile life-form?" Lunzie asked, and was generally hooted down by the others.

"What, attack ferrets?" Elessa held up the blackfurred kittisnake, which curled around her hands, cooing breathily to show its contentment. "If the pirates are after Ambrosia when FSP has scarcely heard of its existence, they already know what's down here, besides us. Sorry, folks."

"Hold it a moment," Bringan said, raising a hand. "Lunzie has made a positive suggestion that merits discussion. Lunzie . . ."

"I had in mind a free bacterium that gets into your breathing apparatus and caulks it up with goo," Lunzie said, warming to her topic. "Five of our officers are down with it already. Nothing, not even breather masks, seems to keep it out. I feel that it's only a matter of time before they die of oxygen deprivation. The organism didn't appear in our initial reports because it's inert, sluggish during the winter months. It dies off in the cold. Now that the climate's warmed up for summer, the bug reproduces like mad. We're all infected. I've just discovered that it's gotten into the ventilation system, housed in the filters. I doubt we'd ever be able to lift off again, with the ship's air-recycling system fouled. I'm putting Ambrosia on indefinite quarantine. Only moral, ethical action possible to a medic or any professionality. Contact between ships is likely to doom them both. In fact, it's my professional opinion that the *ARCT-10* is in real danger since Zebara and Wendell were on board to report to Admin. Their lungs were already contaminated and the air they exhaled from their lungs would now be in the *ARCT's* air-recirculation system. Lungs are always warm— until the host is dead."

"What? What are you talking about?" demanded Vir, paling.

"What's this bacterium?" Elessa demanded. "I never observed one here and I prepared all the initial slides!"

"It's called *Pseudococcus pneumonosis.*" Lunzie smiled slyly. She was rather pleased with the astonished reaction to her little fable. "I've just discovered it, you see. A nicely non-existent but highly contagious condition, inevitably and painfully fatal. It might just stall them. It will certainly make them pause a while. If we can be convincing enough." Then she chuckled. "If we get out of this alive, someone better check with the old *ARCT* and see just who scrambled to the infirmary, requiring treatment for a fatal lung disease."

Zebara and Bringan chortled and, when the rest of the crew realized she'd been acting out a scenario, they gave Lunzie a round of applause. Laughter eased the tension and indicated renewed hope.

"That just might work," Bringan agreed after several moments of hard thinking. He gave Lunzie a warm smile. "Would we have trouble with them understanding medical lingo?"

Lunzie shrugged. "If I could fool you for a few minutes, I maybe can fool them. You see, Bringan only's a xeno-medic. He diagnosed it as vacation fever: personnel pretending to be sick so they could lounge in the sun. Once we got back here, with me, a human-medically trained person, I began to suspect a serious medical problem. By then it was too late to contain the bacterium. It was widespread. And, for all I know, loose on the *ARCT-10* as well.

"Sorry about this, folks, but I'll make it extremely personal: heavyworlders get it worst." She warded off the violent protests until Zebara bellowed for silence.

"She's got a valid reason to pick on us."

"I said I was sorry, heavyworlders. I'm not disparaging you but it's a fact, piracy has attracted many heavyworlders. Look, I'm not starting an argument . . ."

"And I'm ending it," Zebara said, showing his shark teeth. The muttering subsided immediately. "Lunzie's reasoning is sound. We take the lumps."

"How do you know so much about the planet pirates?" Dondara wanted to know, his eyes narrowed and unfriendly.

"Not my choice, but I do. Sorry about this."

"I'll forgive you if it works," Dondara said, but he gave her a wry twist of a smile.

"I think she's come up with the best chance we've got," the xenobiologist said approvingly. "Unless someone has thought up a better one just recently? Who delivers this deathless message to the pirates?" He looked at Zebara.

"I think I'd better," Zebara replied. "Not to decry Lunzie's dramatic abilities, but because the report of a heavyweight will be more acceptable to them than anything a lightweight could say."

"I hate such an expedient." With a fierce expression, Dondara exploded to his feet. "Do we have to compound the insult to all honorable heavyworlders who abhor the practice of piracy?"

With a sad expression on his face, Zebara shook his head at the geologist. "Don, we both know that some of Diplo's children have been weak enough to go into the service of unscrupulous beings in order to ease the crowding of our homeworlds." Dondara started to protest but Zebara cut him off. "Enough! Such weaklings shame us all and the good carry the disgrace along with them until the real culprits can be exposed. I intend to be part of that exposure. And this is one step in the right direction." He turned to Lunzie. "Brief me, Doctor Mespil!"

The plan, as plans do, underwent considerable revision until a creditable script was finally reached. With the help of the garment synthesizer and Flor's copious history diskfiles, Zebara was tricked out in the uniform of an attaché of Diplo, the heavyworlders' home planet. On a simple disk blue tunic, Flor attached silver shoulder braid and a tight upright collar of silver that fastened with a chain suspended between two buttons. As Zebara was dressed, Lunzie rehearsed him on details.

Meanwhile, Flor and Wendell were tinkering with the scout's black box, trying to mask, shield, electronically alter or scramble its identification signal. Neither wanted to tamper with the box because that could lead to other problems.

With a prosthetic putty, Bringan sculpted a new nose for Zebara and broadened his cheekbones to enhance his appearance to a more typical heavyworlder cast. Lunzie was stunned by the result. It changed him completely into one of the dull-faced hulks that she remembered from the Mining Platform.

"Zebara, they've achieved parking orbit," Flor called. "The lead ship will be directly overhead in six minutes."

The last touches of his costume in place, the heavyworld captain swaggered into the communications booth and took his place before the video pickup. Out of sight, Lunzie sat next to Flor in the control room and watched as a hail was sent to the two strange ships.

"Attention to orbiting ships," Zebara announced in a rasping monotone. "Arabesk speaking, attaché for His Excellency Lutpostig the Third, the Governor of Diplo. This planet is proscribed by order of His Excellency. Landing is forbidden. Identify yourselves."

On the screen before them, Lunzie and Flor saw a pattern shimmer into coherency. It was not a face but rather an abstract computer-generated graphic.

"So, they can see us, but we can't see them," Flor muttered to Lunzie. "I don't like this," the communications officer added miserably.

An electronically altered voice shivered through the audio pickup. Lunzie tried to guess the species of the speaker but it spoke a pure form of Basic with no telltale characteristics. Possibly computer-generated, like the graphic, she guessed.

"We know of no interdiction on this planet. We are landing in accordance with our orders."

Zebara gave a rasping cough which he only half covered with one hand. "The crew of this ship have contracted an airborne bacteria. *Pseudococcus pneumonosis.* This life-form was not, I repeat, NOT, mentioned in the initial landing report."

"Tell me another one, attaché. That report has been circulated."

Zebara's second cough lasted longer and seemed to rake his toes. Lunzie was impressed.

"Of course, but you should also know that the reports were made during the cold season in this hemisphere. Since the weather has warmed, the bacteria has awoken and multiplied explosively, infiltrating every portion of our ship." For good measure he managed a rasping gagging cough of gigantic proportion.

The voice became slightly less suspicious. "The effect of this warm season bacteria?"

"It infests the bronchial tubes, in a condition similar to pneumonia. The alveoli become clogged almost immediately. The first symptom is a pernicious cough." Zebara demonstrated, gagging dramatically. "The condition results in painful suffocation leading to death. Five of my crew have died already.

"We heavyworlders appear to be particularly susceptible due to our increased lung capacity," Zebara continued, injecting a note of panic into his voice. "First we tried to filter the bacterium out by using breather masks, but it is smaller than a virus. Nothing keeps it out. It can live anywhere that is warm. It flourished in the ventilation system and the filters are so caulked up that I doubt we will be able to cleanse them sufficiently to take off again. Ironic, for cold slows and kills it. Unfortunately, living pulmonary tissue never becomes cold enough. It even lingers in the lungs of the deceased until the boby itself has chilled."

There was murmuring behind the whirling pattern of colors on the screen, then the audio ceased completely.

"Zebara." Pollili's voice came over the private channel. "I now have readings on their ships. They're big ones. One of them is a fully loaded transport lugger, full of cold bodies. There must be five hundred deepsleepers aboard. It's the smaller one that's leaking energy. An escort, carrying enough firepower to split this planet in two."

"Can you identify the life-forms?" Lunzie asked.

"Negative. They're shielded. I get heat traces of about a hundred bodies, but my equipment's not sensitive enough to identify type, only heat emanations." Pollili's voice trailed off as the pirate spoke again.

"We will consider this information."

"I warn you, in the name of Diplo," Zebara insisted, "do not land on this planet. The bacterium is present throughout the atmosphere. Do not land."

Zebara slumped back into the padded seat and wiped his forehead. Flor hastily cut the connection.

"Bravo! Well done," Lunzie congratulated him, handing him a restorative pepper.

The rest of the crew crowded into the communication station.

"What will they do?" Vir asked nervously.

"What they said. Consider the information." Zebara took a long swig of the pepper. "One thing sure. They're not likely to go away."

"First of all, they'll check their source files to see if there's any mention of the bacterium," Bringan enumerated, ticking off his fingers. "That alone should make it hot for the people who sold them the information and forgot to mention a potentially fatal airborne parasite here. Second, they'll try to get a sample of the bacterium. I think we'll see an unmanned probe scooping the air, looking for samples to analyze."

"Third, they might try to put a volunteer crew down to test the effects of living beings," Elessa offered, bleakly.

"A distinct possibility," Flor said. "I'll just rig a repeater signal to broadcast the Interdict warning over and over again on their frequency. Might make them just a teensy bit more nervous."

Her fingers flew over her console, and then clicked on a button at the far left side. "There. It'll be loud, too."

Lunzie grinned. She was becoming more impressed with the imagination and ingenuity of this EEC Team. "I can't imagine that 'volunteers' will be thick in the corridors. But they will figure out all too soon that there isn't anything. Shouldn't we grab some rest while we can?"

"Well, I can't," Bringan said. "When they don't find what they're expecting, they'll ask us to identify it, so I better design an organism. Vir, you're a good hack, you can help me."

"I'll help, too," Elessa volunteered. "I wouldn't be able to rest with those vultures circling, just waiting to land on top of us."

"I'll authorize sedatives to anyone who doesn't think he or she can sleep," Lunzie offered, with a look toward Zebara for permission. The captain nodded.

Those who weren't involved in designing the pseudobacteria scattered to their sleeping cubicles and left the others wrangling over mouse-controlled Tri-D graphics program.

Lunzie lay down on her bunk and initiated Discipline technique to soothe herself to sleep. She got a restful few hours before tension roused her. There had been bets as to when another transmission from the pirate vessel would arrive.

After a twenty-four-hour respite, tempers began to fray. The design team had an argument, ending with Elessa storming out of the scout to sit in tears behind a tree, agitatedly soothing her pet kittisnake.

Wendell took a nap, but he was so tense when he

awoke that he asked Lunzie for a sedative. "I can't just sit around and wait," the pilot begged, twisting his hands together, "but if there's any chance of us lifting, I also can't be frazzled or fuzzy-minded."

Lunzie gave him a large dose of a mild relaxant, and left him with a complicated construction puzzle to keep his hands busy. Most of the others bore with the tension more stoically. Zebara alternated between popping mineral tablets and drumming on a table with an air of distraction and running the ships' profiles through the computer records. He badgered Flor with frequent updates on the *Zaid-Dayan*'s eta.

The outer two heavyworlders paced the common area for all the world like caged exotics; then Dondara irritably excused himself. He left the ship and headed downslope in the sled.

"Where's he going?" Lunzie asked.

"To break rocks," Pollili explained, turning her palms to the sky. "He'll come back when he can hold the frustration in check."

Dondara had been gone for nearly two hours when Flor appeared at the door of the common area. Zebara raised his head. "Well?"

She grimaced. "They've launched an unmanned probe. It's doing the usual loops." Then she really grinned. "I got good news, though." Everyone in the room snapped to. "I just stripped the beacon of a reply from the *Zaid-Dayan*. They say to hold tight. They ought to be here within three hours."

Ragged cheers rose from the crew when suddenly a low-pitched beeping came from the forward section.

"Uh-oh," Flor said. "The upstairs neighbors ahead of schedule!" She turned and run forward, followed by the rest of the crew. The filtered voice came through the audio monitors.

"Diplomat Arabesk. I wish to speak with Diplomat Arabesk."

Zebara reached for the silver-collared tunic but Lunzie grabbed his sleeve.

"You can't talk to them, Zebara, you're dead. Remember! Heavyworlders are more susceptible. The bacterial plague has claimed another victim. Pollili, you talk to them."

"Me?" squeaked the telemetry officer. "I can't talk to people like them. They won't believe me."

Flor was wringing her hands with nervousness. "Someone's got to speak to them. Soon. Please."

Lunzie hauled Pollili by the hand into the communications booth. "Poll, this can save all our lives. Will you trust me?"

The heavyworlder female looked at her beseechingly. "What are you doing to do?"

"I'm going to convince you that what you are about to say is one hundred percent the truth." Lunzie leaned forward and put a comforting hand, the one in the cast, on the other's arm. "Trust me?"

Pollili shot a desperate look at the beeping console. "Yes."

"Good. Zebara, will you clear everyone else out for a moment?"

Puzzled, the captain complied. "But I'm staying," he announced when everyone had left.

"As you wish." Lunzie resigned herself to his presence. "Flor can't hear us, can she?"

Zebara glanced at the set of indicator lights above the thick quartz glass panel. "No."

"All right. Poll, look at me." Lunzie stared into the heavyworlder's eyes and called upon the Discipline techniques she had learned on Tau Ceti. Keeping the small hypospray out of Flor's line of sight, she showed it to Pollili. "Just something to help you relax. I promise you it's not harmful." Pollili nodded uneasily. Lunzie pressed the head of the hypospray against the big woman's forearm. Pollili sagged back, her eyes heavy and glassy. Flor stared curiously from the other side of the panel and reached for a control. Zebara forestalled her with a gesture and she sat back in her chair, watching.

Lunzie kept her voice low and gentle. "Relax. Concentrate. You are Quinada, servant and aide to Ienois of the Parchandri Merchant Families. You landed here with a crew of twenty-five. Eight have already died of the bacterial plague, all heavyworlders. Arabesk, the Governor's personal representative, has just succumbed. Nine lightweights, the oldest and weakest ones, are also dead and the clone-types are showing at least the first symptoms of infection. You have a pernicious, deep-lung cough which strikes whenever you get excited. The bacteria is found only within thirty feet of the ground." Lunzie turned to Zebara. "That's too low for a probe to fly safely. With topographical variances, it's more likely to crash into a tree or a rock outcropping." Zebara nodded approval.

Lunzie turned back to programming Pollili. "The bacteria multiplies in direct relation to warmer temperatures. It's 22 degrees Celsius here right now. Optimum breeding time. You, Quinada, have connections with the faction in the Tau Ceti sector. You are something of a bully so you are not easily cowed by the inferior dogsbodies of any pirate vessel." Now Lunzie signalled to Flor to open the channel to the communications booth. "Remember, your name is Quinada, and you don't take guff from anyone, especially the weakling lightweights. You respect only your master, and he is one of those who is ill. You know and trust those of us here in the ship. We are your friends and business associates. When you hear your real name again, you will regain your original memories. I will touch you now and you will reply as circumstances require."

"We seek Diplomat Arabesk," the tinny voice said again. Pollili roused the instant Lunzie touched her arm. The medic leaned out of range of the video pickup and crept from her side.

"Arabesk is dead. Who is this?"

"Who speaks?" the voice demanded, surprised.

"Quinada!" Pollili said with great authority and some annoyance.

"Who is this Quinada?" Zebara asked in a low voice as Pollili's expression assumed a suitably Quinadian scowl.

"Just who I said she is," Lunzie whispered, crossing her fingers as she watched the heavyworlder female lean forward, prepared to dominate. "She works for a merchant who knew about Ambrosia more than two weeks before I left Tau Ceti for the *ARCT-10*. I must now assume that Ienois has direct lines with pirates from here, the *ARCT-10* and Alpha Centauri. Since he's got such a wide family, I'd be willing to bet someone of his kin were involved in setting up the Phoenix double-deal."

"This Quinada must have made quite an impression on you," Zebara replied wryly. "However did you impose her on Poll?"

"A Discipline technique."

"Not one of which I've ever heard. You must be an Adept. Oh, don't worry," Zebara assured her as she began to protest. "I can keep secrets. More than one, if your information on this merchant is true."

"Do I have to repeat everything to you dense-heads? I am Quinada," Pollili said, scowling and pulling her brows together in an excellent imitation of her model. "Servant to Ienois, senior Administrator in the eminent Parchandri Merchant Families. Who are you to challenge me?" There was a long pause during which the audio was cut off.

"We know of your master and we know your name," the voice announced at last, "though not your face. What are you doing on this planet?"

"My master's affairs. My last duty to him," Pollili

answered crisply. "No more of that. Arabesk is dead and I speak for those still alive."

"Where is your master?"

"The lung-rotting cough took him yesterday. The puny lightweight stock from which he springs will probably see the end of him before the week is over." Pollili delivered the last with an air of disgust overlaying her evident grief. Lunzie nodded approvingly from her corner. Pollili's own psyche was adding to the pattern Lunzie had impressed on her mind. Fortunately, there weren't the same dangerous leanings in Pollili's makeup that repulsed Lunzie in the original Quinada but the telemetry officer sounded most convincing.

"Quinada" confidently answered the rapid-fire questions that the voice shot to her. To consolidate her position, "Quinada" put up on the screen the genetic detailing of the bacterium which Bringan and the others had created. She explained what she understood of it. As Pollili, she knew a good deal about bacteria but the Quinada overlay wouldn't comprehend that much bioscience.

With her headset clasped to one ear, Flor gestured frantically for Zebara to join her in the soundproof control station. "Sir, I'm receiving live transmission from the *Zaid-Dayan*. They're approaching from behind the sun after making a triple jump! Those must be some fancy new engines. They'll be here within minutes!"

"Keep them talking!" Zebara mouthed through the glass to Pollili.

The woman nodded almost imperceptibly as she ordered the bio-map off the screen.

"It may interest you to know, Citizen Quinada, that we have taken atmospheric samples and find no traces of this organism which you claim has killed five of your colleagues." The voice held a triumphant note.

"Eight," "Quinada" corrected him. "Eight are dead now. The organism hovers within ten meters of the surface. Your probe didn't penetrate far enough."

"Perhaps your entire complement is alive and well, with no cough at all. We have noticed no difference in the number of infrared traces in your group between our first conversation and now."

"Dammit," Bringan groaned. "I knew we forgot something."

"Quinada" had an answer for that. "We have placed some of the sick in cold sleep. You are picking up heat traces for the machinery." "Quinada" coughed pointedly.

"You are not fooling us," the pirate sneered. "Your ship's identification signal is being scrambled. We suspect it is EEC, not Parchandri or Diplo. We have doubts as to your identity, Quinada. Your bio-file will be in our records. If it *is* yours."

Nervously, Zebara began to drum on the doorframe. The sound affected Lunzie's nerves. Tension began to knot up her insides. She forced herself to relax, to set an example of calm for the others. In the communications booth, Flor was white-faced with fear. Bringan paced restlessly in the corridor.

Under strain from her interrogator, "Quinada" started coughing. "You dare not accuse me of lying! Not if you were standing here before me. Come down, then, and die!"

"No, *you* will die. We will broil you and your make-believe organisms where you lie." The voice became savagely triumphant. "We do not look kindly on those who deceive us. We claim this planet."

The team members looked at one another with dismay.

"Attention, unidentified vessel." Another voice, crisply female and human, broke into the transmission. "This is the Fleet Cruiser *Zaid-Dayan*, Captain Vorenz speaking. Under the authority of the FSP,

we call upon you to surrender your vessels and prepare for boarding."

Pollili sat, eyes on the swirling pattern on the
screen, without reaction. Scarran dashed for the telemetry station, the others right behind him.

"There is another blip! Phew, but the *Zaid-Dayan*
is a big mother," he said.

The light indicating the FSP warship was fast closing with the planet from a sunward direction. On
screen, it projected the same intensity as the transport ship but with much more powerful emanations.
Statistics scrolled beside each blip. The enemy must
have been reading the same information on its screens,
because the two pirate vessels veered suddenly, breaking orbit and heading in different directions.

Tiny sparks erupted on the edge of the pirate
escort facing the FSP cruiser as the transport ship
broke for the edge of the Ambrosian system.

"What's that?" asked Lunzie, indicating the flashes.

"Ordnance," Timmins said. "Escort's firing on the
ZD so the lugger can escape."

Answering flickers came from the FSP ship as it
increased velocity, coming within a finger's width of
the pirate.

"They've got to stop the lugger from getting away!"
Elessa exclaimed.

"It can't get them both," Vir chided her.

"I'd rather the ZD took out the armed ship, myself. We're not safe and home yet."

"Oh, for a Tri-D tank," Flor complained. "The
coordinates say that they're miles apart but you can't
get the proper perspective on this obsolete equipment."

The transport zipped off the edge of the screen in
seconds. The two remaining blips crossed. For a
moment they couldn't tell which was which, until
Scarran reached over and touched a control.

"Now they're different colors. Red's the pirate,
blue's the *Zaid-Dayan*."

Red vectored away from Blue, firing rapid laser bolts at the larger ship. The blue dot took some hits, not enough to keep it from following neatly on the tail of Red. Now it was Red's turn to be peppered with laser bolts. Then a large flash of light issued from the blue dot.

"Missile!" Scarran exclaimed.

A tiny blip joined the larger two on the screen, moving very slowly toward the red light. The pirate vessel began desperate evasive maneuvers which apparently availed nothing against the mechanical intelligence guiding its nemesis. At last, Red had to turn its guns away from Blue long enough to rid itself of the chasing light dogging its movements.

The *Zaid-Dayan* sank a beautiful shot in the pirates' engine section. The red blip yawed from the blow but recovered; the pirate had as much unexpected maneuverability as weaponry. But the FSP cruiser inexorably closed the distance between them.

The speakers crackled again. "Surrender your vessel or we will be forced to destroy you," the calm female voice enjoined the pirate. "Stop now. This is our last warning."

"You will be the one destroyed," the mechanical voice from the pirate replied.

"They're heading into the atmosphere," Flor said, and indeed it seemed that the pirate was making one last throw of the dice, a desperate gamble with death.

"Turn on visual scan," Zebara ordered.

The communications officer illuminated another screen which showed nothing but sky. Gradually they could catch the shimmering point of light growing larger and larger in the sky to the north.

"Increase contrast." Flor complied, and the point separated into two lights, one behind the other. "Here they come."

Even at a thousand kilometers the scout team could hear the roar of the ships as they plunged through the atmosphere in controlled dives. On the screen, the two ships resembled hot white comets, arcing from the sky. Laser fire scored red sparks in the blazing white fire of each other's hulls.

"They're coming in nearly on top of us," Flor said in a shriek.

Red fire lanced out of the lead ship on the screen. Instead of pointing backward at the pursuing vessel, it blazed toward the planet's surface. There was a loud hiss and an explosion from outside the scout. Fragments of stone flew past the open hatchway. The force field protected those inside, but it would not hold for long. A smell of molten rock filled the air.

"Bloody pirates!" Zebara roared. "Evacuate ship! Now!" He lunged for the command console, ripping it from its moorings, and made for the exit.

"Well, I expected retaliation," Bringan replied, cradling something against his chest as he followed the captain. "Everybody out!"

The rest of the team didn't wait to secure anything but dove through the hatch. Lunzie was nearly to the ground before she realized that Pollili still hadn't moved.

"Come on!" she yelled, urgently. "Hurry! Come on—*Pollili!*"

The woman looked around, dazed and incredulous. "Lunzie? Where is everyone?"

"Evacuate, Poll. Evacuate!" Lunzie shouted, waving her arm. "Get out now! The pirates are firing on us."

The heavyworlder shot out of the booth like a launched missile. On her way down the ramp, she picked Lunzie up with one muscular arm about her waist and flung them both out of the hatchway. They hit the dirt and rolled down the hillside as another streak of red light destroyed a stand of trees to the left of the ship. The next bolt scored directly

on the scout's engines. Lunzie was still rolling
down the slope when the explosion dropped the
ground a good three feet underneath her. She landed
painfully on her arm brace and skidded down into
the stream at the bottom of the hill, where she lay,
bruised and panting. The only part of her which
wasn't abraded was the forearm protected by the arm
brace.

Pollili landed beside her. They flipped on their
force-screens and covered their heads with their arms.
The pirate escort made a screaming dive, coming
within sixty feet of the surface. Its engines were
covered with lines of blue lightning like St. Elmo's
fire. It had sustained quite a lot of damage.

The pirate was followed by a ship so big Lunzie
couldn't believe it could avoid crashing.

"The *Zaid-Dayan!*"

The two ships exchanged fire as they changed
direction, headed out toward Dondara's rock flats
before ascending once more into the sun. Radiant
heat from their passage set fire to the trees on the
edge of the plateau. The pirate and the cruiser continued to blast away even as they touched the bottom of their parabola and veered upward toward the
sky. They were completely out of sight in the upper
atmosphere when Lunzie and Pollili felt air sucked
away from them and then heard a huge *BOOM*! A
tiny fireball erupted in the middle of the sky, spreading out into a gigantic blazing cloud edged with black
smoke. The explosion turned into a long rumble
which altered to a loud and threatening sibilation.

"Into the water, quickly!" Lunzie gasped.

The two women were just barely under the surface
when hot fragments of metal rained down around
them, hissing angrily as they struck the water. The
fragments were still hot when they touched the edge
of their protective force-screen envelopes and passed
through harmlessly.

Lunzie's lungs were beginning to ache and her vision to turn black by the time the pieces stopped falling. When she finally crawled up the bank, her legs still in water, she gratefully pulled in deep breaths.

Pollili emerged next to her and flopped on her back, water streaming out of her hair and eyes. There were burns on the fabric of her tunic, and a painful-looking scorch mark on the back of one hand.

"It's over," Lunzie panted, "but who won?"

"I sure hope we did," Pollili breathed, staring up at the sky as the thrum of engines overhead grew louder.

Lunzie rolled over and dared to look up. The FSP warship, its spanking new colors scorched and carbonized and lines etched into its new hull plates by the enemy lasers, hovered majestically over the plateau where the destroyed scout had once rested, and triumphantly descended.

"We sure did." Pollili's voice rang with pride.

"That," declared Lunzie, "is the most beautiful thing I've ever seen. Singed about the edges, scorched a bit, but beautiful!"

The *Zaid-Dayan* carried the scout team to rendezvous with the *ARCT-10*. Zebara's team was lauded as heroes by the Fleet officers for holding off the pirate invasion until help could arrive. Pollili especially was decorated for "performance far beyond the line of duty."

"It should have been for sheer invention," Dondara muttered under his breath.

Pollili was uncomfortable with the praise and asked Lunzie to explain just what she had done which everyone thought was so brilliant.

"I trusted you; now tell me what you trusted me to do," Pollili complained. When Lunzie gave a brief resume, Poll frowned at her, briefly resuming her

"Quinada" mode. "Then you should take some of the credit. You thought up the deception."

"Not a bit," Lunzie said. "You did it all. I did nothing but allow you to use latent ingenuity. Chalk it up to the fact that people do extraordinary things when under pressure. In fact, I'd be obliged if you glossed over my part in it to anyone else."

Pollili shook her head at first but Lunzie gave her a soulfully appealing look. "Well, all right, if that's what you wish. Zebara says I can't ask how you did it. Only at least tell me what I said that I don't remember so I can tell Dondara."

Lunzie also reassured Dondara that his mate could not snap back into her "Quinada" role. He'd missed it all since he was just returning to the scout just as the ship was blown up. He had been set to wade into the molten wreckage and find some trace of Pollili. He was very proud that his mate was considered hero of the day and constantly groused that the computer record of her stellar performance had been destroyed along with the scout ship. Lunzie was relieved rather than upset and eventually gave Dondara a bowdlerized description of the events.

The other team members had suffered only bruisings and burns in their escape, treated by Fleet medical officers in the *Zaid-Dayan*'s state-of-the-art infirmary. Bringan's hands and feet were scorched and had been wrapped in coldpacks by the medics. In his scramble from the scout ship, he had been so concerned to preserve the records he salvaged that he hadn't turned on his force-belt. He also hadn't realized that he was climbing over melting rock until the soles of his boots began to smoke. He'd had a desperate time trying to pry the boots off with his bare hands.

Zebara had a long burn down his back where a flying piece of metal from the exploding scout had plowed through his flesh. He spent his first eight

days aboard the naval cruiser on his belly in an
infirmary bed. Lunzie kept him company until he
was allowed to get up. She called up musical programs from the well-stocked computer archives or
played chess with him. Most of the time, they just
talked about everything except pirates. Lunzie found
that she had become very fond of the enigmatic
heavyworlder.

"I won't be able to give you the protection you'll
need once we're back on the *ARCT-10*," Zebara said
one day. "I'd keep you under my protection if I
could but I no longer have a ship." He grimaced.
Lunzie hastened to check his bandages. The heavyworlder captain waved her away. "I had a message
from the EEC. I have number one priority to take
the next available scout off the assembly line but if I
break my toys, I can't expect a new one right away."
He made a rude noise.

Lunzie laughed. "I wouldn't be surprised if they
said just exactly that."

Zebara became serious. "I'd like to keep you on
my team. The others like you. You fit in well with
us. To reduce your immediate vulnerability, I'd ad-
vise that you take the next available mission *ARCT*
offers. By the time you come back, I should be able
to reclaim you permanently."

"I'd like that, too," Lunzie admitted. "I'd have the
best of all worlds, variety but with a set of permanent companions. I think I would have enjoyed myself on Ambrosia. But how do I queue-jump past
other specialists waiting to get on the next mission?"

Zebara gave her his predatory grin. "They owe us
a favor after our luring a pirate gunship to destruction. You'll get a berth in the next exploration available or I'll start cutting a few Adminstrators down to
size." He pounded one massive fist into the other to
emphasize his point, if not his methodology.

Chapter Fourteen

Zebara was right about the level of obligation the EEC felt for the team's actions.

"Policy usually dictates non-stress duty for at least four weeks after a planetary mission, Lunzie," the Chief Missions Officer of the *ARCT-10* told her in a private meeting in his office, "but if you want to go out right away, under the circumstances, you have my blessing. You're lucky. There's a three-month mission due for a combined geological-xenobiological mission on Ireta. I'll put you on the roster for Ireta. With the medical berth filled by you, there are only two more berths to assign. It leaves in two weeks. That's not much turnaround time. . . ."

"Thank you, sir. It relieves my mind greatly," Lunzie said sincerely. She had come straight to him after that talk with Zebara. The scout captain had depressed the right toggles.

Then she had to give the Missions Officer her own report on the Ambrosia incident, with full details. He kept the recorder on through the entire interview, often jotting additional notes. She felt quite exhausted when he finally excused her.

She later learned that he had interviewed each member of the team as well as the *Zaid-Dayan* officers. Apparently the fact that the lugger with its cold sleep would-be invasion force had escaped didn't concern him half as much as he was pleased that the overgunned escort had been destroyed. Most of those *ARCT-10* Ship-born felt the same way. "One less of those hyped-up gunships makes space that bit more safe for us."

The rest of Zebara's team was given interim ship assignments until a replacement explorer scout ship was commissioned. Lunzie, waiting out the two weeks before she could depart on the Iretan mission, found herself with one or more of the off-duty team, and usually Zebara himself. To her amusement, a whisper circulated that they were "an item." Neither did anything to dispel the notion. In fact, Lunzie was flattered. Zebara was attractive, intelligent, and honest: three qualities she couldn't help but admire. She was duly informed by "interested" friends that heavyworlder courting, though infrequent, was brutal and exhausting. She wasn't sure she needed to find out firsthand.

During his convalescence, Zebara strained his eyes going through ship records, trying to locate doctored files. The rumor of a bacterium on Ambrosia killing the landing party one by one had indeed made the rounds of the *ARCT-10* before any report had come back from the *Zaid-Dayan*. It was arduously traced back to Chacal, Coe's asocial friend in communications. He was taken in for questioning but died the first night in his cell. Although the official view reported it as a suicide, whisper had it that his injuries couldn't have been self-inflicted. Lunzie felt compassion for Coe, who felt himself compromised by his "friend's" covert activities.

"Which gets us no further than we were before," Bringan remarked at Lunzie's farewell party the night before she embarked on the Iretan mission.

"Somebody's got to do something positive about those fardling pirates," Pollili said, glowering about the room.

Lunzie was beginning to wish that she'd never imposed the Quinada personality on Pollili. Some of it *was* sticking. She devoutly hoped it would have worn off by the time she returned from her three months on Ireta.

At the docking bay while they were waiting for the *ARCT-10* to reach the shuttle's window down to Ireta's surface, she had a moment's anxiety as she saw six heavyworlders filing in. Stop that, she told herself. She'd got on just fine with Zebara's heavyworld crewmen. This lot could be similarly sociable, pleasant and interesting.

She concentrated hard on the activity in the docking area for there were several missions being landed in this system. A party of Theks including the ubiquitous Tor were to be set down on the seventh planet from the sun. A large group of Ryxi were awaiting transport to Arrutan's fifth planet which was to be thoroughly investigated as suitable for colonization by their species. Ireta, the fourth planet of the system's third-generation sun, was a good prospect—some said a textbook example—for transuranic ores since it appeared to have been locked into a Mezozoic age. Xenobiological surveying would investigate the myriad life-forms sensed by the high-altitude probe, but that search was to take second place to mining assay studies.

The teams would contact one another at prearranged intervals, and report to the *ARCT* on a regular basis by means of a satellite beacon set in a fixed orbit perpendicular to the plane of the ecliptic. The *ARCT-10* itself discovered traces of a huge ion storm between the Arrutan system and the next one over. They intended to track and chart its course.

"We'll be back for you before you know it," the deck officer assured them on his com as the Iretan shuttle lifted off and glided out of the landing bay. "Good hunting, my friends."

Ireta was named for the daughter of an FSP councillor who had been consistently supportive in voting funds to the EEC. At first it seemed that the councillor had been paid a significant compliment. Initial probe readouts suggested that Ireta had great potential. There was a hopeful feeling that if Ambrosia was lucky, Ireta would continue the streak. It possessed an oxygen/nitrogen atmosphere, indigenous plant life that ingested CO_2 and spat out oxygen: probe analysis marked significant transuranic ore deposits and countless interesting life forms on the part surveyed, none of which seemed to be intelligent.

A base camp was erected on a stony height and the shuttle positioned on a massive shelf of the local granite. A force-screen dome enclosed the entire camp and the veil constantly erupted in tiny blue sparks where Ireta's insect life destroyed itself in clouds on the electrical matrix. Sufficient smaller domes were set up to afford privacy, a larger one for the messhall-lounge, while the shuttle was turned into a laboratory and specimen storage.

And then there was the extraordinary stench. The air was permeated with hydro-telluride, a fiendish odor like rotting vegetation. One source was a small plant, which grew everywhere, that smelled like garlic gone berserk. No one could escape it. After one good whiff when the shuttle doors had opened on their home for the next three months, everyone dove for nose filters, by no means the most comfortable appliance in a hot, steamy environment. Soiled work clothes were left outside the sleeping quarters. After a while, no amount of cleansing completely removed the stench of Ireta from clothes or boots.

The stink bothered Lunzie far less than the feeling that she was being covertly watched. This began on their third day dirtside when the two co-leaders, Kai on the geological side and her young acquaintance Varian as xeno, passed out assignments.

The remainder of the team was a mixed bag. Lunzie knew no one else well but several of the others by sight. Zebara had personally checked the records of everyone assigned to that mission and she'd been delighted to learn that Kai as well as Varian and a man named Triv were Disciples. She was as surprised as Kai and Varian when three children had been included for dirtside experience on this mission. Bonnard, an active ten-year-old, was the son of the *ARCT-10*'s third officer. The gen was that she was probably glad to have him out of her hair while the *ARCT* explored the ion storm. Cleiti and Terilla, two girls a year younger than Bonnard, were more docile and proved eager to help.

Kai and Varian had both tried to set the children aside.

"That's an unexplored planet," Kai had protested to the mission officer. "This mission could be dangerous. It's no place for children."

Lunzie was not proof against the crushing disappointment in the young faces. There would be a force-shielded camp: there were plenty of adults to supervise their activities. "Oh, why not? Ireta's been benchmarked. No planet is ever completely safe but it shouldn't be too dangerous for a short term."

"If," Kai had emphasized that, holding up a warning finger at the children, "they act responsibly! Most important of all, never go outside the camp without an adult."

"We won't!" the youngsters chorused.

"We'll count on that promise," Kai told them, adult to adult. "It isn't uncommon for children to join a mission," he said to the others. "We can use the extra hands if we're to get everything done."

"We'll help, we'll help!" the girls had chorused. "We've never been on a planet before," Bonnard had added wistfully.

The last-minute inclusion of the children was curiously comforting to Lunzie: she'd missed so much of Fiona's childhood that she looked forward to their company. Lunzie preferred making new acquaintances, for strangers wouldn't know any details of her life. The team leaders, of course, knew that she had experienced cold sleep lags, for those were on her file. Varian considered her somewhat mysterious.

Gaber was the team cartographer and endlessly complained about the primitive facilities and noxious conditions. Lunzie usually greeted these outpourings with raised eyebrows. After the scout ship on Ambrosia, their quarters, not to mention the privacy of a separate small dwelling, seemed positively elaborate. However, Lunzie was willing to tolerate Gaber because he had been able to achieve long-term (for an ephemeral) friendships with the oldest Theks on the *ARCT-10* and she would divert his complaints to the relationships which fascinated her. She assisted Kai in making certain that the cartographer remembered to wear his force-belt and other safety equipment. That much was out of pure selfishness on Lunzie's part, for Gaber had to be constantly treated for insect bites and minor lacerations.

Trizein was a xenobiologist whose infectious enthusiasm made him popular with everyone, especially the youngsters, as he would patiently answer their many questions. Trizein applied the same amazing energy to his work though he was absentminded about safety precautions. Lunzie would be assisting him from time to time and had no problem with that duty.

Dimenon and Margit were Kai's senior geologists who would locate Ireta's deposits of useful minerals. They were specifically hoping for transuranics like plutonium which paid the biggest bonuses. Ireta's preliminary scan clearly displayed large deposits of radioactivity. Dimenon's crew was eager to get to work laying detective cores. Triv and Aulia and three of the heavyworlders, Bakkun, Berru and Tanegli, completed the geologists, while Portegin would set up the core-receiver screen and computer analysis.

Lunzie made no immediate efforts to approach the six heavyworlders. They didn't seem to mix with the lightweighters as easily as Zebara, Dondara and Pollili. The captain had instilled his team with his own democratic, bootstrapping ideals and, while on the *ARCT-10*, they had not limited their acquaintances to heavyworlders.

Paskutti, the security officer, was of the sullen, chip-on-the-shoulder type who would prefer a ghetto in the midst of an otherwise tolerant society. Lunzie wasn't sure if he was just sullen or stupid, but he ruled the female Tardma's every action. Lunzie refused to let him worry her. Her time with Zebara had shown that the attitude problem was theirs, not hers. Fortunately, as time passed Tanegli and another heavyworlder named Divisti became more sociable though they remained more distant with lightweights than Lunzie's comrades on Zebara's team had been. Bakkun and Berru were a recent pairing and it was understandable if they were much engrossed in each other.

Lunzie could not quite dismiss her lingering anxieties: Orlig's death still haunted her. Chacal, who had proved to be a spy, could never have strangled the heavyworlder. Knoradel and Birra, the Ryxi, when questioned, had both adamantly insisted that Lunzie had insulted Birra and then attacked Knoradel, who had gone to her assistance. Birra had left with the Ryxi settlers and Knoradel transferred off the *ARCT-10*.

Far from being a wonderland, Ireta's landscape became downright depressing after the novelty of it wore off. The purple-green and blue-green growth overhung the camp on every side. What looked like a flat, grassy meadow beckoning to the explorer usually turned out to be a miry swamp. The fauna was far more dangerous than any Lunzie had seen on Ambrosia or on any of the planets she had so far visited. Some of the life-forms were monstrous.

The first sled reconnaissance flights sighted large bodies crashing through the thick green jungle growth but, at first, no images were recorded, just vast shadowy forms. When at last Varian's team saw examples of Ireta's native life, they got quite a shock. The creatures were huge, ranging from a mere four meters to over thirty meters in length. One long-necked, slow-moving swamp herbivore was probably longer, but it hardly ever emerged from the marsh where it fed, so that the length of its tail was still in dispute.

Lunzie watched the xenob films with disbelief. Nothing real could be that big. It could squash a human being in passing, even a heavyworlder, and never notice. Small life there was in plenty, too. Lunzie held morning and evening surgeries to treat insect bites. The worst of them was a stinging insect which left huge welts but the most insidious was a leechlike bloodsucker. Everyone activated their personal force-screens outside the camp compound.

Instead of a second balmy paradise like Ambrosia, Ireta had more nasty surprises and anomalies than Purgatory. Stunners were issued to the geology and xeno teams although Varian made far more use of telltale taggers, marking the native life-forms with paint guns trying to amass population figures. Anyone out on foot wore his lift-belt, to remove himself quickly from the scene of trouble.

Lunzie found it curious that there were so many parasites with a taste for red, iron-based blood, when the first specimens of the marine life forms which Varian or Divisti brought in to be examined proved to have a much thinner, watery fluid in their systems. To test the planet for viability, foragers were sent out for specimens of fruits and plants to test and catalog. More than curiosity prompted that for it was always wise to supplement food stocks from indigenous sources in case the EV ship didn't get back on time. In this task, the children were useful, though they were always accompanied by an adult, often Lunzie, frequently Divisti who was a horticulturist. Whenever she thought about the ion storm which the *ARCT-10* was chasing, Lunzie pressed herself to find safe sources of indigenous foodstuffs. Then she chided herself for half believing her "Jonah" reputation. That had been broken by the fortuitous outcome of the Ambrosia incident.

Because her skills did not include mapping or prospecting, Lunzie took up the duties of camp quartermaster. She spent hours experimenting with the local foods when she wasn't overseeing the children's lessons or doing her Discipline exercises. She didn't mind being the camp cook for it was her first opportunity to prepare food by hand since she had left Tee. Making tempting meals out of synth-swill and the malodorous native plants provided her with quite a challenge.

Lunzie and Trizein also combined their skills to create a nutritious green pulp from local vines that filled all the basic daily requirements. On the one hand, the pulp was an extremely healthful meal. On the other, it tasted horrible. Since she had concocted it, Lunzie bravely ate her share but after the first sampling no one else would eat it except the heavy-worlders.

"They," Varian declared, "would eat anything."

Lunzie managed a chagrined smile. "My future efforts will be better, I promise. Just getting the hang of it."

"If you could just neutralize the hydro-telluride," Varian said. "Of course, we can always eat grass like the herbivores. D'you know, it doesn't stink?"

"Humans can't digest that much grass fiber."

On one of their supervised "foragings," the children had spotted a shy, hip-high, brown-furred beast in the ferny peat bogs. All their efforts to capture one of the "cute" animals before an adult could follow the active children, were circumvented by the quadrupeds' native caution. Varian found that odd since there was no reason for the little animals to fear bipeds. Then a wounded herbivore too slow to escape with the others was captured. A pen was constructed outside the camp for Varian to tend and observe the creature. On the next trip, Varian brought back one very small specimen of a furry quadruped breed. It had been orphaned and would have fallen prey to the larger carnivores.

The two creatures proved to compound Ireta's anomalies. Trizein had been dissecting clear-ichored marine creatures, styled fringes because of their shape. The large herbivore, savagely gouged in the flank, was red-blooded. Trizein was amazed that two such diverse species would have evolved on the same planet. Trizein could find no precedents to explain red-blooded, pentadactyl animals and ichor-circulating marine creatures cohabiting. The anomaly didn't fit the genetic blueprint for the planet. He spent hours trying to reconcile the diversities. He requested tissue samples from any big creature Varian's team could catch, both carnivore and herbivore, and he wanted specimens of marine and insect life. He seemed to be constantly in the shuttle lab, except when Lunzie hauled him out to eat his meals. He'd have forgotten that minor human requirement if she'd let him.

Meanwhile, the little creature now named Dandy and the wounded female adult herbivore called Mabel had to be tended and fed: the children assumed the first chore. Lunzie had synthesized a lactose formula for the orphan and put the energetic Bonnard in charge of its feeding, with Cleiti and Terilla to assist.

"Now you kids can't neglect Dandy," Lunzie told them. "I don't mind if you treat it as a pet but once you take responsibility for it, you'd better not forget that obligation. Understand me? Especially you, Bonnard. If you're interested in becoming a planetary surveyor, you must prove to be trustworthy. All this goes down on your file, remember!"

"I will, Lunzie, I will!" And Bonnard began issuing orders to the two girls.

Varian chuckled as she watched him grooming Dandy and fussing over the security of his pen while the girls refilled its water bucket. "He's making progress, isn't he?"

"Considerable. If we could only stop him bellowing like a bosun."

"You should hear his mother," Varian replied, grinning broadly. "I don't blame her for dumping him with us. I wouldn't want him underfoot if I was charting an ion storm."

"How's your Mabel?" Lunzie asked casually although she had another motive for asking.

"Oh, I think we can release her soon. Good clean tissue around the scar once we got rid of all the parasites. I wouldn't want to keep her in a pen much longer or she'll become tame, used to being given food instead of doing her own foraging."

"Mabel? Tame?" Lunzie rolled her eyes, remembering that it had taken all the heavyworlders to rope and secure the beast for the initial surgery.

"Odd, that injury," Varian went on, frowning. "All the adults of her herd had similar bite marks on their haunches. That would suggest that their predator doesn't kill!" Her frown deepened. "And that's rather odd behavior, too."

"You didn't by any chance notice the heavyworlders' reaction?"

Varian regarded Lunzie for a long moment. "I don't think I did but then I was far too busy keeping away from Mabel's tail, legs and teeth. Why? What did you notice?"

"They had looked . . ."—Lunzie paused, trying to find exactly the right adjective—"hungry!"

"Come on now, Lunzie!"

"I'm not kidding, Varian. They looked hungry at the sight of all that raw red meat. They weren't disgusted. They were fascinated. Tardma was all but salivating." Lunzie felt sick at the memory of the scene.

"There have always been rumors that heavyworlders eat animal flesh on their home planets," Varian said thoughtfully, giving a little squeamish shudder. "But that group have all served with FSP teams. They know the rules."

"It's not a rumor, Varian. They *do* eat animal protein on their homeworlds," Lunzie replied, recalling long serious talks she'd had with Zebara. "This is a very primitive environment, predators hunting constantly. There's something called the 'desert island syndrome.' " She sighed but made eye contact with the young leader. "And ethnic compulsions can cause the most civilized personality to revert, given the stimulus."

"Is that why you keep experimenting to improve the quality of available foodstuffs?" Lunzie nodded. "Keep up the good work, then. Last night's meal was rather savory. I'll keep an eye out for a hint of reversion."

A few days later Lunzie entered the shuttle laboratory to find Trizein combining a mass of vegetable protein with an *ARCT*-grown nut paste. She swiped her finger through the mess and licked thoughtfully.

"We're getting there, but you know, Tri, we're not real explorers yet. I'm sort of disappointed."

Trizein looked up, startled. "I think we've accomplished rather a lot in the limited time with so much to analyze and investigate. We're the first beings on this planet. How much more explorer can we be?"

Lunzie let the grin she'd been hiding show. "We're not considered true explorers until we have made a spiritous beverage from indigenous products."

Trizein blinked, totally baffled.

"Drink, Trizein. Quickal, spirits, booze, liquor, alcohol. What have you analyzed that's non-toxic with a sufficient sugar content to ferment? I think we should have a chemical relaxant. It'd do everyone good."

Trizein peered shortsightedly at her, a grin tugging at his lips. "In point of fact, I have got something. They brought it in from that foraging expedition that was attacked. I ran a sample of it. I think it's very good but I can't get anyone else to try it. We'll need a still."

"Nothing we can't build." Lunzie grinned. "I've been anticipating your cooperation, Tri, and I've got the necessary components out of stores. I rather thought you'd assist in this worthy project for the benefit of team morale."

"Morale's so important," Trizein agreed, exhibiting a droll manner which he'd had little occasion to display. "I do miss wine, both for drinking and cooking. Not that anything is likely to improve the pervasive flavor of Iretan food. A little something after supper is a sure specific against insomnia."

"I didn't think anyone suffered that here," Lunzie remarked, and then they set to work to construct a simple distillation system, complete with several filters. "We'll have to remove all traces of the hydrotelluride without cooking off the alcohol."

"A pity acclimatization is taking so long," Trizein said, easing a glass pipe into a joint. "We'll probably get used to the stench the day before the *ARCT* comes for us."

They set the still up, out of the way, in a corner of Lunzie's sleeping dome. With a sense of achievement, they watched the apparatus bubble gently for a time and then left it to do its job.

"It's going to be days before there's enough for the whole team to drink," Trizein said in gentle complaint.

"I'll keep watch on it," she said, her eyes crinkling merrily, "but feel perfectly free to pop in and sample its progress."

"Oh, yes, we should periodically sample it," Trizein replied gravely. "Can't have an inferior product."

They shut the seal on Lunzie's dome just as Kai and Gaber burst excitedly into the camp.

"We've got films of the monster who's been taking bites out of the herbivores," Kai announced, waving the cassette jubilantly above his head.

The lightweights watched the footage of toothy monsters with horrified interest. Varian dubbed the carnivores "fang-faces" for the prominent fangs and rows of sharp teeth. They were terrifyingly powerful specimens, walking upright on huge haunches with a reptilian tail like a third leg that flew behind them when they ran. The much smaller forepaws might look like a humorous afterthought of genetic inadequacy but they were strong enough to hold a victim still while the animal chewed on the living prey. Fortunately the fang-faces on film were not savaging herbivores in this scene. They were greedily eating clumps of a bright green grass, tearing them up by those very useful forelimbs, stuffing them into toothy maws.

"Quite a predator," Lunzie murmured to Varian. She ought to have hauled Trizein away from his beloved electro-microscope. He needed to have the contrast of the macrocosm to round out the pathology of his biological profiles.

"Yes, but this is very uncharacteristic behavior for a carnivore," Varian remarked, watching intently. "Its teeth are suitable for a carnivorous diet. Why is it eating grass like there's no tomorrow?"

As the camera panned past the fang-face, it rested on a golden-furred flying creature, eating grass almost alongside the predator. It had a long sharp beak and wing-hands like the Ryxi but there the resemblance ended.

"We've seen avian nests but they're always near water, preferably large lakes or rivers," Gaber told Lunzie. "That creature is nearly two hundred kilometers from the nearest water. They would have to have deliberately sought out this vegetation."

"They're an interesting species, too," Kai remarked. "They were curious enough to follow our sled and they're capable of fantastic speed."

Varian let out a crow. "I want to be there when we tell that to the Ryxi! They want to be the only intelligent avians in the galaxy even if they have to deny the existence of others by main strength of will."

"Why weren't these species seen on the initial flyby of Ireta?" Divisti asked in her deep slow voice.

"With the dense jungle vegetation a super cover? Not surprising that the report only registered lifeforms. Think of all the trouble we've had getting pictures with them scooting into the underbrush."

"I wish the *ARCT* wasn't out of range," Kai remarked, not for the first time. "I'd like to order a galaxy search on EV files. I keep feeling that this planet has to have been surveyed before."

Dimenon, as chief geologist, was of the same opinion. He was getting peculiar echoes from signalling cores all over the continental shield. Kai managed to disinter an old core from the site of one of the echoes. Its discovery proved to the geologists that their equipment was functioning properly but the existence of an unsuspected core also caused consternation.

"This core is not only old, it's ancient," Kai said. "Millions of years old."

"Looks just like the ones you're using," Lunzie remarked, handling the tube-shaped core.

"That's true enough, but it suggests that the planet has been surveyed before, which is why no deposits of transuranics have been found in an area that should be rich with them."

"Then why no report in the EV files?" Dimenon asked.

Kai shrugged, taking the core back from Lunzie. "This is slightly more bulky but otherwise identical."

"Could it be the Others?" Dimenon asked in a hushed voice.

Lunzie shook her head, chuckling at that old childish nightmare.

"Not unless the Others know the Theks," Kai replied. "They make all the cores we use."

"What if the Theks are copying the science of the older technology?" Dimenon argued defensively.

While it was hard to imagine anything older than Theks, Lunzie looked at Kai who knew more about them than she did.

"Then the ancient core has to mean that Ireta was previously surveyed? Only who did it? What do the Theks say?"

"I intend to ask them," Kai replied grimly.

A few days later, Varian sought Lunzie out in her dome. The young leader was shaking and very disturbed. Lunzie made her sit and gave her a mug of pepper.

"What's wrong?"

The girl took a deep sip of the restorative drink before she spoke.

"You were right," Varian said. "The heavyworlders are reverting to savagery. I had two of them out on a survey. Paskutti was flying the sled as we tracked a fang-face. It chased down one of the herbivores and gouged bites out of its flank. It made me sick, but Paskutti and Tardma exhibited a grotesque fascination at the sight. I insisted that we save the poor

herbivore before it was killed. Paskutti promptly
blasted the fang-face with the sled exhaust, showing
his superiority like an alpha animal. He did drive it
off but not before wounding it cruelly. Its hide was a
mass of char."

Lunzie swallowed her disgust. As surrogate mother-
confessor and psychologist for the team, she knew
that a confrontation with the heavyworlders was required to discover exactly what was going on in their
minds, but she didn't look forward to the experience.
Right now she needed to refocus Varian on her mission, to take her mind off the horror.

"The predator just took the animal's flesh," she
asked, "leaving a wound like Mabel's? That's interesting. A fang-face has a tremendous appetite. One
little chunk of herbivore oughtn't to satisfy it."

"They certainly couldn't sustain themselves just by
eating grass. Even though they do eat tons of it in
the truce-patch."

Lunzie stroked the back of her neck thoughtfully.
"That grass is more likely to provide a nutrient they're
missing. We'll analyze anything you bring us."

Varian managed a laugh. "That's a request for
samples?"

"Yes, indeed. Trizein is right. There are anomalies
here, puzzles left from eons past. I'd like to solve the
mystery before we leave Ireta."

"If we leave," Gaber said irritably later that day
when Lunzie invited him to share a pot of her brew
of synthesized coffee. "I don't intend ever signing up
for a planetary mission again. It's my opinion that
we've been planted. We're here to provide the core
of a planetary population. We'll never get off."

"Nonsense," Lunzie returned sharply, ignoring his
basic self-contradiction to concentrate on reducing a
new rumor. "The transuranics of this planet alone
are enough to supply ten star systems for a century.
The FSP is far more desperate for mineral wealth

than starting colonies. Now that Dimenon is prospecting beyond the continental shield, he's finding significant deposits of transuranics every day."

"Significant?" Gaber was skeptical.

"Triv is doing assays. We'll have evaluations shortly," Lunzie said in a no-nonsense tone. Gaber responded to firmness. "Add to that, look at all the equipment we have with us. The EEC can't afford to plant such expensive machinery. They need it too badly for ongoing exploration."

"They'd have to make it look like a normal drop, or we all would have opted out." Gaber could be obstinate in his whimsies.

Lunzie was exasperated by the cartographer's paranoia. "But why plant us? We're the wrong age mix and too few in number to provide any viable generations beyond grandchildren."

Gaber sat gloomily over his mug of coffee. "Perhaps they're trying to get rid of us and this was the surest way."

Lunzie was momentarily stunned into silence. Gaber had to be grousing. If there was the least byte of truth to his appalling notion, she was a prime candidate for the tactic. If eighteen people had been put in jeopardy just to remove her, she would never forgive herself. Common sense took hold. Zebara had checked the files on the entire mission personnel: she had been a late addition to the team and, by the time she was included, it would have been far too late for even a highly organized pirate network to have maneuvered a planting!

"Sometimes, Gaber," she said with as light a tone as she could manage, "you can be totally absurd! The mission planted? Highly unlikely."

However, when Dimenon returned from the northeast edge of the shield with his news of a major strike, Lunzie decided that tonight was a very good

occasion to break out the quickal. There was enough
to provide two decent tots for each adult to celebrate
the discovery of the saddle of pitchblende. The upthrust strike would provide all the geologists with
such assay bonuses they might never have to work
again. A percentage was customarily shared out to
other members of an exploratory team. Even the
children.

They had to be content with riches in their major-
ity, and fruit juice now in their glasses. However,
they were soon merry enough, for Dimenon brought
out the thumb piano he never travelled without and
played while everyone danced.

If the heavyworlders had to be summoned from
their quarters by Kai to join in, they did so with
more enthusiasm than Lunzie would have believed
of the dour race. They also appeared to get drunker
on the two servings than anyone else did.

The next day they were surly and clumsy, more of
a distraction to the survey teams than a functioning
part. There was physical evidence that the alcohol
had stimulated a mating frenzy. Some of the males
sported bruises, Tardma cradled one arm and Divisti
walked in a measured way that suggested to Lunzie
that she was covering a limp.

Lunzie spent hours over comparative chemical analysis and called the heavyworlders in one at a time
that evening for physical examinations, trying to determine if their mutation was adversely affected by
the native quickal. To be on the safe side, she added
one more filter to the still. Nothing else which could
be construed as harmful was left in the mixture. She
took a taste of the new distillate and made a face. It
was potent, but not potent enough to account for the
heavyworlder behavior.

Lunzie lay in bed late that night staring up at the
top of the dome and listening to the bubbling of the
still.

If, she mused, aware that the quickal had loosened a few inhibitions, Gaber should be correct, I might be planted but I haven't lost anything. I've nothing left of my past except that hologram of Fiona in the bottom of my bag. I started my travels with that: it is proper for it to be with me now.

I wonder how Fiona is, on that remote colony of hers. What would she say if she could see me now, in an equally remote location, escaping yet another life-threatening situation, complete with fanged predators? Lunzie sighed. Why would Fiona care? She knew that when she had escaped from Ireta back to the *ARCT-10*, she'd join Zebara's team, stop running away, and have an interesting life. No big nasty pervert has dumped nineteen people on a substandard planet just to dispose of one time-lagged ex-Jonah medic.

Which brought her right back to the underlying motivation. The planet pirates. They were to blame for everything that had happened to her since her first cold sleep. They had unsettled her life time and again: first by robbing her of her daughter, trying to kill her and making her live in fear of her life. Somehow, even if it meant turning down a place on Zebara's team, she was going to turn matters around, and start interfering with the pirates, instead of them messing up her life all the time. She'd managed to do a little along those lines already: she just had to improve her efficiency. She grinned to herself. That could be fun now that she had learned to be vigilant. The Ireta mission had a few more weeks to run.

With a sigh, she started the Discipline for putting herself to sleep. In the morning, she kept her mind busy with inventorying the supply dome. As she checked through, small discrepancies began to show up in a variety of items, including some she had had occasion to draw from only the day before. She turned over piles of dome covers, and restacked boxes, but there was no doubt about it. Force-belts, chargers, portable disk reader/writers were missing. Stock had also been moved around, partly to conceal withdrawals. Quickly, she went over the foodstuffs. None of the all-important protein stores were gone, but quantities of the mineral supplements had vanished as well as a lot of vegetable carbohydrates.

The missing items could be quite legitimate, with secondary camps being established for the geology teams. There was no reason they couldn't just help themselves. She would ask one of the leaders later on.

From the hatch of the dome, Lunzie saw Kai coming down the hill from the shuttle and met him at the veil lock. "You look tired."

"Thek contact," Kai said, feigning total exhaustion. "I wish Varian would do some of the contacts but she just hasn't the patience to talk to Theks."

"Gaber likes talking with Theks."

"Gaber wouldn't stick to the subject under discussion."

"Such as the ancient cores?"

"Right."

"What did they say?"

Kai shrugged. "I asked my questions. Now they will consider them. Eventually I'll get answers."

Varian joined them as they walked to the dome. "What word from the Theks?"

"I expect a definite yes or no my next contact. But what in the raking hells could they tell me after all this time? Even Theks don't live as long as those cores have been buried."

"Kai, I've been talking to Gaber." Lunzie took the co-leaders aside. "He's heard a rumor about planting. He swears he has kept his notion to himself, but if he has reached that conclusion on his own, you may assume that others have, too."

"You're smarter than that," Kai snapped. "We haven't been planted."

"You know how Gaber complains, Lunzie," Varian added. "It's more of his usual."

"Then there's nothing wrong in the lack of messages from the *ARCT-10*, is there?" Lunzie asked bluntly. "There's really been no more news from our wandering ship in several weeks. The kids especially miss word from their parents."

Kai and Varian exchanged worried glances. "There's been nothing on the beacon since they closed with the storm."

"That long?" Lunzie asked, taken aback. "They couldn't have gotten that far out of range since we were dropped off. Had the Theks heard?"

"No, but that doesn't worry me. What does is that our messages haven't been stripped from the beacon since the first week. Look, Lunzie," Kai said when she whistled at that news, "morale will deteriorate if people learn that. It would give credence to that ridiculous notion that we've been planted. I give you my word that the *ARCT* means to come back for us. The Ryxi intend to stay on Arrutan-5 but the Theks don't want to remain on the seventh planet forever."

"And even though the Theks wouldn't care if they were left through the next geologic age," Varian said firmly, "this is not the place I intend to spend the rest of my life."

"Nor I," was Lunzie's fervent second.

"Oh, there can't be anything really wrong," Varian went on blithely. "Perhaps the raking storm bollixed up the big receivers or something equally frustrating. Or," and now her eyes twinkled with pure mischief, "maybe the Others got them."

"Not on my first assignment as a leader," Kai said, making a valiant attempt to respond.

"By the way," Lunzie began, "since I've got the two of you at once, did you authorize some fairly hefty withdrawals from stores?"

"No," Varian and Kai chorused. "What's missing?" Kai asked.

"I did an inventory today and we're missing tools, mineral supplements, some light equipment, and a lot of oddments that were there yesterday."

"I'll ask my teams," Kai said and looked at Varian.

She was reviewing the problem. "You know, there have been a few funny things happening with supplies. The power pack in my sled was run down and I recharged it only yesterday morning. I know I haven't used up twelve hours' worth of power already."

"Well, I'll just institute a job for the girls," Lunzie said. "They can do their studies at the stores' dome and check supplies and equipment in and out. All part of their education in planetary management."

"Nice thought," Varian said, grinning.

Dimenon and his crew returned from their explorations with evidence of another notable strike. Gold nuggets glittering in a streambed had led them to a rich vein of ore. The heavy hunks were passed from hand to hand that evening at another celebration. Morale lifted as Ireta once again proved to be a virgin source of mineral wealth.

A lot of the evening was spent in good-natured speculation as to the disposition of yet another hefty bonus. Lunzie dispensed copious draughts of fruit ale, keeping a careful eye on the heavyworlders although she was careful not to stint their portions.

In the morning, everyone seemed normal. In contrast to the drunken incompetence they had displayed the last time, the heavyworlders were in excellent spirits.

A different kind of emergency faced Lunzie as she emerged from her dome.

"I can't take it! I can't take it!" Dimenon cried, clutching first his head and then falling on his knees in front of us.

"What's the matter?" she demanded, alarmed by the distortion of his features. What on Earth sort of disease had he contracted? She fumbled for her bod bird.

"That won't help," Kai said, shaking his head sadly.

"Why not?" she said, her hand closing on the bod bird.

"Nothing can cure him."

"Tell me I'm not a goner, Lunzie. Tell me." He waved his hands so wildy that she couldn't get the bod bird into position.

"He doesn't smell Ireta any more," Kai said, still shaking his head but smiling wryly at his friend's histrionics.

"He what?" Lunzie stopped trying to scope Dimenon and then realized that she hadn't had time to put in her own nose filters. And *she* didn't smell Ireta either. "Krims!" She closed her eyes and gave a long sigh. "It has to come to this, huh?"

Dimenon wrapped his arms about her knees. "Oh, Lunzie, I'm so sorry for both of us. Please, my smeller will come back, won't it? Once I'm back in real air again. Oh, don't tell me I'll never be able to smell nothing in the air again . . ."

"An Ambrosian shadow crab by another name will still get you wet," Lunzie muttered under her breath. Nothing for it but to play out the scene. She picked up Dimenon's wrist and took his pulse, shone the bod bird in first one eye, then the other. "If the acclimatization should just happen to be permanent, you could install an Iretan air-conditioner for your shipboard quarters. The *ARCT-10* engineers are very solicitous about special atmospheres for the odd human mutation."

Dimenon looked as if he believed her for a long, woeful moment but the others were laughing so hard that he took it in good part.

Despite the installation of Cleiti and Terilla as

requisitions clerks, the depletion of supplies did not cease. More items than those checked out by the girls continued to go missing: some were vital and irreplaceable pieces of equipment.

Coupling that with the increasingly aberrant behavior of the heavyworlders, Lunzie pegged them as the pilferers. At the rate supplies were being raided, they must be getting ready to strike off on their own. They were physically well adapted for the dangers inherent on Ireta. This wasn't, she admitted to herself, the usual way in which heavyworlders usurped a full planet. Perhaps her imagination was going wild. There were only six heavyworlders, not enough to colonize a planet.

But the Theks were still in the system, and the Ryxi. So the system was already opened up in the conventional way. The *ARCT-10* would soon be back to collect them, and if the heavyworlders wished to indulge in their baser instincts until that time, they were no real loss. There were still five qualified geologists and she, Trizein, Portegin and the kids could help Varian complete her part of the survey.

With Bonnard as Varian's record taper and with the possible alteration of the camp in mind, Lunzie assisted Trizein in his studies of the now-obsessive anomalies of Iretan life-forms.

Today's first task was to lure Dandy into the biologist's lab so he could take measurements of its head and limbs, and samples of hair and skin from the shy little animal. The beast kicked and whistled when Trizein scraped cells from inside its furry ears. Lunzie took it back to its pen and rewarded it with a sweet vegetable. She stayed a moment calming and caressing it before returning to Trizein, who was peering into the eyepiece of a scanner. He gestured her over in excitement.

"There is something very irregular about this

planet," he said. "You just compare these two slides: one from the marine fringes and the other fresh from the little herbivore." Obediently Lunzie looked and he was right; the structures represented radically differing biologies. "Judging by the eating and ingesting habits, I have no doubt that the square marine fringes are native to this planet but Dandy and his friends don't belong here.

"I have a theory about the primitive yeasts we've been documenting," Trizein went on in a semi-lecturing mode. "It's been plaguing me all along that there was something familiar about the configuration."

"How can that be?" Lunzie asked, racking her brains. "I'll grant you that the Ssli are a tad like the fringes but I've never seen anything like Dandy before."

"That's because Dandy is the primitive form of an animal you're used to in its evolved state: the horse. The Earth horse. The species is not only pentadactyl, it is perissodactyl."

"That's impossible!"

"I'm afraid there's no other explanation though it doesn't explain how the creatures got here—he couldn't have evolved on this planet, but here he is."

"Someone had to have conveyed the stock here," Lunzie mused.

"Precisely," the biologist said. "If I were to ignore the context and study only the data I've been given, first by Bakkun, and now from this little fellow's living tissue, I would have to say that he is a hyracotherium, a life-form which became extinct on old Earth millions of years ago!"

The sound of the sled interrupted them. Lunzie hurried to the shield controls to admit Varian and Bonnard. She informed them that Trizein had news that he wanted to share with them. It was his triumph and he should be allowed to enjoy it by himself. The absentminded biologist was seldom outside his laboratory except to eat or to visit with Lunzie or Kai and had been largely unaware of the other facets of the team.

To the amazement of his small audience, he displayed the disk showing an archival drawing of a hyracotherium from his collection of paleontological files. There was no doubt about it: Dandy was unquestionably a replica of an ancient Earth breed from the Oligocene era.

"Let's see if there's more alike than just the furred beasts," Varian said, leading Trizein to the viewscreen. Varian promptly sat the bemused biologist down to watch her tapes of the golden fliers. Trizein launched into raptures as the graceful creatures performed their aerial acrobatics.

"No way to be certain, of course, without complete analysis, but this unquestionably resembles a pteranodon!"

"Pteranodon?" Bonnard made a face.

"Yes, a pteranodon, a form of dinosaur, misnamed, of course, since patently this creature is warm-blooded. . . ." One by one, he identified the genotypes of the beasts Varian and the others had recorded. Each of the Iretan samples could be matched to a holo and description from Trizein's paleontological files. He did point to some minor evolutionary details but they were negligible alterations.

Fang-face was a Tyrannosaurus rex; Mabel and her breed were crested hadrosaurs; the weed-eating swamp dwellers were stegosauri and brontosauri. The biologist became more and more disturbed. He could not believe that they existed just on the other side of the veil which he himself never crossed. When Varian gave him the survey tapes she'd compiled, he shook an accusatory finger at the screen.

"Those animals were planted here."

"By who?" gasped Bonnard, wide-eyed. "The Others?"

"The Theks planted them, of course," Trizein assured the boy.

"Gaber says we're planted," Bonnard added.

Trizein, in his mild way, was more saddened than disturbed by the suggestion. He looked to Varian.

"We're not planted, Trizein," the young co-leader assured him and gave Bonnard a very intense and disapproving glare.

Kai was urgently summoned back from the edge of the continental shield to hear Trizein's conclusions, leaving Bakkun alone on the ridge. Varian particularly wanted Kai separated from the heavyworlders, for by the time he returned, Trizein had given her even more disturbing news.

Paskutti had asked Trizein to test the toxicity of the fang-face flesh and hide, a question which was not mere idle curiosity. Varian now had films of a startling atrocity. That day, Bonnard had led her to Bakkun's "special place." It proved to be a rough campground where five skulls and blackened bones of some of the fang-faces lay among the stones.

Lunzie knew how quickly the parasites of Ireta disposed of carrion. That meant these were very recent. There could be little doubt that the heavyworlders had killed and eaten animal flesh. The situation narrowed down to how well Kai, and Varian, could control the heavyworlders until the *ARCT-10* retrieved them.

Chapter Fifteen

With a grim expression, Varian began emergency measures. She ordered Bonnard to remove all the sled power packs and hide them in the bushes around the compound. The packs had been depleted at an amazing rate and now she had the answer. Overuse by the heavyworlders. They'd have to have sledded to reach their "secret place," for the ritual slaughter and consumption of the animals.

Kai met them in the shuttle at the top of the hill, puzzled at the unusual urgent summons. He was horrified when he heard Varian's conclusions. Lunzie confirmed the continued drain of supplies which led her to believe that the heavyworlders had reverted to primitivism.

"We're lucky if it isn't mutiny," Varian finished. "Haven't you noticed in the past few days how their attitude toward us has been altering? Subtly, I admit; but they show less respect for our positions than before."

Kai nodded. "Then you think a confrontation is imminent?"

Varian affirmed it: "Our grace period ended last restday."

The heavyworlders could take over. As Lunzie

367

drily pointed out, the mutated humans were far more able to take care of themselves on wild Ireta than the lightweight humans.

"I realize I'm repeating myself," Lunzie added, "but if Gaber felt he had been planted, the heavy-worlders must have come to the same conclusion." She paused, hearing the whine of a lift-belt in the distance and listened harder. Who'd be using a lift-belt now?

"Bonnard and I also saw a Tyrannosaurus rex with a tree-sized spear stuck in his ribs," Varian said, shuddering. "That creature once ruled Old Earth. Nothing could stop him. A heavyworlder did, for fun! Furthermore, by establishing those secondary camps, we have given them additional bases. Where are the heavyworlders right now?"

"I left Bakkun working at the ridge. Presumably when he's finished he'll come back here. He had a lift-belt . . ."

Lunzie glanced out of the shuttle door and saw the whole contingent of heavyworlders coming toward them up the hill. The drawn concentration on their heavy-boned faces was terrifying. They looked dangerous, and they harbored no good intentions for the lightweights in the ship. She shouted a warning to Kai and Varian. She saw the door to the piloting compartment iris shut almost on Paskutti's foot.

As she flattened herself against the bulkhead, she noticed the imperceptible blink that told her the main power supply had been deactivated and the shuttle was now on auxiliaries. Was it too much to hope that one of the leaders had managed to get a message out?

"If you do not open that lock instantly, we will blast," said the hard unemotional voice of Paskutti, blaster in hand.

He was fully kitted out with many items that had so recently gone missing from the stores. Of course,

Lunzie told herself; she realized too late that most of that purloined equipment had offensive capability.

"Don't!" Varian's voice sounded sufficiently fearful to keep Paskutti from pulling the release but Lunzie knew the girl was no coward. It did no good for either of them to be fried alive in the compartment.

The hatch opened and massive Paskutti reached through it. He seized Varian by the front of her shipsuit and hauled her out, flinging her against the ceramic side of the shuttle with such force that it broke her arm. Grinning sadistically, Tardma treated Kai the same way.

Lunzie caught Kai and kept him upright, forcing her mind into a Discipline state to calm herself. This was far worse than she could have imagined. How could she have been so naive as to think the heavy-worlders would just go quietly?

Then Terilla, Cleiti and Gaber were unceremoniously herded into the shuttle, the cartographer babbling something about how this was not the way matters should proceed and how dared they treat him with such disrespect.

"Tanegli? Do you have them?" Paskutti asked into his wrist com-unit.

Whom would the heavyworlder botanist have? Lunzie answered her own question—the other light-weights not yet accounted for.

"None of the sleds have power packs," said Divisti, scowling in the lock. "And that boy is missing."

"How did he elude you?" Paskutti frowned in annoyance.

"Confusion. I thought he'd cling to the others." Divisti shrugged.

Good for you, Bonnard, Lunzie thought, seeking far more encouragement from that minor triumph than it really deserved.

"Start dismantling the lab, Divisti, Tardma."

Trizein came out of his confusion. "Now wait a

minute. You can't go in there. I've got experiments and analyses going on. Divisti, don't touch that fractional equipment. Have you taken leave of your senses?"

"You'll take leave of yours." With a cool smile of pleasure, Tardma struck Trizein in the face with a blow that lifted the slight man off his feet and sent him rolling down the hard deck to lie motionless at Lunzie's feet.

"Too hard, Tardma," said Paskutti. "I'd thought to take him. He'd be more useful than any of the other lightweights."

Tardma shrugged. "Why bother with him anyway? Tanegli knows as much as he does." She went toward the lab with an insolent swing of her hips.

Lunzie heard the scraping of feet on the rocks outside and Portegin with a bloody head half carried a groggy Dimenon across the threshold. Bakkun shoved a weeping Aulia and a blank-faced Margit inside. Triv was stretched on the floor when Berru tossed him there, grinning ferociously at his gasps of pain. Inaudible to the heavyworlders, Lunzie could hear Triv begin the measured breathing which led to the trance state of Discipline. At least four of them were preparing for whatever opportunities arose.

"All right, Bakkun," Paskutti ordered, "you and Berru go after our allies. We want to make this look right. That com-unit was still warm when I got here. They must have got a message through to the Theks."

Methodically the heavyworlders continued to strip the shuttle. Then Tanegli returned. "The storehouse has been cleared and what's useful in the domes."

"No protests, Leader Kai, Leader Varian?" sneered Paskutti.

"Protests wouldn't do us any good, would they?" Varian's level controlled voice annoyed Paskutti. He shot a look at the obviously broken arm and frowned.

"No, no protests, Leader Varian. We've had enough

of you lightweights ordering us about, tolerating us because we're useful. Where would we have fit in your plantation? As beasts of burden? Muscles to be ordered here, there, and everywhere, and subdued by pap?" He made a cutting gesture with one huge hand.

Then, before anyone guessed his intention, he grabbed Terilla by the hair, letting her dangle at the end of his hand. When Cleiti jumped up at her friend's terrified shriek and began to pummel his thick muscular thigh, he raised his fist and landed a casual blow on the top of her head. She sank unconscious to the deck.

Gaber erupted and dashed at Paskutti who merely put a hand out to hold the cartographer off while he dangled the shrieking child.

"Tell me, Leader Varian, Leader Kai, to whom did you send that message? And what did you say?"

"We sent a message to the Theks. Mutiny. Heavyworlders." Kai watched as Terilla was swung, her screams diminishing to mere gasps. "That's all."

"Release the child," Gaber shouted. "You'll kill her. You know what you need to know. You promised there'd be no violence."

Paskutti viciously swatted Gaber into silence. His neck smashed into pulp, Gaber hit the deck with a terrible thud and gasped out his dying breaths as Terilla was dropped in a heap on top of Cleiti.

Horrified, Lunzie forced herself to think. Paskutti had to know if a message had been beamed to the beacon. How would that information alter his plans for them? Triv had now completed the preliminaries of Discipline. Lunzie wished for a smidgeon of telepathy so that the four of them could coordinate their efforts.

"There isn't a power pack anywhere," Tanegli said, storming into the shuttle. He seized hold of Varian by her broken arm. "Where did you hide them, you tight-assed bitch?"

"Watch it, Tanegli," Paskutti warned him, "these lightweights can't take much."

"Where, Varian? Where?" Tanegli emphasized each syllable with a twist of her arm.

"I didn't hide them. Bonnard did." Tanegli threw Varian's suddenly limp body to the deck.

"Go find him, Tanegli. And the packs, or we'll be humping everything out of here on our backs. Bakkun and Berru have started the drive. Nothing can stop it once it starts."

Lunzie wondered what he meant and whether she dared to go over to Varian and examine her. The heavyworlder leader snarled at Kai.

"Get out of here. All of you. March." Paskutti kicked Triv and Portegin to their feet, gesturing curtly for them to pick up the unconscious Gaber and Trizein, for Aulia and Margit to lift the girls. Lunzie bent to Varian, managing to feel the strong steady pulse and knew the girl was dissembling. "Into the main dome, all of you," he ordered.

The camp was a shambles of wanton destruction from Dandy's broken body to scattered tapes, charts, records, clothing. The search for Bonnard continued, punctuated by curses from Tanegli, Divisti and Tardma. Paskutti kept glancing from his wrist chrono and then to the plains beyond the force-screen.

With Discipline-heightened senses, Lunzie caught the distant thunder. She spotted the two dots in the sky: Bakkun and Berru, and the black line beneath, a tossing black line, a moving black line, and suddenly, with a sinking heart, she knew what the heavyworlders had planned.

The Theks might get the message but they wouldn't reach here in time to save them from a fast approaching stampede. Paskutti was shoving them into the main dome now but he caught Lunzie's glance.

"Ah, I see you understand your fitting end, medic. Trampled by creatures, stupid, foolish vegetarians like yourselves. The only one of you strong enough to stand up to us is a mere boy."

He closed the iris lock and the thud of his fist against the plaswall told them that he had shattered the controls. Lunzie was already checking Trizein over, briefly wondering if "your fitting end, medic" meant this whole hideous mess had been arranged to destroy her.

"He's at the veil," Varian said, peering over the bottom of the far window, her arm dangling at her side.

Trizein groaned, regaining consciousness. Lunzie moved on to Cleiti and Terilla and administered restorative sprays.

"He's opened it," Varian reported. "We ought to have a few moments when the herd tops the last rise when they won't be able to see anything for the dust."

"Triv!" Kai and the geologist jammed Discipline-taut fingers into the fine seam of the plastic skin and ripped the tough fabric apart.

Lunzie got the two girls to their feet. Gaber was dead. She gave the near hysterical Aulia another jolt of spray.

"There are four on lift-belts in the sky now," Varian kept reporting. "The stampede has reached the narrow part of the approach. Get ready."

"Where can we go?" Aulia shrieked. The thunderous approach was making them all nervous.

"Back to the shuttle, stupid," Margit said. "NOW!" Varian cried.

Stumbling, half crawling, they hurried up the hill. Trizein couldn't walk so Triv slung him over his shoulders. One look at the bobbing heads of crested dinosaurs bearing down on them was sufficient to lend wings to anyone.

The shuttle hatch slammed behind the last human as the forerunners flowed into the compound. The noise and vibration was so overwhelming not even the shuttle's sturdy walls could keep it out. The craft was rattled and banged about in the chaos, death and destruction outside.

"They outdid themselves with the stampede," Varian said with an absurd chuckle.

"It'll take more than herbivores to dent shuttle ceramic. Don't worry. But I would sit down," Kai added.

"As soon as the stampede has stopped, we'd better make our move," a voice piped up from behind the last row of seats.

"Bonnard!"

Grinning broadly, the dusty, stained boy appeared from the shuttle's lab. "I thought this was the safest place after I saw Paskutti moving you out. But I wasn't sure who had come back in. Am I glad it's you!"

"They'll never find those power packs, Varian. Never," Bonnard said, almost shouting above the noise outside. "When Paskutti smashed the dome controls I didn't see how I could get out in time. So . . . I . . . hid!"

"You did exactly as you should, Bonnard. Even to hiding," Varian reassured him with a firm hug.

Another shift of the shuttle sent everyone rocking.

"It's going to fall," Aulia cried.

"But it won't crack," Kai promised. "We'll survive. By all the things that men hold dear, we'll survive!"

When the stampede finally ended, it took the combined strength of all the men to open the door. The carnage was fearful. They were buried under trampled hadrosaurs. It was full night now. Under the cover of darkness, Bonnard and Kai slipped out and, using lift-belts, managed to bring the power packs back to the shuttle.

"Bonnard was right. We've got to make a move," Kai told them as the survivors huddled together, still shaken and shocked by their ordeal. "Come dawn, the heavyworlders will return to survey their handi-work. They'll assume the shuttle is still here, buried under the stampede. They won't be in any hurry to get to it. Where could it go?"

"I know where," Varian said.

"That cave we found, near the golden fliers?" Bon-nard asked, his tired face lighting.

"It's more than big enough to accommodate the shuttle. And dry, with a screen of falling vines to hide the opening."

"Great idea, Varian," Kai agreed, "because even if they used the infrared scan, our heat would register the same as adult giffs."

"And that's the best idea I've heard today," Lunzie said briskly, handing around peppers which had been overlooked by the heavyworlders in the piloting compartment.

It required a lot of skill to ease the shuttle out from under the mountain of flesh but Lunzie knew it had to be done now while Kai and Varian held on to their Disciplined strength. The two managed, with Bonnard assisting in the directions since he'd been outside.

By dawn they had reached the inland sea and maneuvered into the enormous cave, every bit as commodious as Varian and Bonnard had said. Not one of the golden fliers paid attention to the strange white craft that had invaded their area.

"The heavyworlders don't even know this place exists," Varian assured them when they were safely concealed.

Triv and Dimenon used enough of the abundant drooping foliage to synthesize padding to comfort the wounded on the bare plastic deck. Lunzie sent them out again to get enough raw materials to synthesize a hypersaturated tonic to reduce the effects of delayed shock. Then everyone was allowed to sleep.

Lunzie was one of the first awake late the next day. Moving quietly so as not to disturb the exhausted survivors, she cooked up another nutritious broth in the synthesizer, loading it with vitamins and minerals.

"Guaranteed to circulate blood through your abused muscles and restore tissue to normal," she said, serving up steaming beakers to Kai and Triv who had awakened. "We've slept around the chrono and half again."

After checking the binding on Kai's arm, she massaged his shoulders to work out some of the stiffness before she ministered in the same way to Triv.

"Thanks. How long before the others rouse?" asked Triv, gratefully working his upper arms in eased circles.

"I'd say we have another clear hour or so before the dead arise," Lunzie answered, holding a beaker of soup to Varian. "I'll need some more greenery to fix breakfast for the rest of them."

They filled the synthesizer with vegetation from the hanging vines that curtained the cave's mouth. Weak sunlight, as bright as Ireta ever saw, shone in on the shuttle's tail through the tough creepers. By the time the others awoke, there was food.

"It's not very interesting, but it's nutritious," Lunzie said as she handed around flat brown cakes. "I'd do more with the synthesizer, but how long can we depend upon having the power last? And the heavyworlders might detect its use."

Varian set the children to keep a lookout at the cave opening, warning them not to hang beyond the vines. Bonnard thought that was wasted effort.

"They're not going to look for people they think they've already killed."

"We underestimated them once, Bonnard," Kai

remarked. "Let's not make the same mistake twice."
Duly thoughtful, the boy took a lookout post.

A very long week went by while the survivors
recovered from shock and injury.

"How long do we have to wait for the Theks to
come and save us?" Varian asked the three Disciples
when all the others had gone to sleep. "They would
have had your message within two hours after you
sent it. 'Mutiny' ought to stir their triangles if
'heavyworlder' didn't."

Kai upturned his hands, wincing at the stab of pain
in his broken wrist. "The Theks don't rush under any
circumstances, I guess. I had hoped they might just
this once."

"So, what do we do?" Triv asked. "We can't stay
here forever. Or avoid the heavyworlders' search
once they realize the shuttle's gone. I know Ireta's a
big planet but it's only this part on the equator that's
barely habitable. Even if we stay here, we've got to
use energy to produce food. We could get caught
either way. They've got all the tracers and telltaggers.
They have everything, even the stun-guns. What do
we do?"

Every instinct in Lunzie shouted "NO" at the
obvious answer but she voiced it herself. "There is
always cold sleep." Even to herself she sounded
defeated.

"That's the sensible last resort," Triv agreed. Lunzie
wanted to argue the point but she clamped her lips
firmly shut while Kai and Varian nodded solemnly.

"EV is coming back for us, isn't she?" Triv asked
with an expressionless face.

Kai and Varian assured him that the *ARCT-10*
would not abandon them. The richness of their sur-
veys was on the message beacon to be stripped when
the *ARCT* had finished following that storm. The
beacon Portegin had rigged outside the cave, camou-

flaged as a dead branch, would guide the search and rescue team to them.

"With the sort of ion interference a big storm can produce, it's no wonder they haven't been able to make contact with us," Varian said staunchly but none of the others looked as though they quite believed her.

Lunzie kept trying not to think of the word "Jonah."

"Good, then we'll go cold sleep tomorrow once the others have been told," Kai decided briskly.

"Why tell them?" Lunzie asked. She would rather get the whole process over with before she lost her courage.

"They're halfway into cold sleep right now." Varian gestured to the sleeping bodies, startling Kai. "And we'll save ourselves some futile arguments."

"It's a full week now and at the rate carrion eaters work on Ireta, the heavyworlders may have discovered the shuttle is missing," Triv said ominously.

"There's no way the heavyworlders could find a trace of us in cold sleep. And there's a real danger if we remain awake much longer," Varian added.

With the other Disciples in agreement with a course she herself had recommended, Lunzie rose slowly to her feet. Unwilling as she was, she went to the cold-sleep locker and tapped in the code that would open it. She really hated to go into cold sleep again. She had wasted so much of her life living in that state. It was almost as bad as death. In a sense, it was a death—of all that was current and pleasant and hopeful in this segment of her life.

But she gathered up the drug and the spraygun, checked dosages and began to administer the medication to those already asleep. Triv, Kai and Varian moved among them, checking their descent into cold sleep as skins cooled and respirations slowed to the imperceptible.

"You know," Varian began in a hushed but startled

tone as she was settling herself, "poor old Gaber was right. We are planted. At least temporarily!"

Lunzie stared at her, then made a grimace. "That's not the comfort I want to take with me into cold sleep."

"Does one dream in cryogenic sleep, Lunzie?" Varian asked as Lunzie handed her a cup of the preservative drug.

"I never have."

Lunzie gave Kai his dose. The young leader smiled as he accepted it.

"Seems a waste of time not to do something," he said.

"The whole concept of cold sleep is to suspend the sense of subjective time," Lunzie pointed out.

"You sleep, you wake. And centuries pass," added Triv, taking his beakerful.

"You're less help than Varian is," Lunzie grumbled.

"It won't be centuries," Kai said emphatically. "Not once EV has those uranium assays. It's too raking rich for them to ignore."

Lunzie arranged the cold-sleep gas tank controls to kick in as soon as its sensors registered the cessation of all life signs. She held her dose in her hand. She wouldn't risk them all if she stayed awake. Her body heat would register as a giff to any heavyworld overflight of the area. She could stay awake.

But if she slept with these, she would, for once, have someone she knew, people she liked and had worked with. She wouldn't be quite so alone when she woke. That was some consolation. Before she could talk herself into some drastic and fatal delay, she tossed the dose down and lay down along one side of the deck, pillowing her head on a pad and settling her arms by her side.

Who knows when they'll come for us, she thought, unable to censor dismal thoughts. She grabbed at another consolation: the heavyworlders didn't get her, or the others. She'd wake again. And there'd be another settlement due her.

The leaden heaviness began to spread out from her stomach, permeating her tissues. The air on her cooling skin felt uncomfortably hot, and grew hotter. Suddenly Lunzie wanted to get up, run away from this place before she was trapped inside herself again. But it was already too late to stop the process. She felt her consciousness sinking fast into another death of sleep. Muhlah!